Discover a place where desire sets
the soul aflame, where love and laughter
warm the heart . . .

Discover the world of
COLLEEN QUINN
and her breathtaking novels . . .

UNVEILED

"Rich in characterization, evocative, warm and tender . . . *Unveiled* is a pleasure from beginning to end." —*Romantic Times*

DEFIANT ROSE

No one could take the circus life out of beautiful Rose Carney—not even the tempting stranger who dared her to love him . . .

"[A] delightful, warmhearted love story that brings to life the magic and excitement of the circus." —*Romantic Times*

"Priceless . . . this story should definitely be on your reading list." —*Rendezvous*

"Delightful . . . sheer joy!" —*Heartland Critiques*

Unveiled

COLLEEN QUINN

DIAMOND BOOKS, NEW YORK

This book is a Diamond original edition,
and has never been previously published.

UNVEILED

A Diamond Book/published by arrangement with
the author

PRINTING HISTORY
Diamond edition/May 1993

ISBN: 1-55773-891-2

Diamond Books are published by The Berkley Publishing Group,
200 Madison Avenue, New York, New York 10016.
The name "DIAMOND" and its logo
are trademarks belonging to Charter Communications, Inc.

PRINTED IN THE UNITED STATES OF AMERICA

10 9 8 7 6 5 4 3 2 1

For Cathy

Special thanks to Gail Fortune, for her enthusiasm, and to the wonderful people of Cape May at the Linda Lee house, the Queen Victoria, and the Mainstay Inn, who shared their homes with me and invited me back another time.

❊ ONE

"Are you absolutely certain? In essence then, I am bankrupt?" Christopher Scott asked as his legal adviser peered up from behind silver-rimmed spectacles. The older man laid down his pencil and closed his ledger with a sigh.

"I'm afraid so, my son. The panic has hit many families hard, as you know. Unfortunately your family's investments have suffered greatly, especially the railroads. Then there are the bills from the estate, taxes, salaries, and upkeep. You are in the red, and with prices deflated, I don't see that situation improving any time soon."

"I see." Christopher digested this information. Ruffling his fingers through the thick black hair that fell charmingly into his face, he gave a grin that the gamblers at the nearby hell halls would have instantly recognized. "So what do you suggest?"

"I would propose you begin searching for employment." The austere, thin-lipped attorney rose to his feet and placed the ledger in his valise. Christopher and his aunt exchanged a glance, then the young man broke into laughter, rose from his seat, and pounded the accountant on his back.

"Good, that's very good. Come now, James, it can't be as bad as all that? What about my South African mines? The silver? The textile mills?"

"I'm sorry." The man paused on the way out, then glanced enviously at the rich room with its green velvet drapes, the Brussels rug, the dark cherry furnishings, and the crystal chandelier. Portraits of elite Philadelphians gazed from the wall, and objets d'art graced the tables. "Perhaps you might consider selling off your assets. That may hold you for a time, but you really need a more permanent solution. I wish I had something better to offer you, but I don't. The facts speak for themselves."

He closed his case with a snide snicker, then followed the butler to the door. Returning a moment later, the butler filled a brandy glass and, without expression, placed it on the table before disappearing.

"I would suggest you drink it," his aunt said sharply. "You will undoubtedly be needing it to get through the next hour."

Sending his aunt a look betraying his lack of appreciation, Christopher gulped the brandy, waiting for the numbing warmth to overcome him. A handsome man, barely thirty years old, he had the self-assured, careless look of one who had never had to face reality. It wasn't that he was unintelligent or incapable. It was just that he'd lived a charmed life, and didn't regret it for a moment.

Tonight, the drink didn't help. Christopher doubted that there was enough brandy in the world to help him cope with what he had learned.

"How the hell could this happen?" he demanded, rising to his feet and pacing the floor. "How could it all be gone? Hundreds of thousands of dollars, dollars that my father made selling that damned soap, how could it have evaporated like one of his bubbles?"

"It happened the way it always happens," Aunt Eunice said dryly, refilling the glass and drinking it herself. "The older entrepreneur dies, leaving a fortune to his dissolute son, who gambles and runs the estate into the ground. It is an old plot; one need look no farther than the nearest penny dreadful to review it.''

''Very funny,'' Christopher said sarcastically. ''I didn't do all this. No one, no matter how dissolute, as you put it, could have run through that kind of money in five years. It would take a lifetime of gambling, drinking, and wenching to lose my father's fortune. Christ, I can't believe it.''

''You must believe it,'' Eunice said sternly. ''It's time you grew up and faced facts. My brother was very successful, it is true. Soaps and perfumes. He understood what women were looking for in cleaning products, and supplied them. Made quite a fortune once the little rose-shaped soaps caught on. For a few pennies, even a serving woman could afford them.''

Christopher nodded. ''Who would have known that the economy would turn sour? All of the profits of the business were channeled into investments. Father realized that the soap business was too fickle for long-term security, so he bought solid stocks and bonds, thinking to provide for us for years to come.'' He smiled sardonically at the irony of that. ''He might as well have spent it wenching, for all the good it did.''

''Do not speak ill of the dead,'' Eunice said sharply, her webbed face taking on an even leaner cast. ''You should be making plans. Your decisions will affect more than just yourself, as you know.''

Christopher stared thoughtfully at his aunt. Though she would die rather than admit it, he was all she had left. And she was a responsibility he couldn't neglect. Aunt Eunice, for all her forthright speech, had a heart of gold. It was she who had interfered when his father was too harsh or impatient with his devil-may-care attitude. She'd made sure that he had the best schooling, and that he'd applied himself when he would have settled for average grades. Long before his mother died, Aunt Eunice had treated him with all of the stern affection she would have given her own child, if she'd had one.

And now she needed him. He knew that she was frightened. She had been poor once, just like his father, desperately poor. He couldn't imagine what her existence must have been like, for she simply shuddered when anyone talked about it, and changed the subject. No, if it was only himself, he could survive. But Aunt Eunice deserved better than an almshouse.

"You're right," Christopher said slowly, not revealing his thoughts. "We do have others to think about. We have a large staff to consider, the butler, the scullery maid, the cook, and the chambermaid. Then there's the stable boy, the gardener, and the grounds keeper. I can't just throw everyone out into the street."

"No, I suppose not." Eunice glanced at the young man and there was almost a sympathetic look on her face. "Then you are thinking of selling the estate?"

"I can't," Christopher said with a sigh. "The house is badly in need of repair. We wouldn't get a dime on the dollar of what it's really worth. Besides, I just can't do that to my father. If he were alive, it would kill him all over again."

Eunice nodded. John Scott had loved this house, with its clean Colonial lines and its red-brick facing and marble steps. It was the realization of a dream, the immigrant gazing from the roads of Philadelphia at the wealthy Walnut Street mansions. He had been determined to belong to that society, and had struggled from his ignoble beginning as a dockworker to accomplish that feat.

"What do you think?"

Eunice peered at her nephew and saw that he wasn't joking, he was genuinely soliciting her opinion. She stared at him thoughtfully, weighing the options, her shrewd mind working frantically. Finally she drew a deep breath. "I think there's only one way out. Marriage."

"What!" Christopher laughed. When Eunice's face did not change, his laughter slowly died, only to be replaced by genuine puzzlement. "Surely you are joking."

"Not at all," Eunice said briskly. "You are of age, and expected to marry. Why, the mothers of every eligible chit in the city see you as a catch. A man of your class is expected to marry a woman of equal upbringing, a woman who happens to be . . . well-off."

"But marriage!"

"I don't think you have much other choice. You are well educated, but like most academics, you are unfit to do anything. You have no knowledge of accounting, you deplore banking, you know nothing of the law or medicine. The entrepreneurial spirit has certainly skipped a generation, and I fail to see you as a sweatshop worker. In short, if you wish to maintain your present life at the least inconvenience to yourself, I would suggest you consider it."

Christopher paled. "What about a bank loan? Surely we could borrow against what the house is worth. That should hold us for some time."

"You could remortgage," Aunt Eunice agreed. "But the debt will have to be paid back and, in the long term, will not provide an answer. No, I think you have your possibilities. Sell the estate, or marry an heiress." At Christopher's glum face, the elderly woman smiled. "It won't be so awful. After all, you aren't a bad-looking man. Those light skirts have been chasing you for years. Perhaps with the right coaxing, you might be able to convince a girl that you are not loathsome."

"But that is so . . . unromantic," Christopher said bluntly.

Aunt Eunice chuckled. "So is starving, my boy. Face it,

you are not cut out to be poor. You like nice clothes, good food, the best drink, and your games. Being poor isn't fun, Christopher. Poor people live on street corners, huddle over barrels of coal in the winter to stay warm, eat scraps, and die young. I was poor once. There is nothing noble about it.'' Aunt Eunice saw his expression and smiled grimly. "Marry for money, nephew. It is your only answer.''

Christopher shot her a look, then took back the brandy glass. There were times when drink was the only answer. This appeared to be one of them.

"Ah. It's you. The madam is expecting you.'' A woman with a thick brogue and a face so well scrubbed that it seemed permanently red, opened the door and scowled.

Katie entered the hallway of the magnificent Victorian cottage, her cold fingers numbly clutching a worn carpet-bag. Barely twenty-five, she looked much younger than that, with her dark black hair, her nose sprinkled with freckles, and her small pink mouth. Her blue eyes usually danced with pure mischief, but today they were cast shyly downward. Unfashionably dressed in a bleak gray muslin that still bore hoops, she looked exactly like what she was: a young Irish girl who had saved her last few pennies to make the long trip from Philadelphia to the quaint little seaside village of Cape May.

"I suppose you're here about the advertisement,'' the woman grumbled.

"Yes.'' Katie unfolded a yellowed newspaper clipping that she'd carefully cut from the *Public Ledger* and handed it to the dour-faced woman along with her papers. She'd read the clipping so many times she knew it by heart, and she was certain she fit the qualifications as a lady's companion.

She had to have this job, she thought desperately as the woman examined the papers. There were others depending on her, particularly a little boy with soft blond hair and a smile that squeezed her heart. God, how she loved him. She was almost afraid to admit that love, for it was the same fickle emotion that had brought her shame. John Sweeney, with his Irish grin and his carefree ways, had won her heart. He'd said that he loved her, that he would never leave . . . but he did. And Philadelphia, for all its grand hotels and streets, was too small for an unwed woman and her child. She held her head high, refusing to allow that thought to continue. She had to survive.

"Humph." The woman frowned, handing back the papers. She examined Katie critically, her eyes almost disappearing into her round face. Katie held her breath until the woman nodded, then continued abruptly, "I suppose you'll do. Your papers are in order. Mind you'll not be making off with the silver. And watch your p's and q's. The old dragon's a stickler for the queen's English."

Katie thrust the papers inside her bag. "Where is Mrs. Pemberton?"

"She's taking her nap." The woman tried to remain gruff, but there was something about Katie that made it extremely difficult to maintain her demeanor. "I don't suppose you've eaten?"

"Not since yesterday." Katie sighed.

The woman rolled her eyes in resignation. "Well, come in until it's time for your interview. To the kitchen with you, and don't be scuffing my floor. My name's Eileen."

Katie nodded and did as she was told, little daunted by the woman's brusque manner. Where she came from, in the Irish ward of Philadelphia, everyone talked like Eileen and had the same lack of affection toward youth. It came from living in the city, where so many young people died long before they reached adulthood. It was as if one didn't prove oneself fit until one overcame that stigma.

Hushing the sound of her boots on the polished marble

floor, Katie gazed in wonder at the ornate rose wallpaper, twirling with leaves and thorns from one wall up to the border and even across the ceiling. Burgundy and gold, it looked grand to the young woman's eyes, as did the hurricane lamps dripping with crystal, the heavy carved furniture, the gold-leaf looking glass that consumed one side of the wall.

The kitchen was at the far end of the house. Katie passed sitting rooms cleverly arranged with intricate chairs and heavily swathed in velvet drapes. Stained-glass windows appeared as if by afterthought, their odd panes gleaming bloodred and sapphire in the morning sunlight.

"Here it is. Sit now at the table and I'll light the stove. Lord would think you would eat first, the long trip and all."

Eileen pinched her arm, indicating the table, and Katie abruptly took a seat, rubbing the abused member. As Eileen bustled about she stared at the sideboard in amazement. Never had she seen so much food. A basket of potatoes waited beside the sink, and a bowl of fruit graced the table. A ham stood near the stove, enticingly pink and juicy. She saw a pitcher of fresh milk in the icebox and a loaf of baked bread on the sideboard. Eileen cut her a thick slice, then lathered it with blueberry jam and thrust it disdainfully at her.

"Eat that until the luncheon is made. I'm going to share my own meal with you. Can't see you go hungry, and the old dragon would begrudge you even that."

Katie smiled in gratitude, then devoured the bread. Nothing had ever tasted so good. She drank greedily of the frothing milk Eileen had placed before her, and was finishing a second chunk of bread before she could speak.

"What is she like?"

Eileen scowled as she placed a good supper of ham and potatoes on the table, then joined the young girl. "Madam? She's about what you would expect. Daft, she is. Forgets one day to the next. But don't let that fool you into thinking you can put one over on her. Sometimes the old lady is as sharp as knives. Cheap as they come, too. Would take the pennies off the eyes of a corpse.''

Katie shuddered, then ate a second slice of ham. "Why does she need a companion?''

Eileen chuckled, then recited the clipping. " 'Elderly lady seeks seaside companion. Must be youthful, trustworthy, etc. Room and board, plus wages. See Ella Pemberton.' Note how they're vague on the last.''

"They?''

"The Pembertons,'' Eileen said with a conspiratorial wink. "The Main Liners can't stand the old lady. So they send her down here, to the shore house, hire a companion, and they're done with the whole situation. Convenient, isn't it?''

"Very,'' Katie agreed. She was about to help herself to another potato when the clanging of a bell startled her and she nearly dropped her spoon. Eileen sighed, then pushed heavily away from the table and gave Katie an inspecting glance.

"Pull your hair away from your eyes. Too bad we don't have time to take a comb to it, the color's lovely. And brush the tips of your boots. Madam can't stand dust. There now.'' Reaching out, she pinched Katie's cheeks, satisfied when she saw the tears start in her eyes and fresh color bloomed just below them. "You'll do. Up with you now. And remember, don't cry. She can't stand sniveling.''

Katie nodded, wincing as her cheeks still stung. She felt Eileen's hand touch her shoulder reassuringly, then the woman shoved her toward the massive staircase. Katie fought the instinct to run. Clutching her carpetbag, she entered the first bedroom that Eileen indicated.

The room was so dark that it took her a moment to realize it was all decorated in rose, from the palest pink to the darkest cherry. The windows, painstakingly shuttered, were clothed in burgundy velvet, refusing to permit even the slimmest shaft of light to enter. Gas lamps hung from the wall, but no flicker of illumination glinted from their opaque glass shades. Even the lace bedspread looked yellowed and old, as if it had shriveled up like a pansy from lack of sunshine.

"Another, I suppose?" Ella Pemberton's voice rasped. She had the same impervious tone as one of the nuns who ran the city's parochial school. "I heard the door. Let's have a look at you, miss."

Katie dropped her bag and stepped forward, grimacing at the thought of the inspection. Up close, Ella Pemberton was even more daunting. Her face, once beautiful, had sharpened with age, chiseling her features until one couldn't help but notice the penetrating eyes, the unforgiving nose, the mirthless mouth. Common sense, lack of humor, and overbearing intelligence were all written there. The old woman's pale eyes peered at the young girl and she gestured to the housekeeper.

"Not much bigger than the last one, is she? I take it her papers are in order?"

"Yes, miss," Eileen said evenly. "She has a good letter of reference from Marjorie Westcott."

"I see." The old lady peered quizzically at Katie, then waved a finger impatiently. "Don't just stand there, turn around! Eileen, light the lamp. I want to get a good look at her."

Eileen complied, then indicated to Katie that she should move closer. Katie stepped into the lamplight and looked directly at Ella Pemberton. She felt like a little girl at school, being inspected by the nuns, then taken to task for the dust on her boots. She winced, waiting for the old woman to find fault, but a profound change seemed to come across Ella.

"My God," the old woman whispered in shock. "Can it be? It is. My dear, dear girl."

Katie stared at the woman in confusion. Ella's profile had lost its harshness and her eyes seemed to soften like wax. Color had drained from her cheeks and there was a look of disbelief mingled with joy on her face as a tear dropped down her lined skin.

"Mrs. Pemberton?" Katie asked softly. She was afraid for a moment that the woman would faint, but Ella chuckled and wiped at the tear.

"Fan. My dear, dear Fan. Please forgive me for not recognizing you immediately. It's just been so long."

Katie glanced at Eileen, who stood in the doorway with her mouth sagging. Ella's voice was full of emotion and had lost its bitterness. She sounded like a young girl and a wistful smile came to her face as she gazed fondly at Katie.

"That's not your niece," Eileen said quickly. "This is a girl answering the advertisement. You know Fan is—"

"Don't you dare," Ella said sternly. She whirled on the housekeeper and poked a jagged finger in the air. "You know I never believed that. It was a tale, that's what it was. They like to see me suffer. No, I have my Fan back and all will be well."

"But—"

"Please put her in her old room, Eileen. There will be no more discussion. My sweet Fan."

Eileen opened her mouth, then closed it abruptly. "This way, Your Ladyship," she muttered, leading Katie out of the room. When they got outside, she turned toward Katie in disapproval. "It looks like you'll be here for a while. She's really addled her brain now. Fan, she called you. Thinks you're her niece."

Katie's eyes widened. "Her niece?"

Eileen nodded, then pushed open a door at the far end of the hall. In spite of her bewilderment, Katie couldn't stop the look of wonder on her face when Eileen led her into a lovely bedroom decorated with chintz and ribbons. Not even the housekeeper's scowls could dim her pleasure as she observed the mirrors and a washstand, a rug so thick her feet sank into it, and a bed filled with down feathers.

"This is for me?" Her voice squeaked and Eileen nodded, her lips tight.

"This is Fan's room. That's where she wants you." Eileen indicated the lovely surroundings. "Enjoy it while you can. Eventually I'm sure she'll realize her mistake."

"What happened to her? Fan, I mean?" Katie asked.

Eileen hesitated, then shrugged. "Frances ran off with a disreputable gambler and was never spoken of again. Word reached the family that she got killed in San Francisco, but the old lady refused to believe that. Fan was her favorite. She cared more for her than the rest of them put together."

"And she's never been heard from since?"

Eileen nodded. "Until you walked in, Mrs. Pemberton seemed to have forgotten her." Scowling again, Eileen indicated the washstand. "Tea is at four. I'm sure the old woman would want her dear niece there."

Eileen stalked out, leaving Katie alone in the room. After kicking off her boots, the young girl flounced onto the quilt and nearly hugged herself in glee.

She'd fallen over the rainbow. And right into the pot of gold.

Two

"Dammit, Jack, after all these years, I can't believe you're telling me this." Christopher stared at the older man who lounged in a richly upholstered chair, his feet resting on a stuffed ottoman.

At Christopher's heated words the man shrugged, then flicked the ash from his cigar into a brass tray. "I'm sorry, Chris, but I can't extend you any more funds. Your account is way past due and already over your limits. I understand your difficulties, but . . ." Hesitating a moment, he continued thoughtfully, "May I be perfectly frank, in light of our friendship?"

Christopher paled, then nodded. Jack Birmingham was the owner of the most reputable gaming hall in the city. The man wielded considerable power and influence, and when necessary, he used them. No policeman had ever shut down his establishment, no politician had ever rallied against the sin of gambling. The reasons were simple: Jack paid them well to support his business, and they complied.

Placing aside his cigar, Jack began quietly. "You're out of money, Chris. I checked with your banker yesterday. It's all right, the man is discreet." He noticed the look of alarm on Christopher's face and spoke reassuringly. "You see, I am entitled to this information because I hold your letter of credit.

It is not common knowledge throughout the city. However, I cannot in all good conscience continue to advance you money.''

''But I can win it back,'' Christopher said desperately. ''I know I can. You know my record—I'm the best cardplayer in the place.''

''I know that. You've made a lot of money for yourself, and the house. You play a fair game, you are a gentleman and have never been caught cheating.'' Jack smiled when Christopher seemed to relax a bit. ''But my answer must remain the same. It is as much for your sake as my own.''

''I don't understand.''

''I know,'' Jack said sympathetically. ''But let me clarify the issue. For reasons I can't explain but have often observed, the winners are men who don't need the money. Once they do, they lose. They give off emotions that other men sense and capitalize on. They reveal their hand because their livelihood depends on the next card. No man can successfully play poker with stakes like that.''

''Then you're saying you won't help me?'' Christopher demanded.

Jack shook his head. ''I don't want to see you get to the point where you can't dig yourself out. It's happened to too many others, men who thought just a few more hands and they'd be ahead. They wind up destitute, slaves to the game they once controlled.'' As Christopher paced the floor Jack spoke softly. ''Why don't you get away for a few weeks, maybe to the seaside, and do some thinking? You need to come up with an alternate plan of action, not just a temporary fix. You are a handsome young man, Christopher, well connected and full of charm.'' He smiled. ''Have you perhaps considered marriage?''

Christopher's mouth dropped, and Jack continued. ''Society doesn't know about your financial woes. And the debutantes often bring a sizable dowry into a marriage. I would consider it, at least.''

''Thanks,'' Christopher said sarcastically. ''I've had the same advice from my aunt. It seems everyone is advocating the marriage market these days.'' He procured his derby and departed without looking back.

Jack Birmingham relit his cigar. Christopher would come to reason. He really didn't have any other choice.

She couldn't do this. She would have to confess to Lady Pemberton that she wasn't her long-lost niece. She was simply Katie O'Connor, daughter of Seamus O'Connor, who drank himself to death shortly after his wife had passed on. She wasn't a Philadelphian first family, wasn't among the Who's Who, wasn't even registered in the church. She had borne a bastard son, and for that deserved to be shunned by all decent people.

''Miss Fan, Lady Pemberton wants you to come to tea,'' one of the maids called through the door. ''And she asks that you wear the pink plush.''

The pink plush? Katie leaped from the bed and opened the chiffonier, gasping at the lovely gowns inside. There were muslins and silks, satins and laces, day dresses and riding outfits. Every imaginable color was represented, and every available fabric had been pressed into the making of this wardrobe. Almost reverently, she touched the sleeve of the pink day dress.

It felt like the finest of cottons, soft and cool to the skin. But there was something eerie about taking another woman's clothes, especially one who was presumed dead. It was almost like seeing a ghost. Swallowing her trepidation, Katie withdrew the dress from its hook, then wrapped the garment lovingly around her and stood before the mirror.

She couldn't prevent the involuntary gasp that came from

her lips. It was gorgeous. The rose color brought out the best of her dark hair and made her eyes seem hauntingly blue. Indecision coursed through her, but the temptation of the dress was too strong. Maybe, for just a few hours, she'd go along with this. After all, who would it hurt?

She got her answer very shortly. Choking for breath as Clarise, the maid, tightened her corset, she straightened, obviously in pain. "Does it really have to be so tight?"

"Yes, miss," Clarise responded, perplexed. "All the young ladies lace their corsets that way. At least you didn't have to lay on the floor. My last mistress needed me to stand on her bottom just to get them tight enough."

"My God, this is like a torture chamber." Katie shrugged into seven petticoats, a bustle, a corset cover, the pink skirt, then a bodice with a detachable lace collar. By the time the costume was complete, she felt like a stuffed rag doll. Each breath was a new experience in pain and every motion made her want to faint.

"You'll get used to it, I suppose." The maid giggled at Katie's expression. "But you look lovely, and you have such a small waist. Look in the glass."

Katie glanced at the mirror. The dress was pretty and fashionable, completely different from the secondhand dress she'd worn for the trip. She turned, observing the way the skirt swept the floor, and she reminded herself to hold it up or else she'd trip. Her hair, pulled up into a simple style, now softly framed her face. She looked like a lady, or at least like the niece of one.

"I'll get the scissors and trim your hair tonight," Clarise said. "It will be easier to dress."

Katie nodded, then started grimly for the stairs. Being wealthy wasn't as easy as it looked. But then, nothing was. That was a lesson Katie had learned long ago.

* * *

"Mr. Bartram, my family's known yours for two generations. We've done business with this bank for years. My father stood for your son's christening! And you mean to tell me I can't have even the smallest loan?"

"I'm afraid not." Clyde Bartram fiddled with his stiffly waxed mustache and stared sympathetically at Christopher. "I'm sorry, but we know what is happening to your finances. Your railroad stocks are worthless, your mortgage payment is past due . . . it is all I can do to keep the creditors at bay now. It is only your reputation and your family's name that has kept the collectors from your door."

"Then it's hopeless." Christopher stared at the beautifully polished mahogany desk before him. "I've tried everything. Overnight I'm a pauper."

"It's worse than that." Clyde pulled a stack of papers from a file on his desk and spread them out for display. "All of these are coming due. Your house is the collateral for a lot of these loans, but the mortgage hasn't been paid. I've been able to keep your secret for the time being, but I can't hold out much longer."

"And then what?" Christopher had to ask.

Clyde shrugged, then examined the papers, refusing to look at Christopher as he did so. "You know the answer to that, son. They'll sell off the house and the assets, pay off the debts, then, if there are any proceeds, pay you the balance. I asked you here today, Christopher, because I've drawn up some preliminary figures. You won't be left with a red cent if you let this happen."

"Isn't there anything you can suggest? No short-term loan, or promissory note?"

The banker looked quietly at the polished young man before him and shrugged. "Have you thought of going into some kind of business? The economy's getting better and—"

"And who would advance me the money for that?"

Christopher snorted. "I don't know where next month's payments are coming from."

"You have a point," Clyde said softly. "And once you start asking for a loan, creditors all over town will hear of your state. And if your reputation is ruined . . . I hate to say this, but Philadelphia is an unforgiving town. You'd be finished. My best advice is—and I know this sounds odd—"

"I know. Marry for money." Christopher put on his hat and extended a hand. "Thanks, Clyde. It's the same advice I've been hearing all over town."

"I'll try to extend your mortgage payments through the summer," the banker said. "But it's not a bad idea, Christopher. Perhaps you should consider it."

Christopher stormed out, slamming the door behind him.

"That dress looks lovely on you, Fan. When I saw you in that horrible costume you arrived in, I nearly lost my wits. What do you expect from that ne'er-do-well. . . . Well, never mind all that. You're back now and that's all that matters."

Katie smiled, then attempted to take a seat on the porch of the elaborate summer cottage. The bustle, made up of yards of fabric and a cagelike contraption, refused to accommodate itself to anything like sitting. She struggled comically with the dress until Ella Pemberton, coughing with discreet laughter, showed her how she could lower herself onto a cushion.

"Thank you," Katie breathed. "I've never had a dress like this. And the petticoats!" She lifted a corner of her skirt, indicating the layers of fabric beneath. "This dress needs seven!"

"We do without a few when it gets very hot," Ella admitted as she leaned forward, pouring the tea from an elaborate silver urn. "There is always a breeze, however, so you needn't worry about the vapors."

Katie nodded. With the way her corset restricted her breathing, fainting was a distinct possibility. Still, the gown was gorgeous, the porch wonderful, and the food plentiful. Eileen brought out the tray, giving Katie a disapproving look as she placed it with the rest.

"Doesn't Fan look lovely, Eileen?" Ella asked.

"Lovely." Eileen's voice was heavy with irony. "But no matter how you change the blanket, it's still the same horse."

"What are you talking about, horses and such rubbish? I think you've been in the sun too long. Do bring Fan and me some fresh tea. We want to enjoy the air."

Eileen departed, giving Katie a sarcastic look, which Katie ignored. As she sipped the tea her mouth watered at the sight of the luscious cakes, the sandwiches, the sugared almonds, and an assortment of fruits. Even if it was just for today, she would enjoying playing Fan, no matter what the housekeeper thought.

"It's so beautiful here." Katie indicated the rows of cottages that stretched along the road. Porch after porch was easily visible, and she could see the lovely women in their soft summer dresses pouring tea and chatting quietly. The porches themselves seemed more an extension of the parlor than anything else, and the best of the house furniture graced the pretty verandas.

"I don't suppose you remember it much from when you were a little girl." Ella smiled, her face softening at the recollection. "You used to play on the beach with your dolls, bringing them tea just like the ladies did. Do you recall the day that horrid Weston boy kicked sand all over your dishes? You didn't cry, but proceeded to drench him in seawater tea. I thought I'd laugh all afternoon."

Katie smiled. The older woman was enjoying herself, there was no doubt about that. And if it wasn't for the dress, she would be as well. She vowed to discard half of the underwear beneath the gown, and she didn't care what

Clarise said, she would refuse to be laced so tightly. Helping herself to one of the cakes, she found she could only eat tiny pieces of it, for the very act of swallowing was difficult with the tightly laced corset.

But it was a small price to pay. She felt beautiful, fashionable, and most of all . . . respectable. It was a feeling she hadn't experienced since her disgrace. Even Father O'Leary, the local parish priest, had confessed that he was disappointed in her. And once she had become noticeably pregnant, many of her friends had deserted her as well.

She frowned at the memory. She would have to tell Ella Pemberton the truth, but she wasn't compelled to do it immediately. The older woman seemed so happy with the illusion. It seemed the least she could do. Unaware of her expression, she flinched when Ella leaned forward and pinched her cheek sharply. "Stop that, you'll make wrinkles. And sit up straight. Here comes the Misses Chandler. Smile, dear."

Katie did as she was told, her lips freezing. If she allowed Ella to introduce her as her niece, it would be that much harder on Ella when the truth was finally discovered. And somehow Katie knew they would know. The Misses Chandler, even from the distance, looked formidable. It was one thing to fool a senile old lady. It was another to fool wealthy society matrons.

Katie was about to feign an excuse when Ella gave her a sharp look. "I don't want any protests, Fan. I know what you think of them, but you must say hello. It will be too rude to run off when they've seen you."

Katie could do nothing but smile as the two matrons approached, their eyes peering inquisitively from behind their bonnets. Appearing like two crows in their somber gowns and haughty manner, they stepped rigidly onto the porch and gave a cool nod to Ella. Immediately they both turned toward "Fan," observing her with the same thoroughness that Eileen had employed when she'd first arrived.

"Ladies," Ella said cordially. "This is my niece. You do remember Frances? Fan, this is Alice and Martha Chandler."

"Charmed," Alice said, then her intonation abruptly changed. "Frances? You don't mean . . ."

"Why yes, this is Fan," Ella said, sitting back in her chair and gesturing to the others. "Do join us. My niece has just arrived and is no doubt anxious to hear all the gossip."

"Fan?" Martha questioned softly. Both of the women turned eager eyes to her.

Katie swallowed hard. Catching Ella's suggestion from the corner of her eye, she nodded. "Ladies. How are you? I'm so glad you could join us. It's nice to be back."

She used the polite, formal tones of the women whose homes she'd once cleaned, fidgeting to keep from giggling. In one of her attempts to make money, she'd worked as a maid. Servants were considered invisible. The rich women had spoken freely around Katie, and she remembered their speech inflections. This was going to be fun, she thought, swallowing a grin. She would have to confess all of this. Tomorrow.

The Misses Chandler exchanged a curious glance, then took the proffered chairs. "We can stay but a minute. We have the Pews visiting this afternoon," Alice said grandly, then turned curiously to Katie. There was a faint disapproval in her voice and an amused mockery that Katie was all too familiar with. "Will you be staying awhile, dear? You've been away for such a long time."

Katie was about to respond when Ella cut in abruptly. "Of course she will. This is her home. Now that Fan is back, I trust you'll see her invited to all the best parties and teas. I want her reintroduced to society."

"I see." Martha coughed delicately. She glanced at Alice, and the two women shared a look, then Martha turned back to Ella. "I don't know quite how to say this. I mean, we'll do everything we can but . . . there is the scandal, you know.''

The silence was palpable. Martha looked down to her feet while Alice blushed a brilliant red. Ella appeared furious.

Katie swallowed hard, all too aware of the feeling of humiliation. She'd dealt with it herself for so long that all of her indignation was aroused on behalf of the missing Frances. These women, and dozens more like them, would scorn Fan simply because of an indiscretion, one that wouldn't raise more than an eyebrow with a man.

She had thought only the poor did this, shunned a woman who didn't quite conform, but she'd been very much mistaken. In some ways, the wealthy were even more cruel. She could just picture the whispers, the snide laughter, and the cutting remarks designed to punish Fan for daring to follow her heart.

Katie burned, her fists clutching her lace handkerchief and balling it into knots. She was about to speak hotly when Ella interrupted, her voice like ice.

"She is not a scandal," Ella said firmly. "She made a mistake. She is young; it has been known to happen."

"I know, I know!" Alice interjected. "And Martha didn't mean to pass judgment. It's just . . . you know how society people are. They could never forget that she ran off like that, with that man."

"I see." Ella fixed the two women with a harsh stare. "Then I suppose I'm obliged to remind them of your niece's little indiscretion, Martha. When she allowed that photographer to take her picture at the fair with the—dare I say it?—actor. Photographs are so inconvenient, aren't they? And I can't imagine what her fiancé would think."

Martha had turned an interesting shade of scarlet, Katie noticed. And Alice looked uneasy, a feeling that was rewarded a moment later when Ella turned to her.

"And I would hate to think they couldn't forget the rumor about your nephew, Alice, concerning the little problem he had in surgery. I know common information blamed that man's death last year on a medication, but I understood it was from Charles's drinking. You see, we both employed the same butler. Your nephew is a prominent physician with a future, especially now that he's a teetotaler. But if word got out—"

"You wouldn't!" Alice gasped.

Ella shook her head. "No, I wouldn't, just as I know you wouldn't refuse to help Fan. She never ran away with any man. Fan was ill while she was away visiting, and now has returned. I know you will both do everything within your power to see her reinstated."

The two women placed their cups down so hard Katie thought the china would break. She stared at Ella Pemberton in amazement. For a woman who was addled, she had a remarkable memory when it suited her, and she certainly handled these two busybodies perfectly. Katie wanted to cheer for her. Instead she got immense pleasure from the Misses Chandlers' discomfort.

Martha recovered first. "I'm so glad we've had this little talk. You are perfectly right, Ella. Fan, would you care to come to a reception tomorrow afternoon? I can quietly invite a few of the best people and begin to reinstate you into our midst."

"And tea on Sunday," Alice added. "I know everyone will want to see you when I explain things."

Katie grinned. "I would be delighted." If she had any misgivings about continuing the charade, they were vanquished. She owed it to Fan, and to women everywhere. And if it meant a little deception, so what? She was giving an elderly woman immense pleasure, and herself the opportunity of a lifetime. After all, Fan traveled in circles Katie O'Connor would never have access to. There was a long summer ahead filled with parties, balls, teas, and rich men. . . .

And for however long it lasted, she was Frances Pemberton. Maybe the luck of the Irish hadn't deserted her after all.

* * *

This is totally ridiculous. Christopher ruffled his hand through his hair and stared out the window of the train car, watching the open New Jersey countryside roll by. That a grown man would be on an expedition like this was almost unthinkable, and for himself it was doubly embarrassing.

"Stop scowling, Christopher," Aunt Eunice said without glancing up from her novel. "It is unseemly, and it won't help matters."

Christopher sent her a look betraying his lack of appreciation. "Well, how am I supposed to feel? We're going to Cape May in the hopes of landing a rich debutante for my wife. Do you know what that makes me?"

Eunice closed the book firmly and gave her nephew a steady stare. "Practical, is what it makes you. We've been through all this before. This is your best option. Cape May is a wonderful place to look for a wife. All of the wealthiest women, daughters of railroad executives, merchants, and builders, come here for the summer. You have every opportunity to meet them, wine and dine them, and under a starlit sky, come to an understanding. With the help of the ocean breezes, the balmy air, the sun-drenched days, even you can make a go of it."

"That's not the point." Christopher glowered. "I've had my share of success with women and you know it. What I am referring to is the reason behind it. This time I'm not courting someone because I care for her company or because I find her pretty. Now it's for her bank account."

"It is amazing how noble we get when confronted with the truth," Aunt Eunice remarked. "Do you really think your brethren, the dashing Philadelphia Main Liners, are not taking financial matters into consideration when choosing a wife? When was the last time one of your college friends married a poor woman? Or one without background? And they all expect a dowry." Eunice smiled as Christopher scowled again. "Grow up, my boy, and face reality. You are only doing the exact same thing."

"You seem to have forgotten one small detail," Christopher said bluntly. "To court a woman means money. I'll need clothes, funds for outings, rent for the house, money to give parties . . . it will require a considerable investment. And my own account is depleted."

"I know," Aunt Eunice said wisely. "I've already taken care of that. I sold some of the paintings and can invest in you through the summer. Don't give me that look, we have no choice. But I plan to see my money back. Like any other investment, I want to recoup the capital plus a dividend." Giving him a charitable smile, Aunt Eunice continued. "Do you think you can manage your part?"

"Yes." Christopher glared, then turned to look once more at the vacant countryside. Already he missed the city, with its fine wines, its good restaurants, tall buildings, and excitement. Cape May was nothing more than a sleepy shore town, bereft of anything but cottages and debutantes. He and his friends, the dashing socialites of the city, avoided the place like the plague. He'd had no time for young, inexperienced girls who wanted to be gently courted with poetry and nosegays. The debutantes bored him to death, the spoiled daughters of rich men who had never taken the time to develop character. He'd spent his childhood with them, gone to school with them, met them at teas and parties. He found their company oddly unfulfilling and didn't have the slightest idea why.

And now he had to marry one. He knew he'd have to someday; it was inevitable. A man of his position in society was expected to marry, and to a woman of the same standing. Aunt Eunice was right. It was his only choice, and this was the ideal place to find a wife.

But he didn't have to like it.

THREE

"God, how I despise these things." Christopher swallowed his brandy in one smooth gulp while his companion chuckled.

"Come now, the party isn't that bad." Charles Pepper grinned, indicating the young people gathering around the piano. "I see one or two girls worth making the acquaintance of, and the dinner was well done. You're making it intolerable."

"No, but it's about to get there now," Christopher said dryly as an elderly matron approached, obviously seeing them as prime candidates for her unwed daughters. Christopher winced. He had been relieved to find that an old college friend was in town on the same mission, and that he would have some tolerable company during his search for an eligible wife. Handsome and kind, Charles had no trouble attracting females, and made Christopher's job that much easier. Still, Charles couldn't make up for the hell he'd been through in the past week.

They were guests at the Drexels' that evening for a dinner party. Since he'd arrived at Cape May, Christopher had been to several dinners and balls just like this one, paying court to the young ladies in hopes of finding one who didn't have him yawning by ten-thirty. So far he'd been dismally

unsuccessful, but word had gotten out that he, Christopher
Scott of the Philadelphia Scotts, was available. Every
mother with marriageable daughters found him with all the
accuracy of a homing pigeon. Holding his brandy glass as if
for protection, he forced a smile as the woman cornered
him.

"Mr. Scott and Mr. Pepper." Mrs. Mitchell inclined her
head as the two young men acknowledged her presence. She
gave them a warm smile, then glanced innocently toward
the young women. "Have you met everyone here? I know
at dinner, conversation is sometimes difficult."

"I believe we have," Charles answered immediately.
"They are all charming, especially your daughters. Mary
and Nellie, I believe?"

"Why, yes," Mrs. Mitchell said, simpering and turning
her attention to Christopher. "Did I mention that Mary is
accomplished on the piano? And that Nellie can sing very
sweetly?"

"Yes, you did. Several times at dinner," Christopher said
bluntly, ignoring Charles's soft cough. "I am sure your
daughters are very talented," he amended, catching the
sharp look Charles gave him.

"They are that," Mrs. Mitchell said, beaming. "I suppose you'd like to dance with one of them later. Might I ask
which one you favor?"

Seeing the look on Christopher's face, Charles interrupted gallantly. "How can he possibly choose, Mrs.
Mitchell? They are both lovely and skillful."

Mrs. Mitchell grinned at him, then gave Christopher a
less-than-kind glance. "I do hope you both plan to come to
our reception next week. I know the girls are counting on
it."

"I will attend with the same eagerness that brought me
here tonight," Christopher responded. He saw Charles

cough again, hiding his laughter, then his companion agreed.

"We both look forward to it."

"Humph." Mrs. Mitchell nodded, then stalked away, aware that some devilry was going on, but not quite sure what. As soon as she was out of hearing distance, Charles laughed openly.

"You've got to stop that, Chris. You can't antagonize the mothers and expect to do well with the daughters."

Christopher frowned. "I know, but have you met them? Her daughters are enough to drive a man to drink. Such silly, vapid females . . . isn't there one woman here with some character, one who isn't afraid to have a real thought? My God, they are like cookie-cutter imitations of women."

Charles shrugged, glancing toward the crowd. There was some justification for Christopher's remarks. Born to a life of leisure, the debutantes were not the most interesting women he'd ever met either, but for himself, beauty and a nice disposition were enough. It was Christopher who wanted more, and Charles could understand his difficulty.

"May I have your attention, ladies and gentlemen?" Mrs. Drexel clapped her hands and the murmurs of conversation died. "We've persuaded Miss Chester, one of our lovely guests, to entertain us tonight on the piano while Miss Mitchell sings."

Everyone clapped while Christopher rolled his eyes as if in pain. Charles nudged him as one young lady took a seat at the piano and the other stood before it. The music began softly. Margaret Chester was a decent enough pianist and she managed to get through the first few bars without error. Christopher was just beginning to relax when Nellie Mitchell opened her mouth and began to sing, her voice like nails scraping on a chalkboard.

He wanted to cover his ears, but everyone else in the room listened with polite attention as the girl positively screeched. This was even worse than he'd anticipated. As always, no one reacted negatively. It was considered the height of bad manners to criticize a young lady's talents. Even Charles was maintaining a polite visage, seemingly oblivious to the girl's tone. When she tried to hit a high note and her voice broke, Christopher winced, unable to hide his reaction. In desperation, he glanced around the room, searching for an exit.

All of the people were smiling politely; all of them clapped softly and encouraged the young girl to perform once more when the torture finally ended. Miss Mitchell giggled, then launched into a second song that was equally atrocious. Christopher was about to retreat in disgust when a woman caught his attention. Seated in the center of the room, she clapped a handkerchief to her face, her body silently shaking.

She was laughing.

Intrigued, he watched her. Clad in a yellow silk dress with a bit of demure lace at the wrist and throat, she struggled to hide her chuckles while her eyes danced with hilarity.

Who was she? Christopher grinned at her, well aware of her source of amusement. She was next to a dowager, and he saw the elderly woman give her a disapproving look as she discreetly wiped a tear from her face. Raven-haired with a nose that was sprinkled with freckles, she stood out from her blond-haired companions like a rose in a field of daisies, but it was her eyes that captivated him. Brimming with mischief, they betrayed her, revealing the thoughts that the handkerchief would have hidden. Feeling his gaze on her, she glanced up, and their eyes met and held for one brief second.

He felt as if he'd been punched in the stomach. The reaction was instantaneous and bewildering, as potent as the strongest whiskey. Perplexed, he saw the same confusion on her face, replaced a moment later by laughter as Miss Mitchell lost another note. Scolded by the elderly woman again, she obediently turned back, but he couldn't tear his gaze away from her.

The music finally died and the assembly clapped politely. Christopher breathed a sigh of relief as Miss Mitchell departed from the piano and the ladies fought among themselves as to who was next.

"Nellie, why don't you—"

"I couldn't possibly."

"Miss Chandler, aren't you singing?"

"Thank you, but my throat is dry. Why not Miss Pemberton?"

"Yes, Miss Pemberton!"

"No, I couldn't . . ."

"Nonsense!"

Christopher had been barely paying attention when he noticed that the woman he'd been admiring was being pressured to sing. She caught his grin as she politely tried to decline. When the women insisted, she didn't have a choice and took her place at the piano while the others clapped softly.

She looked uneasy, her black hair shining in the gaslight, her nose crinkled as she arranged her dress. Settling back against the wall with his drink, Christopher smiled. At last, entertainment. He didn't have the faintest idea as to whether or not Miss Pemberton could sing, but he couldn't wait to find out after her amusement at Miss Mitchell's expense. She whispered something to Margaret, who gave her an odd look from the piano as she rustled through the sheet music. A few minutes later strains of soft, beautiful music filled the room, and Miss Pemberton's voice with it.

The song was "Greensleeves." Christopher recognized it instantly as the young woman sang, her voice hauntingly beautiful and full of emotion. It was an odd choice for a fashionable young lady, but no one seemed to care as the ancient song struck a chord in everyone's heart. Christopher detected the trace of a soft Irish accent in her words; that in itself was strange and he wondered again about Miss Pemberton. Spellbound, the audience listened with rapt attention as she deepened the song, her lilting brogue filling the air with visions of Ireland and its soft green fields, magical mists, and silver lakes. There wasn't a dry eye in the room when she finished, and the applause was thunderous.

"That was lovely, dear," Mrs. Mitchell said, wiping at her eyes. "I haven't heard that song since I was a little girl. Tell me, though, how did you manage to imitate a brogue so well?"

Katie started to reply, but it was Ella Pemberton who answered.

"Isn't she clever? She has only to hear an accent once and she can imitate it. Fan was always so bright, you know."

The assembly crowded around her, begging for another song as Miss Pemberton demurred. Observing her from the end of the room, Christopher turned to Charles, his cocky tone completely vanquished.

"Who is she?"

"Miss Pemberton?" Charles looked at him with some surprise. "You mean you haven't heard?"

"Heard what?"

"About the scandal." Charles lowered his voice. "Everyone's talking about it."

"What scandal?" Christopher glanced at Miss Pemberton once again, more interested than ever.

Charles sighed, then launched into the story with obvious misgivings. "It seems that Frances Pemberton disappeared years ago. You may have heard your parents mention it—the incident was in all the papers. The official story was that she met with an accident while away on a trip. But it was common knowledge that Fan ran off with a man.''

''I see.'' Christopher's eyes narrowed. For some reason, it bothered him to think of her loving a man, both physically and mentally. Ridiculous, he told himself. You haven't even met the chit. Still, he wished he had another brandy.

''Ella Pemberton took her back in recently. No one really knows where she's been or the identity of the man. The Missus Chandler are reinstating her into society, giving the story that she has been ill. You know their position; they are one of the first families and the wealthiest. No one dares dispute them.''

''How odd.'' Christopher's eyes couldn't leave the woman now. Laughing merrily at one of the men's outrageous compliments, she was obviously having a good time. He had the feeling she always did. ''I wonder what induced them to do that?''

''Probably Mrs. Pemberton,'' Charles said. ''They say she is devoted to the girl. The Pembertons have quite a bit of money themselves. If one didn't mind the scandal, the girl could be quite a catch.'' He smiled, watching Christopher's expression.

''Charles,'' Christopher said with a grin. ''I was thinking the exact same thing.''

He was incredibly handsome. Katie had to tear her eyes away from the man who watched her so covertly from the far side of the room.

He couldn't be interested in her. He was so . . . urbane, so cultured and sophisticated. He was dressed in a dark suit and a spotless white shirt that brought out the best of his polished black hair and whiskey colored eyes. But it was the amusement on his face, the joke that they'd shared, and the flash of longing she could have sworn she'd seen just before she'd turned away that mesmerized her.

Who was he? He was talking quietly with Charles Pepper,

a man that all the other girls agreed was the catch of the
season. In the past few weeks, she'd been having a
wonderful time as Fan, escorted to dozens of parties and
favored with attention from many of the upper class society
men. Still, she'd never seen him before. Curious, she
watched him, aware of a certain carelessness in his stance
and a devilish charm to his grin. A rogue, a rake and a
scoundrel—she would have bet her life he was all of those,
but there was something else about him that compelled her
to look back again and again.

"He is handsome, isn't he?" Bertrice Merriweather
commented, seeing Katie's interest. "That's Christopher
Scott, of the Philadelphia Scotts. He usually never comes
to these affairs, but rumor has it that he's looking for a
wife."

"What is he like?" Katie couldn't help but ask.

Bertrice shrugged, then giggled. "That's what we'd like
to know. All of the girls are in love with him, but he hardly
gives any of them a glance. Mrs. Mitchell has asked him to
supper for Nellie and Mary, but he hasn't really paid
attention to either of them."

"Why? When he wants to get married?"

"That's just it. No one can figure it out. He's either very
particular, or there's more to it. He spends most of his time
in the city, and his family is old money. Soaps, they say."
Bertrice sniffed indignantly. "I heard he's just fast."

Katie glanced back at Christopher. She saw the look of
amused tolerance on his face as Mrs. Merriweather joined
him, then turned to point out Bertrice. He seemed emphat-
ically bored, and it occurred to her that he considered
himself above all this. Glancing at Bertrice, he gave her a
polite smile, then his eyes met Katie's again with a warm,
sensual grin that sent shivers up her spine.

Shuddering, Katie turned away. The last thing she needed

was involvement with a man who was fast. She'd already had her heart broken once.

She wasn't looking for it to happen again.

The scandal. That explained it, Christopher thought dryly as he made his way to the dance floor. That was why Miss Pemberton seemed so different, so intelligent and so . . . interesting. She'd had some of life's experiences and was unique among the innocent young girls who surrounded her.

No wonder she'd captured his attention so completely. She was a woman with a past, one that was notorious from what he'd heard. He noticed that she wasn't without dancing partners and immediately understood why. Other men knew what he knew. While they might not court her, they would certainly try to bed her, a Pemberton or not.

His mouth tightened. She would be grateful if he offered marriage. This really was an ideal solution to both their problems. He would have the dowry he needed and she would have his name, an impeccable one at that. No doubt she would fall into his arms at the very thought.

"It's him, he's coming this way! It's Christopher Scott!" Bertrice whispered in a frenzy of feminine excitement. "Do you think he'll ask me to dance? I saw my mother talking to him earlier."

"I'm sure of it." Katie grinned, then accepted a glass of punch from a servant. Sipping the sweet brew, she watched Christopher approach, aware that he was even more handsome up close.

"Ladies." He bowed, suppressing a grin as Bertrice simpered, her face scarlet.

"Mr. Scott! I'm sooo pleased that you c-could join us!" Katie winced as Bertrice stuttered, fanning herself energetically. "It's suddenly so warm in here, I feel faint. Will you excuse me? I need to sit down."

Christopher nodded, watching with amusement as Bertrice backed away, then deposited herself on a chair, fanning her cheeks breathlessly. He turned back to Katie. "I do hope, Miss Pemberton, that you aren't inclined to the vapors?"

"Not in the least," Katie answered briskly, then grinned. "I couldn't manage a faint if I tried."

"Good." He took the glass from her hand and boldly placed it aside. "Will you dance, then?"

He was already leading her onto the floor, his manner sure and confident. Amused at his audacity, Katie wasn't in the least surprised to discover that he was a magnificent dancer. Lean and well proportioned, he moved with an easy grace that put to shame many of the other men who'd asked her to dance in the past few weeks.

"That was a wonderful song you did earlier this evening," Christopher said, whirling her around the floor. "Odd choice, however. Most of the young ladies pick something repulsive like 'I Dream of Jeanie with the Light Brown Hair.'"

"I'm not very fond of popular music," Katie answered truthfully, not adding that she seldom heard it. "I sing what I like."

"You have a very pretty voice. I could have sworn you had a touch of a brogue."

"I spent some time among the Irish," Katie said quickly, wanting to end this line of conversation as soon as possible. "Have you ever been abroad, Mr. Scott?"

"Christopher." He nodded. "Several times. You know, I was thinking tonight that I don't remember you too well. Did you come here often as a child?"

This was getting sticky. Katie nodded, trying to remember what little information she had about Fan. Ella did say she'd been here, so that much was safe. Still, there was something about the penetrating way that Christopher questioned her that made her uneasy. She had to divert him, and the sooner the better.

"Many times," she responded, trying to sound confident. "I am so disappointed that you don't recall, but they say age does that. Speaking of relics, just how old are you, Mr. Scott?"

Her ploy worked. Startled into laughter, he shrugged. "Almost thirty. I don't know if that counts as a relic, but it's old enough."

"Elderly," she agreed, but her eyes twinkled.

He grinned at her, holding her even closer. "So, Miss Pemberton, how long have you been back?"

He knew. With that one simple question, Katie was sure he'd heard of the scandal. It was the talk of the town, so she shouldn't have been surprised. Glancing up at him, she saw there was no censure in his face, no disapproval. Instead there was acceptance and, surprisingly, amused interest.

"For a few weeks now. It was very hard on my aunt with me gone. I really shouldn't have stayed away so long, but I was just too ill."

His face changed slightly with an expression that she didn't recognize. He seemed to tense, as if it mattered to him personally. But that was ridiculous, he didn't even know her. Whatever it was, the expression was gone in a moment and he shrugged, letting his hand gather hers as the music ended.

"Bertrice was right about one thing, it is very warm in here. Would you join me on the porch?"

Katie stiffened. As Fan, she'd had several invitations like this one, and they all meant one thing. Usually some sophomoric lad with peach-fuzzed cheeks, hearing the rumors about her, would entice her away and try to make love to her. She'd sent one man into the boxwood shrubs just the previous night at the Pews, another into the fountain behind the Swarthmores' cottage. If Christopher intended nothing more than a crude seduction, she would rather know it now.

"All right." She followed him outside, breathing deeply of the fresh sea air and the cool breezes. Cape May was beautiful at night, the sky studded with stars like crushed crystal on black velvet, reflected in the ocean below. The ornate cottages of the railroad executives lined the beach like gingerbread houses, each with an identical charming porch, cupola, and a witches' cap tower. It was enough to make one believe in fairy tales, but Katie knew better. For her, there was never a happily-ever-after. Apparently there wasn't one for Fan either.

Disappointed, she turned to Christopher expectantly, waiting for a fumbling attempt at a kiss or a grope. Strange, she had expected better of him, but then one never knew. Apparently lechers came clothed in fifty-dollar suits as well as dock workers' caps.

Christopher didn't touch her. Instead he leaned against the porch railing and stared pensively at the tossing ocean. "Miss Pemberton," he began, his tone confident and businesslike. "I believe in being up front and right to the point. I am, as you have observed, of marrying age. I come from a good family and have many of the right connections within the city. I've heard I'm not an unhandsome man and, when the mood strikes me, am even considered congenial."

Katie stared at him in stunned surprise, then he continued in the same voice.

"You, on the other hand, need a husband. I know all about the scandal . . . and you have my word that it doesn't concern me in the least. You seem pretty enough, and if tonight is any indication, you are certainly accomplished. But I am aware that marriage proposals aren't very likely to come your way. You need respectability—I can provide that. I need a wife." He took a deep breath, then shrugged, turning toward her with a cocky grin. "In short, what I'd like to know is . . . will you marry me?"

❊ FOUR

Katie stared at him for a moment in stunned silence, then burst into laughter, her giggles loud and infectious. Christopher frowned, his lack of amusement clear as she continued to chuckle helplessly. She laughed until she cried and was forced to retrieve a lace handkerchief from her pocket and wipe her tears.

"What is so funny?" he demanded, growing more annoyed by the moment.

"I'm sorry," Katie said, though she continued to giggle. "I didn't mean to offend you. It's just that I've never had such a romantic proposal before. I suppose you just swept me off my feet and I don't know how to act."

A wry smile came to his face as he surveyed her, her last words whispered with the soft innocence of a southern belle. Even in the dim light he could see her eyes dancing with amusement, and the joke was definitely on him.

Yet he had to admit she had cause. In his eagerness to see the matter done and behind him, he hadn't approached her with any finesse. Most other women would have been flattered; it wasn't every day the most eligible bachelor in town offered to marry them. Yet Fan saw through to the ridiculousness of the situation and didn't seem at all impressed by the grand nature of his offering.

"I see," Christopher said, his smile deepening when she finally managed to stop laughing. "Then it wasn't my proposal you were rejecting, just the manner in which it was offered."

"I didn't say that," Katie responded quickly. There was something in the way he looked at her, with a devilish kind of interest, that made her uneasy. "I have to admit, though, that I'm not used to men asking me to marry them after one dance. And in spite of the desperate nature of my predicament, I am not in such dire straits that I would agree to a proposal, though I appreciate your kindness."

"I suppose you're right." Christopher nodded, turning toward her. He didn't miss the emphasis on the word "kindness," and he had to stop himself from laughing with her. Instead he spoke in a grave tone. "I could get down on one knee—would that make it acceptable?"

Katie gasped when he did exactly that, then clasped her hand in his with an earnest expression on his face. Horrified, she glanced toward the window, trying to retrieve her hand while he held on to it tightly.

"What do you think you're doing?" she hissed, her brogue deepening. "Do you want someone to see you?"

"I can't help it," he protested, gazing up at her with feigned devotion. "Ever since I met you tonight, I knew there could never be anyone else. Dare I say it? I think I'm in l—"

"Get up!" Katie hauled him to his feet and snatched back her hand. Margaret Chester peered out through the lace curtains and Katie smiled at her and waved, indicating the cool night air as the reason for their presence on the porch. Margaret nodded, then closed the curtains with a knowing expression.

"Now you've done it," Christopher said. "You've drawn the attention of the most notorious gossip in town. Now you'll have to marry me to avoid another scandal.

When would you like to set the date—I've always liked winter weddings, don't you?''

Katie stared at him, aghast. ''I wouldn't marry you if you were the last man on earth! Now, if you will get out of my way, I would like to rejoin the party.''

''Then you leave me no choice, Miss Pemberton.'' Katie tried to pull past him, but he caught her hand once more and held her firmly. ''I will have to give in and court you. I really thought that since we were two responsible, mature adults, we could skip such formalities, but I see that such is not the case. I am disappointed, however. I thought here is finally a woman who's not afraid to break tradition, who knows her own mind and goes after what she wants. Now I'll have to convince you in the old-fashioned way. I suppose it would stop the gossips.''

''I think you've lost your mind,'' Katie said in wonder. ''Were you always such a gentleman? Or did it come by degrees?''

He laughed then, throwing back his head and chuckling with such masculine mirth that had she been in another frame of mind, Katie would have laughed with him. ''Miss Pemberton, I assure you I am one hundred percent sane. I will call on you tomorrow and bring you—what is it that's acceptable? Candy or flowers, I believe?''

''You can go straight to the devil.'' Katie's eyes flashed and she pulled hard, trying to break away from him. This time he let her, and as she stormed into the house he grinned, watching the swish of her skirts and the gleam of her glossy hair.

She was everything he'd hoped she'd be and more. Fan Pemberton promised intelligence, passion, a sense of humor, and a bit of mystery. He frowned as he recalled her accent, growing deeper when she got angry. And ''go to the devil''? That was hardly a phrase a wealthy lady would use. For all her appearance of propriety, Fan Pemberton was ten times more interesting than her prim and proper counterparts. She was a treasure of contradictions, one that promised to endlessly baffle him, frustrate him, and tease him.

Her violent objection to his proposal didn't daunt him in the least. If anything, he was more determined than ever to win her. Marriage to Fan Pemberton was the perfect solution.

To both their problems.

"Are you bathing today, dear?" Ella Pemberton said when Katie descended the stairs, clad in a candy-striped bathing costume and robe. Ella, seated in the parlor playing solitaire, gave Katie a fond smile.

Pulling the wrapper more closely around her, Katie grinned mischievously. "This is a lot cooler than the petticoats. I think I'll find an excuse to go bathing every day."

"Humph." Eileen plunked down the tea tray with disapproval, making more noise than the action merited. Ella glanced at her from her cards, one eyebrow raised. "Looks scandalous to me," the maid remarked.

"Nonsense," Ella said firmly. "It's what all the other young ladies are wearing, and Fan needs to be up on the latest styles. Who are you going with?"

"Margaret Chester, Mary and Nellie Mitchell. They are sending their carriage around for me."

"That's so nice," Ella said, ignoring Eileen's scowls. "They are sweet young ladies and can help you meet a lot of other friends, though it doesn't appear you'll need their assistance. Another bouquet arrived for you this morning."

Katie grimaced as she glanced toward the array of flowers and dozens of boxes of candy that graced the parlor table. "Mr. Scott?"

Eileen nodded, showing her the latest offering, a pretty bundle of daisies. "That man must be addled, sending you all these things. If he only knew—"

"I think it's kind," Ella said with a twinkle. "He is very handsome, you know, and charming."

"So are snakes," Katie said, wrinkling her nose. "He is obnoxious, overbearing, has the manners of a tomcat . . ."

"Really?" Ella smiled pleasantly. "I thought him rather nice. And he is certainly taken with you, miss. He's sent something every day. Either you'll have to marry that man or open a flower shop."

Katie shrugged, but couldn't resist a glance at the flowers. They were lovely, and she had to admire his determination. In spite of the extremely negative impression he'd made on her that night at the Drexels' party, he was certainly going out of his way to redeem himself. But then she remembered him laughingly saying he'd go through with a courtship, as if the ending were already certain. What a conceited and arrogant man!

"And he's from one of the wealthiest families on the Main Line." Ella yawned, as if the matter didn't concern her one way or the other. "They are definitely gentry."

"And, like most gentry, know the difference between a Thoroughbred and a hack horse," Eileen said pointedly.

"You talk such nonsense these days, Eileen," Ella said sharply. "One would think you're addled instead of me. Have a good time, child." She smiled as the carriage rolled up.

Katie was glad to escape. Christopher Scott was not a subject she cared to discuss. Now or ever.

The coach looked like a flower cart, crammed with girls of varied ages and sizes, all of them garbed in the daring new bathing costumes that were similar to Katie's. Katie joined them, carrying with her some towels and a brush. After tossing them into the center of the floor, she sat beside Bertrice Merriweather. She and Bertrice had quickly become good friends in the past few weeks. With her appealing blond looks and large blue eyes, Bertrice had her own share of admirers, and she appreciated Katie's wit and good humor. Katie found Bertrice sweet and unfailingly kind.

The Misses Mitchell were another story. Jealous of Katie's attention from Christopher, they deliberately shunned her until Bertrice persuaded them otherwise. Now they tolerated her, but were far from friendly, while Margaret was downright vicious.

Having spread the rumor about the scandal, Margaret made sure everyone knew about Katie's indiscretion with Christopher on the porch. Irrationally insecure, Margaret was only happy when she was the center of attention, no matter how that was accomplished. Since Fan was under the protection of the Misses Chandler, she had to be careful, but Margaret was used to such complications. Always appearing kind, she nevertheless knew how to cause a great deal of trouble and usually did.

It was Margaret who commented first on Katie's costume. "I'm so glad you got something appropriate to wear," she said sweetly, though her voice was filled with venom. "That outfit you had last week was positively ancient."

Katie smiled, though she had to fight her Irish instincts and not punch the girl. "Much of my clothing was not appropriate for this climate. I was out west, you know—there wasn't much reason for a bathing costume among the cows."

The other girls broke into laughter and began teasing Margaret. "Did you think she'd be swimming in some water hole?"

"There isn't exactly an ocean out in the desert!"

"Margaret missed geography—she was too busy making eyes at Willie Todd!"

All of the girls dissolved into laughter again, but Katie

didn't miss the flash of anger in Margaret's eyes, which was directed at her. Katie gave her a huge smile, which only infuriated the girl more. Thankfully the coach pulled up to the beach and the girls piled out, then raced to the water.

The surf was a brilliant blue green, the water so clear that one could easily see the sand. There had been a storm the previous night, and the beach was lined with seashells of every imaginable shape and hue. Seaweed floated through the water like a mermaid's tresses, waving gently with the ebb and flow of the sea, while starfish glided through the surf like fallen angels. It was beautiful, restless, and exhilarating. It was also freezing.

The girls laughingly ran into the waves, then shrieked as the cold water plastered their swimming costumes to their bodies. Nellie Mitchell scooped up a handful of water and doused Katie, who quickly returned the favor. A water fight broke out until all of them were soaked, then they fled to the beach to towel themselves dry.

A gull cried overhead and sandpipers ran toward the waves, their little feet scampering comically. Katie sat on her towel as the other girls joined her, talking quietly or dozing in the warm sun. She couldn't stop the tightness in her throat as she envisioned her six-year-old son, running through the waves, laughing and playing in the ocean. God, he would love this. She missed him so much, and even knowing he was well cared for didn't stop the ache in her heart as she realized that he'd never know this life, never know anything but pain and hard work. Why was it that some people had so much and others so little?

She remembered asking her father when she was little and had seen a fancy carriage passing by, filled with beautiful ladies in silk dresses. Seamus O'Connor grew quiet then, staring at his little daughter dressed in frayed cotton, her feet bare, knowing she would never have such a dress. He got roaring drunk that night and sang "I'll Take

You Home Again, Kathleen'' outside the mayor's house. Katie always knew that the two events were connected, but it was something they never talked about.

May you be at peace, Pa, she thought. A tear started in her eyes and stung the back of her throat as she envisioned the run-down area of Philadelphia, the lines of laundry stretching from one dingy row house to another, the broken piles of wood from dilapidated buildings that filled the alleys and provided homes to dozens of rats, the tin washtubs that hung on the outside of the walls, waiting for a weekly bath.

There was one lamp on the street, one light that drew people like moths to a flame and illuminated the gloomy alleyway. When the first star appeared, she would sit there with her child, hearing the cacophony of voices, the passionate Italian marketers hawking their wares, the pugnacious Irish who were always ready for a joke or a brawl, the guttural German accents that, as the night progressed, grew softer with beer. It was their one escape from an existence that offered no others.

Ryan O'Connor, her brother, couldn't take it anymore and disappeared out west in search of gold. Moira, her aunt, worked in the kitchens of the wealthy. At night, she would drink raucously and dress up in her one good gown and insist she was Lillie Langtry. Her mother took in laundry, struggling to see in the dim light. She was old well before her time, and Katie saw herself in Catherine's webbed face and lifeless eyes. . . .

And Katie hated it. When John Sweeney approached her, with his cocksure charm and handsome face, she couldn't have resisted him any more than she could have resisted a twenty-dollar gold piece lying in the street. He had plans, plans that would take them away from all this. The dashing Irishman with the devil's own wit made her believe. She knew it was wrong, but when he touched her hair, her face and lips, she no longer cared.

This time she couldn't hide the sniffle that choked her. It had all been lies. God, she had been such a fool. He had left her, in spite of his words, in spite of everything that had passed between them. He had used her, then discarded her like an old rag. Even when he learned of his child, he hadn't come back, hadn't tried to help her, hadn't even come to see his own son. Ah, but she learned, even if it was the hard way. She didn't have anything else to do with men, and they didn't have anything to do with her. She was Irish, poor, had a child, and was alone. She could expect nothing else.

Until now. Somehow fate had thrown gold in her direction, and for as long as it lasted, she, Katie O'Connor, was Frances Pemberton. She sensed something good would come of this, that she would find a way to help her family, and hope for her son. Perhaps she really wasn't such a bad person . . . maybe God had forgiven her after all.

A noise broke her thoughts and she glanced up, quickly wiping a tear. Several young men were approaching, dressed in hunting pants and carrying rifles. It was common sport among the gentry to shoot at the little sand snipes, and it seemed that the gentlemen had been occupied doing that when they stumbled along this beach.

"Oh my." Nellie smoothed her hair and reddened, reaching quickly for her robe. "It's Christopher Scott, Charles Pepper . . . and I think one of the Forrester boys. Oh, and there's Peter Tyler."

"It's scandalous for them to see us like this," her sister chimed in, snatching up her own robe. "My Lord, when Mother hears of this . . ."

"Well, she won't unless you tell her," Margaret responded. "I certainly don't plan to tell mine. Why, Bertie, I think you're blushing. Don't worry, I think Charles would be delighted to see you in your costume. Yoo-hoo!"

Margaret waved broadly, attracting the men's attention. They approached the girls, chuckling as Bertrice dived beneath the umbrella and Margaret stood up, displaying her costume to its best advantage. Katie stayed where she was, picking up a dime novel and pretending to be engrossed in the story. A shadow fell across her page and she was forced to look up, observing Christopher's wicked smile.

"I'm charmed, Miss Pemberton. I had no idea you'd be here today."

Katie closed the book. "Most gentlemen avoid this beach in the morning," she said, emphasizing the word "gentlemen." "They know we come to bathe."

"My apologies. We had no idea. Although I can't really say I'm sorry." Christopher gave her a look that seemed to sear right through the thin costume she wore and she had to fight to keep from crossing her arms over her breasts.

"Mr. Scott," she whispered so she wouldn't attract the others' attention, "you have got to be the rudest, most insulting man I have ever met."

"I know." He seemed saddened by her appraisal, but she didn't miss the laughter in his eyes. "So are you saying you've agreed to marry me?"

Katie gasped. "I wouldn't marry you if you were the last man on earth."

"I see." He smiled back, not in the least insulted. "What would it take, then? Aren't I rich enough, handsome enough? I've already proven my charm."

"And humility," Katie agreed.

"Then perhaps I just haven't presented myself well. I am Christopher Scott, of the Philadelphia Scotts. I live on Walnut Street in the family estate. I play a good game of poker, terrible billiards, and mediocre chess, unless there is money involved."

"That's very noble of you."

"My friends call me Chris."

"Of which you have many, I'm sure." Katie opened her

book and resumed reading. "Please feel free to go on, Mr. Scott. I find this horribly fascinating."

"Do you believe her?" he asked Bertrice, who was still hiding from Charles beneath the umbrella. "I daresay I get more sympathy from a pit bull."

"Mr. Scott." Margaret flounced up beside him. "It is so hot out here, and I was just saying to Mr. Pepper how nice a walk would be. Would you care to accompany us?"

Christopher hesitated for a moment, just long enough for Katie to peer up from her book and give Margaret a scathing glance. Chuckling quietly, he rose from one knee and brushed the sand from his trousers.

"No, I think not. Thank you, anyway. There's a brace of snipes a few miles down. I think I'll engage in some real sport this afternoon, one where I stand half a chance."

Katie merely nodded when he made his farewells while Margaret joined Charles and started down the beach. Bertrice emerged a moment later, obviously upset.

"I can't believe he just went off with her like that."

"Don't worry, Margaret is just like that," Nellie said reassuringly. "I know Charles likes you. He was looking at you the whole time."

"Do you think so?" Bertrice asked anxiously.

Katie agreed. "I think he only left with Margaret because he didn't think you were interested. You have to stop hiding from him. You're giving him the wrong idea."

"That Mr. Scott sure seems intent upon you," Bertrice said happily. "Why, no matter what you said to him, he kept coming back for more. I've never seen a man more taken with a girl."

Nellie and Mary exchanged a look, but Katie simply shrugged.

"He just wants what he can't have, just like most men. I should tell him yes and really upset him." She shivered, though the idea wasn't as distasteful as it should have been.

Christopher Scott was beginning to get on her nerves. And he was a distraction she couldn't afford.

Margaret returned much more quickly than anyone would have anticipated, Katie thought in satisfaction. The lunch was eaten, and the girls stretched out on their blankets for an afternoon nap. Within moments they were all asleep. Katie was unable to find that refuge for herself, even with the help of the book. Used to a vigorous life, she found the leisure of the wealthy excessive and could seldom find the need for a daytime nap.

Getting to her feet, she decided to walk along the surf, enjoying the weather and the water. Kicking the waves, she was oblivious to everything until she reached a small inlet several hundred feet away. A motion in the water caught her attention and she gasped, realizing she wasn't alone.

A man was in the ocean.

Katie watched in shocked fascination as he stood in the waves like an Adonis. His body was partially hidden by the water, but even from the distance she could tell that he wore little or nothing. When the surf seemed just right, he turned and dived into the water, allowing the waves to carry him to shore.

Katie reluctantly admired his form. He was a good swimmer, obviously used to this life and having ample time to polish his skill. As he rose she saw that he was in excellent shape, his body lean and muscular, moving with a deceptive grace. Wading into the ocean again, he swam out to the deeper part, his body slicing through the waves like a half-human, half-sea creature.

She didn't know when she recognized him, but within moments, knew it was him. Vexed that he swam as well as he danced or probably anything else, she nevertheless couldn't take her eyes from him as he moved expertly through the water.

A dark pile of something on the beach caught her attention, and when he had his back to her, she crept closer and saw that it was his clothes. The temptation was overwhelming. A mischievous impulse possessed her and she snatched them up, tossing them behind a sand dune. She managed to get back to the beach, where her friends were slowly awakening, and she strolled forward, whistling in pure innocence.

"Fan! I was worried about you," Bertrice said, obviously relieved. "I awoke a few minutes ago and you were nowhere in sight."

"I was walking," Katie said, managing to hide her laughter. "In fact, you all must come. I thought I saw a dolphin."

"A dolphin!" Even the Misses Mitchell were excited, and for once Margaret had no sarcastic comments. Snatching up their robes, the girls then donned them and ran down to the water's edge to admire the creature.

Katie hid her laughter as Christopher looked up, obviously startled by his unexpected company. He glanced quickly to the shore and saw that his clothes had disappeared. Hearing feminine giggles, he could do nothing but stand waist-deep in the water while the girls tittered in embarrassment.

"Why, it's Mr. Scott!" Katie cried out innocently. "I didn't recognize you without your cravat."

The girls hid their faces and laughed while her eyes boldly met his. A slow smile came to his face as he quickly envisioned what had happened, and who was behind it. Sketching a bow that was not as graceful as it might have been under other circumstances, he braced his hands on his hips and gave them a bright smile, determined to make the best of the situation.

"Good afternoon, ladies. I would invite you in, but I think *Godey's* would frown on that, don't you?"

Bertrice nearly fainted with embarrassment while the Misses Mitchell dissolved into laughter. Katie grinned, then waved her hand.

"Why don't you join us, then? We don't mind the company." She gave him a smile as brilliant as his own, her face a study in innocence.

"Why, I think I will." He started to walk toward the shore, then stopped when Bertrice began fanning herself as if she really would faint. "I'm just joking, ladies, though it may come to pass if I have to stay here much longer. I'll be wrinkled through to the knees."

The girls laughed, then, red-faced, ran toward the beach where the picnic awaited. "Miss Pemberton!" Christopher called. There was something in his voice that made Katie stop and she turned, looking at him with such a droll expression that he had to laugh himself. "Where are my clothes?"

"I don't have the faintest idea," Katie said, widening her eyes. "And I have to join my friends—"

"Get them," he said sternly. "Or I will come out now. And that will make two scandals for Fan Pemberton."

Katie sighed, then retrieved his clothes and tossed them on the beach. Running away without looking back, she heard his laughter behind her, but she didn't care in the least. She'd won this round, and it was worth every risk to see the confident Mr. Scott become uneasy, even for a moment.

❈ *FIVE*

Katie was still chuckling when she came down to dinner that night. Every time she pictured Christopher in the water, and his expression when he realized she'd taken his clothes, she couldn't help but laugh. Although she'd never admit it, a part of her had been a little distracted by his very masculine form. No armchair philosopher, he evidently led a vigorous life and it showed. A surge of feminine excitement tingled through her as she envisioned him in the ocean, his lean body only partially concealed by the gray-blue water. Stop it, she told herself. The fool was conceited enough without her admiring him. Still, to see him discomfited was worth any price.

"That dress is lovely, Fan. The blue really sets off your eyes and hair," Ella said with a fond glance at her niece. She indicated a chair. "I must say you've enjoyed your outing today. I've never seen you in such high spirits."

Katie smiled softly as she took the seat. It was getting easier and easier to think of herself as Fan Pemberton, and she found that she responded to that name almost as quickly as she would to her own. "We had a great time. I saw Mr. Scott today in the ocean. I have to say it was very revealing."

Eileen brought in the dinner plates, then slammed them

out on the table. "Sounds like a fool notion to me," she remarked. "Bathing in that ocean near naked! In my day young ladies wouldn't think of such a thing."

She emphasized the word "ladies." Katie gave her a sharp look while Ella nodded.

"In your day you would have been perfectly correct. But these are modern times, and doctors now approve of exercise. And all of the fashionable young ladies are so engaged. It is a good way to socialize, outside of the formal customs of a dance or a ball."

Before Eileen could argue, there was a knock on the door. "I believe that is our dinner companions," Ella said sweetly, with an absentminded air. "Would you mind setting out two extra places? I think I forgot to mention that we were having guests."

Katie looked at Eileen in confusion, but the housekeeper seemed to have no more idea than she about their dinner plans. With a shrug, Eileen left the room to answer the door, then returned a moment later.

"Yes." Ella nodded, then turned to Katie. "Mr. Scott is here, with his aunt. Let's join them in the front room, dear, and leave Eileen to her work."

Katie froze, staring at Ella Pemberton in disbelief. It was he—Christopher Scott! She knew she would run into him again; it was inevitable. But she wasn't quite prepared to meet him the same day she had set him up so admirably.

Swallowing hard, she glanced quickly into the mirror, wondering how Frances would handle this. What she saw didn't help. She was too tall, her hair unfashionably black, her nose sprinkled with freckles. She looked like a poor Irish girl, not the niece of this wealthy woman. And now she had to get through a dinner with Christopher Scott and his aunt seated across the table from her!

"Miss Pemberton." Christopher gallantly greeted the older woman first, his expression a model of politeness.

Dressed in an immaculate dark suit with a sparkling white shirt, he looked every inch the gentleman and entirely too handsome. Katie didn't wonder at the attention he received from the other girls. When he finished greeting Ella, he turned to her and his smile deepened. She could hear the laughter in his voice as he bowed to her, then insisted on taking her hand.

"My dear Miss Pemberton. It has been too long since we've . . . seen each other."

Katie fumed, longing to snatch back her hand, but there was no way she could object without attracting Ella's attention. She noticed his aunt was looking at her closely, as if curious about her reaction. Katie forced a sweet smile.

"Yes, it has been. Did you enjoy your swim today, Mr. Scott? I noticed you seemed right at home in the water. Much like a shark, or a barracuda, I would think."

He threw back his head and laughed, while taking a seat beside Ella and Eunice. "Yes, I am an accomplished swimmer. I must say the tide was very rough today. It carried off just about everything, including some personal articles. Did you have any such problem?"

He wouldn't . . . he wouldn't tell Ella what she'd done. She could just imagine the older woman's reaction when she heard that her genteel niece had carried off the clothing of this gentleman, just to make him a laughingstock. Somehow Katie was sure Ella wouldn't get the joke. Fighting to keep her composure, she managed another bright smile, though her eyes implored him.

"No, I can't say that I did. Would you like a drink or something, Mr. Scott? Mrs. Scott? Wine before dinner?"

He smiled broadly, then nodded. "That would be very nice, Miss Pemberton."

Eunice and Ella declined, and Katie left, glad to escape. She was forced to wait on him, but that was nothing compared with what he could do to her. Grimacing, she envisioned a meal full of his innuendos and barbed comments. She had it coming, that much she knew. But it didn't make the prospect any pleasanter. Christopher apparently intended to retaliate for her prank, and there was nothing she could do about it.

Bringing the glass back to the parlor, she paused in the doorway, surprised to see him playing cards with Ella and his aunt. Ella turned over a card, then blushed and laughed at her choice while Christopher applauded her strategy. Eunice made a sharp remark, then they all laughed, Christopher obviously enjoying himself. Katie frowned. Somehow his generosity with the older ladies didn't fit the picture she had of him as a heartless rogue, especially when, a few moments later, he let Ella win the hand.

Ella was still blushing and laughing when Katie reentered with the wine and handed him the glass. He gave her a grin when he took it, his fingers gently brushing hers as he accepted the drink.

"I almost thought you weren't returning," he said, implying that retreat was her first tactic. "I just got duly trounced by your aunt."

"You are too generous," Ella said, though Katie could tell she was pleased. "I've been practicing, but I've yet to equal your skill."

"Yes, but you did win. My congratulations."

Ella couldn't have been happier. Flattered by Christopher's attentions, she was like a young girl again. Katie followed them into dinner, watching thoughtfully as he pulled out the chair for the older women. Yet there was nothing contrived in his actions. Instinctively, she knew that he did this as a matter of respect and genuine affection.

Reluctantly she thought of her own grandfather and her elderly aunt. Patrick O'Connor told endless tales of the old country and his career in the sassenach army. Moira was more than a little daft and didn't care who knew it. Yet they loved Katie and her son unconditionally, and it always hurt her to see them given less attention or respect than they deserved. Christopher, she realized in astonishment, would probably treat them courteously, in spite of their eccentricities.

Katie took the seat farthest away from him. It was just too unnerving to be close to him, especially now when she was forced to change some of her notions about him. She withdrew from the conversation, answering only in monosyllables, but the three of them managed just fine without her. Watching him covertly, Katie had to admit that he was the perfect guest. Ella and Eunice begged him for gossip and spoke at length about everything from tea tables to the Main Line families.

"It is so nice to have a gentleman present for dinner!" Ella said gratefully when the first course was cleared away. "I always say we are too much alone, just us women in the house. Tell us about your business, Christopher, your investments and such. I am always so interested in such doings, and don't hear nearly enough about them."

Katie glanced up, aware that she knew very little about him. Christopher shrugged casually. "I'm . . . investing in art these days," he said slowly.

"Art!" Ella turned to Katie enthusiastically. "Fan once took drawing lessons! She really is quite good, though I haven't been able to prevail upon her to paint for us since she's been back." When Katie refused to respond, she turned back to her guest. "What kind of art are you working with?"

"I'm presently in the business of selling some paintings," Christopher said quickly. "When I've raised enough capital, I'm thinking of a merger of assets. Enough to start another enterprise."

"I see," Ella said in confusion while Eunice had a coughing attack.

"What he means is, he is thinking of forming a mutually beneficial conglomerate," Eunice explained. "Enough about business, though. I find the conversation tiring. I would like to hear more about Fan's painting. Are you fond of the new French Impressionism, dear? I don't quite understand it myself."

Katie gulped, aware that all eyes were on her. She hadn't the faintest idea of what they were talking about, but she had the feeling that the real Frances would. Seeing Christopher's interested gaze, she shrugged, determined not to let him see her defeated.

"I don't quite care for it myself," Katie said thoughtfully. "I think there is something too bold about it."

"Whatever do you mean?" Eunice questioned bluntly. "I've always thought Impressionism to be very subtle. The slightest shading of color lends a whole new meaning to the subject. I can't imagine it being described as bold."

Flustered, Katie glanced at Ella, but even the older woman seemed puzzled. Somehow she had to think of a way out of this one. Amazingly it was Christopher who saved her.

"I think what Fan means is that the idea is bold," he commented. "Now that we have photographs, we don't have the same need for realism in painting. The Impressionists, by using only light and color, convey much more than a true-to-life oil."

"That's it exactly," Eunice said, delighted with her answer. "And one is never quite sure what the hues represent. One is simply left with a feeling, an emotion, which is what good art is all about. What a wonderful observation, Fan."

Katie gave Christopher a look of profound gratitude, which immediately earned her a charming smile, one so dazzling she had to hide behind her glass. A strange fluttering started in her stomach, which she attributed to the wine. It couldn't be anything else, but when she dared to look again, she couldn't stop the thoughts that entered her mind.

He was so good-looking, perfectly handsome, in fact. She winced as she pictured the dock workers from the city, the boys she'd grown up with who hooted when she walked to her job. None of them, not even the rugged Carey Murphy, whom all the girls drooled over, could hold a candle to Christopher.

All right, so he was handsome. And charming when he wanted to be. Rich. And funny. She had to hold back a giggle as she remembered his proposal on the Drexels' porch. Why was she fighting this? He was, in fact, everything a girl dreamed of. Then why was she so afraid?

Because he might find out. Because he'd hate you if he did. Because you're not Fan Pemberton, but a poor Irish maid who cleans houses and hires out as a ladies' companion. You have a child, you don't have money . . . you've never even had a husband. My God—she shook herself. What are you thinking? There was not a happy ending for women like her, and she'd best not forget it.

"Frances, Mr. Scott is speaking to you," Ella said firmly.

Katie glanced up. "Oh? I am sorry. What did you say?"

"I said there is a small theater troupe playing in the hotel tomorrow night. It is not as grand as Philadelphia, but it should prove entertaining. Would you care to go?"

"Oh, how lovely for you, dear!" Ella exclaimed. "And I happen to know you are not engaged tomorrow night. You will have such a good time!"

Katie forced a smile. "I am sorry, but Aunt Ella, you forgot that the Misses Mitchell are coming by for dessert. I can't possibly go."

"No, dear, they canceled," Ella said brightly. "I received a note from them earlier."

"Perhaps if Miss Pemberton really doesn't care for the

play, it is impolite to force her,'' Eunice said sharply, hiding a smile behind her coffee cup. "Christopher, I think you should withdraw the invitation.''

Everyone waited expectantly. Christopher stared at Katie while she gulped the hot coffee, burning her tongue. If she refused, she'd make him look like a fool. If she accepted . . .

If she accepted, she risked everything. He was too cool, too urbane, too handsome and dangerous. He posed more of a threat than John Sweeney, for she could sense that Christopher's charm could be deadly. And if he found out too much about her, she would lose it all. Like Cinderella, the midnight hour would toll and she'd turn once more back into a scullery maid.

Everything practical told her to refuse. Everything emotional told her she couldn't walk away from this. You have one chance at happiness, Katie, her father had told her. Just one life. Don't be afraid to take risks, to laugh and to love. . . .

"I am free tomorrow,'' she heard herself answering. "I will be glad to go.''

"Fine,'' he said. "I'll call for you at seven, then.''

He gave her a dazzling smile and Katie had the distinct impression that she was sinking into quicksand without a rope. Christopher Scott was a threat to her in every way possible.

God help her.

✿ Six

She was perfect. Christopher couldn't stop the contented smile on his face as he sat across from his aunt in the carriage heading home. Sharp-tongued and witty, sensual and pretty, Fan Pemberton was like a rich wine, heady and full of delightful contrasts.

Her expression when she'd met him for dinner was priceless, especially after the stunt she'd pulled earlier. No other woman of his acquaintance would have dared such a thing as stealing his clothes. Most of the debutantes seemed notoriously ignorant of a man's body, and often pretended that the human form stopped below the neck. Yet Fan's earthy approach to the situation and her courage to play such a joke intrigued him more than all the simpering blushes in the world.

And it wasn't as if she was that experienced. There was a maidenly shyness about her that appeared at unexpected times that made him think she wasn't the wanton that the scandal implied. He'd known women at the gambling halls who enjoyed lovemaking simply for the experience. They didn't turn their head from him, nor did their eyes cloud in confusion when he smiled. They met his invitation head-on, aware of what he offered and willingly accepting. Fan wasn't like that, yet from what he'd heard, she wasn't totally ignorant of love either.

He grinned when he recalled the conversation about painting and knew instinctively that she had been over her head. That didn't surprise him; many of the girls he knew spent their educational time in other pursuits, such as gossip or playing. And most of the mothers and aunts exaggerated their daughters' or nieces' accomplishments. Fan apparently excelled at singing, but didn't give a hoot about painting, which didn't deter him in the slightest.

No, life with Fan Pemberton would be anything but boring. And by the softening of her expression, he knew he was finally making some headway with his courtship. He would win her; he was determined to do that. He was smiling self-confidently when Eunice interrupted his thoughts.

"Still mooning over that girl, I see." Rapping him sharply with her cane, Eunice nodded when he glanced up in annoyance and rubbed his leg.

"What are you talking about? I thought you wanted me to find a wife."

"I do. So you've settled on Miss Pemberton?" When Christopher nodded, she paused thoughtfully. "She's a fine girl, intelligent and with backbone. I have a feeling she'll need it."

"What's that supposed to mean?" Christopher said indignantly.

"Nothing at all, dear boy. I have looked into the financial implications of the matter, and they are promising. Fan is the favored niece of Ella Pemberton. Besides a dowry, she stands to receive a goodly inheritance from the woman. Not only will it solve your current problems, but will ensure your future as well."

Something about his aunt's manner bothered him. Staring out the window at the rugged shoreline, he shrugged. "I'm glad, but do we have to be so practical about it? You make me sound like a kept man.''

Eunice chuckled sharply and pounded her cane on the floor. ''We have to be practical, dear boy. I've sold off the last of the Scott portraits, which will provide enough money to wine and dine Miss Pemberton through the summer. I cannot afford mistakes, however, or a change of heart. Are you certain this is the woman?''

Christopher's mind ran over all of the other debutantes he knew, then Fan. She was stunning, earthy and fun. Best of all she made him laugh. In the face of a lifetime commitment, that became extremely important. The whole thought process took less than a few minutes and he nodded firmly.

''Good. We won't have enough income to allow you to court more than one woman in style, so it's best if you are certain. There remains one other difficulty, however.''

''What's that?''

''Whether you can make her want you. Don't give me that look, my boy, I'm just assessing the financial practicalities of our endeavor. Fan may interest you. She has certainly more depth than other young women of your acquaintance and I'm aware that she presents a challenge. Everything has always come too easily to you. Here is a woman who doesn't swoon at your feet, who sees you exactly for what you are and isn't afraid to give back as good as she gets. What worries me is the possibility of failure.''

''That won't happen.'' Christopher's eyes darkened in annoyance, but Eunice noticed the way his foot tapped uneasily on the carriage floor. ''Fan is more difficult than other women, but that doesn't mean anything. I've already made her soften toward me—it's only a matter of time before she surrenders.''

''Ah,'' Eunice said. ''I'm sorry, but I can't let you throw away our one chance at success because you are behaving

like a typical man. This fortress shall be conquered and I'm
the one to do it!'' Christopher sent her a sardonic look,
which Eunice ignored. "We don't have the time or the
money to indulge you. Why don't you try an easier woman?
Like one of the Mitchells?"

Christopher's face tightened and he stared at his aunt
pointedly. "I agreed to this plan, but not under the impression that you would choose my bride. I will, however,
acknowledge your concerns. If I can't convince Fan within
the month to be my wife, then I will reconsider. Is that
fair?"

Eunice nodded. "Yes. Just remember to keep our objec-
tive in mind. You are marrying for money, Christopher. Not
for your heart's desire."

Christopher grimaced. There was truth in his aunt's
remarks. But Fan Pemberton promised much more than a
monetary solution. And now he had less than a month to try.

"A perfect woman, nobly planned, to warm, to comfort
and command; and yet a spirit still and bright, with
something of angelic light."

Katie burst into chuckles as she read the love note
Christopher had given her. He stared at her in confusion as
she smoothed the creamy paper and broke into renewed
peals of laughter. "Whatever is so funny?"

"I'm sorry." Katie grinned, wiping her eyes. "I guess
I'm just not used to being courted so . . . poetically."

She didn't tell him she had never been courted at all, nor
that the local brawling pub boys would hardly declare her
angelic. And they both knew she was far from perfect. Still,
the elegant note with its lacy borders was beautiful and the
gesture touching.

Christopher looked amused, but a little bewildered. "You
don't like it? I believe it's Wordsworth. Love letters are
expected, as part of the ritual."

Katie gulped, aware that she'd revealed her ignorance. Frantically she tried to recall what she knew of Fan's past, and seized on that as a possible explanation.

"I'm sorry, I guess it's just I've been away so long and never properly courted. And given the nature of our relationship, it does seem odd."

That seemed to satisfy him, for he laughed in agreement. "Yes, we have come a long way from hiding my clothes." Then his smile softened and he lightly touched her face. "But in this case, the poet is right. You do have spirit, though hardly the way he intended."

Katie grinned, then sat back to enjoy herself. Seated in the front row of the theater next to Bertrice and Charles, dressed in a cream lace gown of such exquisite beauty that she couldn't help touching the spidery intricacy of the material, she still couldn't believe she was here. The play was astonishing, and Katie was entranced by the tale of a man's ruin from drink and his wife's noble belief in him. The whole experience was heady and exciting, and she never wanted it to end.

Best of all was the attention Christopher gave her. He'd greeted her at Ella's house and immediately presented her with a jewel-encrusted fan; in honor of her name, he'd said laughingly. Still, it was beautiful, and Katie couldn't help flirting with it and giggling at the result. Yet it was the little things he did, the way he held doors for her, the touch of his hand on her arm, the admiring glance he gave her when seated in the dim light, that made her feel special and appreciated.

She didn't know what would come of all this and she didn't ask. For this one brief shining moment she was no longer Katie O'Connor but Frances Pemberton. She'd been thrust into a perfect world, and although she knew it couldn't last, she was enjoying it to the fullest. She'd decided to stop fighting this, to let fate take its course, and so far the trip had been delightful.

Only one thing dimmed her pleasure, and that was the longing she felt for her family and especially her son. Still, she had been able to send them funds, so they were well taken care of. She missed them terribly, but knowing she was helping them assuaged her guilt.

"Are you ready?" He stood aside for her and indicated the aisle. "We can all have a late dinner and then I'll take you home. You must be starved."

"I couldn't eat a thing," Bertrice declared, then reddened when Christopher looked at her in amusement. She was laced so tightly that she really couldn't eat, though her mother had insisted that real ladies never did anyway.

"I'm famished," Katie confessed. "It must be the weather here—I always want to eat."

"Here's the carriage," Charles announced as they walked to the end of the line. "We'll get some food in no time."

Smiling, Katie entered the coach with Christopher and gave Bertrice an encouraging look. The young girl blushed, then glanced shyly at her companion. Please, Katie thought. Let this work out for her. Bertrice was trying so hard that she sometimes made Charles nervous, and Katie had to fill in gaps in the conversation.

Glancing out the window, Katie heard the crash of the sea, saw the bright glimmer of the moon on an ink-black ocean. The breeze was warm and sultry, carrying the scent of summer flowers and the unrelenting smell of the ocean. The sand wrapped around the water like the stole on a woman's shoulders, and night sounds of crickets and shore birds mingled with the music of the waves.

They stopped at a small inn that was known for good food. The waiter led them to a small table clothed in white linen with a vase of fresh roses in the center. He took Charles and Bertrice's order, then turned to Christopher.

"Do you mind if I order?" When Katie shook her head, Christopher spoke to the young waiter. "Bring us the sea trout, a baked potato with cream, and whatever fresh vegetables you have. And a bottle of your best white wine."

The waiter nodded while Katie glanced around the pretty room. Done in a stylish ornate wallpaper, it would have been oppressive like so many other houses, but the colors were all pastels. The effect was beautiful instead of gaudy, and the windows were open, allowing the soft breeze to billow the curtains.

"It's so beautiful," Katie commented, turning to Bertrice. "Don't you think so?"

"Yes," Bertrice said. "I always thought this place was lovely."

"Not nearly so lovely as you," Charles said gallantly.

Bertrice turned even redder, then fanned herself quickly. Katie held her own breath as she saw Bertrice grab her chair as if for support, her color dropping alarmingly. Charles stared in confusion as the young girl gasped, her eyelids fluttering.

"No, Bertrice!" Reaching for her friend, Katie blushed in mortification for her as Bertrice slipped into a faint and tumbled to the floor.

"Waiter! Bring some water!" Christopher shouted, and together he and Charles lifted the young girl back to her seat.

"Damned stays!" Charles swore. "She always laces them too tightly. Women's clothes these days are like torture chambers!"

Silently Katie agreed. She helped Bertrice sip the water that the waiter brought, then the young girl looked around the room, obviously disoriented.

"Where? Oh no, Fan, I didn't . . ." Humiliated beyond belief, Bertrice looked up at Charles as if she wanted to die.

"You're all right," Charles reassured her. "You had the vapors. Would you like to lie down?"

"I can't—" Bertrice staggered to her feet and raced for the door.

"I'll go after her," Charles volunteered, leaving Katie and Christopher behind.

"Do you think we should follow?" Worried, Katie still stared in the direction of the door. To her surprise, Christopher chuckled.

"No, I don't think so. Bertrice's problem has always been too much solicitous help. A few moments alone with Charles could do what would otherwise require two months of courtship. I have a feeling that our young friend isn't as dim-witted as everyone thinks." He gave her a grin. "Besides, that means I have you all to myself."

Suppressing a smile, Katie hoped that he was right. Bertrice needed all the help she could get with her confidence, and if a faint helped, she was all for it. A thrill of excitement went through her as she thought of Christopher's words. It was scandalous, dining alone with a man. Yet it was also . . . wonderful.

The waiter returned, bringing them wine. Katie sighed, drinking deeply of the delicate liquid. She could barely eat the food, for Clarise had insisted on lacing her tightly, so she had to be content with drinking and taking tiny bites of the dinner. The room took on a fuzzy hue and she felt a delicious warmth penetrate her toes. Christopher really was so handsome, she thought dreamily, admiring the way the gaslights shone on his black hair. And charming. And kind . . .

"Are you having a good time, Fan?"

He said her name softly, and Katie wished she could tell him the truth, have him look at her that way and call her by her own name. "I am," Katie said, reminding herself that he could never know who she truly was. "I love the shore. It's so pretty here."

"There's a legend about Cape May, that Blackbeard's treasure is buried here." He grinned at her incredulous expression. "Men come here and dig for it. Some of the locals even sell maps, all of them authentic, of course."

"Of course." Katie smiled, entranced by the prospect of treasure. "Do you think it's true?"

"Here, anything is possible." He appeared withdrawn for a moment, as if thinking to himself, then he glanced at her and shrugged. "Who knows?"

He was so good-looking. Katie nearly drowned in his eyes. Something in his grin told her she was revealing her thoughts, so she drank down the rest of her wine quickly, trying to sound intelligent, and as if his presence didn't affect her in the least. "Can you imagine having all that money? A pirate's treasure must be worth a fortune."

He stared at her strangely for a moment, then sipped from his coffee cup. "Well, I should think you could imagine," he said carefully. "After all, the Pembertons aren't exactly broke. Your family has a good deal of money. I think you would know exactly what it was like."

For some reason it was getting difficult to talk. "Yes, I know we Pembertons are rich. But the treasure just seems so much more romantic, or something."

"Money is money, in whatever shape or form. And in this time and this country, it means everything. No one can do without it. It changes a bricklayer into nobility, a pauper into a prince. We worship a golden idol in America, that much is for certain."

There was something odd about his voice. Katie shivered, wondering what made the fabulously wealthy Christopher Scott sound so philosophical. As if reading her mind, he continued. "Enough of that. I recall earlier you had some difficulty discussing Impressionist paintings. Were you skipping class on the days they lectured on modern art?''

His smile was so charming that Katie grinned back, unaware that her smile was slightly lopsided. She only knew that the world had taken on a special glow, and that it had something to do with herself and Christopher. She fought to remember what they were talking about, and not notice that his hair was even a deeper black than she had imagined, or that his muscles looked exceptionally well formed beneath his coat, like one of those statues. . . . Art! That was it. ''I wasn't very good at painting,'' she admitted.

''I thought as much. I picture you more as a tomboy, interested in tossing snowballs and playing hopscotch, than as a bluestocking. Am I right?''

Katie nodded. ''That's it exactly. What about you?''

''I was a ne'er-do-well,'' he confessed without approbation. ''I thought life was a game for me to enjoy. It wasn't until I grew up that I found out differently.'' He shrugged as if the matter wasn't worth much thought. ''I think we're all wise as children. It's only later that we mess things up.''

There was something so appealing about him in this mood. Christopher's brand of charm was all the more dangerous because it was uncontrived. She couldn't imagine his childhood, filled with toys and pleasure, without any worry of the next meal. She closed her eyes as she thought of her son. God, what she wouldn't do to have him grow up like Christopher—happy, carefree, and easy. Instead he would know nothing but work and poverty.

He smiled and something in his expression took her breath away. Maybe it was the wine, but for a moment she thought that he would kiss her, so intent was his look. Instead he signaled for the waiter and ordered coffee and brandy.

''Now this,'' he said with a grin, ''is the only way to drink coffee.'' Taking up the snifter of brandy, he poured a liberal amount into his cup and an equal amount into hers.

Katie grinned back, then tried the concoction. The brandy added a unique flavor to the pungent brew and warmed her even more. Used to whiskey and beer, she knew how much of those liquors she could imbibe without trouble, but fine wines and French brandies were another matter. Katie drank down the coffee, barely aware that her brogue had deepened, or that she was gazing at Christopher with something close to adoration.

"Isn't it wonderful, having money?" she asked, then hiccuped softly. She seemed surprised at the sound that emerged from her mouth and she shrugged, giving up on conjecture as to how it happened.

"Yes, it's wonderful," Christopher agreed. "I think I should call for the check."

"Oh, yes, let's get our waiter back. He's very nice, don't you think?"

Amused, Christopher watched as Katie called the waiter, then greeted him with a dazzling smile. "Sir, I must ask you, what is your name?"

The waiter stared at her imperviously. "Cartwright, Miss. William Cartwright."

"Ah, just like my old uncle Willy. He used to drink and sing from the rooftops. A chimney sweep, I believe." Katie hiccuped again and grinned. "Do you have an uncle like that?"

"I believe not, miss," the waiter said, though he struggled to remain stern. Understanding, Christopher indicated the check and the waiter produced a bill.

"That's a shame. Isn't that a shame, Christopher? He doesn't have an Uncle Willy. Everyone should have one."

"Yes, you're right, we should all have Uncle Willys. Come on now, Fan. I think I should take you home."

Katie pouted, but when she rose, she noticed that the room was a little unsteady and that Christopher seemed amused by something. He led her to the coach and she giggled as she nearly missed the first step. Christopher caught her and she fell into his arms, loving the way he felt against her, warm and secure.

"Did your mother come from Ireland . . . ?" she sang loudly, her voice lilting and beautiful. She barely noticed that he chuckled, or that he helped her into the coach and called to the driver. Instead he sang with her, his own rich voice blending with hers. Giggling, Katie led the chorus, ending the song on her front porch as they somehow managed to stop, disembark from the coach, then clamber up the steps.

"Not bad, Christopher Scott. Of the Philadelphia Scotts." Katie grinned, then balanced herself against the door. That proved easier than standing alone, and she found she could almost do it without his help, though he continued to hold her.

"You're not bad yourself, Miss Pemberton." He grinned at her expression. "You know, I think I'm glad you forced me to court you. I'm having a pretty good time." She tried to take a swing at him, but he easily caught her arm before she could make contact. The laughter left his eyes and he looked serious, almost intent. "I meant what I said, Fan. I want you like I've never wanted another woman. And I mean to have you. Resign yourself to that."

Katie shivered. It was almost prophetic the way he spoke. It wasn't until he started laughing that she realized perhaps he was joking. But something inside her told her he wasn't.

He paused for a moment, then reluctantly released her hand. Barely touching her face, he brushed aside a stray wisp of dark hair and spoke softly. "Good night, Fan."

His head bent and his lips gently brushed hers, giving her just enough of a kiss to make her want more. Sighing, Katie reached up on her toes and slid her arms around his neck. His response was immediate and left her breathless. Tight-

ening his embrace, he deepened the kiss, making her gasp
with astonishment and pleasure.

It was perfect. His mouth left hers to brush her neck
lightly, creating wonderful sensations that raced through her
blood. When he finally released her, Katie was trembling.
She heard his husky laughter as he tipped her face up to his,
and his eyes had darkened to the color of raw whiskey.

"I'd better leave," he said softly. "Before I can't. Soon
I won't have to leave you at all." His hand lightly touched
her nose, then lingered, brushing against her lips. Then he
turned and walked down the stairs, almost physically
forcing his body from hers.

Confused, Katie watched him go. What was happening to
her? Not even John Sweeney had affected her like this,
though his kisses had been pleasant enough. Exhilaration
rushed through her and she swirled on the porch, her dress
floating around her. Never had she felt so beautiful, alive
and full of joy. Something wonderful was finally happening
to her. Maybe God had forgiven her.

Maybe she had been given a second chance.

❈ SEVEN

"**W**ell, it's about time, miss. A little late for Frances Pemberton, don't you think?"

Startled, Katie opened her eyes and immediately shaded them from the bright sunlight. She pulled a pillow over her head and moaned. "Will you shut those curtains? My head feels like a carriage has run over it."

Eileen shook her head. "It's nigh past ten. The madam's been up for two hours and been fretting about ye, though I could have told her the truth. Out drinking and roaming the town with Mr. Scott. And singing at the top of your lungs like some fishwoman! Scandalous, that's what I say! The blood will show, that it will."

"I did no such thing!" Katie sat up abruptly, the pillow tumbling from her head. The throbbing inside her brain increased, but reality was even worse. It couldn't possibly be true and yet . . .

"You most certainly did. I couldn't sleep, what with all that racket on the porch, so I fixed myself a pot of tea. Didn't expect to hear that kind of noise, and I imagine all the neighbors did as well." Eileen scowled as Katie winced in embarrassment. "Are ye trying to create another scandal for Frances?"

"No," Katie said quickly, then grasped her head. The

slightest movement made it throb like a thousand pinpricks. "Christopher . . . I mean, he ordered this wine, and then brandy in the coffee. I'm not used to drinking such things."

"Ach, and you've not the head for it, either. I've got a glass of tomato juice with a jigger of whiskey in it. Used to do it for me own Johnny when I was a girl. Damned fool notion! Going out with that gentleman and getting stinking drunk like an old sot."

Katie winced, then managed to sit up and take the noisome potion from Eileen's tray. The housekeeper nodded as she wrinkled her nose and took a sip. "Drink it all. It will help take the poison from your blood. I managed to hide this from the madam, though I suppose she'll hear about it from the gossips."

Katie obeyed, choking at the awful taste of the stuff. But she drank it all down, her stomach rumbling alarmingly. The nausea soon passed, and within a few minutes she was feeling almost human.

"Good. The color's come back to your face. Damned foolishness!" Eileen's expression grew stern and she eyed Katie like an unhappy schoolmarm. "Now that you're feeling better, I think it's time you and me had a little talk."

Katie grimaced. Her head hadn't stopped pounding and she looked at Eileen pleadingly. "Does it have to be now!"

Eileen nodded. "When my Johnny had a bad head was the only time he made sense. What I want to know, miss, is what are ye up to?"

"What do you mean?" Katie asked, puzzled.

Eileen scoffed. "You know what I'm asking. I am the only person who seems to realize that you are not Fan Pemberton. You are Katie O'Connor, you live in the Irish ward of the city, and you've worked as a maid. I checked your references. Mrs. Westcott had nothing but good things to say about you, as did your previous employer, so we needn't worry about the silver. But I want to know what you think you're doing. Carrying on, posing as Frances . . ."

"It makes Mrs. Pemberton happy," Katie said defensively.

"It does make her happy, and that's what has me worried. What do you think can come of all this? When you were just acting as Fan, that was one thing. But allowing Mr. Scott to see you! He will find out the truth, I know that as sure as I know Killarney's green. And what will happen then?"

Katie shrugged. "I'm not doing anything wrong! Mr. Scott knew Fan Pemberton. If he wants to spend some time with me, I don't see how that could hurt—"

"He's courting you, miss!" Eileen said, aghast. "Do you really mean to marry that man?"

"No!" Katie gasped in surprise. "I know things have gotten out of hand," she admitted when Eileen gave her an odd look. "I never meant for any of this to happen. It just sort of . . . snowballed."

"Well, it's time you did something about it now. Fooling with that man can only lead to trouble. He has a background, schooling, money—"

"Are you saying I'm not good enough for him?" Katie asked indignantly.

Eileen snorted. "I'm saying nothing of the kind. If anyone knows that money doesn't make the man, it's me. No, I'm saying that it's one thing to fool a senile old woman. It's another to fool a rich society man." At the doubt on Katie's face, she continued: "I know you've got your own troubles—the Irish are born with them. Is it worth the risk just to have the young man's company? When it comes to lust, one man's as good as the next. Do you need to be playing with Mr. Scott?"

"Enough," Katie snapped, unwilling to listen to any more. Eileen was like a walking conscience. "I'll think about it. Now, if you'll kindly hand me my robe, I am going

to try to dress before Madam Pemberton gets too worried.
Do you mind?'' She indicated the door.

Eileen sighed. There were some folks who were determined to get themselves into mischief. And Katie O'Connor was apparently one of them

Katie waited until the door closed, then sank down on the feather bed. She had really done it this time. Mortification flooded through her as she pictured the previous night. She could remember herself hanging on Christopher's words, gazing at him from across the table . . . My God, he must be laughing this morning! she thought.

Then the singing. Although she wanted nothing more than to deny Eileen's words, she could remember herself warbling on the way home, belting out the lyrics of an old, romantic Irish tune.

And then . . . Katie paled as she recalled their goodbye. Although most of it was fuzzy, she had no difficulty remembering their passionate kiss, and Christopher's sensual assurance that soon he would never have to leave her.

Katie wished the bed would open up and swallow her. Frances Pemberton would never have done such a thing. She would have delicately sipped her wine, eaten next to nothing, then politely bade him good-bye. She never would have gotten tipsy, sung at the top of her lungs, and then permitted him to take liberties on the front porch. Katie had revealed herself as fully as if she were naked. My God, what had she been thinking?

She couldn't see him again. Christopher Scott was too dangerous. Unlike Ella Pemberton, he was already suspicious of her—she could tell that by the probing questions he asked and the confusion he manifested at some of her answers. Even the most obtuse man would have a few questions at this point, and Christopher was far from stupid. If he started asking around, he could arouse suspicion, cause more inquiries . . . perhaps even make Ella Pemberton look more closely at the situation.

Katie sighed. She couldn't start over, not now. She had sent most of her money back home to take care of her son. She'd be hard pressed at this point to come up with transportation money to return to Philadelphia, and her own private scandal awaited her there. Wealthy women were not willing to overlook the fact that she had a child out of wedlock. She had managed to stay one step ahead of her reputation, but it always, inevitably, caught up with her. No, she simply had to keep this job.

So she would have to discourage him. Katie closed her eyes, swallowing down the tightness in her throat. She didn't remember everything about the previous night, but she did know one thing. She had enjoyed it. Christopher had made her feel beautiful, special, and respectable. He had acted like the luckiest man in the world just to be with her, a feeling that was even more intoxicating than the wine. And when he kissed her . . . Katie recalled the awesome feeling of being taken out of herself, given a glimpse of a world that she had suspected existed but never really experienced. She'd made love only once before, and it had not been pleasant. But Christopher's kiss promised something altogether different, and the woman in her already mourned for the loss of that experience. But she had no choice. Christopher Scott had become too much of a threat.

And more than she could risk.

"What do you mean she isn't home?" Christopher stood on the doorstep of the huge wraparound porch and stared at the maid, his bouquet drooping in his hand.

Eileen folded her arms and faced him like a watchdog guarding her home. "I mean she isn't home. I am sorry, sir. Would you like to leave the flowers? I'll make sure she knows you were here."

"But she hasn't been home in days! Is she ill, or away?" Christopher persisted impatiently.

Eileen stared at him regally. "I'm sorry, sir, but it isn't for me to question my betters. Frances Pemberton is not home. Would you care to leave your card?"

"Fine." Thrusting his calling card into the maid's hand along with the flowers, he turned and stormed down the porch steps. After marching out to the sandy road, he turned and glanced back at the house, mentally calculating which room was Fan's. A curtain twitched suspiciously at the far left bedroom, and a cold smile curved on his face.

So that was it, she was avoiding him. Remembering their last night together, he wasn't totally surprised. Fan was probably embarrassed, and was now treating him like he had the plague.

He grinned openly now. Every time he thought about that night he laughed. Fan had gotten more than tipsy—and probably had a colossal headache the next day to show for it. And no self-respecting woman got flushed and treated the town to a delightful rendition of an Irish folk song. But then again, there weren't many Frances Pembertons in Cape May.

If he didn't know better, he would think she was from the Irish wards. But Fan was Fan, a delight to him, a scandal to society. He had never met a woman who was more real, more alive, and so intriguing. He chuckled out loud as he recalled the Misses Mitchell asking him pointedly about their outing, hoping to hear something outlandish. Instead he had told them the truth. Fan was simply the most interesting woman he'd ever met, and he was really looking forward to seeing her again.

He frowned as he stared at the house, the curtain still twitching. If Fan had taken it into her head to avoid him, she could easily dodge him for weeks. She hadn't been to any parties in the last few days, had avoided the beach, had even been absent from Bertrice Merriweather's picnic that afternoon. That's when he had decided to take matters into his own hands and demand to see her. But other than barging into the house, he hadn't many alternatives if she chose not to be at home to him.

He had to do something. He was quickly running out of time and money—and couldn't afford to lose either.

"I was so glad that you suggested we get together for tea," Ella Pemberton said softly as Eunice Scott poured her a steaming cup. "I've been wanting to speak with you for some time. I think it's important that we get to know each other."

"My feelings exactly." Eunice smiled, then poured herself a cup. Glancing furtively around the interior of the summer cottage, she hoped that Ella wouldn't notice the lack of rich furnishings, and especially the absence of artwork in the room. But Ella seemed oblivious to the barren walls and was obviously delighted to be present.

"I'm very pleased that your nephew and my niece have become friends," Ella continued. "I've known Christopher for many years now, and have always thought him to be such a nice young man, in spite of what everyone says. I never believed him a gambler for a moment!"

"Christopher's reputation, like that of most men, is greatly exaggerated," Eunice said smoothly. "He is neither as bad as they say, nor as good. But that is a topic I'm sure you are aware of. I think Frances is delightful, and you have my complete assurance that any discussion of her past falls on deaf ears with both myself and my nephew."

"I am very pleased to hear that." Ella's face softened and she smiled sadly. "Fan has always been the kind of girl who follows her heart. From the time she was a child, there was something so special about her, so touching, that very few people could know her and not be moved. Why, just the other day I wasn't feeling well and Fan insisted on staying with me. She read a Dickens story, and acted out the parts so cleverly that I couldn't stop laughing. Yet those same qualities make her vulnerable to the wrong people. I fear for her sometimes.''

Eunice patted the other woman's hand. ''You have no need for concern. I sense there is a genuine affection between Frances and my nephew. In fact, I think he is more than casually interested in her. May I be so blunt as to take you into my confidence?''

Ella looked surprised, but nodded. ''By all means.''

''Christopher wants to marry Fan, and the sooner the better. To say he is anxious doesn't convey the depth of his eagerness.''

Ella's fact lit up and she withdrew a lace handkerchief from her pocket. ''I am so happy to hear that! I didn't dare hope, but in the past few weeks they seem to have grown so close!'' Ella's smile faded and she gazed at Eunice with obvious concern. ''But things haven't been going well recently. I don't know what happened between them, but Fan won't even bring up Christopher's name. And when I've tried to inquire discreetly, even my housekeeper discourages the conversation. I don't know what to make of it all.''

''I know.'' Eunice nodded in agreement. ''I've noticed the same thing. Young couples, especially when courting, can often let a little disagreement or misunderstanding grow entirely out of proportion. I know Fan is a sensitive girl, and she may be feeling a little shy around Christopher. Do you know''—Eunice leaned forward as if imparting important information—''that she is no longer home to him?''

Ella gasped. ''No, I wasn't aware that it had gotten to that point. I just know that Fan was incredibly happy until recently. Now she stays around the house, doesn't visit much, doesn't even socialize with her friends. I've been so worried, but she simply laughs and tells me not to be concerned.'' She sighed, then sipped her tea. ''The last thing I want is for her to be unhappy here.''

''My word, no,'' Eunice said sharply. ''If that happened, she might even be tempted to . . . leave once more.''

''I can't bear to think of it.'' Ella's wrinkled face grew even tighter. ''I can't lose Fan again. Having her back in my life has brought me so much joy.''

''I know.'' Eunice nodded, then hid a smile behind her teacup. ''Then I think we have to take matters into our own hands. We've let the young people handle things, and they've only managed to botch up the entire affair.''

''You're right,'' Ella said firmly. ''I know Fan has feelings for Christopher. She is cutting off her nose to spite her face, to quote something so vulgar as a cliché. But still, what do you suggest we do? If she refuses to see him, our hands are tied.''

''Not necessarily.'' Eunice grinned. ''There are ways to help nature take its course. Even with someone as stubborn as Fan or Christopher.'' She clanked down her teacup as if she had a sudden inspiration. ''Didn't you tell me that the Mitchells are giving a reception tomorrow evening?''

''Yes,'' Ella said in confusion. ''But Fan won't—''

''Let me handle the arrangements,'' Eunice said confidently. ''By the time we're through, this marriage will be a fait accompli. You mark my words.''

Katie gently clipped the thorns from the stem of a rose and placed it into her basket. Sunlight poured into the garden, illuminating all of the secret nooks and crevices where morning glories and columbines struggled to bloom. But the soil was perfect for the roses and they unfolded about her, filling the air with a heady perfume.

''There you are, my dear,'' Ella said softly as Katie

glanced up. "Eunice and I have been looking all over for you. I thought I might find you here."

Katie straightened, then forced herself to smile at Christopher's aunt. This was something she hadn't counted on. She had been successful for several days now in avoiding Christopher, but Eunice was something else again. The older woman had a way of peering straight into one's heart, and Katie knew better than to tangle with her.

"Aunt Ella. Miss Scott. I was just leaving—"

"Stay, please," Ella said, her voice firmer than Katie had heard before. "The garden is so beautiful this time of day and we'd welcome your company."

"I really have some things I must see to—"

"Now, Frances, I insist that you remain," Eunice said sharply, though she smiled as she spoke. "You haven't favored any of us with your company for days. You have refused to even see my nephew, you've avoided me, and you're distressing your aunt. Would you mind telling me why?"

Katie gulped, unprepared for the confrontation. "I've . . . been ill," she said, using the first excuse that came to mind.

"Nonsense!" Eunice declared. "You seem uncommonly fit to me. Now, what is it? Have you decided suddenly to become antisocial?"

Katie glanced pleadingly at Ella, but the other woman seemed as interested in her response as Eunice. Belatedly she realized that Fan probably would have approached things differently and would have spoken to her aunt privately first. Now there was nothing to do but think of something. Fast.

"Well . . ." Katie shrugged. "I don't want to cause a problem for your nephew," she finished quickly, thanking God and Fan for the inspiration. "He and I have become friends. And I'm sure you are aware of the . . . incident in my past?" When Eunice nodded, she continued quickly, "I have no desire to see him embroiled in the same gossip. Christopher has a reputation to consider. I thought it best if I didn't see him for a while. I don't wish to cause him trouble.''

Somehow Katie managed to sound convincing. Even Ella paused as Eunice frowned and rapped her cane on the ground.

''Young lady, you know I don't pay heed to idle chatter, and neither does my nephew. Neither of us cares about the scandal. While it is noble of you to try to protect him this way, I assure you that Christopher is a grown man and makes his own decisions.''

''I appreciate that,'' Katie said solemnly. ''However, I simply cannot allow your kindness, nor that of your nephew, to result in your injury. No, I must remain firm on this point. I cannot see Christopher—it is as simple as that.''

Ella looked pained while Eunice grinned, her sharp eyes dancing.

''But, my dear, no one has suggested any such thing. I have not come as Christopher's emissary—in fact, I understand that he is spending a good deal of time in Margaret's company these days. I had come to speak to you of another matter entirely.''

Katie nodded, but annoyance filled her. Christopher certainly hadn't wasted any time in finding a new love interest. And Margaret, of all people! Recalling Margaret's vicious comments and snide looks, Katie could just imagine the rest. She probably ran into his arms and was laughing behind her back, sure she had bested Fan Pemberton.

''I want you to come to the Mitchells' reception tonight,'' Eunice said shrewdly, aware of the impact of her news concerning Christopher. ''You see, Charles Pepper has developed an interest in Bertrice Merriweather.''

''That's wonderful,'' Katie said sincerely. She genuinely liked both of them, and the thought of Bertrice finding happiness greatly pleased her. "But how does that concern me?"

Eunice smiled softly. "As you know, the young girl is given to fainting spells, especially if she is within an arm's distance of a handsome young man. Charles may lose patience with her. As her friend, I thought you might give her the courage to proceed."

Katie sighed. Eunice had her there. Bertrice was her best friend in Cape May, and the girl was honestly nice and as sweet as she appeared. She deserved someone like Charles, and he was perfect for her. She owed it to her friend to help her, in spite of her own feelings.

"All right," Katie agreed, ignoring Ella's triumphant grin.

"Good." Eunice nodded. "I knew you wouldn't let me down. Oh, by the way, I do believe my nephew will be present. He will not be alone, but since you don't care a farthing for him, that shouldn't present a difficulty, should it?"

Katie fumed, but there was nothing she could do. As Fan Pemberton, she was trapped within her own politeness and couldn't possibly refuse now without revealing everything. "Not at all," she replied. "I'm certain I'll have a wonderful time."

✤ EIGHT

"**D**o you really think he likes me?" Bertrice whispered, glancing toward Charles with a giggle. The handsome young man returned her look with a warm smile, then resumed his conversation with the elderly woman beside her.

"I'm sure of it," Katie said with a grin. "Why wouldn't he? You are the nicest and one of the prettiest girls here."

Bertrice smiled nervously, then straightened immediately as her mother approached.

"There you are, dear. I've been looking everywhere for you. Good gracious, Bertrice, how many times do I have to tell you to stand up straight? You're slouching again. And stop fussing with that dress—you'll mess up the bustle."

Katie winced as she saw the slight confidence that Bertrice possessed a moment ago disappear beneath her mother's disapproval. Bertrice glanced uneasily at her dress, then self-consciously straightened again, even though her posture was perfect.

"I am so thirsty," Katie remarked. "I'd love a glass of punch, but I hate to walk across by myself. Will you come?"

"Sure," Bertrice answered in confusion. If there was one word that didn't apply to Frances Pemberton, it was shy, and Bertrice couldn't imagine why Fan needed someone to accompany her.

Katie smiled, then led the way. As long as Bertrice's mother lingered near them, shredding her daughter's confidence, Bertrice would never get anywhere. She didn't think that her friend's mother was being deliberately mean, it was just that she was so eager for her daughter to be successful that she tried too hard.

Katie sighed, allowing the servant to pour them each a glass of punch. In some ways, this society was much harder than her own. There, the struggle for survival came first and social concerns lagged far behind. It was true that most of them managed to find a mate, but it wasn't the primary concern of their lives, nor were the rules so stringent. If a man was interested in a woman, he might bring her flowers, have dinner at her home, take her for a walk through the narrow city streets, and buy her a whiskey at the local tavern.

Here, however, finding the right mate was the number-one occupation of all the young men and women. All of the parties, the receptions, the dances, and the picnics were designed for that purpose. Women were taught how to speak, how to think, how to move and dress. The lines of propriety were carefully drawn and, as Fan Pemberton had learned, could not be crossed.

And for girls like Bertrice, it was agonizing. Katie felt nothing but sympathy for her as she triple-checked her gown and forced a smile. As the only daughter of a wealthy shipping merchant, Bertrice was expected to make a good match, and the pressure was tremendous.

Katie glanced up and saw Charles watching her friend discreetly, then his attention returned to the group of people surrounding him. Katie saw the Mitchells, Eunice Scott, the Drexels, Margaret Chester, and . . . Christopher.

He was standing close to Charles, and had obviously just

arrived. Katie felt her breath catch in her throat as she admitted dismally just how handsome he was. Dressed in a dark suit, his sparkling white shirt a sharp contrast to his hair and tanned complexion, he looked inordinately happy, throwing back his head and laughing at something Charles said.

And on his arm was Margaret. Katie's stomach felt ill as she saw the young woman laugh with him, then pat his arm familiarly when he responded in turn. As if feeling her gaze, Margaret glanced up and gave her a look of such vicious satisfaction that Katie had to fight her Irish instincts and not box her one there and then. A slow smile crept across her face as she envisioned the havoc that would cause, but the expression faded quickly as Margaret indicated the dance floor.

Taking her punch glass, Katie turned away, her heart sinking. Why did she feel this way? She didn't want him to court her, didn't want his attention, had done everything in her power in the past few days to avoid him . . . Did she really expect him to stop seeing other women, especially now?

"Fan, are you all right?" Bertrice asked in concern.

Katie nodded quickly, then waved her hand as if overly warm. "It's just so hot in here. I feel like these stays are sticking to my legs. Why can't women dress practically, like men do?"

"I don't think they're much better off," Bertrice confided. "Those high collars look dreadfully uncomfortable." She gasped when she spotted Christopher and turned to Katie in sympathy. "That's why you're upset! I don't believe it! That Margaret is such a snake!"

"She's not doing anything wrong," Katie said firmly. "Christopher can escort whomever he wants."

"But she knows he's courting you! She's just trying to

make you mad—look at her face!'' Bertrice huffed, indignant. "She knows you're the one he wants!"

Katie glanced over and felt the wrenching inside her once more. Margaret was a snake, a viper, a shrew . . . but she was a lady. She wasn't an imposter like Katie, a poor girl from the slums. She deserved to have a man like Christopher. She didn't have to worry about being found out, about getting her feelings involved, about being an unwed mother. Margaret was the appropriate choice. Why then did the thought make her furious?

"There's Charles," Katie said, grateful to discover that the other man was alone. "Why don't we go over and talk to him before the dancing starts?"

"I can't!" Bertrice said in a panic. "I would be so embarrassed!" She stared longingly across the room, seemingly flustered at the very thought.

"Of course you can," Katie said decisively. "Besides, I can't let Margaret and Christopher see me standing here like a wallflower. We have to do something quickly."

The tension eased from Bertrice's face as she realized the truth in Katie's words. It was one thing to think about her own fear; it was another when Katie needed her. Ignoring the trembling inside of her, Bertrice squared her shoulders and braved the ten feet across the floor to Charles, giving Katie a reassuring nod. She ignored Margaret as they walked past, and managed to give Charles a welcoming smile as they approached.

"Miss Merriweather! And Miss Pemberton." Charles grinned, delighted with their presence and with Bertrice's bravery. "I'm delighted to see you. You both look lovely tonight."

Katie grinned, then took a step back, allowing Bertrice to move closer. To her delight, the young girl smiled and took the more intimate spot, all the while making sure that Katie was included in the conversation. She was playing the role perfectly, to assist Fan Pemberton, but in the long run she was helping her own cause, and no one was happier than Katie.

"Thank you, Mr. Pepper. Frances and I were just speaking of women's fashion. I think I missed you at church yesterday. Were you present?"

"Yes, indeed I was. I was seated behind you, but I could see you perfectly. I wanted to ask you to breakfast, but you left before I could."

Bertrice beamed, her face blushing prettily. "Perhaps next week."

Within a few moments the two young people were chatting easily. The dancing began, and Katie found no lack of partners as the word spread that she and Christopher had apparently broken up. Katie found herself the subject of gossip again as the notorious Fan Pemberton was blamed, and more than one curious suitor tried to discover who Christopher's rival was.

Katie smiled and flirted, laughed gaily, and danced until her feet hurt, especially when she saw Christopher dancing with Margaret. Being sought after and pursued was like a balm, and she managed to look like she was enjoying herself. By the eighth dance, even she was exhausted and she excused herself, seeing Bertrice with Charles, and took refuge in the library.

The quiet of the room was comforting, and the cool sea air blowing through an open window felt wonderful on her warm skin. Fanning herself breathlessly, she removed her slippers, aware that real ladies wouldn't have dreamed of such a thing, but she no longer cared. She would never have the things that a real lady would, and had been gifted with gold for as long as the charade lasted. It would burst one day like a soap bubble, and she would have to return to being Katie O'Connor. It was a fact that she couldn't forget.

"I'm surprised to find you alone."

Her heart thudding in her chest, Katie turned to find Christopher closing the door behind him, an odd smile on his face. He glanced toward the floor and saw her slippers, then the skirts that she held aloft in the hopes of catching a cool breeze. Flustered, Katie let her gown drop and indicated the door.

"I came because I wanted to be alone. Now, if you don't mind . . ."

"Ah, but I do." Christopher stepped closer and Katie swallowed hard, feeling trapped. It was one thing to dodge him at Ella's house, to refuse his calls and his gifts. It was another to be alone with him. She stepped back, aware of the amusement in his smile.

"You see, I was concerned about you. Every time I tried to see you, I was told you were ill." He leaned closer and pressed his hand on her forehead. "You seem uncommonly well to me."

Trapped against the library table, she gave him what she hoped was a noncommittal smile. "It must have been something I ate," she said sweetly.

"Miraculous," Christopher agreed, though she saw the smirk in his eyes. "And eight dances! I would say that you've recovered completely."

"It must be the sea air," Katie said innocently, indicating the open window. "I hear it does wonders for the infirm. The salt water is well-known as a cure for many ailments. Why, before I came here, I had all sorts of stomach distress. And now—"

"In about two minutes I'm going to cheerfully strangle you," Christopher said with a grin. "Why don't you just admit the truth? You're embarrassed that you got tipsy the other night and don't want to face me."

"That's not true!" Katie said defiantly. "Just because a woman doesn't care for your company doesn't mean that she's got some other motive."

"I see. Then you've decided, after the last few weeks we've had together, that you don't want to see me?"

Katie felt her throat constrict, but she didn't have a choice. If she continued to see him, she risked everything. She thought of her son, of the people at home who depended on her, and she fought the ache that welled up inside of her.

"That's right. I don't want to see you again. It was pleasant, but it's over."

The laughter left Christopher's face and he stared into hers, his jaw tightening. "May I ask why?"

Katie shrugged. She was tempted to tell him she was seeing someone else, but it was too easy for him to discover the truth and she'd be caught in another lie. Instead she sighed, then managed to respond sincerely.

"I just don't feel anything more than friendship for you. I am honored that you considered me for a wife, but in spite of the practical nature of your offer, I don't think it's fair to accept. I am sorry."

He studied her for a moment, more puzzled than upset. "Then it is because of the scandal. For the reasons you gave my aunt."

Katie nodded. "Whether you want to admit it or not, my background will cause you nothing but trouble." That much was the truth, and it enabled her to continue honestly. "I like you too much to let that happen. I think it's better that we go on as friends."

"I see." Christopher shrugged. "Then there really isn't any point, is there?" Katie stared at him, wanting to say much more, but knowing she couldn't. "I'm sorry, too. I really thought we would do well together. I'd better go. I believe Margaret's waiting."

There was something about his voice, tinged with disbelief and amusement, that made her temper rise. He started for the door, looking unbearably handsome, his manner unconcerned as if they'd been discussing the weather. Unreasonably Katie couldn't resist a parting shot.

"I'm so glad you managed to find a replacement so quickly. I wish you happiness."

Christopher closed the door and faced her triumphantly. "You're jealous. I knew it! I could tell by the look on your face when we walked in."

"I am not!" Katie gasped, realizing too late her blunder. "It's just that your protests seem insincere—"

"You're jealous! Come on, admit it!"

"You're dreaming." Katie tried to back up, but she had reached the end of the table long ago and had no retreat. "You are imagining things. If you want to think that, go ahead."

"Am I?" Christopher grinned. "When I looked across the floor, I thought you were going to kill either me or her. Come on now, admit it. You can tell me."

"Of all the . . . You are the most conceited, wretched excuse for a gentleman I've ever seen!"

"Don't forget rude. And insulting," he supplied helpfully.

"If you'll excuse me, I believe the others are waiting . . ."

She tried to brush past him, but he stopped her. He was shaking with laughter, which only made her more furious. "I'm sorry, but you can't expect me to let you walk out of here like this. I told you before, Fan. I want you. And you want me. Or am I imagining this as well?"

Katie opened her mouth to protest, but he was kissing her, his lips covering hers, taking from her all rational thought. Her defenses weakened, Katie could no longer think or reason. Her body, ignoring any mental arguments, melted against his and her arms seemed to creep about his neck as if by their own accord.

It was crazy, but Katie could no longer deny it. She

wanted him; it was as simple as that. Her response was genuine, and contained none of the resistance that he had expected. Instead she returned his kiss warmly, responding with all the affection that she'd hidden, unable to conceal what she felt.

Slowly she came back to earth as he withdrew from her, though his arms still held her. The room seemed unsteady and she was forced to hold on to him. If the kiss he'd given her before was perfect, this one was even more so, for she had no excuse of alcoholic intoxication. This time it was real, and the woman in her gave him the answers he sought.

"I didn't think so," he said softly. "I didn't think I imagined all this. You are so different, Fan. So warm and real. It's no wonder I can't let you go."

Mortified, Katie glanced up, aware that Frances Pemberton had just made another social mistake. But Christopher didn't seem at all displeased. Her voice sounded far away when she spoke, and she scarcely recognized it herself.

"Why? Why do you want me? I can only cause you trouble. I'm Fan Pemberton, the notorious woman, the one who ran away with a man, who drinks and sings at the top of her lungs, removes her shoes in libraries, and allows you to kiss her."

"I think I've already answered that," he said warmly, his eyes like sherry. "Resign yourself, Fan. I always get what I want. I always have."

Katie sighed. Why was she fighting this? She was taking a chance no matter what. There were no guarantees for her, no promises, no assurance for a tomorrow. Whether she lived with Ella Pemberton as her long-lost niece or Christopher Scott as his wife, she was still playing a role.

And she wanted him. If she'd learned anything in the past few hours, it was that. While she wasn't in love with him, she did like him. And the thought of being his wife, of waking up beside him, living in the same house, laughing with him, growing old with him . . . It was almost too good to be true. She thought of the women she knew, shackled to men who drank too much, who beat them and died young, always desperately poor . . . to Katie, such a life was no life at all. She'd risk social ostracism rather than have such for herself.

And he was so damned sure of himself. Katie smiled inwardly, thinking she ought to say yes, just to teach him a lesson. And it was her best option. Christopher promised her something she desperately needed—security. At any time Ella could realize she was mistaken. Katie wasn't foolish enough to believe she could delude everyone forever. Yet as Christopher's wife, she would have his protection, and so much more. . . . She would be able to help her family, to care for her son, to give him a stability that she would be hard pressed to find any other way.

Take it, Katie, her father's ghost urged her. Don't be a fool.

"All right," she said softly, returning his gaze. "I'll marry you, Christopher Scott. But don't say I didn't warn you."

✵ NINE

"**F**an! Where is she! I can't wait to see her!"

"Ella's really gone mad this time. The old lady's been addled for years."

"You don't suppose she really came back and left that gambler—"

"Nonsense! Frances Pemberton would never leave San Francisco and return here, due to the scandal!"

Eileen rolled her eyes and ushered in the Pembertons, hoisting their bags and innumerable wraps. Grace Pemberton waited behind as Ella descended the stairs, watching with her lips pursed disapprovingly and all hell in her eyes. Ella was obviously unconcerned and smiled at Eileen.

"I see they've all come. Amazing, isn't it, that it takes a wedding or a funeral to reunite the Pembertons! Plenty of tea, Eileen. My dear family can eat."

"Ella, I demand that you stop this nonsense at once!" Grace slammed down her carpetbag with a thud and put her hands on her hips, prepared to do battle. A woman of fifty years, she wore the perpetually worried expression of one whose life was always in someone else's control. Yet she had been pretty once, as evidenced by the classic lines of her profile, the finely cut nose, the soft mouth. She was not at all happy about what was transpiring, and didn't bother to hide it.

"Come in, Grace. You're always in an uproar about something. It's bad for your bowels. Hello, George," Ella said sweetly, hiding a yawn behind a lace-covered hand. An elderly man pressed a kiss to Ella's cheek, then joined the others, apparently determined to stay clear of this fight.

Grace's color deepened and she faced Ella, obviously furious. "Forgive me if I seem out of line, but it is my understanding that you are marrying off my daughter, Fan Pemberton, to Christopher Scott! My daughter, when everyone knows that Fan—"

"Do not even attempt to say it." Ella's expression lost its perpetual sweetness and she glared at her sister-in-law with no apparent love lost.

"Ella, I must speak with you. Alone," Grace said in an imperious tone, ignoring the protests around her. She closed the door to the parlor, shutting out the rest of the family, then turned to her sister-in-law. "I know, dear, how much you've wanted Frances to return," Grace continued in a reasoning tone that one would use with a cranky child. "We've all wanted that. But it just isn't going to happen. Fan is living with a disreputable gambler. She has made her bed and now she must lie in it. No one knows that better than Fan. She will never return, not now, not ever."

"You are wrong," Ella said determinedly, her features becoming sharper and more emphatic. Gone was the sweet senile woman that the Pembertons all took for granted. No, Fan was being threatened, and like a tigress, Ella was determined to protect the girl she loved as a daughter. "Fan has returned, and is going to be wed." She studied Grace for a moment, then smiled coldly. "Why don't you just admit it? You don't want Frances back. You know a good share of my money is promised to her, money that would be yours if Fan chose not to return. None of you want her back."

"How dare you! How could you suggest such a thing? As if I, her mother, wouldn't want my own daughter?"

"Fan's return is the last thing you want," Ella said wearily, as if tiring of the conversation. "You never liked her, not even when she was a little child. Fan was so lively, so pretty, so full of life and energy. You couldn't stand having the limelight taken away from you, even for a moment."

Grace's mouth thinned and she struggled to maintain control. "My relationship with my daughter is none of your concern," she said evenly. "But there is some truth in what you say. I never did like Fan, but not for the reasons you assume. Fan is a liar, a self-centered fraud, and a manipulator. She uses people the way you would use an old dishrag. But once you were no longer of any purpose, she had no compunction about tossing you aside. May God forgive her wherever she is now."

"Enough of this talk," Ella said firmly. "I've summoned Fan. You will soon see for yourself."

Grace nodded. "Good. Everyone wants to see her. None of the Pembertons can believe that you've done this, that you've allowed a perfect stranger to stand in my daughter's place as if she was one of us. We won't allow it, Ella. Not now or ever."

"We'll see about that," Ella said firmly, losing none of her resolution. She opened the doors to the parlor as Katie descended the stairs. "Fan, dear, please come in. I'm sure you remember everyone."

Katie stood outside the door of the parlor, nervously clutching a lace handkerchief. Clad in a yellow silk dress, her black hair pulled back and a few discreet curls escaping, she looked lovely, and every inch a lady. Ignoring the gasps around her, she entered the room with a grace and elegance that a few months ago would have been impossible. But in so many ways, she had learned to be Fan Pemberton, and she drew on that knowledge now.

The room was so quiet that she could hear the rustle of a mouse. They were all there, every last Pemberton from the oldest uncle to the tiniest newborn baby held in his mother's arms. Katie stared back at the sea of faces, seeing the disbelief and shock on all of them. It was as if she were a ghost, the ghost of Fan's past.

"My God," a male voice said in astonishment. "It is Fan!"

Time stood still as an older woman approached, her fingers pressed to her lips. There was a fear in her eyes as she lifted Katie's face, then she sighed with relief.

"You are not Fan. I knew it! I knew it couldn't be. Who are you? Who do you think you are, masquerading as my daughter?" She stared at Katie coldly in disbelief and outrage.

"Grace, if you dare slander this girl one more time, I will have you thrown from my house," Ella said. "If you don't wish to acknowledge your daughter, that's your business. But you won't do it under my roof. That is Fan, and anyone who says otherwise can answer to me."

Chaos broke out as everyone began talking at once. Katie stood in the center of the room like a bewildered child, examined from all sides by the eager throng. When an elderly man approached her sympathetically and took her hand, she smiled at him gratefully.

"Now, now. You're all upsetting the poor girl. I would like to have a word alone with Miss Pemberton. Do you mind?"

Ella and Grace glanced at each other, then Ella shrugged. "No, of course not. But don't keep her too long. Fan and I have plans to make."

"George, you can't mean to accept this . . . this harlot,

acting as Fan! Frances herself is bad enough, disgracing us all, but this . . . this . . . I won't allow it!''

"I just want to speak with this young woman. Is there anything wrong with that?" Grace could raise no other objection and helplessly watched as her brother led Katie out of the room and into the adjoining sitting room. Closing the doors behind them, he let out a deep breath before turning to Katie.

"I am George Atwater, Grace's brother and a Pemberton by marriage," the man said with a twinkle in his eye. "And what I'd like to know, young lady, is who you are and what you're up to."

Katie stared at the man before her, wondering what in the world she would do now. George Atwater calmly poured himself a drink, then took a seat and sipped the whiskey, his eyes never leaving hers. He was watching.

And waiting.

Shrugging, Katie decided that she couldn't bluff her way out of this one, and that the truth was her best defense. They would find out anyway. Taking a deep breath, she spilled forth the facts.

"So you were looking to hire on as a ladies' maid. Well, I have to admit you accomplished that. Ella has been very happy since you appeared. And given the resemblance, I can see how this all happened." George swallowed the entire contents of his glass, then gazed at the pretty young woman before him. "The question is, what do we do about it now?"

"I don't know," Katie confessed miserably. "I never meant for this to go so far. And now—"

"Now we have a real problem to consider." George stood up and paced the room, leaving Katie to stand in the center. "Grace received a letter from Eunice Scott. She is delighted with the prospect of your wedding. You see, she has wanted Christopher to marry for years. He is the last male heir to the Scotts' estate, and without children, the name would die. Yet it seemed any kind of commitment was the farthest thing from his mind. That is, until he met you.''

Katie glanced up and saw the puzzled expression on George Atwater's face. ''And when you tell them the truth—'' her voice whispered.

George shrugged. ''They won't like it, Eunice especially. The Scotts are very influential in the city. They are one of Philadelphia's first families, and have always been given the utmost respect. I don't know what the repercussions would be. And Fan Pemberton cannot afford another scandal, no matter how it happened.'' He looked at Katie and continued softly. ''And I worry about Ella. Her grip on reality has never been strong. Learning the truth about you might just push her over the edge.''

Katie gasped. ''I never wanted to hurt her! I really do care for her. I only went along with all this because it seemed to please her. I thought—''

''It wasn't your fault. The whole situation is out of your control. I suppose we never should have let her come down here alone, to hire her own companion. But frankly Ella and Grace do not get along. And Ella is the matriarch of the family. No one can risk offending her. This seemed the best solution at the time.''

Katie stared at the elegant gentleman, aware of what he meant. Ella had become inconvenient, an embarrassment to them. Eileen had been right. They shuffled her off to the shore, glad to have her out from underfoot, not really concerned of what became of her. She, as Fan Pemberton, she realized in astonishment, might well be the only one who cared about Ella.

''So what will you do?'' Katie whispered in dread.

George Atwater poured himself another drink. ''I haven't the faintest idea.''

* * *

"Frances, will you take me up? I'm ready for my nap," Ella Pemberton interrupted, seeming not at all unhappy to have done so. George Atwater opened his mouth as if to speak, then closed it, obviously changing his mind.

"Of course." Katie excused herself, took Ella's hand, and led her up the stairs into the pretty bedroom. George watched them go, aware of the trust Ella placed in Katie, then sat back down with his drink.

Inside the bedroom, Katie closed the door and helped Ella undress, struggling with the laces and the corset that the older woman insisted she still wear. When the undergarments were removed, Katie pulled a fresh cotton nightgown over Ella's body, then put her to bed.

Smiling, Ella closed her eyes, the stress gone from her expression. "You're so good to me, Fan," she whispered softly as Katie dimmed the lights. "Stay by my bed for a few minutes. You know I don't like to be alone."

Katie took the seat that she'd occupied almost every day since she'd come to this place and she softly brushed the white curls from Ella's forehead. The older woman's hair, which Katie had washed just that morning, glistened like spun sugar. She looked so pretty, so fragile, so . . . vulnerable.

"The family," Ella began softly, her eyes closed. "Don't let them disturb you, Fan. I've told them if they don't accept you, they are no longer welcome here. Including your mother."

Katie's breath stopped and her hand lingered on Ella's cheek. Guilt overwhelmed her. It had gotten so complicated so quickly. Once, she was certain she was doing right, being here and assuming Fan's identity. But now—

"Aunt Ella," Katie said quietly. "I have to tell you something."

"No." Ella smiled in her repose, her eyes still closed. "I

know what you are going to say. Do not let them do this, Fan. Don't be a party to their schemes. Don't hurt me.''

''I'd do nothing to hurt you,'' Katie said, surprised at the depth of her own feeling. ''You know that.''

''Yes.'' Ella sighed quietly. ''Do you know what my life was like before you came back, Frances?'' When Katie shook her head, Ella continued. ''I sat at the window here, in this room, every day. I would go there after breakfast, and stay until sundown, the curtain moved exactly three inches from the window. Do you know what I was doing?''

''No.'' Katie choked, immensely saddened by the picture Ella painted.

''I was waiting. Waiting for something to happen. Waiting for someone to come into my life, for some kind of happiness. I could see the ocean there. It was restless and beautiful, the waves crashing to the beach, then withdrawing to renew themselves once more. I watched those waves for hours, wondering why I was still alive. My family wants me dead, you know.''

''Don't say that!'' Katie said, appalled. ''I'm sure they love you—''

''They care for nothing but the money,'' Ella said tiredly, without emotion, as if the idea didn't brother her at all. ''They are tolerating me, waiting for the day when I draw my last breath and the executor reads the will. I live just to thwart them.''

Katie gasped, feeling her throat tighten. She hadn't been in the Pembertons' company for long, but she had the feeling that Ella was exactly right. For the first time she understood why Fan left, why someone so young would risk everything on a life with a disreputable gambler. But Fan must have felt a lot of the same things Ella was feeling, and had wanted to escape.

''So you mustn't leave, Fan. You mustn't let them influence you, and they will try. Since you've returned, it is as if Eileen opened the shades and let the sunshine in. I'm addled, so they say. And old, and incompetent. But I know what makes me happy.'' Her eyelids opened and she stared at Katie, her smile vanishing. ''Don't let them take you away from me.''

''I won't,'' Katie found herself promising. ''Not now, not ever.''

Ella nodded, then her smile returned and she sank down onto her pillows. Her breathing quieted, and within moments she was asleep.

Katie watched her, her throat tightening. My God, what kind of people were these, to treat one of their own in this manner? The Pembertons, for all their money and influence, knew nothing about Ella and didn't care. They merely shuffled her off to this cottage, glad to have her out from underfoot. As horrible as it sounded, Katie knew that Ella was right. They were waiting for her to die.

A sob caught in her throat as she thought of her own family. For all their faults, they had stayed together, from her grandfather to her own little son. She couldn't imagine any of them behaving in such a manner. Even when she was pregnant and bore Sean out of wedlock, her family hadn't been happy, but they stood by her, often going without so that she could have an extra cup of milk or a warm pair of socks.

What was wrong with these people? Grace Pemberton, for all her elegant airs, appalled her the most. There was a coldness about her, a ruthlessness, that made Katie shudder. Was Paul like her? Or was she like Ella, a sweet human being who just couldn't stand it another minute?

Katie couldn't tell. In any case, she was staying. After meeting the Pembertons, Katie was certain of one thing.

Ella needed a friend. Her.

''I've been to see the Scotts,'' George announced. The other Pembertons stared at him expectantly. Ella had gone to bed, and the family was holding a secret meeting to determine their next course of action. "The news is not good."

"How could it be any worse?" Stephen Pemberton, Grace's son, asked coldly. "We have a perfect stranger in our midst, masquerading as Fan. Ella is convinced she's back and, if angered, will doubtless write us all out of the will. How, may I repeat, could it be worse?"

"The Scotts adore her," George said bluntly. "Eunice thinks Fan is charming and the perfect mate for her nephew. And as for Christopher, the man is obviously infatuated. When I merely hinted that the family might not be supportive of this wedding, on the grounds of Fan's name and reputation, both of them nearly attacked me. I think we stand to make powerful enemies if this match does not proceed."

Gloom settled over the room. Each Pemberton looked to the one beside him, but no one had any answers. Finally it was Grace who spoke up, but even she was less certain than normal.

"Perhaps we should risk their anger," she said slowly. "After all, there are only Eunice and Christopher. Even if they are offended, they don't represent all of society. Then we could go on as before."

Eileen clattered the tea tray. George looked at her searchingly, then spoke.

"That is true, but there are other considerations. Ella's frame of mind, for one. She is set on this wedding, and to thwart her may cause more damage than we can deal with. I don't think any of us is prepared to move in with her and care for her, are we?"

This time the Pembertons looked to the floor. Used to a life of luxury and money, they did not relish the thought of providing help to a senile old lady.

"Then there is another problem. Ella has had Fan

reintroduced to society. Everyone here believes she is
Frances. Some of the women have even helped in this effort.
I don't think they'd take it too kindly to find out they'd been
tricked by the old woman.''

"But we don't even know her!" Ida Pemberton protested, holding her squalling newborn. "We don't know if
she's a common thief, or worse. My God, this woman could
be any tramp off the streets! Do you actually expect us to
take her into our midst as if she were family?''

This time Eileen placed the dishes down with a clunk.
She turned to the Pembertons like a massive boat pulling
into harbor. ''Begging your pardon, miss, but I couldn't
help overhearing. It is none of my concern, but it might
interest you to know that Miss O'Connor's references are
impeccable. She worked for several families as a maid, and
all of them have nothing but good things to say about her.''

"That's a relief," Grace said, though she gave Eileen a
sharp look. "Such recommendations do not come easily. At
least she is trustworthy.''

"I think, after giving the matter thorough thought, that
we should let the wedding proceed," George said firmly,
ignoring the gasps around him. ''And all of the reasons are
obvious. We all stand to lose too much by making a fuss
over this. And in reality, by marrying her off to the Scotts,
we rid ourselves of the problem. Miss O'Connor will then
become their concern, not ours.''

The protests died and the Pembertons began to smile.
Even Stephen, who up until this point was the most vocal,
grinned and patted his uncle on the back.

"You sly old fox! I see what you're getting at. This way
Fan won't be our responsibility. We won't have to worry
about her cutting in on our money. And she really can't
damage Fan's name any more than Fan herself has already
done. Now the old lady is happy, and the girl certainly

won't tell. God, she stands to gain everything. Well done, man. You've come up with the answer.''

Even Grace nodded as the realization came to her. As Frances Scott, Kate O'Connor posed much less of a threat. It was a solution that satisfied everyone.

❖ *TEN*

"**W**hat's the matter, Chris? Wedding nerves?" Charles Pepper grinned at his friend while Christopher struggled to tie his cravat. Giving up after the fifth attempt, he sighed in resignation and let Charles do the honors.

"No, I just don't understand why we need such a fuss. Why can't two people quietly marry? My aunt has notified every newspaper in the country. The house is full of relatives, ones we haven't seen in years. The cook is in a frenzy, trying to keep them all fed, and I have to wear this ridiculous outfit, just to say 'I do.'" He gestured impatiently at the black coat and ascot he wore.

Charles laughed. "I have to admit that I didn't think you'd be the one marrying so soon. And you knew Eunice would never let you off without a big wedding. She's waited years for this." Charles handed him his coat. "You're a lucky man. Fan is something else."

"Yes, she is, isn't she?" The exasperated look left Christopher's face and he smiled warmly. "You know, Charles, she's so different, so vital and alive. She enjoys every minute as if she can't believe it all won't disappear. I've never met anyone like her."

"She's a hell of a girl," Charles agreed. "Then what's the problem? You aren't having second thoughts?"

"I wouldn't say that." His black hair falling into a charming curl across his forehead, Christopher glanced into the mirror and brushed the errant lock into place. What he saw in the mirror only made him frown. He was handsome, startlingly so. He'd been told that since he was a child, and his looks, combined with an easygoing charm, had made him popular and somewhat casual in his morals. So he wasn't acquainted with the feeling that he had today, that what he was doing wasn't quite right. He frowned at his reflection, then turned to Charles.

"Did you ever wonder why we only court the Main Line girls? I mean, women with money?"

Charles shrugged. "Who else would we court? We go to school with them, live with them, see them at the same parties and receptions. It seems only natural that we'd choose one for a wife. Why?" He stared at his urbane friend, obviously perplexed.

"I was just thinking about it, that's all. You know we really limit ourselves and our choices by doing that. And you have to wonder how many matches are made by convenience, family ties or money rather than love."

"Are you saying that you don't . . . love Fan?" Charles questioned cautiously. "You know, Chris, you don't need to rush into anything if you're not sure. Marriage is a lifetime commitment. After today, you and Fan will be husband and wife. You'll live together, have children, grow old . . . if you have doubts, by God, you'd better express them now."

Christopher grinned. "Relax. I don't have any doubts where Fan is concerned. I knew from the moment I saw her that I would wed her. There was never even the slightest hesitation." His eyes grew darker and he pulled on his jacket. "I was just thinking of the process. You know, the criteria we use to decide on a wife. Whether we admit it or not, money plays a big part in it. For instance, could you imagine the reaction if you picked a . . . maid, or a scullery girl as a bride?''

"God, don't even think about it." Charles laughed. "My mother would have the vapors and take to her bed for days. I don't understand what you're getting at with all this, though. If you're happy with your choice, and she has all the qualities your family would want, then I'd call that a perfect situation.''

Christopher grinned, losing his serious demeanor. ''You know, you're right, Charles. And those are odds that any gambler could live with. Let's go, my friend. I believe it's time.''

Charles nodded, then followed Christopher down the stairs. It was nice to know that even the sophisticated, self-confident Christopher Scott harbored doubts on his wedding day. It made him seem far more human and more sensitive than Charles would have given him credit for.

I miss you, Mommy. Grandpa says you will be home at Christmas. That's too long. I have new pants to show you. Aunt Moira said she'll get me real suspenders. She's helping me write this. And a tie. I'm going to wear them to church on Sunday. Billy O'Leary has a new tie, but no pants.

Grandpa says to tell you we're fine. I'm doing what you said and saying my prayers. I'm going to school, but I hate it. The sisters are mean. They won't let me clap erasers because I hit Jimmy Reilly on the head.

Can you come home soon? I'll comb my hair for you and brush my teeth like you asked.

Love, Sean

P.S. Katie—everything's fine, don't worry. Sean just misses you. We're thankful for the extra money you've been sending. I'm glad the new job is good. Moira.

Tears sprang up into Katie's eyes and she shoved the letter into her pocket as Eileen entered the room. Wiping at her face, she turned quickly away so the maid wouldn't see her crying.

"My, you look grand." Eileen beamed, turning up the gaslight and surveying Katie. "You are the prettiest bride I think I've ever seen."

"Do you really think so?" Katie glanced down at the dress, smoothing the creamy satin. Tiny seed pearls and iridescent beads were scattered all over the gown in floral outlines, complementing the lace overlay and the sheer sleeves that reached down to her fingertips. "This dress is beautiful. It belonged to Ella, you know. She never wore it."

"I know." Eileen sighed, tucking a pleat of the gown and arranging the material more carefully. "She should have had a wee one of her own. As it is, she thinks of you that way."

Katie took a deep breath and turned, facing Eileen directly. "I know you haven't been sure about all this," she said slowly. "But I want you to know that I'm thinking of Ella, too."

"I know that," Eileen answered. "And I've come to the conclusion that you are far better for Mrs. Pemberton than all the Pembertons put together. Damned fools! They're down there now, eating everything in sight. I don't know which one of them's worse, from Grace, Fan's mother, the old witch, to Stephen. He's an excellent argument for why alligators eat their young."

Katie chuckled, glad for the relief from the tightness in her throat. "You always make me laugh, Eileen."

"Well, it's the truth," the woman said firmly, planting her hands on her hips. Her eyes met Katie's. "Just don't lose sight of who and what you really are. You may need to fall back on it one day."

"I know." Katie nodded, smoothing her dress. When she glanced back up, her face showed her concern. "Eileen, do you think . . . I mean, does God understand all this?"

Eileen hesitated. To the Irish, God was as close as the nearest leaf, so it wasn't an odd question. And Katie, posing as Fan, was definitely practicing a deception. Taking a deep breath, Eileen nodded. "I think so. After all, you aren't hurting anyone. Mr. Scott is delighted that you will be wed, and so is his family. Mrs. Pemberton is very happy. The only ones unhappy about it are the Pembertons. I don't think the Lord would object to that situation at all."

Katie lightly touched the letter inside her dress. God might be able to understand, but would Sean? How could she explain to her son that she was going to be wed, masquerading as another woman? And that she was doing it as much for him as for anyone else?

She missed him terribly. Katie pictured her son's sandy-blond hair, his irrepressible smile, his freckled nose. There was so much about him that she relived, from the noise he made playing his tin horn to the way he would curl up beside her and sleep with all the trust of a tiny kitten. Would he ever understand that she had to do this, that it was her only hope of ever giving him the life she'd dreamed of?

It was a question without an answer. But every time she thought of him, wretched with poverty, she knew what she had to do.

May God forgive her.

"Are you ready, lass?" Eileen leaned forward and adjusted her veil as Katie nodded.

"As ready as I'll ever be."

Eileen smiled. "I have a good feeling about this day. I woke with an ache in my leg, and that always portends well. I think everything is going to work out fine."

Katie only wished she could be as sure.

*   *   *

The church was more of a hall than anything else, but it was decorated with summer flowers and the sunshine poured through the windows, making it beautiful. Katie smiled, glad that her wedding was not taking place in one of the grand yet intimidating churches in Philadelphia.

Her wedding. The thought made her cold for a moment. She was never to have one. She remembered the remarks she'd had to endure when Sean was born, that she was sullied and could never be a bride. Even her parish priest, Father O'Leary, had told her she could never wear a white dress or be married in a church. She had sinned in the eyes of God and had to pay for that sin.

Rebellion rose up in her. It was so unfair! Why was it only women were penalized like this for a mistake? Only women were scorned for having lived, loved . . .

But somehow she'd escaped even that. A sniffle choked her and she wiped it back, wishing that her father could somehow see her. He'd be so proud of her, his Katie O'Connor, wed in a real church, even if it was not a Catholic church. She could just see his expression, bursting with pride and happiness. By pretending to be Fan, she'd won something very important—freedom from her own past. It was worth more than the money, the gown . . . than anything.

The music started and she heard Eileen's faint whisper. ''Now, lass. Do us all proud.''

George Atwater adjusted her veil, then leaned closer and offered her his arm. ''Ready?''

Katie nodded. Placing her hand through his arm, she started down the aisle, aware of the eyes on her. In truth, she wasn't aware of how beautiful she really looked. Her black hair, shining in the sunlight like polished ebony, looked wonderful behind a veil that concealed her beauty like a misty cloud. The crowd gasped as she started down the walk, but Katie wasn't aware of them or of the man beside her. All she could see was Christopher, standing in the front of the church, waiting.

For her.

He was so handsome. Katie smiled softly, aware even from a distance that he smiled back. She thought of the first time she'd ever seen him, and the peculiar sensation that had rushed through her, as if she'd known him. It was odd at the time, but it seemed doubly so now. It was as if some part of her recognized him as a future mate and had responded with a primitive instinct.

Katie shuddered with anticipation. She would be married within a few moments, would be Mrs. Christopher Scott and all that it entailed. A shred of doubt passed through her, then she glanced in his direction and all doubts evaporated. He looked so happy, and so appreciative, as if lucky to be waiting there for her.

It was heady. Quelling the excitement that grew inside of her, she walked toward him as if drawn to his side. The minister waited until she had reached the altar, then George Atwater stepped back, allowing Christopher to take her arm.

"Brothers and sisters, we are gathered here today to witness the holy union of matrimony. If there is anyone who has reason why the ceremony should not proceed, let him speak now or forever hold his peace."

A slight murmur went through the crowd. Katie tensed, feeling the emotion behind her. Christopher patted her hand reassuringly. When no one spoke, the priest continued.

"Do you, Frances Pemberton, take this man as your lawful wedded husband, to have and to hold . . . from this day forward?"

Katie nodded. "I do."

"And do you, Christopher Scott, take this woman as your lawful wedded wife . . . ?"

Christopher hesitated, then when Katie glanced at him, he grinned. "I do."

"I now pronounce you man and wife." The minister leaned closer, his smile beaming. "You are a beautiful couple. You may now kiss the bride, son."

Christopher hesitated, then turned toward Katie. He lifted the veil, then his lips brushed hers warmly, softly, enticingly. Katie was reminded of that kiss on the porch, when he'd taken her out of herself and made her feel things she never thought possible. It was unbelievably warm and sweet, and she no longer cared that the church was filled with people who weren't entirely approving. Her eyes lifted and met his, and they were filled with the same emotion.

Joy.

The minister coughed, breaking the spell, then gave them a fond look as Christopher took her hand and started down the aisle. Katie felt as if she were in a dream. Even the Pembertons looked happy, as if they couldn't help but smile at the handsome couple as they passed by. And Ella, with her flower-trimmed bonnet and her soft pink dress, looked ecstatic, the sunshine illuminating a face that was so filled with pleasure that it seemed to glow on its own.

And Katie couldn't have been happier. Maybe God was finally showing her that it was all right, that she was forgiven for Sean and John Sweeney and all of the lies and deceptions. When she stepped outside and the air was filled with late-summer sunshine and the scent of the sea, she was almost positive. The whole world seemed to rejoice, and she just couldn't harbor any more doubts under the circumstances. For some reason fate had brought her to this time and place, and she was meant to follow its course.

Katie giggled as rose petals floated to the ground around her, tossed by some of the guests. Eunice smiled with tears in her eyes, Ella beamed, and Bertrice grinned broadly. They winked at each other, as if each had taken a part in all this and was personally responsible.

"Are you happy, Mrs. Scott?" Christopher leaned closer to her and whispered in her ear.

Katie shivered. "We really are married, aren't we?" She stared up at him, trying the name. "Mrs. Scott. Of the Philadelphia Scotts."

"Almost as impressive as Frances Pemberton." Christopher laughed. "Yes, we're really married. And it's too late to change your mind."

"That's the last thing I'd want to do," Katie said easily, but when their eyes met, she realized she'd meant it. Christopher was kind, gentlemanly, witty, and fun, but best of all, he made her laugh. She still had a hard time believing that of his own free will he had wanted her. True, he thought she was a Pemberton, but all that aside, he'd chosen her as his wife from all the Philadelphia debutantes.

And now they were married. She had to look away when she thought of their wedding night. Somehow she knew it would be good, special and unique. His kiss promised that. But she had been with another man and borne his child. She wondered quickly if that would make a difference. He'd never asked much about that, even knowing that Fan had run away with someone, yet she knew he must have thought about it.

I'll just have to face that when it comes, Katie decided, determined not to let her insecurities ruin the day.

Katie could smell the delicious scent of cooking food before they entered the house. Sniffing appreciatively, she gasped at the sight of the table laden with roast chicken, beef, fresh fish, innumerable cakes, vegetables, and cheese. There was late-summer fruit, wine, pitchers of punch, and trays of cookies. Eileen, red-faced from the effort, directed the maids with all the efficiency of a drill sergeant.

Katie couldn't resist giving her a hug. "Eileen, it looks beautiful. Thank you."

The maid blushed with pleasure. "It ain't nothing," she

said, though Katie could tell she was pleased. She then glanced sternly at Christopher and raised her ladle. "You've got yourself a good girl there, sir, if you don't mind my saying."

Christopher smiled. "I am of the same feeling," he said truthfully. "Thank you for everything, Eileen."

"Humph." The maid rolled her eyes, then, as if embarrassed by her emotions, turned to a serving girl. "You don't put the fishes next to the dessert tray! I don't know where they learn their trade." She scuttled away, replacing the dishes, leaving Katie and Christopher to melt into laughter.

The house slowly filled with guests from the church. The Pembertons mingled with the Scotts, and as the evening progressed and the wine was poured, they got more and more amiable. Musicians softly played from the corner of the huge dining room as the guests devoured the food and sent congratulations to Christopher and Katie. As they visited each family member, one at a time, Katie held her breath, waiting for a sharp remark or a cutting look, but it never came. For some reason the Pembertons had resigned themselves to this wedding and were apparently determined that it proceed without incident.

Christopher never left her side. As Katie accepted the gifts and warm wishes from the guests, he helped her with the presents, brought her a plate of food, insisted that she eat, and saw that her wineglass was refilled (within reason). When she turned to laugh with him at the sight of a little boy sneaking a cake, or Ella Pemberton's glistening eyes, his expression made her breathless. His hand rested casually on her shoulder in a gesture that was almost possessive, and his fingers lightly touched a lock of her hair, playing with the silky texture with a reverence that made her stomach do strange things.

The attention was intoxicating, more so than the wine she drank. Katie felt his breath as he lightly kissed her neck and she glanced up, suppressing a shiver as his eyes promised her so much more. When she could look away, she saw Margaret watching her with an open vindictiveness while Bertrice beamed at her, obviously happy for her friend. Margaret turned away quickly, hiding her disappointment, and for once Katie almost felt sorry for her. No matter what happened, Margaret would never be happy unless she let go of her hatred and jealousy, and Katie could only feel pity for anyone who didn't feel what she felt today.

"Are you having a good time?" Christopher asked.

Katie pressed his hand and returned his smile. "Wonderful," she answered truthfully. She couldn't remember ever having a day that was so perfect.

"Will you dance, then?" His voice was a seductive whisper that made her blush.

"But no one else—" She gestured to the guests, who were still happily eating, and the musicians who were waiting in the corner.

"Come," Christopher commanded, taking her hand and leading her to the door. Katie tossed aside her napkin with abandon, laughing with him as they escaped to the ballroom, accompanied by the musicians, who reacted to a signal from Christopher.

The carpets had been rolled and pulled out of the way, and the floor was lightly sanded. The gaslights were very dim, in anticipation of the later arrival of the guests when the dancing usually began. Katie reached to turn it up, but Christopher stopped her.

"Leave it. They'll all be in here soon enough. Today I wanted the first dance with you. Alone."

Her heart pounding in her chest, Katie found it difficult to breathe. She nodded quickly, tears coming to her eyes as the musicians began to play "Greensleeves."

Christopher was so romantic, so charming, and so handsome. She'd have to be careful, for he could easily steal her heart, and Lord knows she couldn't go through that again. But Katie couldn't resist running her hand down his arm as he reached for her, feeling the muscles beneath his coat. She giggled, recalling the day when she'd hidden his clothes, and he glanced down at her, smiling fondly.

"What?"

"I was just thinking that I certainly gave you a run for your money," she said with a grin. "Most men would have given up long ago."

"I always get what I want," Christopher said. His tone was earnest, but he still smiled. "You never had a chance."

His voice had grown husky, and when she looked back up, his expression took her breath away. It was smoldering with sensuality and desire, and she realized that she was feeling the exact same things. He gathered her closer to him, and she noticed that they fit perfectly together, his long lean body leading her, swirling, over the dance floor.

It couldn't be any better than this, Katie thought dizzyingly, but then it was. She could smell the sweet scent of his limewater, feel the crispness of his dark hair against her fingers. The movement of his body, so warm and close against hers, nearly made her faint with anticipation. And as the music continued, hauntingly beautiful, she moved effortlessly with a grace she never knew she possessed.

"My God," he whispered. "You are so sweet."

No man had ever said that to her. Katie glanced up at him and what she saw made her tremble. The emotions on his face were so intense, so powerful that she was reminded of the first time they'd met. It was like glimpsing the future with an unearthly power that was all the more hypnotic as it was inexplicable.

They didn't realize when the musicians had finished. Instead they swirled around the dance floor long after the music had died, wanting nothing more than to stay in each other's arms. Katie never wanted it to end. She wanted to stay here, like this, forever, safe and secure, knowing that Christopher Scott wanted her and thought she was sweet.

"What are you doing in here with the lights out?"

A small boy skidded into the room and Katie laughed, breaking the spell. Christopher groaned, and reluctantly released her when it was obvious that the child wasn't about to leave. Bending down, Katie took his hand and addressed him solemnly, the same way she talked to Sean.

"You are right, we are silly, aren't we?" When the little boy nodded in agreement, Katie continued. "Then you must fetch us some company. Why don't you tell Ella and the Scotts that we all need to dance?"

The little boy grinned, obviously pleased to be treated seriously and given a task of such importance. He slid back out of the room, delighted with the sandy floor, which provided a wonderful skating rink.

"Now you've done it," Christopher said. "Now we'll never get rid of them."

"We're not supposed to." Katie grinned, her freckles crinkling. "This is a wedding, remember?"

"Yes, but I wanted you all to myself. I guess I'll just have to wait until later."

Katie blushed at his bold reminder of the night to come. She was rescued from further comment as guests returned with the little boy, eager to dance. Charles Pepper stole her out from Christopher's arms, ignoring his friend's scowl, while the others sought out partners.

The music began in earnest, and Katie smiled as she saw the other couples gliding beside her. Christopher was almost as sought after as she, for as the missing Fan Pemberton, she could not claim a recent acquaintance with many of the guests while Christopher could. Nor did he shirk his responsibility to the older women. Katie noticed that he sought them out deliberately, especially Eunice and the other matrons who were there alone. They were so grateful to be asked to dance, especially by the young and handsome groom, and Katie found herself beaming at him from the dance floor. When he asked Ella to dance, treating her with all the courtliness of a medieval knight, she wanted to kiss him then and there.

Christopher looked up and, seeing her expression, finished the dance with Ella and came to her side. She was dancing with Stephen Pemberton by then, laughing at something he said. The train of her white gown was tossed over her arm, her bridal veil having been removed long ago, and her hair gleamed in the gaslight like polished onyx.

"Come," he said, interrupting her dance, heedless of Stephen's indignant expression. "I think it's time we said good night."

❊ ELEVEN

The champagne lace peignoir felt wonderful against her damp skin. Katie brushed out her long, black hair, then added a touch of scent behind her ears the way Eileen had shown her.

A glass of wine waited beside her in the dressing chamber of the hotel. Katie drank of it deeply, thinking of the night ahead. She was now Christopher's wife. A pleasurable rush swept through her, followed by an uneasiness. Would he be gentle? Would he be kind and considerate, or would he take advantage of the situation?

Katie recalled the time she'd slept with John Sweeney. She had been barely eighteen, and he had been so handsome, so charming with his wild Irish grin and his jokes. She had thought she was in love, for no one made her feel the way he did. And when he'd taken her in his arms and promised her he'd never leave her, she'd believed him. She gave him the most precious gift she could have offered any man: herself.

And he took it.

Katie cringed as she remembered what followed. It wasn't that he was rough or unkind. It was just that the entire act seemed distasteful and unfulfilling. She didn't know what all the fuss was about, what all the books and poets and songs referred to. It couldn't have been that painfully embarrassing moment when John Sweeney tried to penetrate her. He thrust himself into her, ignoring her gasp of pain. He groaned, his pleasure almost immediately spent, then he lay on top of her, breathing hard.

"God, Katie darlin'," he'd whispered. "What a woman you are!"

A woman. Tears came to Katie's eyes as her lover lay in her arms, her fingers brushing his dark curls. She felt cheated and empty, as if her initiation into womanhood should have been more meaningful. And when she'd found out she was pregnant, he'd left her alone to fend for herself, taking her heart with him.

It's in the past, Katie told herself. Tonight was a new beginning, a fresh start. Finishing her glass, she placed it on the table and walked out to the bedchamber, determined to be brave.

Christopher saw her approach and his breath stopped. If she had looked beautiful as a bride that day, she looked breathtaking now. Her hair, brushed until it shone, was a glossy black against her fair skin. Her nose, turned up and sprinkled with freckles, was a delight, and her eyes, bluer than the sea, sparkled with sweet anticipation.

"Fan, you look gorgeous," Christopher said, obviously sincere.

"No, you do." Shyly she indicated his satin robe, decorated with a rich paisley pattern and trimmed with red edging. "That's pretty. It looks so luxurious. It suits you."

"You never cease to amaze me," Christopher said with a chuckle, taking her in his arms. "You've grown up with so much money, so many riches, and you always appreciate them as if seeing them for the first time. I think it's what I like best about you."

Katie managed a smile, aware that she'd have to be more careful. She was Fan Scott now, and had to stop thinking like Katie O'Connor. He pressed a kiss to her forehead, then withdrew for a moment, returning with a wrapped package in his hand.

"I know you received a lot of wedding gifts, but I wanted you to have something from me. It's not much, just a remembrance of this day."

Tears filled Katie's eyes and she opened the box excitedly, tearing at the fragile paper and the silver ribbons.

Inside, on a bed of velvet, was a necklace. A gold shamrock glittered from the end of the long chain with a solitary emerald winking from a heart-shaped leaf. Picking it up with reverence, Katie saw the inscription on the back. *To the beginning. May it always be this wonderful. Christopher.*

A tear dropped down Katie's cheek and her eyes lifted to Christopher's. "It's beautiful," she breathed, admiring the gift. "I've never had anything like it, and I'll treasure it always."

"The shamrock's for luck," Christopher said, indicating the charm. "Although I don't think we'll need it. Fan, there's a lot of things that we've never talked about, but I want you to know that I really mean to make this marriage work. We get on well together, we have a lot of fun, and we both like to laugh. I want to keep that alive between us."

Katie nodded, her eyes glistening.

"And I want to start a family. I've always liked children, my reputation to the contrary, and I'd like to have a few of my own. When I saw you talking to that little boy at the wedding, I knew you'd make a wonderful mother. I'd like to give you a son of your own."

The pounding started in Katie's chest and she thought her heart would break. God, how she longed to tell him that she already had a son, a wonderful child that he would adore. But how could she ever? How could she confess the existence of an illegitimate child?

"I'd also like to become more established. True, we'll have your dowry and all that goes with it, but eventually I want more. All of that is none of your concern, however. But I do want you to know that I think we've made a good beginning, and that we have a splendid future ahead."

What was he talking about? Katie was so disturbed by the mention of children that she scarcely noticed. But then he took her in his arms and kissed her slowly, leisurely, with a barely restrained passion that made her want to cry out with pleasure.

No one kissed like Christopher. Katie firmly believed he possessed some kind of magic, for as soon as his mouth touched hers, she forgot everything, all of her trepidations and uncertainties. He demanded a response from her and she gave it, forgetting John Sweeney, forgetting the past, forgetting everything but how much she wanted him.

"Fan . . ." His voice was a hoarse whisper, revealing everything he was feeling. He nuzzled her throat. "Fan."

"Please," she whispered. "I know it's silly, but just for tonight, would you call me Kate?" When he looked at her searchingly, she managed a smile. "My father used to do that when I was little. He always wanted to name me Katie, but my mother wouldn't hear of it."

"Of course, if that's what you want. Kate." His mouth met hers and Katie sighed with pleasure. She didn't think she could have gone through with this if he continued to call her by someone else's name. No, she needed to know that he was kissing her, wanting her, loving her.

He kissed her again and all rational thought left. She could only feel, her body keenly aware of the cool linen beneath her, the scent of Christopher's limewater, the crackle of the fireplace behind her as he lowered her to the bed. When his mouth left hers and his hands began to untie the laces of her gown, she lifted slightly, making it easier for him to loosen the lush fabric and pull it away from her overheated skin. Katie cried out when his mouth made intimate contact with her flesh, trailing enticingly from her throat to the soft valley between her breasts.

Every part of her was alive, tingling with warmth and sensation and want. The nerve endings of her skin seemed to cry out for him, responding to his touch with a wild pleasure that she'd never before experienced. She could sense that he was forcing himself to go slowly, teasing her subtly until she was practically sobbing.

When his mouth took one of her nipples, even the sound of his suckling seemed like an aphrodisiac and powerfully erotic. Blindly Katie reached for him, wanting to return the pleasure, wanting to make him feel as out of control as he was making her. She heard his soft laugh, then he held her hands at her sides.

"No, Katie. Not yet. Please. I won't be able to hold on if you do."

Frustrated, she had no choice but to obey him. Still, the pleasure was delirious as his hand swept over her, down from her breasts that were swollen and aching and wet, down to her belly and lower.

Katie gasped as his hands caressed her thighs, making her cry out, desperately wanting more. His fingers teased her, touching her everywhere except where she was throbbing and needing him, exploring the silken inner flesh of her thighs and the soft black curls above. When she thought she couldn't stand it another moment, his fingers slipped lower, giving her what her body unashamedly pleaded for.

A grateful ooh tore from her throat and she arched her back unconsciously, wanting every sensation, everything he could possibly give her. His mouth continued to caress her, placing burning kisses along her belly and legs. And when he replaced his hand with his mouth, she thought she'd go out of her mind.

Her fingers buried in his hair and she writhed in pure

pleasure. Her breathing came faster, her voice caught in weak little gasps as the tension mounted. Her aching flesh responded wickedly to his mouth, and she cried out as wave after wave of pure pleasure flooded through her.

Never had she felt so drawn out of herself, lost to a world that she'd never dreamed existed. Her body contracted, her fingers dug into the sheets, her toes curled against the mattress. He seemed to know exactly what was happening to her, and by the time she opened her eyes, stunned by the intensity of what she was feeling, he was reverently kissing her breasts once more.

"My God," he whispered, softly caressing her cheek. "I just can't get enough of you."

Katie flushed, but her eyes held him, aware of the firelight in their dark depths and the emotion they contained. She was his then. Whatever he wanted, she would return this incredible pleasure.

Her hands reached out and caressed him boldly, hearing the sharp intake of his breath as she touched him where he was hot and throbbing and almost painfully hard. Smiling back at him, Katie took control and imitated his actions, returning his kisses with a passion that made his blood boil. When her hair brushed his thighs and she returned his intimacy, he almost lost control.

"Stop," he commanded, drawing her up on top of him. "I want you so badly. Please . . ."

He entered her, her body still astride him, and Katie gasped with the joy of it. She was so warm, so aroused, and so ready for him that it began again almost instantly for her. Hearing the soft sounds she was emitting, Christopher lost all control and thrust deeply into her. Katie's breath caught and she swallowed hard as intense erotic pleasure swept through her. She clung to him, moving with him as a ritual older than time possessed them, taking them past the physical into a realm where reality didn't exist.

They didn't speak, but something changed between them. From this moment on, Katie knew she wouldn't be afraid again. Somehow everything would work out. When their passion was spent and she collapsed into his arms and he stroked her sweat-streaked hair, she knew that it had happened.

God had finally forgiven her.

She awoke to the soft sounds of the church bells ringing and the crash of the waves on the shore. For a brief second she couldn't remember where she was, for the bed was so luxurious and the linen as fine as silk. She was even more astonished when she realized that she was not alone. She struggled up on one elbow, a rush of joy sweeping through her.

Christopher. He was still asleep, his eyes closed, his breathing quiet as he lay on the snowy pillow. Somehow she hadn't thought about this, that she'd awaken beside him, but it was heavenly and she didn't want to move, afraid of breaking the spell. He looked so innocent, his wavy black hair falling over his forehead, tempting her to touch it. His mouth was perfect, full and generous, and his body, barely covered with the sheet, brought a blush to her face as she remembered the tremendous pleasure he had given her last night.

Her wedding night. Katie sighed, aware that no wedding could ever have been as wonderful, or the night that followed as romantic. It was almost too perfect, and the Irish in her was afraid.

Live, Katie darling. Be happy

Katie smiled, wiping at the tears of joy that misted her eyes. It was foolish to be anxious. She was married now, and the life that could have disappeared at any moment was now hers. She was Mrs. Scott, and no one could say otherwise.

A delicious giggle surged up within her. She would awaken like this every day, with Christopher at her side. Aye, she may not love him yet, but she wanted him. Last night had proven that. Love would come, she was certain. She had the rest of her life to make this work, to form some kind of a new family. And somehow she would find a way to bring Sean into their lives so that he could grow up like Christopher, happy and secure. She wasn't sure how she could accomplish that, but she'd think of something. Katie had learned to stop questioning fate. She had been meant to answer that ad, to become Fan Pemberton, to marry Christopher. It had all happened for a reason.

Christopher rustled in his sleep and she smiled fondly at him. Ah, he was so good-looking, so carefree. There were times when she felt so much older than he, having lived as she had, but she didn't begrudge him his money. She allowed herself the pleasure of looking at him, her eyes memorizing every small detail as if he would disappear. . . .

"Did I pass inspection?"

Katie gasped as she realized he was fully awake and was watching her with a grin. She tossed her pillow at him, hearing his laughter, but before she could stomp out of the bed, he caught her wrist, dragging her back against his chest.

"You should have said something!" Katie chided, then melted into laughter as he rolled her onto her back, trapping her effectively beneath him.

"Why? You seemed to be having a good time. The last thing I want to do is interfere with your pleasure."

"You are the most conceited, swellheaded—"

"Unscrupulous," Christopher supplied helpfully. "Egotistical—"

"Excuse for a husband," Katie finished, still laughing. She wrapped her arms around him, delighted with the way his body warmed hers, and the sensual way he kissed her.

When his face lifted to hers, she shivered at the smoldering desire she saw in his eyes.

"Are you happy?" he asked softly, taking her hand and kissing her fingers.

Katie's breath caught and she gazed up at him, amazed that so simple an act could make her stomach contract and her legs feel weak. "Very," she managed, closing her eyes as his mouth caressed her palm, arousing her in a way she'd never dreamed possible.

She must be a wanton. Surely he didn't mean to take her again, in broad daylight on Sunday morning, and surely she didn't want him to! No decent woman felt what she was feeling. She'd heard the whispered conversations of other women, about a wife's duty and a man's privilege, and she was certain that her first sexual experience with John Sweeney was common. Squirming, she managed to extricate herself from his embrace.

"Fan? What's wrong?"

Katie blushed, especially when he called her by that name. Good Lord, she couldn't do this, especially with the church bells ringing! She clutched the sheet more tightly about her naked body and gestured to the window.

"The bells. We have to get ready for services."

Christopher shrugged, toying with the edge of the sheet. "We have time. There is a second service at ten."

"We have breakfast," Katie said quickly. "Remember? Your aunt is giving a breakfast in our honor this morning."

"Brunch," he corrected her. "And that isn't until eleven. Fan, what's wrong?"

Katie shrugged, growing more embarrassed as she remembered the previous night. Fan Pemberton would not have reacted to him with such abandon. Real ladies didn't derive pleasure from sex, only taproom whores did that. And last night her response had been unmistakable. Surely he must be thinking the worst. . . .

"It's not decent," she said shyly.

Christopher frowned, staring down at her in disbelief. "Fan, you've lived with another man. A gambler, they say." His eyes darkened as if this fact troubled him immensely, but he continued in the same tone. "That's almost the same as being married. Surely in all that time you made love in the morning?"

Katie swallowed hard. He expected her to have much more experience than she did. "Not really," she murmured. "It was . . . not the same."

"In what way?" When she didn't answer, he continued softly. "Fan, I've never asked you about your past. I know about the scandal, have heard the rumors, but would like to hear it from you. What was he like? Did you love him so much to leave everything? Why did you come back?"

Katie gulped. She had unwittingly opened Pandora's box, but there was no escape now. Christopher waited expectantly, and she knew she owed him an explanation. Yet how could she possibly continue this lie and tell him about a past she knew nothing of?

She couldn't, Katie decided. She would tell him the truth, but only about her own experience. Taking a deep breath, she answered quietly.

"I thought I did love him." Her eyes squeezed shut as she thought of John Sweeney, and fresh tears started as the pain began all over again. "I would have done anything for him. Surely you can understand that? He was the first man to make me feel that way, as if I really meant something to him."

"I see," Christopher said, his tone dry. "What happened then?"

"I was too young," Katie said softly, knowing that for the truth. "And I didn't really understand what love meant. When he, you know . . ." She couldn't bring herself to say it, and thankfully Christopher nodded. "I didn't feel anything. Not like last night. I thought that's the way it is supposed to be. Then he left me, and I realized he never loved me at all. He couldn't have. So I came home.'' She forced a smile, though there was a glistening of moisture in her eyes. "Fan Pemberton and the scandal.''

Christopher said nothing, but saw the shame in her face. Reverently he picked up her hand and kissed it, then he looked directly at her.

"The man was a fool, Fan, a damned fool. What happened between us last night was wonderful, and nothing for you to be embarrassed about. We have the rest of our lives together, and I intend to spend it making you happy. I can only do that if you let me. Do you trust me enough?''

Katie looked at him through her tears, past the charming facade that most people saw, to the urgent and compelling man beneath. She nodded, her fears evaporating. For some reason she did trust him. His smile returned and he pulled her into his arms. Katie sighed. It felt so good, so natural to be there that, wanton or not, she could no longer deny him.

"Come then. Show me that you mean it.'' His voice was warm and compelling.

Katie did.

TWELVE

"Oh God, Christopher! Isn't it beautiful!"

Christopher smiled indulgently as Fan stood in awe at the sight of the brunch. It was true, the hotel was pretty, with the view of the ocean sparkling through the windows and dozens of white candles illuminating the soft linen tablecloths and crystal. And the food, fresh sea trout, eggs prepared with several interesting sauces, tea cakes and rolled sandwiches, coffee and sugared almonds, was well done and exceptionally served. Fan had attended dozens of brunches just like this one. Yet she brought a freshness to everything she did, as if it was the first time, and he thought it delightful.

Christopher grinned as he recalled Fan on her knees that morning in church, her hands quietly folded in prayer, a far cry from the woman she'd been in his arms. Her response had delighted him, for he knew it was real and honest, and his blood quickened as he realized that he could make her feel that way. And when she'd reciprocated, making love to him in the most intimate way possible for a woman to love a man, he thought he'd go out of his mind. Yes, he'd done exactly the right thing when he married Fan Pemberton. She was funny and witty, charming and mischievous, but best of all she was real, one of the few women in his acquaintance that he could truly say that about.

"There you are. Everyone is waiting. You looked beautiful yesterday, dear, and even prettier today." Aunt Eunice pressed a kiss on Katie's cheek, then gave her nephew a wink. "Well done, my boy. Seems we finally have made you respectable."

Christopher gave her a dry smile. "There was never any question in the matter. Now, if you don't mind, Aunt, my bride and I are starving."

Katie grinned as Christopher led the way, nodding to the Pembertons and the Scotts. She nearly giggled when they reached the table and he groaned in frustration.

"If it was up to them, we'd never eat. You'd think they'd have some pity—we've only been married a few hours. Don't look now, but here comes Margaret and the other girls."

Katie grimaced as Margaret approached. Bertrice saw her expression and with a subtlety that would have been unheard of a few months ago managed to distract her by indicating a torn hem. Katie melted into laughter as Margaret was forced to follow Bertrice into the outer room, where, apparently, the hem could be repaired.

"I can't believe the change in Bertrice," Katie commented happily at Christopher's quizzical glance. "Charles has been a grand influence on her. She's really come out of her shell."

"I'm glad, too. They seem to make a nice couple, and Charles really likes her. I think we may hear of another Cape May wedding soon."

Katie smiled. Nothing could have made her happier. Bertrice deserved a man like Charles. She was still beaming when she noticed Ella rise unsteadily, then pause as if unable to go on. The older woman stared about her in confusion, then took several deep breaths while clinging to the back of the chair. Her smile fading, Katie put down her napkin and immediately got up.

"I'll be right back," she whispered to Christopher, then walked across the room. She took Ella's hand and helped her to the door. "Are you all right?" Katie whispered softly.

Ella nodded, but Katie could see the strain in her eyes and a bluish tinge around her mouth. Her hands were cold, and when she glanced up at Kate, she looked afraid.

"I'll be fine," she said, but her voice quavered. "It's just the excitement. I think I need to rest for a while."

Katie nodded. "You overdid it yesterday. I wanted you to take it easy—"

"And not dance at your wedding?" Ella managed a smile, then grasped the chair once more. "You're right, I did too much. I have an odd pain in my arm. I just need to lie down."

One of the maids escorted Ella to the hotel sitting room while Katie watched, concerned. When she rejoined Christopher, she couldn't hide the way she was feeling.

"Is she all right?"

"I don't know," Katie said, suddenly very glad to have someone to share this with. "She doesn't look well."

"I'm sure it's just the excitement." He squeezed her hand reassuringly. "If she continues to do poorly, I'll send for our personal physician in the city. He's very good."

Katie smiled gratefully. Christopher seemed to know exactly what to say to make her feel better. She turned to say good-bye to Bertrice and the other guests. When only the families remained, Eunice stood up.

"I'd like to make a toast to the bride and groom. May you have many days as happy as this one. Long life, long love to you both!"

Everyone clapped, then sipped champagne and orange juice. Katie blushed, embarrassed by the attention, but her eyes met Christopher's. She felt a surge of emotion rush through her. He smiled, his eyes soft and full, as if sharing the feeling with her. Katie didn't think it was possible to be this happy. She broke away from his stare, aware of the sound of an altercation from the front part of the dining room.

"I'll not listen to anything! Take your hands off me When they hear what I have to say—"

"Madam, you can't go in there. It is a private party!"

"Really! Well, this is my party, and I'll go where I damn please!"

"Madam!" The waiter rushed up and glanced apologetically at Christopher. "I'm sorry, but I tried to stop this woman. She insisted upon coming in."

"That's right!" The woman barged in, her face a mask of hatred. "Don't you understand, you fools! You've been duped! I'm Fan Pemberton!"

The only sound that followed was the clatter of Katie's fork as it fell to her plate. Time stood still as she stared in astonishment at the woman before her.

It was like looking at a mirror image. Fan Pemberton had the same glossy black hair, the same blue eyes, the same nose, the same freckles . . . even the same dimples. Katie swallowed hard, blinking, sure the apparition would vanish, but it did not. An eerie fear crept over her, a feeling that was reflected in the angry face that stared back at her. It was as if she were no longer an individual, no longer the only Katie. Good God, a perfect replica stood right before her.

Katie wanted to run, to hide, to get away from this woman who seemed as incredulous as she. But there was no escape. Already she could hear the buzz from the wedding guests as they, too, recovered, and the reality began to sink in. She couldn't even look at Christopher, but her heart pounded as she sensed his confusion.

"What the hell's going on here?" he asked, glancing from one woman to the other in disbelief.

Grace Pemberton spoke first, coming forth from her table to examine the woman who had barged in. The two women eyed each other with an obvious lack of affection. In one cursory glance, Grace was satisfied and she turned to the others with a sarcastic tone.

"*This* is Fan." She spoke in a smug voice. "I told you *she* wasn't my daughter. This is the real Fan."

Bedlam broke out. The Pembertons' voices rose in an uproar as they demanded explanations and reprisals while the Scotts stared in dignified disbelief. Eunice stepped forward, still glaring at Fan as if she couldn't believe her eyes, then she turned toward Katie.

"Who are you?"

Some of the noise quieted as Katie struggled to answer. "I'm Kate. O'Connor. Katie O'Connor." She could hardly talk, her emotions were so intense.

Eunice glared at her. "Where did you come from? Have we ever seen—"

"No," Katie said quickly. "I live in the poor section of Philadelphia. I am a ladies' companion."

"My God." Eunice fanned herself with her napkin, looking as if she would faint. She glanced accusingly at Christopher. "Then that means you've married a pauper? She has no dowry, no money? That all our plans were for nothing?"

"Unfortunately, Miss O'Connor, or should I say, Mrs. Scott, is not from our circle," George Pemberton interrupted, wisely stepping between Eunice and the young couple. "But that should make little difference to you, Eunice, monetarily, at least. I think our biggest problem right now is what to do with two Fan Pembertons."

"You don't understand." Eunice wrenched her handkerchief and stared at her nephew. "Christopher, do you know what this means? We're ruined, absolutely ruined."

"Fan." Christopher turned to Katie, his eyes blazing. "You're coming with me. I'm getting to the bottom of this. Now."

Before Katie could say a word, Christopher hauled her toward the conservatory at the side of the hotel. Slamming the door behind him, he faced her with his hands on his hips, his breath slowing as if he was forcing his temper under control. His jaw was tight, and there was something besides anger in his expression that Katie couldn't immediately identify.

"I want to know the truth," he said quietly, his voice deadly. "All of it."

Katie nodded, fighting the tears that stung the back of her throat. She had known this day would come, that she couldn't get away with impersonating Fan forever, but somehow she didn't think it would be like this. Struggling to find the right words, she poured it all out quickly.

"My real name is Kate O'Connor. I'm not rich, I'm not from the Main Line, I live in the Irish ward with my family."

He stared at her, as if trying to make sense of what she was saying. She could see the disillusionment in his eyes. "The Irish ward . . . No wonder everything seemed so new to you—it was! If you're saying what I think you are, you've never been a part of this society." When Katie nodded, he continued in the same odd voice. "How did all this happen?"

Katie still couldn't bring herself to tell him everything, but she decided to tell him the main facts, especially those he could easily verify. "I applied for a position as a ladies' maid with Ella Pemberton this summer, and she mistook me for Fan. I tried to tell her the truth, but she just wouldn't listen."

"So you lied." He sounded incredulous. "You took

advantage of a senile old woman and lived as Fan, never stopping to think what would happen to her if the truth came out. Why? Why did you do it? You were the one woman I'd thought was real and honest, yet you used Ella to gain entry into society. . . . My God, I don't even know you!''

"It wasn't like that!" Katie tried to take his hand, to make him listen, but he pulled away from her in disgust. "You can ask Eileen. I did try to tell her, but it was no use. It's true, I enjoyed acting as Fan. Is that so hard to understand?" Her voice choked. "Christopher, I had nothing. No money, no clothes, nothing but a lifetime of hard work. And here, like the leprechaun's pot of gold, I had everything given to me. More gowns than I could imagine. Plenty of food. A nice room. And best of all, I was admitted to a world that before I could only glimpse. Can you imagine what that was like?"

She could see a small bit of the anger leave him, but his eyes were still like ice. "That doesn't excuse what you did. Ella Pemberton didn't ask for this betrayal."

"That's not fair!" Katie wiped at her cheeks with her fists, hating the stinging tears that sprang to her eyes. "I never meant to hurt Ella. It was partially for her sake that I went along with everything. Christopher, you didn't see her. She was so thrilled to have Fan back, so happy. She told me that before I came, all she could think about was dying. How could I have told her that my existence was only a figment of her imagination?"

"You still could have told *me* the truth," Christopher said, his tone fierce. "I would have kept your secret. You married me, slept in my arms last night. . . . Was all that just part of the plan, too?"

"And what would have happened then?" Katie looked at him defiantly. "Are you saying that you would have still married me? Me, Katie O'Connor, who is a nobody?" She laughed bitterly. "I don't know everything about your world, but I've learned that much. There's no way you would have wanted me."

"I couldn't have married you." There was a strange tone in his voice and he looked at her with a mixture of rejection and longing. "No matter what I would have wanted, I couldn't have married you."

"Why?" Katie stared at him, her eyes wide with pain. "Because I wasn't good enough? Because my bloodlines weren't Fan Pemberton's, because my family doesn't own real estate? Tell me, dammit, I want to hear it from you."

"I couldn't have married you because I haven't any money!"

Katie's mouth opened in astonishment as Christopher dropped onto a garden bench, then sank his face into his hands. No money? Her mind whirled in a torrent of confusion. But he was Christopher Scott, of the Philadelphia Scotts, of the Main Line, whose family made their fortune in soaps and perfumes. What he'd just told her made absolutely no sense, but from his stricken posture, she knew he was saying what he believed to be the truth.

Katie suddenly recalled Eunice's words moments before when Fan had shown up. She'd said something very similar, about them being ruined, about a dowry. . . .

"Christopher," Katie said softly. "What did Eunice mean? Why don't you have any money?"

Without lifting his face from his hands, he spoke quietly. "My family lost everything in the 1873 panic. We were heavily invested in railroad stocks, and if you know anything of what happened, they aren't worth the paper they were printed on. I was on the verge of losing everything. I tried to borrow, to gamble, but there was no hope. My only option was to marry for money."

"But the courtship, the dinners, the flowers . . ."

"We sold our paintings," Christopher said bluntly, looking directly at her for the first time. "Aunt Eunice auctioned off our collection of portraits. That provided enough money for the summer.''

Katie couldn't believe what she was hearing. ''So you thought that Fan Pemberton, with her soiled past, would have welcomed you, and you would have the money you needed. It was all perfect, wasn't it?''

''Yes, goddammit!'' Christopher rose to his feet and glared at her. He seemed as angry with himself as with her. ''I didn't want to do this! And I didn't choose Fan until I got here. Until I met you. I thought I was so damned lucky, that I found a woman that I wanted as well as one who had money. But I didn't count on being deceived! I'm married to you, and I suddenly realize that I know nothing about you—''

''And what of you?'' Katie cried, fighting the pain that threatened to humiliate her. ''You lied, too! You let me think you were rich, that you hadn't a care in the world! Well, it seems Christopher Scott had a few little secrets, too!''

''Enough!'' Christopher bellowed. ''I can't hear any more of this! I need to think about it and decide what I want to do. And I suggest you do the same.'' He looked at her as if she was beneath contempt. ''Now, if you don't mind, I prefer that you leave. I don't want to go back to the hotel room and be reminded of last night. I'm sure it won't bother you.''

Katie turned on her heel and left, letting the sobs overwhelm her. He wanted to think about it; she knew what that meant. He was contemplating divorce.

And there was nothing she could do to stop him.

''. . . and I can't believe you were all taken in by this . . . this imposter! Why, she doesn't look anything like me! Didn't anyone think to check her credentials? My God, any tramp off the street could walk in here and you would take her into your bosoms without so much as a fare-thee-well!''

"Oh, Fan, shut up." Grace plunked down into a seat and stared at her daughter. Fan returned the petulant look, but stopped her tirade long enough to shove several rich cakes into her mouth. "You know," Grace said tiredly, watching her daughter with distaste, "you've created a bit of a problem, though I doubt that overly concerns you. Fan Pemberton now stands to have two scandals. I don't think the society papers will forgive that."

Fan's mouth dropped and she quickly reached for a glass of wine to wash down the cakes. "I can't believe this." She wiped her lips with her sleeve and glared at her mother. "I come back after all this time to find myself replaced by some—what did she say she was? A ladies' companion. She's slept in my room at Aunt Ella's, been introduced everywhere as me, married with my name, and all you can care about is the scandal?''

"It is a consideration," George Pemberton broke in while the others nodded in agreement. "It is a problem not just for us, but for the Scotts." He glanced sympathetically at Eunice, who still stared at the real Fan Pemberton in confusion. "It's not that we aren't concerned about you, Fan. And of course, we're all happy you're home. But we have to be careful how we handle things. Many a publicity rag would love this story, and there are others who would take advantage of our dilemma and use it against us. I, for one, have too many business deals pending with society's elite to risk involvement in any more scandals.''

"And I'm trying to get into the Wissahickon Club," Stephen Pemberton remarked. "There is a lot of competition for membership. If word leaks out . . .''

"Everyone has a lot at stake. We do, after all, have two Fan Pembertons. We can't let that continue.''

"You're damned right!" Fan said bluntly, seating herself

beside George with an outraged glare. "That tramp has enjoyed herself enough! There's no way this farce will continue!"

"The other question is, how do we tell Ella?" The murmurs in the room died as George glanced suggestively toward the door where the matriarch had exited. "God only knows what this will do to her. We all know how attached she's become to the girl."

"That's ridiculous!" Fan snapped. "I'm back! Ella will be happy when she discovers the truth!"

Everyone's eyes went to Fan. The traveling garment she wore, still stained from the trip, was a garish and cheap yellow-and-black-striped affair with black lace at her face and throat. Black kohl lined her eyes, and the suggestion of rouge tinged her cheeks. She boldly tapped a fan against the side of the table, heedless of her crossed legs or exposed ankles.

Everyone's eyes met, and there wasn't the slightest disagreement that Ella would not be pleased to see that the real Fan was back. Katie O'Connor may not have had breeding or money, but she had been kind to the older woman, and had been a friend. Moreover, she was a lady, which Fan for all the privileges she had enjoyed, was not.

"By the way, Fan, no one has had the opportunity to ask you yet just why you came back." Grace's voice was thick with insinuation as she eyed her daughter thoughtfully. "I understood you had found true love."

Fan flushed, then returned her mother's stare with a look that wasn't exactly kind. "Things didn't work out, that's all. I thought it best to come home."

"I see." Grace nodded, obviously seeing a lot more. "So out of the goodness of your heart, and your suddenly remembered familial duty, you rushed back—"

"We ran out of money." Fan slammed the table and got to her feet. "You want to know? I'll tell you. Frank ran out of luck in Frisco. We lost. Big. I took to waiting tables in the saloon while he tried to rustle up some cash. It was useless. Frank isn't a miner or a rancher, and I don't intend to waste the rest of my life being pinched by some randy cowboy who's had three beers.''

"Frances!" Eunice said, appalled. "You worked as a waitress? In a saloon?"

Grace waved a hand. "Go on."

"What else is there to say? I got on the next train for home, and here I am." She grinned, seeing the shocked faces around her. "I thought this is where I should be. Especially since I'm in the family way. That's right; you're all going to have another little Pemberton.''

"My God, Grace, fetch my smelling salts." Anita Pemberton, one of the younger nieces, fanned herself breathlessly and stared at the young woman before her as if seeing a demon.

Grace snorted. "There's no time for that. Is that all, Fan? Or is there any other sordid little fact that escaped you?"

"That's it." Fan shrugged. "I've said my piece, though God knows, I hated to come back to this place. Frisco is my kind of town, not this crummy little backwater or stuffy Philadelphia. But it seems my reappearance is well timed, that's for sure.''

"Frances." George spoke softly, though his voice was thick with disdain. "Am I to understand that you would prefer living in California? And that if it wasn't for the money, you would go back there?"

Fan stared at him for a moment, then nodded, obviously confused. "That's right, I hate it here. I always did."

"Well, what if you could go back?"

"Oh, no." Fan rose, suddenly aware of what they were all thinking. "No. You're not sending me back and keeping that slut here in my place. You can't make me—"

"Don't be so sure, Fan," Grace broke in, her voice stern.

"This really is the best solution. No one outside the family has seen you yet. Fortunately you arrived after the other guests left. Kate can go on as Fan Pemberton while you can live in San Francisco as anyone you wish. No one else has to know anything."

"No. Absolutely not," Fan said stubbornly. "I won't let her—"

"We'll cut you off without a cent," George said quietly. The other Pembertons nodded in agreement as Fan glanced quickly around the room. There was no support anywhere. "Think about it, Fan. You'll have nothing. No money. No clothes. No friends. Why, you might even have to wait tables here for a living."

Fan glared in hatred at them all, then slammed her fan down on the table and stormed for the door.

"You won't get away with this! I swear. . . ."

Grace smiled softly as the door slammed shut. "I think we may have just solved our problem."

From the hotel sitting room, Ella Pemberton stood at the window and watched as the footman hailed a carriage. A dark-haired woman dressed in a cheap yellow gown stepped into the cab. She seemed none too happy, and when she glanced back at the window, her expression showed her outrage.

Ella let the curtain fall from her hand as the carriage retreated. Her heart pounding, she closed her eyes, remembering a scene exactly like this one that had happened many years ago. It was the same situation, the same face, the same woman. She could see it all clearly, Grace's indignant expression, her daughter's defiant one. Yet it had all come around, and was happening once again.

A small smile crept across Ella's face and she reclined once more against the back of the comfortable chair. They all thought she was senile, that she had lost her wits. Sometimes she wished it was true, for it would make everything easier. Yet it often worked to her advantage.

Like this time. This time they wouldn't win. And no one could be happier than Ella.

THIRTEEN

Katie unbuttoned the lovely gown she wore, a gown that she could no longer call her own. It was all so unreal, that her entire world could be shattered so quickly and so completely. But it had happened. Like Cinderella, the hour of midnight had struck and the coach was now a pumpkin.

Sniffling, Katie placed the dress back with the others and stood looking at the wardrobe. She had no claim to it now. All of it would revert to its rightful owner, the real Fan Pemberton, and there was nothing she could do about it.

Maybe it was for the best. Katie thought of her son, of how much she missed him, and realized that she couldn't have continued this farce, no matter how much she wanted to. She wanted her son around her, wanted to see her family again, even if it meant returning to scrubbing floors and cooking for the Main Line rich.

And Ella. A painful throb surged inside her as Katie thought of the older woman. Ella had become much more to her than a rich employer. Still, Ella had the real Fan back now. If Katie stayed, she would only add to the woman's grief, to discover that she'd been deceived. She had no choice.

A glimmer caught her eye and she glanced into the mirror, seeing herself clad in her corset and petticoats. The necklace Christopher had given her glittered in the morning sunlight, the gold shamrock twinkling with the emerald. A sudden tightening came to her throat and she felt so ill she had to sit down on the edge of the bed.

It had meant so much to her, this gift. Katie knew it was ridiculous, but it was almost as if she thought it would bring her real luck. It wasn't as if she loved Christopher; she wouldn't lie to herself about that. Still, she genuinely liked him and enjoyed his company. And last night . . . she couldn't even think about that, it just hurt too much. Yet it had all been lies. First her lies to him, then his about his financial position. None of it had been what they'd pretended. She should be glad it was over, glad that she wouldn't see him again. Why then did she feel so much like crying?

Ah, Katie, it's just the Irish in ye. The gods weren't happy with her deceit, and once again she was being punished. She, Katie O'Connor, wasn't good enough to hang her hat with decent people. She was being sent back to where she belonged, on her knees, to a life of repentance and dirty floors. . . .

"Mrs. Scott? It's George Pemberton. May I come in?" A slight knock sounded on the door and Katie wiped her eyes, then snatched up her robe.

"One minute!" Katie tied the garment firmly around her waist, then opened the door cautiously. "Mr. Pemberton," she choked self-consciously, but allowed the older man to enter.

"Kate." George nodded, his gaze falling on a small pile of clothing in the center of the bed. "May I ask what you're doing?"

"I'm packing." Katie fought the tears that threatened and kept her voice firm. "I'm only taking my own things, so you can tell the Pembertons not to worry. Fan won't miss anything from her own wardrobe."

"I see." George frowned as Katie continued to pack, placing a ridiculously small amount of clothing into a battered valise. "May I ask where you're going?"

Shrugging, Katie continued her work. "Home. To Philadelphia. I haven't many other choices, and it seems the most logical thing to do."

"Back to your old life?" George sounded incredulous. "Is this something you want?"

"It doesn't matter what I want." Katie gave him a tired smile. "I appreciate all your kindness and concern, but the fact is that Fan has come home. I can't stay."

"What if I told you that she hasn't come home? That she never left San Francisco?"

Katie stared at him as if he'd lost his wits. George chuckled softly. "No, I'm not insane, and neither are you. As it happens, the family . . . encouraged Fan to go back. No one has seen her; no one knows the truth. We could go on as before."

Katie's mouth parted, but no sound came forth. She sank into a chair, trying to make sense of what this man was saying. "You mean . . . I couldn't possibly . . ."

"Why not?" George asked amicably. "Ella cares a lot for you. She would be quite happy having you here. Of course a dowry is out of the question, since everyone knows the truth. But still, with Christopher's money . . ."

Katie shook her head. "It wouldn't work."

"Why ever not?"

"For reasons I can't go into." No matter what else had happened, she owed Christopher that much loyalty. She wouldn't divulge his family secret. "Don't even ask me. I just can't say."

"I see." George frowned. He obviously hadn't counted on this. "Are you sure you're just not being stubborn?"

Putting the last piece of clothing into the valise, Katie

nodded. "Christopher was so disillusioned when he learned the truth that I don't think he'll ever trust me again."

"He'll recover," George said quickly. "Anyone would react that way initially."

"You don't understand." Katie smiled sadly. "You didn't see his face. He thinks I'm nothing more than a liar and worse. You can't base a marriage on that kind of feeling. Christopher wouldn't listen to me; he doesn't care. He can't see past his own hurt. I don't think anything would make a difference."

"I'm sorry to hear that." George rose to his feet and took Katie's hand. "Isn't there anything I can say to change your mind?"

"No," Katie said. "I have to go."

George nodded, then squeezed her hand softly. "Good luck to you, Katie. I have a feeling we'll meet again someday."

"I hope so." She couldn't look at him when he left. When the door closed, she sank down onto the bed and sobbed, feeling as if her heart were breaking. Someday she'd learn not to expect much from life.

Maybe then it wouldn't hurt so much when she was proven right.

"Hit me, James."

Christopher relaxed back in his chair as the dealer replaced two of his cards, then glanced around the table to the other men. Tucking the cards into his hand, he grinned with anticipation, then downed a whiskey, smiling at the bargirl who kept his glass comfortably full.

This was his life. He had been ridiculous to think he could make it anything else. Here, at the gentlemen's club of Cape May, in a room filled with cigar smoke and rich men eager to indulge in a game of poker, he was at his best. This was familiar territory, where lying and cheating were part of the rules and everyone knew the score.

The whiskey burned his tongue, but he didn't care, especially when it settled like a warm sun in his belly, dulling the ache. Word of his financial condition hadn't reached this gambling hall yet, and even though a few of the men thought it odd that he should be playing on the day after his wedding, he didn't care. There was no way he was going back to that hotel, to listen to Eunice's fears and Katie's explanations.

Katie. A sour taste started in his mouth whenever he thought of her. It was bad enough that his financial plan had gone awry, and that he and his aunt were in worse straits than ever. But to think that she had lied to him about her entire identity almost made him insane.

Never would he have believed it of her. Katie was so forthright, so honest, so carefree and easy. He'd never forget the first time he saw her, when she alone laughed at one of the Mitchell girls as she'd screeched her way through a song. Everyone else had been simply polite, but his Katie couldn't help what she thought and it was right there, on the surface.

Anger tightened his throat and he quickly drank more of the whiskey. He had been a fool. He had been taken in by a pretty face—a lovely face, he amended silently. And now he was paying the price. All of their artwork was gone. To start over would mean selling the furnishings of his father's estate. And even that wasn't practical . . . however could he explain to a new bride that half his furniture was gone? He wanted to redecorate and just couldn't find the right thing?

And that was if he could get out of the marriage. Oh, Christopher had no doubt that he had a real case of fraud. But if Katie chose to fight him, to tell perhaps another lie in court and claim that he knew all along . . . he couldn't bear to think of the rest. Judges didn't look too kindly on men deserting their wives, whatever the reason. And the marriage had been consummated. . . .

That thought made him more furious and he put down his cards, barely caring that another player called. Was that all part of the lie? He wasn't sure anymore what was real. Had Katie feigned the passion she displayed in his arms as part of her scheme? Much as he hated to admit it, that hurt worse than the lack of money, to think that she'd simply used him in the coldest way possible. A small voice in the back of his mind reminded him that he had done the same thing, but he stubbornly refused to listen. No, Katie was the deceiver here, and he'd best not forget it.

"Chris, why don't we take a break and go for a walk?" Charles asked softly, concerned when Christopher carelessly threw another chip into the pile, his own dwindling at an alarming rate.

Christopher glanced up through a haze of smoke and alcohol. "Now? My luck's about to change, I feel it. If I can just win a few hands, I'll be right back on top."

The dealer hesitated, then seeing Charles's reluctant nod, dealt out the cards. Christopher grinned, looking at four high cards, all hearts. One more card, and he'd have a royal flush.

The bargirl leaned over and peeked at his hand, then gave him an encouraging smile. His eyes wandered appreciatively over her lush curves and tinted red hair. Dressed in a brilliant green gown with a peacock plume waving in her curls, she was a woman who was exactly what she appeared to be. Her eyes met his and he saw the invitation there, the calm assurance that she would provide no lack of feminine companionship. Her attention was like a balm to his wounded ego, and when she leaned close to pour him another drink, her breasts rubbed suggestively on his arm.

"One." Throwing his card onto the table, Christopher accepted a replacement, exhaling in relief when he saw the ten of hearts. Hiding his expression, he casually tossed a pile of chips onto the table and waited.

The other players glanced at each other, then back at their hands. The tension hung heavy as one after another folded, leaving but one man sitting across from him. Christopher didn't know the portly gentleman, but some of the players had come from New York, having tired of Saratoga Springs. Normally his gambling instincts would have warned him about the man's deadpan expression, his lack of drinking, his seemingly endless fund of money. But not tonight. Dulled by whiskey and disillusionment, Christopher felt nothing but a gambler's need to score a win.

"Call." The gentleman met his bet and glanced at Chris. "Let's see what you have, son."

Christopher smiled, then unfolded his hand, betraying the flush. The gentleman nodded and gave him a congratulatory smile. "Well done. Barkeep, another drink for my companion."

Scooping up the chips, Christopher ignored Charles's concerned frown and sipped at the whiskey, the bargirl crooning in his ear. It felt good to be home again.

Ella was sleeping. Katie saw her in the little sitting room she'd retreated to, wrapped in a shawl that was as finely spun as a spiderweb, her face wistful in repose like a young girl's.

Katie smiled, though tears came to her eyes. She had come to care about this woman, to know her secret fears and loneliness. Long ago Ella had ceased to be her employer and had become what she'd pretended to be—a dearly loved family member. Katie wished there was a way she could maintain some kind of relationship with the older woman, but that seemed impossible. Rich people didn't associate with poor Irish like herself. And it would only upset Ella more to know the truth.

It was better this way, Katie thought. Ella would learn that she'd returned to San Francisco, much the way the real Fan had done. She would be upset for a while, but would go on with her life and forget, the same way she had done so long ago. Only this time, hopefully, she had some new memories to cherish.

Opening her valise, Katie withdrew the sparkling fan that Christopher had given her and placed it beside the old woman. Ella would know and understand that this was her way of saying good-bye. Choking, Katie pictured the woman seated at her window once more, only this time cooling herself against the hot summer breezes with this implement. It was a vision that greatly upset her and she had to leave the room quickly.

Ella Pemberton would soon forget. And maybe then Katie wouldn't feel so haunted.

"What do you mean, she's gone?"

Grace Pemberton stared at her brother-in-law with an obvious lack of affection. "She can't be gone! What does she plan to do? Go back to working as a maid?"

"Impossible." Eunice Scott shuddered, then glared at the Pembertons. "There hasn't been a Scott working as a menial since I was a girl. And the new Mrs. Scott, imposter or otherwise, cannot think of such a thing."

"She might be working for one of our friends!" Ida Pemberton gasped. "Pass me the salts, Grace!"

"You couldn't talk some sense into her?" Grace asked shortly, still staring at George in disbelief. "Did you explain?"

"Yes. I told her everything, just the way we discussed. That Fan isn't coming back, that she is safe to assume her identity. The chit wouldn't listen. Seems to feel the breach between herself and Christopher can't be mended."

Eunice nodded, aware that there was more to the story

than that. She glanced at the others and shrugged. "My nephew spent the night in a gaming hall, and as of yet, hasn't come home. Fan, I mean Katie, is on the train back to Philadelphia this morning. It seems they are hell-bent on destroying any chance of a marriage."

"What is going on here?" Ella walked into the hotel sitting room, looking more fragile than ever. The morning sunlight made her curls glisten softly like angel hair, and her blue eyes looked ethereal, almost otherworldly. Carefully taking a seat in the middle of the group, she nodded to the waiter for tea and looked at them all with a peculiar, penetrating glance.

"What do you mean?" Grace asked nervously. "Everything is fine. We were just discussing—"

"Everything isn't fine." Ella cut her off imperviously. "When I wake up and hear Eileen crying in her room, see that Christopher hasn't come home, then I know something is amiss. Now, why don't you tell me what everyone else seems to know."

Grace glanced at the others and shrugged. "You're right, Ella. There's no sense hiding the truth. Fan and Christopher have quarreled. Fan left this morning."

"Ah." Ella digested this, then glanced up once more. "Just this morning?" When they nodded in response, she continued questioning. "Has no one spoken to her? Tried to persuade her?"

"I have," George said. "She won't listen to reason. Fan seems to think she and Christopher will never make up, and given his disappearance last night, she may be right. We've done everything that we could."

"Bring him to me."

Grace looked at George, who frowned, puzzled. "But Ella, we've already tried—"

"Bring him to me. What nonsense is this, anyway? Two young people get married, and at the first simple argument, everyone is willing to let them call it quits. In my day, such a thing was unheard of. These young people have no sense of responsibility anymore. What kind of man lets his wife leave him after a simple misunderstanding? I want to see him. Now.''

George nodded, then retreated to find Christopher. Ella said nothing but accepted a cup of tea and sipped thoughtfully while the other Pembertons and the Scotts murmured among themselves. Senile, she might be, but Ella was still the family matriarch.

And the one who held the purse strings.

''Oh, my God, my head,'' Christopher groaned, holding his aching forehead between his hands. ''What the hell did I drink?''

''Everything.'' Charles sat on the edge of the bed, eyeing his friend with sorely strained patience. ''Whiskey mostly. Those bargirls know how to keep your cup full.''

At the mention of bargirl, Christopher's brow furrowed and he glanced hastily at the bed beside him. Thankfully it was empty. A peacock plume dangled sinfully on the opposite pillow, but the pillow itself remained undented and there was no cloying scent of perfume or alcohol on the linens.

Seeing Christopher's bewildered expression, Charles hastened to reassure him. ''Nothing happened with the girl. I'm afraid the gentleman you were playing with was a bit of a riverboat gambler. You accumulated a sorry debt, then passed out from drinking, with plenty of help and encouragement. Lola and I put you into bed.''

''Thank God.'' Christopher grimaced, then sank back into bed, obviously in pain. ''If that's the case, then why are you here? I don't have any pressing appointments.''

''Ella Pemberton wants to see you right away. Eunice says if I didn't bring you back, she'd come for you herself.

I figured out of the two of us, you'd sooner tolerate my company.''

''Thanks.'' Christopher groaned again. ''Ella? What does she want?''

''I don't know, but I suggest you make yourself ready. That is one lady I wouldn't care to cross. There's much more to her than everyone thinks.''

''You're right about that.'' Christopher forced himself away from his bed and yanked on his clothes. Pressing a cold cloth to his face, he glanced into the mirror, groaning yet again when he saw his appearance. ''God, I could haunt houses today. Oh, I have to see Mr. Oldacre before I go.''

''I took care of it,'' Charles said slowly, seeing Christopher's expression turn cautious.

''The debts? All of it?''

Charles nodded. ''Mr. Oldacre grew concerned when you began drinking too much. He was afraid you wouldn't be able to honor your debt. Apparently he began asking questions. For the sake of your reputation, I thought it better if I paid.''

Christopher stiffened, then turned to his friend slowly. ''Then you know.''

Charles nodded. ''I'm sorry. I know how embarrassing this must be for you. But I surmised as much from Eunice and Ella's conversation.''

''It's a damned shame when a man's misfortune becomes public news,'' Christopher said bitterly. ''When will they learn to keep their mouths shut?''

''They didn't mean anything,'' Charles said gently. ''They are both concerned. Chris, if a few dollars will help you get through—''

''Thanks.'' He laughed shortly. ''But it will take more than a few dollars to dig me out of this mess. Christ, nothing is ever the way it seems to be. First the investments. Then this marriage. And Fan.''

The pain on his face was obvious. Charles nodded and spoke cautiously. "You know, she's gone. I understand she left for Philadelphia. Ella is distraught, and Eunice is furious."

"Philadelphia?" Christopher digested this for a moment and stared at Charles in disbelief. "What does she think she'll do there? Did she say anything about her plans?"

"Not a word, but I suppose you can guess. Whatever she did before, I imagine. Frankly I'm worried about her. I don't know what her past is, or what kind of life she had, but she must have been desperate to resort to posing as another woman."

"She'll survive," Christopher said bluntly, but his face betrayed concern.

"Sure, I suppose she will. Maybe. It isn't easy for a woman out there with no resources, which I assume she hasn't. Other than the name Mrs. Scott, she hasn't taken anything else with her."

Christopher winced. It was true; Katie was still his wife, like it or not. And Mrs. Scott was out there somewhere, on a train to a city that didn't love immigrants, despite its name. Would she really go back to scrubbing floors or worse? Could he bear the thought?

"Katie will do what's best for her, just as I will. I appreciate your concern, Charles, but at the moment it's misplaced."

"Right," Charles said coldly. Christopher picked up his good wool coat and indicated the door.

Katie was a problem he'd have to deal with. And it all boiled down to trust.

❊ FOURTEEN

The odor of boiled ham and cabbage stung her nostrils as she walked through the door of the two-story row house, and Katie breathed deeply of the welcome scent. She stood there for a moment, taking in the well-worn sofa, the lace shawl draped over the back of it to hide the wear, the candlelight struggling to illuminate dark corners, and the gin bottle waiting welcomingly by the table. A rosary dangled from a lamp, and a score of books, dog-eared from being read and reread, waited invitingly by the couch. She was home.

They were all there, gathered around the table, laughing, arguing, and joking, their food quietly disappearing at the same time. Katie's eyes filled as she saw her grandfather and her aunt, but her gaze went swiftly to the little boy at the end of the table.

Clad in pants that were an inch too short and preoccupied with shoveling food into his mouth, he grinned at something her grandfather said, then gulped his milk with abandon.

Sean. Katie thought her heart would burst as she stood in the doorway, watching her son. Although he had grown since she'd last seen him, every freckle on his face, every strand of the glistening blond hair, every scrape on his muscular little body was etched into her soul. She had to take a deep breath, overcome with emotion and longing.

It was as if he sensed her. Sean put down his spoon and turned quickly, then his little face lit up and he ran toward her, heedless of the chair that overturned or the milk that spilled. "What the hell—" her grandfather began, but his words were drowned with the plaintive cry of "Mama!"

Katie sobbed, her arms wrapped around his little body, her heart pounding. He felt so good, smelled so good, all dirt and sand and little boy. She could barely hear the others, the surprised questions and inquiries, and she didn't care. She was holding her baby again, the way she'd dreamed so often, and none of it mattered.

"Sean. Sean." Katie didn't even try to stop the tears until she was sobbing so hard that her son looked up, alarmed.

"Mama? Aren't you glad to see me?"

There was such serious concern in his tone that Katie had to laugh, then she buried her face against him. "Yes, I'm glad to see you. Very glad."

"Then why are you crying?"

Katie smiled, wiping at her eyes. "Because I'm glad. Sometimes grown-ups cry when they're happy."

"I don't want you to cry. Are you staying for good?"

The table grew quiet as the others waited for her answer. Katie ignored them and nodded, still holding her son. "Yes, I'm staying with you. For good."

He beamed back at her, and once again she thought her heart would break. How could she have left him? Even though she knew it had been necessary, right now the thought seemed impossible. He was part of her, as necessary as breathing, and it had taken a major sacrifice on her behalf to try to give him a better life.

She smiled then, holding him back a few inches so she could really look at him. "These are your new pants . . . you've grown so much this summer!"

"Aunt Moira says I'm growing like a weed. Don't you, Auntie?"

Katie smiled, then tore her eyes away and looked up at her family. They were waiting expectantly, allowing her time to become reacquainted with her son. It was her grandfather who spoke first, and his voice was thick with emotion.

"Come, lass, have some supper and we can talk then. Let your mother have something to eat, Sean."

Katie went to the scarred and familiar table, seeing the questions in her aunt's and grandfather's eyes. She forced a smile, then accepted the plate that Moira handed her. Finally, when Katie was finished with her meal, she kissed Sean on top of his head and turned to the others.

"All right, ask."

They both started at once, until her grandfather interrupted and cleared his throat. "Are you really home for good, Katie?"

She nodded. "Did you get the money I sent?"

"All of it." Patrick smiled for the first time. "It bought new shoes for your son. Books for school. Pencils and paper. And even a few things for the house. 'Tis well you managed to save so much. I know how dear things are down at the seaside."

"It was all like a dream. Clothes like I never imagined. Food aplenty. Nice people. And they treated me well. Unlike . . ."

"Unlike folks here." Moira slammed a dish then wiped her hands on a flannel. "Damned fools! Well, I'm glad you had a good summer, though the boy's missed you something dreadful."

"You had clothes? Nice gowns?" Sean sat closer, obviously entranced. "Did you keep them?"

"No, I left them. I only kept what was mine. I didn't want any of them to say anything wrong later."

"And the house?" Moira questioned softly. "You said it was grand. Tell us."

Katie smiled and described the chandeliers, the enticing gardens, the well-equipped kitchens, and the lovely bedroom. The room was still as she spoke, and the O'Connors stared in wonder at the one who'd glimpsed Eden. Finally Patrick shrugged, then wiped his mouth on his sleeve.

"It sounds like a grand place, for sure. Why then, Katie, did you leave?"

"Things didn't work out." Katie couldn't bear to tell them the full extent of her deception. Her grandfather would have been appalled, and Moira further disillusioned. No, she would keep that much a secret. "I grew to really like Ella Pemberton, but there was a disagreement within the family about me. I thought it best if I left."

"Ah." Moira nodded wisely. "'Tis a rare shame, that's for sure. But it couldn't go on forever. Nothing in this world does."

Katie swallowed hard as she thought of Christopher. Strange, but her aunt had always been overly perceptive. At times she even seemed to have "the sight." Still, she was right, and it was something she should have remembered. For Katie, at least, nothing good ever went on forever.

Patrick sat back and reached for his pipe. He lit it, then puffed thoughtfully. "Your brother is doing all right, though not as well as he'd have us believe."

"Ryan?" Katie asked in surprise. Ryan was such a determined, strapping lad that she had been sure he would be incredibly successful on his own.

"It seems he couldn't make his fortune out west, the way he'd planned," her grandfather continued as Moira poured all of them a healthy drop of homemade gin. "He's working in the mining camps in Colorado. Still waiting for the big strike."

The luck of the Irish, Katie mused. She sipped from her

cup, watching her son leave the table, scampering after a kitten. Patrick lit a fire and they retreated to the parlor. The flames threw ghosts on the walls and floor, the gin warmed her, the supper had filled her. Her grandfather spoke of his day at the gardens, where kindly Mr. Foster kept him employed long after his eyesight had failed. But he was as sturdy as an old oak and as vigorous. Katie couldn't remember a day when he'd been ill.

Sean, tiring of the kitten, curled up beside her on the sofa and fell quickly asleep. Moira disappeared upstairs, then returned in a worn yet elegant gown. She took her familiar place by the fire, and as the liquor disappeared, would become convinced she was indeed Lilly Langtry. Patrick's voice grew richer as he spoke of the old days, when he was part of the sassenach army, and of the places he saw.

It was as if she'd never left. Katie had a feeling that no matter where she went, or for how long, this six-room house would still be waiting, these strange and wonderful people still here, the gin jar beside the sofa. After weeks of being a Pemberton, Katie saw it all differently, and yet was reassured. They would never be a part of Christopher's society. They would never fit in with those elegant and cultured folk, who would look at their old clothes, their rich brogues, their odd appearance and would whisper with disdain. Yet these people loved her, accepted her, no matter what.

They were a family.

Christopher felt as if he was on trial as soon as he entered the room. Placing a kiss on his aunt Eunice's head, he nodded politely to Ella and took a seat in the sitting room beside the window, where the light would cause him the least damage. He had barely lowered himself into the chair, his head pounding fearfully, when Ella fixed him with a stare that would have impaled a more timid man.

"So I understand Fan has left you."

Christopher nodded, groaning as his head seemed about to burst. "Ella, I am sorry, but there are problems. Do we really have to talk about this now?"

"I should say so." Ella glared, putting her dainty teacup aside. There was nothing sweet or soft about her this morning, Christopher observed with alarm. Even his own aunt was facing him with a cold look.

"Do you realize what has happened here? Your wife, the new Mrs. Scott, Fan Pemberton, is gone and no one has done a thing about it. Even her husband spent the night gaming and wenching, instead of looking for her."

"I was not wenching!" Christopher shouted, then was rewarded with a splintering pain that made him grab his head. When he could speak, he continued more softly, "I did drink. And gamble. But that is hardly a crime. I didn't know Fan had gone until this morning."

"I see." Ella and Eunice exchanged a look, then Ella continued in a voice dripping with sweetness. "And now that you know, what do you plan to do about it?"

That was the question of the year. Christopher swallowed hard, then leaned back in his chair and responded truthfully. "I don't know. I'm sorry, Ella, I know that's not what you want to hear. There are problems between Fan and me that I am not at liberty to fully discuss. Even if I were to track her down and haul her back here, I'm not sure it would do any good."

Ella took a sip from her cup and then placed it thoughtfully aside. She stared at Christopher with the same penetrating look, then spoke quietly. "I know they all say I'm senile, that I don't know what I'm talking about, but they're wrong. I'm going to ask you something once, and I want you to give careful consideration to your answer. I'll know if you're lying, Christopher, so don't waste my time. What do you feel about Fan?"

Christopher looked up in surprise. He had been expecting a discussion of his finances, but Ella was deadly serious. He took a deep breath and answered easily.

"I was infatuated with Fan from the first day I saw her. I never met anyone like her. She is so different from the other girls, so fresh and full of life. I wanted her badly. If you don't believe me, ask my aunt."

Eunice nodded in agreement. "That is the truth, Ella. In fact, I tried to dissuade him from pursuing your niece, in that Fan would be a more difficult conquest. Christopher wouldn't hear of it."

"In that case, why are you willing to allow your wife to leave you like this?"

Christopher groaned, then looked at his aunt for guidance. Eunice would not meet his eyes, so he looked directly at Ella. There was nothing left but to tell the truth, what he could without doing more damage.

"I'm sure you've learned of my financial difficulty." When Ella nodded, he continued softly: "Fan found out that the Scotts have no money. She had also kept a few things from me. Both of us were severely disillusioned. As a gentleman, I cannot tell you her secrets, but you have mine. Do you understand now why it's senseless to go after her?"

"Not at all," Ella said firmly. She stood up and faced him, looking as if she wanted to box his ears. "Christopher, you are going to learn that these frustrations are a part of life. Nothing more, nothing less. I understand that you thought to receive a dowry with Fan. Given the circumstances, coupled with your behavior, I don't feel comfortable giving Fan the full allotment now. However, I can provide an income for one year, one thousand dollars, enough money to allow an enterprising young man such as yourself the opportunity to get on his feet. Should you do that, and should Fan desire to remain married, the rest of the dowry will be disbursed."

Christopher gaped in astonishment. Ella was being more than generous; even he could see that. And while it wasn't everything, it would provide a way to keep food on the table until he could think of something else. And Ella still thought of Katie as Fan. Everyone else knew the real Fan had returned to California. Was it fair to let Ella go on being deceived, when so many others knew the truth?

He glanced at his aunt and Eunice nodded as if reading his mind. She gestured him to silence, and he immediately understood. Ella loved Fan, and she loved Katie as Fan. The old woman didn't have that much longer to live. What good would it do her to know the truth?

And Katie. Christopher winced as he thought of her, back in Philadelphia, working as a menial for the people he associated with. He couldn't bear the idea, and if he had to be truthful, he somehow felt responsible for her. Like it or not, she was his wife, and although he was furious with her, he owed her something. Whether Katie would agree to come back was something else.

Ella saw his expression and smiled. "I don't know if you will be able to convince her to return. Frances can be most stubborn. However, I want her back and I want this resolved. If she doesn't agree to those terms, then she can come home and we will see about an annulment. However, I have the feeling that the two of you would make quite a team if given the chance. I'm willing to provide that opportunity. The question is, have you the courage to make it happen?"

Christopher glanced at his aunt. Eunice looked so hopeful that it made him feel guilty. "I think it's an extremely generous offer," she said quickly. "And you'd be a fool not to take it."

Christopher nodded. "All right, I'll find her. But I can't promise anything else. Frances Scott will do what she wants. That's one lesson I've already learned."

*   *   *

The murky water of the Delaware River splashed against the docks, lending a quiet rhythm to the sound of drinking inside the tavern. Workmen, their knees and elbows thick with grime, sat at the cratelike tables and drank deeply of the bitter ale. Few of them had the money for whiskey. A meager fire burned on the grate, roasting a piece of beef, and a black and white dog scoured the ashes for a bit of meat before being booted away by a dockworker.

John Sweeney sipped from his mug, watching the river below without interest or awareness. Handsome still, despite the years of wenching and drinking, he nevertheless ignored the glances he received from the serving girl and quietly lit a cigarette, drawing deeply on the cheap tobacco.

It just wasn't fair. All John Sweeney had ever wanted was to make it big. He knew he was cut out for more than this. He had more looks, more charm, and more brains than half the men he knew. Instead he carried bricks for the row houses that were popping up by the score in the city—dozens of bricks. He could mortar them, applying the thick gray cement in just the right amount on the previous row, then slap a wall together with a precision that had made him the envy of many a new apprentice. But it still wasn't enough. It never would be. John could wall himself away from the view of the house on Rittenhouse Square, but it was never far away in his mind.

And someday he'd have it. Rubbing his scarred hands on his trousers, he took another sip and swore to himself. If it was the last thing he did, he'd live in one of those houses and watch other poor struggling wretches like himself build homes for a living. He'd wear a good wool coat and have a new derby, like the gentlemen on Walnut Street, and he'd talk of something other than the weather and lack of food.

"Like the same for your supper tonight, Johnny?" The

serving girl grinned, displaying a lack of teeth, and John Sweeney returned her smile.

"Sure, Elsie, lass. Ah, you're a pretty one." He watched her giggle as she walked away, knowing she was sure to bring back an extra helping of potatoes, which she knew he liked, and an extra beer when no one else was looking. Women were so easy. One compliment, a few admiring words, and they ate out of his hand.

The girl returned a moment later and placed a newspaper on his table. John unwrapped it stealthily, then slipped the bread he found inside beneath the crate. He unfolded the paper and pretended to read it, all the while stuffing his mouth with the bread.

He had the society page. John almost snorted at the detailed descriptions of the rich folk's comings and goings. The charity ball. The Association for the Preservation of whatnot. The hunt club and the polo match . . .

It was then that he saw her picture. At first the bread nearly fell out of his mouth, but he closed it quickly and studied the image before him. It was impossible, but there could be no mistake. It was the same eyes, the same nose tilted with an Irish ancestry, the same mouth, barely suppressing the laughter that was always just beneath the surface. . . .

Katie O'Connor. John Sweeney had to wash the bread down with his ale and nearly choked in the process. The serving girl pounded him helpfully on the back.

"Are you all right, mate?"

John nodded, his eyes swimming as he gestured to the picture. "The paper. How old is it?"

"I'd say a few weeks. We gets them from the old gent down the street, the one that carts them away for a penny. Why?"

"I'm just asking." He stared again, this time aware that he was reading something about a Fan Pemberton. It was odd that he should have the skill to read, but one of his women, a schoolteacher, had taught him. He scanned the accompanying article in confusion. There was something about a seaside wedding, a full description of the gown, the food, and the ceremony itself, but very little about the bride. It seemed the *Public Ledger* had assumed that everyone would know Fan Pemberton as well as Christopher Scott.

It couldn't be, yet his eyes returned again and again to the picture. He wouldn't forget that face; he couldn't. It had been a short affair, yet for all that, the girl had been a virgin. She'd been in love, or so she had thought. John Sweeney didn't take the word too seriously himself. If a girl took his whispered promises as truth, so be it. All women knew the score. A man did what he could to get what he wanted. It was as simple as that.

Later she had come to him about the child. He had been incredulous at her happiness, and even more amazed that she'd expected him to marry her. Him! John Sweeney, who could have any and all of the women of the city, if he chose. It was all he could do not to laugh then, and it still made him chuckle now.

"Who's the girl?" The serving wench leaned closer, indicating the picture. "Someone you know?"

His grin broadened and he nodded. "Yes, I'd say I know that girl. And guess what, Elsie me love. It looks like she fell into a pot of gold. And I know just the man she should share it with."

✴ FIFTEEN

Christopher walked through the streets of Philadelphia, a Philadelphia he'd never really seen. Horses and trolleys clattered over the cobbles, heedless of pedestrians, children, or barking dogs. Row after row of shops and houses spilled onto the street, becoming a part of the road itself, with vendors hawking everything from fresh produce to tea. A Chinese laundry, Hong Way, was the only one that kept within its boundaries and revealed that there was indeed a sidewalk.

The cacophony and the commotion were endless. This part of the city, far from the more sedate sections that he frequented, teamed with life. There was music from an organ grinder, calls from merchants, responses from the customers. Thick brogues, Italian and German accents lingered through the streets, and he had but to turn a corner to hear one or the other. A melting pot, the city had been called, but it was obvious to Christopher that nothing had truly melted.

Where the hell could she be? Damn her, she had an aptitude for getting into trouble. He knew only that her name was Katie O'Connor, she lived in the city, she was Irish . . . that he should have known the first time he heard her sing. It still appalled him that she'd betrayed him so completely, but some of his anger had died. In truth, walking through these streets, he was beginning to understand.

Could he really blame her? He shuddered as he pictured her, cleaning a house, scrubbing a floor, walking through these streets, always afraid and wondering where her next meal would come from. That was Katie O'Connor's life until she'd met Ella Pemberton. Given the choice of remaining herself, or assuming Fan Pemberton's identity, could he honestly say he would have done differently?

Absently he kicked at a piece of newspaper blowing in the street, barely aware of the curious glances he received. He could understand why she had assumed Fan's role, especially when he witnessed her affection for Ella. But was he just part of the same scheme? Did she marry him just to be able to continue her new life?

That was the part that ate at him. Sure, he was doing much the same thing, marrying her to secure his own position. But deep within his heart, he knew there was something more. Katie had captivated him from the beginning. He was too jaded to believe in love at first sight, but it was something very close to that. If he had been strictly concerned about the money, he could have easily married one of the Mitchell girls, Margaret Chester . . . any number of them would have welcomed him. And although he was still furious at Kate, he couldn't just let her leave like this, especially now. Ella had given them a second chance, and he was damned sure they were going to take it.

"Peaches, gent? You want some fresh peaches?"

"Ale? I got the best beer in the city. Chilled, too!"

They saw his good jacket, his polished shoes, and flocked to get his attention. Christopher ignored them and walked into the nearest dram shop. Several loiterers stared at him curiously, but he went to the man behind the counter and spoke in an authoritative voice.

"Have you ever heard of a family named O'Connor? Seems they live somewhere in the area."

The burly man exchanged a glance with those waiting inside the doorway, then shrugged, all the while polishing a bottle. "Can't say that I have." He squinted suspiciously. "You the law or something?"

Startled, Christopher glanced around and realized why the man had asked. He was well dressed in the poor section of town, obviously a stranger, asking for information about one of them. The man standing beside him spat onto the floor and returned his stare with a challenging smile.

They weren't going to tell him anything. Embarrassed, Christopher bought a bottle of brandy, then nodded to the man and walked out, aware of the silence that followed.

On the steps of the dram shop, he looked down the street. There were rows and rows of brick houses, any of which could contain the elusive O'Connors. He knew nothing of them, nothing about her family. Were they tradesmen, bricklayers, horsemen, or all servants? He didn't know where in Ireland they came from, or what part of the city they called home.

A cart passed by, rolling very near the step, and splashed a puddle of water and horse excrement all over Christopher's polished boots. Outraged, he trudged over to a cab that was waiting at the curb. Somehow he'd find Katie O'Connor.

If it was the last thing he did.

"Now, miss . . . what did you say your name was?"

"O'Connor," Katie replied. "Katie O'Connor."

"That's right." Florence Eldridge nodded. "Funny, I can never get the names of my servants straight. You will be expected to keep all twenty-seven rooms in the house clean, and I am very exacting. I want them dusted, the rugs beaten, the floors swept, the windows done monthly. The housekeeper will wash the linens, but I want them changed weekly and scented with lavender. Do you understand all this?''

''Yes.'' Katie nodded, smoothing her white apron over her worn black work dress.

The woman stared at her for a moment, then her brow wrinkled as she examined Katie's face. ''I swear I've seen you somewhere before. . . . No, it couldn't possibly be.'' At Katie's questioning silence, the woman continued: ''In the newspaper there was a picture of a society wedding, the Scotts and the Pembertons, I believe. It's the oddest thing, but you look exactly like the bride.''

Katie gulped, but smiled incredulously. ''Like Mr. Scott's wife?''

Florence laughed. ''Oh, but it couldn't be, of course. Frances Pemberton is a society debutante. It's just that the resemblance is remarkable. They say everyone has a twin.''

Katie continued to smile, but dropped her eyes. ''I'm sure, mum,'' she said, keeping her voice low and appropriately subservient. She hadn't missed the cause for Florence Eldridge's amusement, that a lowly woman like herself could ever be considered as anything other than a servant. It was an attitude she had become used to over the years, but now it grated on her.

Two small children scrambled down the steps, tumbling at their mother's feet. Florence smiled fondly and straightened them, then indicated Katie.

''This is our new maid. She's going to help Eleanor with the housework, and with you two as well.'' As if in afterthought, she looked at Katie. ''You said you didn't mind children, didn't you?''

''Of course not.'' Katie smiled at the two little ones. They returned her smile, but Katie saw a secretive glance between them that instantly alarmed her.

"Jonathan?" Florence questioned softly. "You didn't shake hands with Miss . . . O'Connor."

The boy extended his hand, and Katie grasped it without thinking. Instantly something sharp pierced her palm and stung her. Gasping, she snatched back her hand and stared at the thistle embedded in her flesh as the children shrieked with laughter.

"Now, Jon, I told you to stop that." Florence grinned at Katie apologetically. "I suppose boys will be boys."

Katie forced a smile, plucking the stinging thistle from her hand. She wished that she was ten years old again; she'd take this little darling outside and prove that boys aren't always boys. Instead she rubbed her palm and pretended that she enjoyed the joke.

"All right, it's time you got to work. Here is Eleanor; she'll show you what to do."

"This way, miss." Eleanor, the housekeeper, looked as sturdy as a bulkhead. She waved her hand and indicated the stairs. "We'll start with the children's rooms. They're always the worst. Then we'll continue downstairs. Madam likes the house very clean, you know." She waited until they were out of earshot, then spoke furtively. "She drinks in the afternoon. Don't mind what she says, then. She always forgets."

Katie forced a smile, then lifted her skirts and followed the housekeeper up the stairs. She was home again, back in her rightful place.

She was beginning to wish she had never known anything else.

"Dammit, Auntie, do you have to sell the sofa?" Christopher watched in disbelief as two burly workmen carted the comfortable seven-foot couch out the backdoor and onto a waiting cart. There was a huge gap where the sofa had been, and Eunice carried a small table with flowers and plopped it into the space.

"Yes, we have to sell the sofa. Otherwise there won't be any food tomorrow." Eunice spoke with the same tone that a schoolteacher would use with an especially dull student. "The bill collectors were here again this morning. We are behind on the mortgage, the taxes, the bank loans . . . in short, just about everything. I managed to hold them at bay for the time being, but we do need to raise some more cash."

"Christ." Christopher sat down on an orange crate, one of the few seats available. "Would you mind turning up the lights, at least? It looks like a morgue in here."

"Oh, that's another thing." Eunice sighed, then sat beside him on a matching crate. "I had the gas turned off." At Christopher's expression, she continued defensively: "We can make do with candles and wood fires. Your parents did for years."

"Wonderful. Let's go back to the seventeenth century." Christopher snorted in disgust and glanced around the near-naked room. The chandelier dangled uselessly over his head, no longer sparkling with light. Patches of faded color stood out from the walls like a macabre checkerboard, witness to the places where portraits once gazed on the room. The velvet drapes had been stripped from the walls and the twilight poured in, making the place seem even more dismal. The only cheerful note was the fire, which threw off a little too much heat for the season.

"I'm sorry, but you have to face facts. No one expected our plan to backfire the way it did. I don't suppose you had any luck in locating Fan—I mean Kate?"

"No." Christopher started to sink back into his seat and nearly fell on the floor. "Damn." He righted himself quickly, then stared bleakly around the ghostly room. "I looked everywhere. The streets. The row houses. I asked at taverns and shops. No one seems to know Kate O'Connor.''

"How odd," Eunice said somberly. "She is our best hope after all. If you and Katie can walk through the Pembertons' door as husband and wife, our troubles are temporarily over.''

"I know." Christopher slapped his leg with his hand. "Where the hell could she be? How could she just vanish like that? I even spoke to the nuns at the convent. Kate O'Connor would have to be Catholic, wouldn't you think?'' At Eunice's nod, he continued. "But even they wouldn't tell me a thing. Sister Ellen Elizabeth just suggested I come back with a warrant if I really needed to know.''

Eunice nodded. "I know. I remember when I was young. Poor people don't trust the rich. They are probably protecting the girl, thinking that you mean her some harm." She frowned thoughtfully. "Have you tried her former employer? I believe Eileen said it was Marjorie Westcott?''

"Yes, it's one of the first places I went. Mrs. Westcott had nothing but kind things to say about Kate, but even she remarked that Kate was strangely secretive, reluctant to provide information about herself. She wouldn't even leave a forwarding address, but simply thanked Mrs. Westcott for the employment and disappeared.''

"That is strange," Eunice agreed. "Even if Kate knew she was applying for the position as Ella's companion, Kate had no guarantee that she would be given the job. You would think she would keep in touch with Marjorie, just in case things didn't work out.''

"Dammit, it's so frustrating! Somewhere in this city is the key to a new start, both for Kate and me. And neither of us can touch it without walking through Ella's door together. It's enough to make me mad.''

Eunice patted his hand sympathetically. The door knocker sounded, and she rose quickly to respond.

"Oh, Eunice," Florence Eldridge said in surprise, her

hand still raised to the door. "I wasn't expecting you to answer."

Eunice smiled. "I was just leaving. I'm sorry, I would ask you in, but I have an appointment." She stared at Florence questioningly. "Had you called earlier?"

"No, I know this visit is sudden." Florence waved her hand apologetically. Eunice could smell the aroma of brandy, smothered in perfume. Florence smiled unsteadily. "And I don't mean to keep you. I was just on my way home and had to tell you something." She leaned closer with a conspiratorial smile and Eunice tried not to breathe. "Do you remember that picture in the paper of your new daughter-in-law?"

"Frances?" Eunice stood very still. "Yes, I recall. It wasn't a very good likeness."

Florence nodded. "I know. I've just hired a girl for my house, and Eunice, you wouldn't believe it. She is the spitting image of Fan Pemberton. Isn't that incredible?"

Eunice gaped, then managed to close her mouth and act only mildly interested. "Yes, that is. Incredible, I mean." Feigning a yawn, she continued, as if bored, "You don't happen to remember her name, do you?"

"Oh, my. Let me see, I'm terrible with names, especially the help. Catherine? No, it's something Irish. Kate O'Connor. That's it. Kate O'Connor."

Florence beamed, proud of her memory, and Eunice nodded. "I can't say I know her. Good evening, Florence. I forgot something and must step inside the house, but I will call on you soon. Thank you for stopping by."

The bewildered Florence Eldridge watched as the door closed in her face and she heard the sound of hurrying footsteps.

She had always heard that Eunice Scott was a little peculiar. Frowning, she returned to her carriage. She'd go home and have another drink. Then she would be able to figure it out.

She always could.

She just couldn't take any more.

Katie pocketed her dollar and put on her shawl, aware of the oncoming nightfall. Her legs hurt from chasing the children up and down the stairs, slipping once when Jonathan put soap on one of the steps. Her bottom was bruised, both from the fall and from Charles Eldridge's habit of pinching her whenever he went by.

Florence Eldridge, although not cruel, nevertheless saw her as having little more importance than the furniture, and she absently gave orders that only interfered with the running of the household and the children. Brandy was her weakness, and more than once Katie saw her gargle cologne in an effort to dispel the scent that was never far away. But in some ways, Katie couldn't blame her. Married to a philandering husband and with two wretched children, she didn't have much of a choice.

Stepping outside the house, Katie sagged tiredly against the backdoor, where the servants entered. It was so hard to assume this role again, to be treated as next to nothing. Sometimes when she closed her eyes, it seemed as if that other life had merely been a dream. Sean begged her to describe the house and its contents over and over again, and to tell him about the seashore, the waves, how vast was the ocean and how blue the sky. He never seemed to tire of hearing it, nor Katie of telling.

She fondled the dollar in her pocket, aware that to the Pembertons this was little more than pocket change. But tonight it would put meat on the O'Connors' table, and maybe even some milk. A pang went through her as she thought of her son. She was with him now, able to be a part of his life, but that didn't keep it from hurting when she saw everything he was forced to do without. She had wanted so much for him, wanted him to know some of the better things in life. She'd had everything within the palm of her hand, and had lost.

Worst of all was when she thought of Christopher. The shamrock still hung around her neck; she couldn't bear to take it off, yet there were times when she could swear she felt it pressing into her flesh. Could she have really started to care for him? When she was completely alone, exhausted in the little bedroom of the six-room row house, lying beneath the covers, only then would she admit the truth: he meant something to her.

And she missed him terribly. Now, when it was over, she could face that. She thought of their wedding night, when he had loved her so thoroughly, so tenderly, and she felt ill. Somehow, in between all the lies and deceit, Christopher Scott had made a place for himself in her heart. It was the worst thing that could possibly happen, the last thing she needed. She'd been hurt once, bitterly hurt. Yet how did one stop caring, stop missing, and stop wanting?

The wind blew uncommonly cool for late summer. Katie sighed, then pulled her shawl around her. There was no use thinking this way. She had gotten what she deserved, and had no one to blame but herself. Kate O'Connor was not meant to be gentry. She'd tried to rise above herself and had landed right back where she belonged. It was that damnable Irish luck.

She started across the street, toward the corner where she could wait for the horse-drawn trolley. The Eldridges' house was a little farther than she usually went in search of work, but the distance, she'd decided, might be of benefit. Perhaps fewer of the people on the outskirts of town had heard of her reputation, and by the time it caught up with her, she could move on. That was how she'd lived the first few years of Sean's life, and it looked as if she'd do the same again.

The cobbles gleamed beneath her feet, but she scarcely noticed. Tears threatened behind her eyes, but she blinked them back. She was done with crying; it didn't do any good. She was also done with dreaming. Even the hansom carriage that waited across the street no longer got her attention. She had stopped looking at the coaches, searching faces, wanting just a glimpse of him.

Her heart froze as her eyes betrayed her and she glanced back. It couldn't be, it just couldn't. Katie stood in the middle of the street, heedless of the traffic that passed, of the carriage drivers who shouted obscenities and ordered her out of the road.

She'd know that face anywhere, that rakish grin, those warm brown eyes just waiting to laugh with her. She saw his look of alarm as a cab careened by, then he reached out and grabbed her, hauling her toward the carriage. Stunned, she couldn't speak, couldn't move, couldn't breathe.

"Katie." Christopher smiled. "I've come to take you home."

❊ SIXTEEN

Katie still stared at him as if he spoke a foreign language. Another carriage raced around the corner, and Christopher indicated the coach.

"Let's get out of the street."

Nodding, she lifted her black maid's dress and followed him inside the elegant carriage, her mind still in a whirl.

He couldn't be back, yet here he was. Her mind tried to make sense of it all. Christopher was in Cape May. He wouldn't have returned to Philadelphia, using the last of his money, just to find her. Had something else happened? Why couldn't he just leave her alone?

As if sensing her confusion, Christopher shouted something to the driver, then as the coach began to move he turned to her and took her hand.

"Katie, we need to talk. Can we go somewhere and have some supper? There is so much I have to tell you."

"Why?" she asked softly. At his puzzled expression she explained. "Christopher, you made it clear that you didn't want anything else to do with me. That you think I'm a liar and a cheat. I don't see much reason to talk."

"Trust me on this," he said. "When you hear everything I have to say, you'll understand."

She didn't have much of a choice. Besides, she was

overwhelmingly curious. Nodding, she watched in confusion as the carriage stopped before a small, yet elegant restaurant. Katie accompanied him inside, wishing she had something other than a shawl to cover her work dress. She saw the curious glances the waiter gave her and her sophisticated companion, but she decided she could ignore them. When they were seated with a cup of hot tea, he spoke quietly.

"Katie, I've done a lot of thinking in the past few days. I realize that I judged you too harshly. Who knows? Given the same circumstances, I might have done the same thing."

Katie sipped the hot tea, not daring to react or hope. Did this mean he'd forgiven her?

"I also understand how everything happened. I've spoken to Ella, and you're right. The woman loves you. I can see how the situation developed and, given the affection between the two of you, why you let it continue."

Katie's mouth dropped, but she closed it quickly. She couldn't believe she was hearing this and wondered frantically how much gin she'd consumed the previous night. Yet even the strongest dose of alcohol couldn't have produced a dream like this one.

"I guess the part that upset me the most was my own fear that you were using me as well. Katie, I can understand the rest of it, but I have to ask you. Was I just part of the scheme, too?"

She shook her head, unable to speak. "No," she managed.

He watched her closely, as if trying to determine whether or not she spoke the truth. It was humiliating, but she had to admit she understood why he might weigh what she said with some caution. Apparently he trusted her word and he nodded.

"Then I think we do have something to talk about. Katie, we are married. Like it or not, that is our legal situation. In a way I am responsible for you. And in truth, it bothers me to know that you're out here, alone in this city, working at God knows what. Katie, I want you back.''

The teaspoon clattered to her dish, but neither of them noticed. A small spark of hope arose inside of her. Was it possible that he was feeling some of the same things she was? ''Back? You want me to come . . . to your home? To live as your wife?''

Christopher nodded, grinning, looking more handsome than ever. ''Yes. Is that so hard to believe? Katie, you and I have a lot in common. I think we both realize that. And we get along well. We were attracted to each other from the first, and I think we still are. Instead of going our separate ways, why not pool our resources and see what we can do as a team.''

Katie felt the rush of joy inside her dissipate. He said nothing of feelings, nothing of caring. In fact, he spoke as if this was a business arrangement. But surely he must feel something for her, or he wouldn't have gone to such lengths to seek her out.

She wanted to believe, but the pain inside of her reminded her of the consequences of such foolishness. She waited until after the serving man had brought her dinner, then she questioned him thoughtfully.

''Is that why you came looking for me? Because you want me to help you?''

For the first time Christopher looked uncomfortable. ''No, that's not the only reason. I think we can help each other.'' At her pointed stare, he sighed, then he held open his hands like a gambler ready to call. ''Katie, we have a chance at a new beginning. Ella Pemberton has agreed to give us a percentage of Fan's dowry, one thousand dollars, enough for one year. If we can make a go of it, we get the rest.''

Understanding seeped through her, and with it disillu-

sionment. This was why he really wanted her. It had nothing
to do with emotions, nothing to do with her. It was for the
money. Again he simply saw her as a means to an end.

"Christopher, I appreciate the offer. And for a girl like
me, it is a really good one. But I have to say no." She
smiled bitterly. "At Mrs. Eldridge's, I get a dollar a day and
meals. And the terms are clear to everyone."

"Katie, that's not what I meant."

"Good evening, Christopher. Thank you for the dinner. I
believe I can find my own way home."

"Katie, listen to me."

But it was too late. She was gone.

"Katie!" Christopher ran after her, but Katie had disappeared into the night as quickly as she'd run out. He looked
down the street, where dozens of little alleyways and
crisscrossing roads provided endless refuge for someone
who didn't want to be found.

Furious, he returned home. He had ruined his chance.
Even if he found her tonight, there was no way she'd listen
to him. Maybe it was best if he waited a day and let her
think about it, then he could try again.

Eunice was waiting when he entered the house. He could
tell by her grim expression that she had guessed the
outcome of the meeting. Hanging his coat on a nail where a
picture once graced the wall, he turned toward her, prepared
to do battle.

"Well?" Eunice looked pointedly behind him. "I notice
you're alone."

"She wouldn't come." Christopher tried unsuccessfully
to keep the frustration from his voice.

"What do you mean she wouldn't come?" Eunice asked
patiently, as if speaking to a half-wit. "Did you explain the
situation? Tell her about the money?"

"Of course I did." Christopher snorted. "She didn't care.

She simply told me she'd rather continue working for Mrs. Eldridge, bade me good-bye, then disappeared into the night like a phantom. Dammit!'' Striding about the room, he couldn't hide his outrage. "It took me days to find her, and she's gone again! She wouldn't listen to reason."

"That's ridiculous," Eunice said blandly. "Katie O'Connor cannot possibly prefer living as a maid to living with you, particularly after working for Florence Eldridge. The woman drinks, you know. And her children." Eunice shuddered at the memory, then eyed Christopher speculatively. "You must have made a very enticing offer for her to reject you."

"I told her the truth," Christopher said. "It is a business arrangement. Together we get the money and can start over. It's as simple as that."

"You didn't tell her like that?" Eunice said, aghast. When Christopher glanced up in confusion, his aunt rolled her eyes. "You did. What a romantic proposition! Why didn't you just offer to buy her instead? I believe there is a name for that profession."

Christopher stared at her, openmouthed. "You don't think—"

"Of course that's what she thought," Eunice snapped. "After all, you already confessed to using her before to get money."

Christopher wanted to protest, but he remembered Katie's hurt expression and the pain in her voice. Surely she knew that there was more to it than money.

Eunice seemed to read his mind. "I suggest you tell this woman what she means to you. Before it's too late."

She had been a fool. Katie couldn't get past that fact as she sat beside the fire in the little row house, trying to get warm. She didn't know why she was surprised, or why she'd expected anything different. For her, it was always the same.

How could she have let herself hope? She thought of the ridiculous flood of pleasure she'd experienced when she saw Christopher, and felt doubly humiliated. He had simply found another way to use Fan Pemberton to get what he wanted. All he needed was her cooperation. And she, Katie O'Connor, a woman alone with a child, was never quite good enough for anything else.

Yet, she realized as she smoothed the threadbare cushions of the sofa, she had been tempted by his offer. She would have a good home again, food, and the respectability that was so important to her. She could provide more for her son, could see that he ate well and went to a better school. She could even help out her grandfather and her aunt. Although they would die rather than admit it, they had put to good use the money she had sent from the shore and sorely missed the extra dollars. And she would be with Christopher.

A month ago she wouldn't have thought twice about it. But she just couldn't do it now. Every time she looked at him, she would know the truth. Pride was the only thing she had left, the only thing they'd never been able to take from her. For all of the slurs she'd had to endure, Katie O'Connor always held her head high.

"Mama?"

Sean came down the stairs, rubbing his eyes. She hadn't seen him earlier; she had come home too late. Katie held out her arms, surprised when he tumbled into them, sobbing.

"What's the matter?" She smoothed his soft blond hair, wondering what strange dream had awakened him this way.

"They hurt me." His words were barely coherent as he spoke through his tears.

"Who hurt you?" Katie quickly disengaged herself from him, then looked at him closely. Gasping, she saw a shiner developing beneath one eye, and a nasty scrape on his cheek.

"The boys at school. Aunt Moira put a cold cloth on it, but it still hurts. They called me that name."

Katie's heart broke. She wrapped her arms around her son fiercely, hating the children who had done this to him. And she knew why, and what name they meant. Sean had no father, and to the street urchins, he was a bastard.

Because of ignorance and poverty, they took their frustrations out on each other. Katie didn't think she could bear it, so intense were her emotions. Gradually Sean stopped crying, then lifted his small face to her.

"It didn't matter, Mama. I hit back like Grandpa told me. I don't like to hurt them. It makes me feel bad."

"I know." Katie rocked him in her arms. "They don't like to hurt you either. Try to stay away from them."

"I will." Sean rose, yawning. "Can I sleep in your bed?"

Katie nodded, aware that he wanted some measure of security. She watched him smile, then go upstairs, the latest drama forgotten. With the resilience of a child, the promise of her companionship erased the damage of his injuries.

Almost. Katie sat in the darkness, letting the fire die. She had to do something to help her son.

Before he grew up just like his father.

"For the love of God, what is this? The place looks like a wake. Moira, take a look at this."

Sean giggled in the bed as Katie awoke and heard her grandfather's grumblings downstairs. The two of them shared a smile, then Katie bustled after Sean, wanting to know firsthand what all the commotion was about.

"Mama . . . look!" Sean stared in amazement when they reached the bottom of the stairs and looked into the parlor.

The room was filled with flowers. In spite of the lateness of the season, summer roses, bunches of daisies, fresh chrysanthemums, and baby's breath brightened the room like sunshine. In the center of them all was a wrapped plant, and as Katie approached she saw that it was a shamrock.

"'Tis for you." Patrick shoved a letter at Katie, then stared at the profusion of flowers in wonder. "Would take me all season just to garden these. Who are they from?"

"A friend." Katie ignored his scowl and opened the note, hearing Moira's pleased comments.

My dearest Kate, the note began in an elegant scrawl that she instantly recognized as Christopher's. *I want to apologize for yesterday. I didn't explain things very clearly, and realized only later what you must have thought. I was trying so hard to be truthful that I omitted what must be the most important fact of all.*

Katie, when I said that I wanted you back, I meant as a wife, truly. I believe we have a future together. I don't know if what I feel for you could be called love, but I will tell you this. You mean more to me than any woman I've ever known.

I want you, Kate, and I think we can be happy. Do you think that we have a chance?

Christopher

Katie grinned, hugging the note to her chest. He cared about her—he had to. She hadn't missed the significance of the shamrock. He, too, thought of their wedding night, and what that simple promise meant. Patrick scowled when she whirled around the room, and Moira laughed, her voice sounding like a young girl's.

"Damned foolishness," Patrick said. "The world could be falling apart and that colleen wouldn't care."

"Let her be, Paddy," Moira said, then turned to Kate. "When is your gentleman calling?"

Katie hesitated. How could she tell them the truth, that she was married to this man? Could she possibly explain her reasons for what she'd done, the sequence of events leading up to her impersonation of Fan that resulted in a wedding they would surely consider immoral?

Yet how could she not?

If there was one thing Katie had learned, it was that evading the truth only led to more trouble. So taking a deep breath, she quickly spoke.

"He isn't. I'm going to him. He is my husband."

Moira looked stunned, while Patrick appeared less surprised. Katie explained the details of her marriage. When she had finished, Patrick frowned, his brows drawn together, looking thunderous.

"Are you saying that you love this man? That you want to go back to him?"

"I'm not certain what I feel," Katie said honestly. "But I think he does care for me."

"Many successful marriages have had stranger beginnings than this," Moira said hopefully. When Patrick grunted, she continued defensively: "Well, it's true. Remember Jimmy Reilly and Winifred Blake? Their marriage was a silver-glove affair. And then there was—"

"What about the boy?" Patrick interrupted Moira, his voice stern.

"Sean is part of the reason that all this happened," Katie responded truthfully. "You know how much I love him. I want something better for him than what I can provide." Her eyes squeezed shut as she thought of those children teasing him. Yes, somehow she would find a way to give him a better life.

"So you've told this society man about him? About your son?"

"Not yet." At Patrick's disapproving frown, Katie hastened to explain. "At first he thought I was Fan Pemberton. I couldn't tell him then. By the time he learned the truth, there was no point. I thought it was over and I left."

"To come here."

Katie nodded. "I will tell him now. He has a right to know."

"Good." Patrick seemed relieved, but he came closer to her and lifted her chin. His hand was like sandpaper, yet it was reassuring. "I just want to ask you one more thing before you go to him. I know you, Katie, and I've seen you hurt before. Does this man make you happy?"

Katie nodded slowly. That much was true. Christopher did make her happy, and always made her laugh. And the one night they had spent together as husband and wife . . . Katie had never felt so close to another human being as she did then. Not even with John Sweeney had she experienced that union, a bonding of spirit as well as flesh.

"Yes," she answered with conviction. "He makes me happy."

"Then go to him. Remember, Katie, we have but one chance at this life. You have to take what happiness is offered and don't question it. Especially you. You've had enough hardship. Take it, Katie. And may God be with you."

The cabdriver knew exactly where the Scotts lived. Katie sank back against the seat in awe as the carriage pulled up in front of the Main Line mansion. Climbing out, she paid the man, then stood in the street, shivering in the wind.

It was every bit as grand as the Eldridges' house. Katie stared at the clean lines of the Federalist mansion, the elegantly curved windows, the dull red brick, the ivy creeping on the south side. An enormous green door with a brass knocker stood before her, and she lifted the metal with some trepidation.

The door opened instantly and Katie gaped in surprise as Christopher stood on the other side, still wrapping a robe around him. He had evidently just awakened. His hair was tousled from sleep, and his chin bore the stubble of a beard. Still, he was so handsome and Katie wondered how it was possible for someone to be born with so much.

"Kate." He seemed surprised and very pleased. "Come in. I suppose you received my message?"

"Yes. Thank you." Katie stood shyly inside the grand house, then glanced around and was stunned to see that it was virtually empty. Christopher didn't seem to notice that there were no furnishings, no curtains, no gaslights or servants. Instead he led her back to the kitchen, talking all the while, and proceeded to light the stove for his morning tea.

". . . so glad you came. I had to go back to the church to find you. It was only when I proved to those nuns that we were married that they would help me. I'm sorry about last night. I didn't think—"

"Christopher," Katie said softly, unable to take her eyes from the crates. "You don't have any tables."

"Oh, that." He waved a dismissing hand. "We sold them. Aunt Eunice and I needed money to live on during the last few months."

"But everything? Even your rugs . . ." She stared down at the bare wood floor. There wasn't even a little throw rug to keep the chill away.

"We had to. We were desperate." He said this in a joking manner, and she stared at him in wonder. "Katie, I meant what I said in that note. I really do want you back."

She nodded, then sank down on a crate to think. Everything she had wanted to say to him went out of her head. She had wanted to talk to him about Sean, to explain, but confronted with this . . . Katie shuddered. Somehow she hadn't envisioned things as being this bad. At the shore, Christopher and his aunt had been able to maintain a facade of wealth. Here, their situation appeared desperate.

"What happens when you have guests?" Katie asked. "Don't they wonder?"

"We haven't entertained since we've been back." He looked at her in confusion. "Katie, none of this matters. If we get back together, we get the money to replace these things. If that's what you want to do."

Her mind was in a whirl. Poverty and financial problems were nothing new to her; they apparently were to him. If she should go along with this plan and the Scotts didn't change their style of living, they would soon be more broke than now. They needed much more than the dowry under these circumstances. Ella's offer, generous as it was, would only give them a start.

"Christopher, I've given the matter a lot of thought. I do think you're right, that we make a good team. And together we could be successful."

He grinned, obviously pleased. "I think so, too. Katie, I really do care about you—"

She held up her hand and looked at him pityingly. He didn't understand. Somehow she had to make him. "Christopher, I will come back, but there are some conditions. I don't know if you've really thought this through, but we will have to make some major changes. Ella's money is only temporary; we have to find a way to reinstate your fortune. Otherwise we will go through the fund in no time at all. Just to refurnish this house, hire servants . . . the cost will be unbelievable."

Christopher nodded, then sat beside her at the table. "I know, but we'll be able to do something. Once we're reestablished."

"We can't wait that long." Katie sighed, aware that her

knowledge would now be extremely useful. "Trust me, I know what I'm talking about, and I know how to survive. I will help you. I'll live with you as your wife, I'll cook and clean and keep house for you. But you've got to listen to me about this."

Christopher nodded. "Sure. Whatever you think."

"Good." Taking a deep breath, Katie accepted his hand and looked him right in the eye. "Christopher, starting today, we've got to find another source of income."

"Like what?"

"Jobs." She smiled at his shocked expression. "You and I must become gainfully employed."

❖ SEVENTEEN

Christopher stared at her in stunned silence, then broke into a light laughter.

"No, no, you don't understand." He spoke quietly, as if explaining the most rudimentary facts to a child. "We are society people. We don't work."

"You do now." Katie smiled, undaunted. "You might still be society, but you aren't rich. And without a plan, that will soon be evident to everyone. We have to get through the next year, Christopher. After that, if we're still together, we get the money."

Eunice joined them, quietly taking a seat and hearing the end of the conversation. Pouring herself some tea, she frowned thoughtfully, then turned to her nephew.

"I'm afraid she's right. Christopher, I've been thinking about the same thing. Ella's money will only last a few months. We need a more permanent solution."

The condescending smile died on Christopher's face as he realized the truth in her words. Worse, he couldn't find a single flaw in their reasoning.

"So what are you two saying?" His eyes lifted to Katie's and he frowned. "You want me to dig ditches or something? If I take a job, people will know I'm poor. We might as well give up now."

"Not necessarily." Katie procured a sheet of paper from the top of a crate and reached for a pencil. Putting his name on top, she gazed at him contemplatively. "Now what are you good at? Gambling, billiards, parlor games. You are a great host, know how to make people comfortable. You are conservative in appearance and have many contacts in the business world."

"Money." Christopher laughed at the irony. "I am good with money. Charles used to say it was the gambler's instinct, but I can usually pick winning investments. If I could get my hands on some damned capital . . ."

"Use someone else's," Katie said, ignoring his look of confusion. "That's perfect! Don't you see? You could be one of those men in banks, who make money for other people!"

"An investment banker." Eunice nodded thoughtfully. "You could manage trusts and estates, like the Wellingtons or the Chesters."

"And produce an income for yourself." Flushed with excitement, Katie put down her pencil and grinned.

Eunice's brow wrinkled thoughtfully. "You know, that could work. Charles Pepper's family owns one of the largest banks in the city. I'm sure he'd help you get started. And it would look natural. Lots of your contemporaries do this kind of work as a hobby. They really don't need the money, but they want to carve their own niche. Stop scowling, dear," Eunice said, seeing his expression. "So if you were to take this kind of position, it wouldn't look like you're destitute."

Katie nodded enthusiastically, ignoring Christopher's thunderous expression. "Now let's do the same for me." She turned over the paper.

"Kate, you can't mean—" Eunice protested.

"Oh, no," Christopher said sharply. "I'm not having a wife that works. Besides, you can't go on cleaning the houses of my friends. Eunice, you can try to cover up with Florence Eldridge, but Kate can't continue that.''

''I wasn't thinking of working as a maid,'' Katie said firmly. ''But we do need a second income, and it would be foolish to pretend otherwise. There has to be a way.''

Kate ignored their disapproving glances and scribbled on the paper. Christopher leaned over her shoulder, reading. ''Katie, this is ridiculous. You can cook and clean, write in a neat hand, take care of others . . . they're all jobs that would fall into one or two categories, and none of them practical for our purposes. What do you propose, to become a cook or a governess? How could we explain that?'' His voice was incredulous.

''I can sing.'' Katie looked up at him, her blue eyes brimming with inspiration. ''I can teach others, either women or children.''

''Are you suggesting that you . . . tutor?'' Eunice asked, though her voice wasn't as disapproving as a moment ago.

Katie nodded. ''It's perfect. I can teach for a few hours in the afternoon. This is respectable, and will provide additional money. And other society women spend their time in such pursuits. It's considered fashionable.''

Christopher looked at her as if she'd gone mad. ''Do you really mean to spend hours with some ill-tempered brat who couldn't carry a note to save her life, just to earn a few extra dollars? I won't hear of it!''

''You haven't a choice,'' Katie said firmly. ''I gave notice to Florence Eldridge, and I've got to get something.'' At his continued frown, Katie persisted. ''Christopher, it's the only way. At this point, pride is a luxury we can't afford.''

''I think she's right.'' Eunice sighed. ''Katie, I hate to see you take on so much responsibility, but I think your plan has merit. And if you two don't mind, I'd like to help. I can run the household, keep in touch with the right people, and make sure the gossip mongers don't get hold of any of this. I can keep our place in society until you two are ready to resume yours.''

Christopher scowled. Somehow he hadn't planned on his reunion with Katie taking this form. Yet even he could see that her plan was necessary. Shrugging in resignation, he spoke. ''All right, I can't fight the both of you. We'll try it. But if it doesn't work—''

''We'll think of something else.'' Katie reached out and shook his hand. ''This is a business arrangement, you know.''

Christopher's eyes met hers and noticed that she quickly looked away. Business arrangement. He wasn't sure he liked the sound of that.

Even if it was his idea.

''Paddy, will you come to the door? There's a strange man here.''

Moira turned back inside the dark row house and indicated the porch. Patrick rose wearily from his seat, his leg stiff from pulling weeds. He had arthritis, but he hid it well and never complained, and had found that a cup of the gin and a pipe worked just as well as reciting his woes.

Outside, someone lounged just beneath the street lamp. Patrick stared at him, a vague remembrance stirring within him at the sight of the handsome young man with the gold hair and a smile that could charm the pennies from the eyes of a corpse.

Yet the memory wasn't a pleasant one. Patrick hated the way his mind seemed clouded these days, and that the worries over the next meal obliterated all else. He knew this man and didn't like him. But he couldn't quite remember. . . .

"Patrick O'Connor." The young man spoke, his grin insolent. "I don't suppose you recall me."

"Can't say that I do." Patrick's heart pounded faster as a premonition came to him. God, it couldn't be, it was so long ago. . . .

"I'm not surprised," the young man continued, stepping closer, and placing a booted foot on the porch steps. "Katie only brought me home once to meet the family. Can't say that I blame her. I wasn't exactly welcome."

"John Sweeney." The words tumbled forth with hatred from Patrick's lips. How could he have forgotten? John still had the devil-may-care attitude, the cocksure grin, the lack of respect that he'd always had. The man was handsome and possessed charm, that was undeniable. Still, there was something about him that had warned Patrick years ago, when Katie had first introduced him. It was the same sensation he'd experienced when he'd seen a snake, long before it struck.

"What the hell do you want?"

John broke into laughter. "Now, Paddy, is that any way to greet an old friend? I just happened to be in the neighborhood and thought I'd stop by. It seemed a kind and friendly thing to do, seeing as we're both from the old sod."

Patrick's fists tightened and he wished he had a shillelagh with him. "It's been six years," he said slowly. "You broke my poor Katie's heart. In all this time you never thought to come by until now. I don't suppose you wanted to see what you'd done to her and her life." He spat into the gutter, barely missing John. "So I ask you again. Now that Katie is happy and is making a life for herself, what do you want?"

"Is she happy?" John's grin didn't vanish, but his eyes lost some of their sparkle. "Bring her on out then so I can congratulate her on her good fortune."

"I'd kill you first," Patrick said softly. He rubbed his

blistered palms together, as if aching to make good his threat. "Stay away from her. I'm warning you."

"All right." John laughed, but this time without mirth. "Calm down, old man. Don't get that Irish temper up." When Patrick didn't respond, he continued quickly: "I don't have to see Katie. My intention wasn't to upset her or your family. I just want to see my son."

For a moment Patrick thought he would pass out, so intense were his emotions. He stared blankly at the young man before him, aware of his light coloring that on Sean was beautiful, his smile that on Sean was dazzling, and his strong build, which his son showed every sign of inheriting. Yet there was a blackness in him that Sean did not possess, an evil that blighted him the way a bruise blighted the most perfect peach.

"No," Patrick said calmly.

John's grin died and he met the old man's stare. "He is my son. I have the right."

Patrick shook his head. "You have no right. You gave that up when you abandoned my granddaughter. Your son is doing fine. We've raised him well without any help from you, and we'll go on raising him well."

"I'd like to see for myself."

Patrick stared at the young man, his eyes searching. He saw John Sweeney's poorly cut coat, his frayed elbows, his ragged trousers. He saw the places where his boots had worn through, and he saw the cloths stuffed inside to keep his feet dry. He saw the dried mortar on his heels, the scraps on his hands from carrying endless bricks. Suddenly he knew this man as if he'd known him all of his life.

"How much?" Patrick saw that John didn't look surprised, and that he'd guessed correctly. "How much do you want to leave my family alone?"

His grin broadening, John slouched against the porch pole. "I would be insulted, except—"

"Except that I am right." Patrick stepped closer, his rugged face expressionless. "I've known dozens of young spaulpeens like you. Worthless, all of them. They use their looks and their charm to get what they want." He spat again, this time not caring that he hit one of John's boots. "You no more want to see your son than a whore wants to see a constable. I want to know how much money you want from us. Then get the hell out."

"Easy now. There's no need to get angry." John shrugged and took a step back. "I could use the money, and Katie's doing so well. If you really don't want me visiting—"

"How much?" Patrick nearly shouted.

"I think fifty dollars will do for a start."

Patrick's face didn't change, but his skin paled. Fifty dollars was all the money he'd saved for the rent, to pay for the next few months. If he gave him that money, they would be forced to leave, to find cheaper housing, maybe in a worse place.

Yet he didn't have a choice. John Sweeney would crush Katie's newfound happiness. If this man showed up on the Scotts' doorstep, making a claim on his son, he could easily destroy their marriage. The Scotts couldn't risk another scandal, and he had no doubt that John Sweeney would create one.

And Sean. John Sweeney would corrupt the lad, turn him into a street urchin with no morals or conscience. That would kill poor Katie and would crush Moira. They'd fought so hard to give the boy a good life. They'd insisted he go to Sunday Mass, made him wash, helped him as much as they could with his schooling. He was a good boy, a kind boy. And it would all be for nothing if his father ever got hold of him.

"I will get the money." Patrick turned to go inside the

house, then paused at the door. "And if I ever see you near the boy—"

"Don't worry." John Sweeney grinned. "I don't look a gift horse in the mouth."

Returning, Patrick shoved the money in John's hands. "Now get out."

John Sweeney pocketed the bills, then doffed his hat and grinned as he turned down the street. Patrick watched him with a sinking heart.

It wasn't the last they'd hear of John Sweeney. Everything Irish in him told him so.

"La, la, la, la . . . la."

Katie winced when Sara Witherspoon's voice cracked as she reached the upper range of the scale. Patiently Katie smiled encouragingly, then hid her reaction as Sara screeched through another octave.

She was beginning to think it wasn't possible to teach some people music. Katie herself had never questioned her own gift; it was something she took for granted and thought everyone else possessed the same talent. She was quickly learning that what came so easily to her was excruciatingly difficult for others.

Yet it provided a job, and everything was working as planned. Christopher was employed at the Peppers' bank, with only Charles knowing the full extent of their need. And Eunice was circulating the story that as well-to-do newlyweds, Katie and Christopher felt so fortunate that they wanted to return some of their new happiness to others. It was all coming together, except . . .

"La, la, la . . . lala."

Except she and Christopher were not living as husband and wife. Katie wondered whether he had really intended to get her back just for the Pembertons' money. It had worked; Ella had been as good as her word. As soon as it was confirmed that Katie had come back to Christopher, Ella had forwarded a one-year portion of Fan's dowry. Eunice had quickly applied the money to pay off outstanding debts, but it was even more obvious that Katie had been right. When the worst of the bills were paid, there was very little left.

So they were living together, but they weren't sleeping together. Katie blushed even to think of it. The Scotts' house was so large that it seemed foolish to suggest sleeping anywhere other than the feminine bedroom that Eunice had indicated was reserved for her. Stripped of most of the furniture, it looked overly big and empty, as if waiting for its real occupant. Katie sat in the huge bed alone at night, wondering if she should speak to Christopher, but she was afraid to bring up the subject. Her own emotions wouldn't stand the light of day, and she had no desire to begin a conversation that might prove painful. She'd been hurt too much in the past to take that risk.

And if she had to be truthful, she hadn't confessed everything the way she'd intended. She'd been so shocked when she first returned to Christopher at the way he lived that she couldn't bring up the subject of Sean. She attempted to at other times, but without a real intimacy between them, it was just too difficult and risky. She was forced to keep her son a secret, and as time went by it was harder and harder even to attempt telling Christopher the truth.

So they lived as polite friends, Christopher going off to his job every day, Katie to hers. She went every morning to her family to see to her son. She hadn't been paid yet, so she couldn't give them much money, but she was worried. Paddy didn't seem himself, and even Moira was distant. Only Sean was the same.

"La, la, la, la . . . lalala."

"Maybe we should try something less difficult." Katie

turned the sheet music on the polished piano and indicated a new piece. "This one should be nice."

"I'm bored," Sara said petulantly, banging the keys with her fingers.

Katie forced a smile. "You're doing fine. Your voice gets prettier every day. And you wouldn't want Melissa Eldridge to outperform you, would you?"

Sara shook her head, her blue bow flapping behind her. Melissa Eldridge had the reputation of being the neighborhood songbird, and like everyone else, Sara couldn't stand her. Newly motivated, the young girl studied the music, then began again while Katie directed. Katie tried not to think of cats howling, but when Sara attempted the new piece, she swallowed hard, in pain.

"There you two are." Jane Witherspoon entered the room, her smile beatific as Sara sang. "My compliments, Fan. I never knew you were so talented. My Sara gives a whole new meaning to the song, don't you agree?"

Katie nodded, straight-faced. It wasn't nearly as difficult to assume Fan's role again as she'd thought it would be. This world was so different from her own that she could easily keep the two separate. Jane patted her daughter's head, then indicated the French doors.

"You can run outside now, Sara. That's enough for today." She continued to smile as her daughter raced off, then she turned to Katie. "I don't know how to thank you for all you've done. Even in a few short weeks, the difference in Sara's range is remarkable."

"Remarkable," Katie agreed, feeling something like a hypocrite.

"I think it's given her new confidence among her friends. Girls are so competitive when it comes to womanly skills, you know. Whereas before Sara refused to sing at church, she now contributes, and quite loudly."

Katie smiled, feeling sorry for the church members. "I'm

so glad you're happy. I know we haven't discussed any permanent arrangements, but I think we should—''

"You are right," Jane said eagerly, placing a fond hand on Katie's shoulder. "Fan, I know you have other obligations. But I really want you to continue Sara's lessons. It's done so much for her, you really have no idea.''

"That's fine." Katie breathed a sigh of relief. It had taken Eunice some time to find this position, and it was perfect. Jane Witherspoon was something of a recluse; she didn't attend the lunches, or the gatherings, or the charity groups that other women frequented. Instead she spent her time among her books, studying and dreaming, and with her daughter, whom she adored. As a result, very few people were even aware that Fan Pemberton was tutoring Sara, and those who were didn't question it further.

"As for compensation, I know you don't need the money. My word, as Mrs. Scott, you have enough for ten families!'' Jane giggled while Katie felt a dread creeping over her. "So to give you money would be the height of bad taste and would no doubt insult all of you. Yet I can't see you coming here so often without receiving some kind of benefit.''

She extended a wrapped package. Katie smiled uncertainly, then opened the gift. Inside were six white linen handkerchiefs, all carefully embroidered and trimmed with crocheted silk.

"Sara made them herself." Jane grinned proudly. "She's even embroidered your initials on the corners. See? F.S. for Fan Scott."

Katie smoothed the cloths, then smiled at Jane Witherspoon. "They are just lovely.''

❊ *Eighteen*

". . . And as a conservative, I deem investments as costly speculation. I think carriages are the answer. People will always need transportation, and horses are the best. Strong, stable carriage shops and horse goods are the answer."

Bartholomew Meade sank back into the leather seat and puffed his cigar, tugging importantly on his waxed mustache. Charles Pepper exchanged a thoughtful look with Christopher, watching in amusement as Christopher opened a file and sifted through the paper. Satisfied, he closed the papers and fixed Bartholomew with a steady stare.

"I agree that carriages have been a good investment. And you're right, people need transportation, and they're likely to continue needing it. Look at what's happening in the city." Removing a map from his desk, Christopher spread the parchment out and indicated the city lines. "West Philadelphia is spreading out rapidly. Center city is developing as a center of commerce and offices. With the exception of the northeast mills, more and more workers are no longer living near their jobs. They will have to rely on transport to survive."

"Then I'm right." Bartholomew puffed.

Christopher smiled. "On that point, yes. However, I

don't agree that horses and carriages are the best long-term investment. There are too many people working on improvements in this area, and that is what I recommend you look at. Take this company, for example.''

Christopher displayed a data sheet for the City Streetcar Company. Bartholomew read the information with open skepticism. When he finished, he tossed the sheet down and shrugged.

''No one will want to ride in those.'' He indicated a drawing of a streetcar. ''I know there are a few operating in the city, but gentlemen would never—''

''What about the working class?'' Charles interrupted, eager to make the point. ''They don't own horses and carriages and often can't afford cab fare. A cab ride from West Philadelphia to center city costs twice as much as by streetcar. The reason is simple. Only one person rides in a cab at a time. By transporting a lot of people at once, the streetcars are extremely economical and provide a handsome profit. Look at the return on investment.''

Bartholomew examined the numbers and his face changed to show he was impressed. ''They look good. But there isn't much money here, or capital.''

''That's why they're selling shares,'' Christopher said quietly. ''The company has been privately held for years. They want to expand and own all of the streetcar lines in the city. There are several which are operating independently. If we can buy them up, this company will have a virtual monopoly on the only mass transportation available, at a time when people will need it the most.''

Bartholomew studied the figures, then looked back at the map. He noticed that the streetcar lines were marked with a pencil, indicating the routes. ''There is some overlap,'' he commented, though his voice was less sure. ''Could the company make them more efficient?''

''That's the first step,'' Christopher said with assurance.

"I've spoken to the owners and they are aware of the situation. By consolidating the lines under one company, not only do you increase capital, you can do it by the most efficient means. We can run more lines where needed, from the outskirts of the city where the people live to where they work. Within a few years we can streamline the whole process, then relax and make money. It's foolproof."

Bartholomew nodded, then reached for his checkbook. "I will trust you. You've already made me money on that other speculation . . . illuminating gas? And the chemical company, Smith, Klein and French, looks promising. Here's the money."

"You won't regret it." Charles stood up and patted the man's round shoulders. "Christopher has an uncanny feel for these things. He hasn't been wrong yet."

"Call it a gambler's instinct," Christopher said dryly.

Bartholomew paused, then realized the joke and guffawed. "That's a good one. Truthfully I don't care where he gets it as long as he does." Grinning, he turned to Christopher. "You're going to make a lot of men rich. I suppose it's easy when you have your own money. You're not as cautious as the rest of us."

Christopher kept a bland expression as Charles led the man from the office. When he returned, he closed the door and rubbed his hands together happily.

"Chris, you did it. And you're perfectly right—the man will make a fortune. But without your investment skills and your selling ability, Meade would have continued to make a poor showing in his portfolio and would have blamed us. We were in danger of losing him, you know."

"I heard." Christopher replaced the man's file, then indicated the map. "That's the secret. Sometimes you have to see the trees in the forest, and people like Bartholomew have trouble doing that. They're scared, and I don't blame them. I know what it's like to lose money in investments that are supposed to be foolproof. I won't recommend anything without weighing all the factors and talking to the experts.''

"And it's working extremely well." Charles beamed, obviously proud. "You're making the bank rich and a lot of customers satisfied. And you're putting in so many hours. If I didn't know better, I'd think you were enjoying yourself.''

"Forget that," Christopher said dryly, although he admitted to himself that Charles touched on the truth. For so long he was considered the spoiled black sheep of the Scott family, unable to do anything of worth. And although the work was hard, it was challenging. It required thinking and research, and for Christopher, whose chief employment of the past few years had been chasing women and drinking, it was a pleasant change.

And it was like gambling. By reading the paper, working with businesses, and forecasting, he was able to predict which companies had growth potential and which did not. As Charles had said, he'd already been very successful, and that was gratifying.

But he had an image to keep up. Scowling, he tossed aside the map. "You know why I'm doing this, so let's not pretend anything else. By the way, while we're on the subject, you alone know why I need this job." Seeing Charles's affirming nod, Christopher asked the question that had plagued him for weeks. "So when do I get paid?"

Charles didn't seem surprised at the question. He squirmed uncomfortably. "Chris, I know how much you need the money. But frankly my father is concerned about the outstanding debts, particularly those you owe me. He's decided to withhold your salary until those debts are paid.''

"What?" Christopher was stunned. "But he can't do that! I need the money now!"

"I know." Charles looked upset. "Chris, I've tried to talk to him, but you know how he is. He was furious when he found out that I'd helped you. I did get him to agree to a small stipend until we're even. It should help keep you going in the meantime.'' Extending a small leather pouch, he let a few coins fall into Christopher's hand.

Christopher stared with disbelief at the pittance that gleamed within his palm. "I can't live on this."

"Of course you can't," Charles agreed. "But at the rate you're going, you'll pay the debts off in no time and start with a clean slate. Please don't give up. Within a few months you'll be back in the black and able to hold your head up. My father feels we should give you that opportunity.''

Christopher pocketed the few coins and departed the office, his heart sinking. Outside, he stood beneath the street lamp, wondering what in the hell to do next. To reestablish himself elsewhere would take months, and he didn't have the luxury of time. And he enjoyed this job. He knew he owed the Peppers money, but dammit! Couldn't the old skinflint wait until he got on his feet?

Then he recalled Charles's father, with his righteous expression, his tight lips, his bulging cash box. He would never understand his position, and would only care that his son was dutifully reimbursed. Christopher felt sorry for Charles as he envisioned the battle that must have ensued when his father delivered his ultimatum. Winston Pepper was an authoritarian, and his son surely suffered because of it.

There was nothing Christopher could do but wait. He swore to himself as he signaled to his driver. He couldn't tell Katie the truth—she might leave, returning to her family, and he couldn't bear that. Yet it wasn't her fault that he'd gotten himself into this position. He couldn't let her go, couldn't admit defeat. He knew he could turn things around if . . . Somehow he had to get through the next few months.

And the next few hours.

*   *   *

The house was dark when he approached, and unusually quiet. Christopher removed his greatcoat, taking a package from the pocket and tucking it beneath his arm. He hung the coat on the nail, then ventured into the kitchen.

"You're home." Katie gave him a warm smile while Christopher stared about him in amazement. She'd covered the crate with a cloth so that it looked just like a table, and two candles flickered enticingly in the center, throwing a warm glow over the plates. The few remaining pieces of good china and crystal glittered on the gingham cloth, and late-summer flowers brightened the center. The aroma of game birds and potatoes filled the air, and there was even an inexpensive bottle of wine chilling in a bucket of ice.

"Eunice went to bed early," Katie explained self-consciously as he stared at the makeshift table. "I know we haven't spent much time together lately, so I thought we could . . . have dinner together."

She suddenly seemed shy and unsure of herself, not at all like the practical joker and confident woman she'd always been. Grinning, he took a step closer and kissed her, breathing in the warm sweet scent of her.

"I was thinking the same thing." Withdrawing the package from under his arm, he handed it to her. "Katie, I know it's not much, but I was passing a pawnbroker's today and thought you might like this."

Eagerly she fumbled with the wrappings and broke open the brown parchment. "Oh, Christopher, it's lovely."

"It's a music box." He turned the polished ivory case in her hands, then opened the lid. Instantly the room was filled with a lilting song that seemed both sad and sweet.

"'Greensleeves.'" Katie smiled, her heart aching.

He nodded, his voice thick with emotion. "I wish I could get you something nicer. My God, it's humiliating to live like this! I barely see you, and when I do, we're both tired and frustrated. There has got to be a better way."

"We're making it," Katie said gently, placing a warm hand on his face. "It will just take time. We're on the right track, but it won't happen overnight."

"I know." Christopher took his seat at the table and waited for her to join him. "But I don't know how to explain. All of my life I took money for granted. There was always enough of it for whatever I wanted, always enough for everyone. And now, when I want to give you something . . ." He glanced at the music box, his pain evident.

Katie smiled. "Christopher, the thought means everything. In all that time when you had money, I imagine you didn't put much effort into finding a gift or giving one." She picked up the box and held it lovingly. "This means much more because you did."

His eyes met hers, and for a moment Katie thought he would say the words she longed to hear from him. Instead he looked away, then admired the succulent quail that she'd placed in the center of the cloth, along with the vegetables. "How did you do all this?"

"Mr. Armstrong, next door. He hunts for sport and asked if we enjoyed game. They look wonderful."

Christopher sampled the fresh meat, then grinned in agreement. "They taste even better. Thank God the old man is such a good shot." Studying Katie, he continued softly: "How are the singing lessons going?"

"Very well," Katie said quickly. The last thing she wanted to admit was that her plan had been a failure. "In fact so well I'm thinking of taking on a few more students. Just a few," she continued when she saw his disapproving expression. "But after all, we could use the money."

There was a long silence after that. Katie poured the

wine, then questioned softly, "And the job? How is that going?"

"Great," Christopher said, but she noticed that he drank a huge gulp of wine when he answered. "The investments are doing very well. Charles is pleased and so is his father. They want me to continue as planned."

"That's wonderful," Katie breathed in admiration. "I knew you'd make it a success."

"Yes," Christopher said dryly. "It seems I do very well at making everyone else money. Now if I can only do that for us."

"It will happen," Katie insisted. "Just be patient."

Christopher reached out and took her hand, shaking his head in amazement. "You are the most remarkable woman. How did I ever find you?"

"At the Drexels' party, remember?" Katie teased, though the contact of his hand on hers took her breath away. "You thought I was Fan Pemberton."

He nodded, grinning. "How could I forget that? By the way, the rest of the world still thinks of you as Fan. I would prefer that they begin to call you Kate. I think we've lived enough lies, don't you?"

Katie shuddered, her own fears resurfacing. He thought he knew the whole truth, but in fact, he only knew part. She had to tell him about her son, but there never seemed to be the right time. If she didn't, and he found out . . .

"So I think I'll start calling you Kate publicly, and just explain that it's my name for you, and your middle name. No one has to know anything else. Is that all right with you?"

Katie beamed at him. "That would be wonderful."

"Good." Finished with his meal, he rose and lifted the lid of the music box. Instantly the room was flooded with song. "I know this isn't the most elegant ballroom, but could I have this dance with my beautiful wife?"

Katie rose, her heart so full she thought she couldn't stand it. Taking his hand, she let him lead her to the vacant floor, where the missing furniture left more than enough room for dancing.

It seemed magical. In spite of the lack of furnishings and lighting, the room was bathed in candlelight and the warm glow of music. Katie felt Christopher's body close to hers, his arm around her waist, and she was filled with longing. She wanted to be close to him, to know she meant something to him, to have a real life with him as his wife.

There had been so many lies, and still were. How could she go on like this? Yet as the lovely strains of the music filled her ears, and he held her closer, she was overwhelmed with emotion.

"Katie. My sweet Katie."

It was just like their wedding night, before everything had been marred with ugliness. Christopher held her, then when she turned her face to his, his mouth met hers in a kiss that was achingly sweet and violently passionate. Stunned, Katie returned the kiss, her own desires, long suppressed, now out of control. Neither one realized that the music box had stopped or that the music had ended. They stood in the candlelight, locked in an embrace that neither of them wanted to break.

"Oh, my God, Kate," Christopher whispered, when he finally eased his mouth from hers. His hands slid caressingly around her, down to her waist, then up her back. His eyes had turned darker, stormy with passion, and when Katie looked into them, she saw the same intense hunger she felt herself.

"Tonight I know I shouldn't ask you this," he continued, his voice ragged and hoarse. "But can I come to your room?"

Katie's blood pounded. She didn't know what this meant, though her mind screamed for answers. Was he truly committing himself to their marriage, or was it simply physical need? She had to know, but couldn't bring herself to ask now, not when her head felt dizzy with desire, or her flesh was aching to feel him inside her.

She wanted him. With that one kiss, he'd made her lose all sense of logic. She nodded, her smile breaking forth, and like two children, they raced up the stairs and into her room. Giggling, Katie shut the door while Christopher approached her.

"Kate." Christopher spoke softly, his voice filled with emotion. "I know I'm not much of a bargain right now, but if you'll give me time, I'll try to set things right. I didn't want to resume our marital relations until then, because I didn't want you to think . . ." He couldn't finish the sentence and Katie, understanding, nodded. "But I can't live in the same house with you and not want you. It's been driving me mad."

Katie sighed as he kissed her once more, then undid the buttons on her dress; slowly, achingly, he pressed a kiss to every area he exposed, taking a long time to remove the cumbersome gown and undergarments. Katie had to help him with the latter, and when the tight corset was finally undone and on the floor with the rest of her clothes, she turned to him, looking breathtakingly beautiful.

"Christopher." She smiled, drawing him into her arms. "I've wanted you for so long, waited for this. I didn't think you wanted me, that I meant anything to you except . . ."

His kiss stunned her with its intensity. Overwhelmed with desire, she rose on her feet and pressed against him, feeling his urgency as he quickly attempted to rid himself of his clothes. Grinning, she helped him, fighting the buttons on his cravat until he managed to tear through them and toss the damned shirt aside. Within moments, he was as naked as she, and standing near the edge of the bed.

They gloried in that moment. If the first time their

lovemaking was filled with idyllic bliss, this time it was more intense, deepened by the bonds that had grown between them. Katie's breath caught and she had to hold him for support when Christopher's hand swept down her, caressing her breasts until they were aching and full, then lower, exploring her until she was writhing against him.

She returned his caresses, astonished to realize that she held the same sensual power over him. Emboldened by her discovery, she shyly touched him, and he closed his eyes in rapture, urging her to continue, wanting more. He taught her the motion while he continued to pleasure her, and the feeling was so intense that she thought she would fall.

It was as if he sensed what she was experiencing, for he slid her onto the bed, then firmly held her hands at her sides.

"But . . ." she whispered in protest, then he grinned at her, his dark eyes mesmerizing.

"I can't let you continue that. It will be over too quickly. Let me pleasure you."

His mouth burned against her skin, and she squirmed in sheer erotic joy. His tongue teased first one breast, then the other, making the nipples hard and prominent. Her body ached, throbbing and wet, wanting him shamefully, and when his mouth met her there, giving her what she longed for, she cried out in ecstasy.

His mouth dazzled her, loving her to the point of oblivion. Her body, youthful and without inhibition, responded wildly, making her arch against him, wanting every moment of joy he was giving her. When her climax made her cry out, nearly sobbing with pleasure, he held her tightly, securely, bringing her slowly back to reality.

No one had ever made her feel this way. Even on their wedding night, the lovemaking hadn't been this wild, this explosive. Wanting nothing more than to provide him with the same pleasure, Katie pressed hot, sweet kisses along every inch of his body, watching with the same erotic tension as he groaned, trying to maintain some kind of control. His hands dug into the covers of her bed as her tongue teased him, making him want her so desperately that he called out her name as if in prayer. And when she slid over him, his hard male warmth entering her with a shock of pleasure so intense that Katie gasped, he held her tightly, forbidding her to move.

"I can't," he said hoarsely, his body struggling for control. "We can't yet . . . the risk . . . Oh, my God, I don't think I can—"

His body surged inside of her, powerfully and almost frantically. Katie's breath caught as the heat flowed within her like hot honey, culminating there where his body slid in and out of hers. He withdrew at the last wonderful moment, and she gave a cry of disappointment as his warmth shuddered against her. She wanted to feel that inside her, to know his pleasure, but when his arms encircled her and pulled her down against him, it was almost as good.

"Oh, Katie." His voice rumbled in his chest a moment later. They lay sated in nirvana like two kittens, seeking each other for warmth. Christopher sighed. "My God, that was wonderful."

She lay in his arms, feeling an overwhelming emotion that she didn't dare confess. It was clear to her why he'd withdrawn from her—he didn't want to risk pregnancy. Now was the time to tell him about Sean, and yet, as he lay beside her in sexual oblivion, she just couldn't. He might be appalled, might hate her or worse. This part of their relationship was too new and too fragile to test that way. And if she should lose him . . .

"Hold me, Christopher," Katie whispered. "I want to feel you close to me."

He did, and for that moment Katie was content.

❋ NINETEEN

*H*e loved her. He had to. Katie turned over in the frilly, feminine bed and saw Christopher stretched across the white linens. He looked magnificent, his dark, muscular body a sharp contrast to the pale bed coverings. Her eyes ran over him, admiringly, and the thoughts of the previous night brought a bright blush to her cheeks.

He had to care for her—last night proved that. Although she wasn't very experienced with lovemaking, she knew that what had passed between them had been special. It was more than mere physical passion; the intensity spoke of something else, something deeper.

Never before had she felt so drawn out of herself. Never before had she experienced such great pleasure. And she knew that he'd felt it, too. The woman in her was reassured that way, for there were some things that a man just couldn't hide. Christopher experienced the same erotic ecstasy last night that she had, and that must mean . . .

If she could just be sure. Worried, Kate bit her lower lip as she watched him sleep. She knew she had to tell him about Sean and soon. Yet she was afraid of what he would say, and worse, what he would do. Too often in the past those few words were enough to send her into disgrace. She wasn't good enough, wasn't worthy to keep company with gentlefolk. She had given birth to a bastard and, in all eyes, rich and poor, had sinned.

He thought he knew everything about her. He'd forgiven her deception about her identity, but could he forgive this? If she was certain of his feelings, she would tell him, but until he said the words, it was just too frightening. If he sent her away, especially after last night, she just didn't think she could bear it.

Katie slipped from the bed and put on a robe. She stood in front of the long paned window, looking out onto the grounds. It was cold and gray, the sky the color of pewter. Summer had long since waned; she could see the curling wisteria vines, naked of leaves. Soon it would be winter. Her family would need coal for the fireplace, Sean needed new shoes. Somehow, she'd have to find a way to help them, without Christopher discovering her secret. She'd tell him, she had to. But not yet. Their intimacy was too new, too fragile to risk with such a confession.

He roused slowly, and looked around the bed in confusion. His eyes met hers as she stood beside the window, and he smiled invitingly. He was so damned handsome, Katie thought.

"Come." He indicated the bed. "It's cold in here without you."

Katie grinned and came to stand close to him. She looked childlike, shy and not at all like the bold woman from the previous night. She indicated the window reluctantly. "It's morning. You have to go to work."

"I know." He grabbed her hand and pulled her into the bed. Shrieking, Katie tumbled beside him, then rose on one arm, giggling with him.

"What am I going to do with you, Christopher Scott?"

He grinned, tracing her freckled profile with his finger. "Last night you managed quite well, Mrs. Scott. Now if you just keep doing that—"

Katie swatted him playfully as he swept her into his arms. "We have to get up. Eunice will be awake, and I have to get breakfast."

"Breakfast will wait." His lips nuzzled her neck and Katie couldn't resist the tingling sensations that thrilled within her at his touch "Till later . . ."

It was much later when they descended, flushed and giggling like two children, carefree and innocent. Their mood remained exuberant until they reached the kitchen, where Eunice sat with a worried expression. She was wearing her reading glasses, and spread around her were several sheets of ominous-looking papers.

"What's all this?" Christopher took a seat beside her and lifted one of the notices. Eunice peered up from her reading and sighed as Katie removed a tin of flour.

"These are bills," Eunice said with a scolding tone. "I've been going through them. Some can wait, but our taxes are due. You know what that means."

Christopher groaned. "They will publish the fact that we're late in the *Ledger*. Everyone will know of our financial state. Dammit, how did we get so far behind? I thought with the dowry . . ."

Katie stopped beating the biscuits long enough to hear Eunice's answer.

"The dowry helped catch up the most pressing bills. I withheld some of it because we have to eat and get firewood for the winter. Katie's been wonderful, she's stretched the food beyond belief, but we're still running low." Adjusting her glasses, Eunice gave Christopher a penetrating glance. "And we just don't have enough money coming in from your jobs yet."

"I see." Christopher and Katie refused to meet each other's eyes and stared at the paper Eunice held in her hand, as if wishing it would disintegrate. "When will they publish the notice?"

"Within the week," Eunice said quietly. "I've kept it out for as long as possible, but the bill is just too delinquent."

"We'll have to think of something else," Katie began.

Christopher glanced up. "Oh, no. No more ideas. No more jobs. I'm not scrubbing floors and neither are you. Don't even consider it."

"But—"

"We're going to do things my way this time. We need some fast cash—there's no getting around it. And that means there is one solution. We gamble."

"What?" Both Eunice and Katie looked at him as if he'd lost his mind.

"We're going to the Ingersolls' party tonight, correct?" Christopher continued, undaunted by their reaction. When Katie nodded, he added, "There is always a gentleman's game that takes place at those parties. I'll play a few hands and win us enough to pay the taxes."

"And what will you use for a stake?" Eunice said bluntly. "You need money to enter a card game, I believe."

"This." Christopher indicated his gold pocket watch. "I can pawn it at the shop in town, then redeem it when I win. It will bring more than enough for a stake."

"But what if you lose?" Katie asked, obviously concerned.

Christopher grinned. "With you on my side, how can I? All I need is a little luck. Don't worry." He saw their faces and hastened to reassure them. "What's the worst that can happen? If I lose, I'll pay out and quietly leave. I'm no worse off than I am now. If we don't do something, we'll be disgraced."

Katie and Eunice exchanged looks. "I don't like it," Eunice said firmly. "I didn't mind your gaming when we had the resources to support it. But now—"

"It's the best way I know to make money fast,"
Christopher said. "Have you two any better suggestions?"

They looked at each other in silence. No one could think
of anything else. No one offered anything else.

"Good." Christopher rubbed his hands in anticipation.
"I know we'll score tonight. It will be an affair to
remember. I just feel it."

The Ingersolls had one of the loveliest houses on the
Main Line. Entering, Katie handed her wrap to the servant
who stood waiting in attendance, then glanced around the
room in appreciation. Black and white marble gleamed from
the floors, while the chandeliers tinkled overhead, blazing
with gaslight. A long white marble staircase led down into
the magnificent hallway, and portraits of ancestors stared
down from the wall above like silent guests.

"Fan! I'm so glad you could come." Emily Ingersoll was
one of the nicest girls Katie had met. Plain but friendly, she
extended her hands. "Come in, everyone's been asking
about you. Bertrice is here, Nellie and Mary . . . I think
you know just about everyone."

Katie shrugged at Christopher's expression and giggled,
helplessly drawn into the crowd of women. Bertrice, who
was officially engaged to Charles, broke off from her
conversation and rushed over.

"Fan! I kept asking when you'd be here. Isn't this house
beautiful? And you look so lovely, let me see that dress."

Katie twirled, silently grateful that Ella had sent Fan's old
clothes. The older woman would be returning from the
seaside shortly, and Katie was looking forward to seeing her
again. Ella was a positive force in this world for her, and she
honestly missed the older woman.

"You look pretty, too." Katie admired Bertrice's rose-
colored gown, delighted to see how nicely she was dressed.

In truth, since her relationship with Charles had deepened, Bertrice had bloomed. She looked radiant and happy.

"Mother didn't like this gown, but the dressmaker and I did, so I insisted. It is pretty, isn't it?" Glancing up, Bertrice's expression changed to chagrin. "Oh, look, that Margaret Chester is here. She is always so hateful, isn't she?"

"I haven't seen her since Cape May," Katie responded. She wasn't looking forward to seeing her, either. Every time Katie thought of Margaret on Christopher's arm, she just wanted to strangle her.

As if knowing they were talking about her, Margaret gave Katie a superior smile, then turned back to her conversation. Katie felt oddly disquieted by that glance. Margaret was never happy unless she was causing some kind of trouble. Something was amiss, but Katie didn't have the faintest idea as to what. But knowing Margaret, she knew she wouldn't have to wait long to find out.

"Dinner is served," a servant announced, indicating the dining room. Katie took Christopher's arm as he approached, and she thought he never looked so handsome. There was a jaunty cockiness about him, a lack of seriousness that made him especially appealing amid so many solemn men. Winston Pepper dominated the conversation, advising everyone concerning their investments, and Katie saw Christopher and Charles exchange an amused glance. She smiled, accepting a seat, aware that whenever she was in his company, Christopher provided the fun.

"Is everyone present?" Emily asked, glancing around the room before signaling for the meal to begin, Margaret gazed up, then, with a smirk, indicated the door.

"I believe Mrs. Eldridge is just coming in. Why, Florence, you will have to tell us that amusing story again, only this time for everyone's benefit. You know, the one about the maid you hired who looks just like Fan Pemberton? The one who recently disappeared?''

Katie felt the color drain from her face and she turned quickly, aware of everyone's eyes on her. Florence Eldridge, obviously the worse for drink, stared at her, but recognition lit up her gaze. She pointed an unsteady finger at Katie and spoke in slurred tones.

''That's her! My maid! What are you doing here? I have floors to be cleaned!''

Katie cringed, unable to think of a decent response. She saw Margaret's face, twisted into a vindictive smirk, then heard the gasps of the other guests. Eunice stood up and faced Florence slowly, like a ship pulling into harbor and preparing to do battle.

''Why, Florence, how dare you insult my nephew's wife that way! Not that being a maid isn't a noble profession, but the woman married to my nephew would scarcely be a menial! Are you suggesting such a thing?''

''Why, I—''

''Now, Florence, why don't you lie down for a while. You look a little peaked. You always do before dinner, don't you, dear?''

The other guests hid their expressions. Everyone knew Florence's reputation for drinking, but had never seen her so openly drunk. Florence clung to the doorway for support, then stared at Katie in confusion.

''I know it's her! I know it! She was here, up until I saw you.'' The facts seemed connected to Florence, but after three brandies, they were much less clear. ''Katie O'Connor. That's her name!''

The guests looked at each other, then chuckled quietly in open amusement. Christopher laughed along with them, then turned to Katie with an affectionate smile.

''Isn't that funny—that's my pet name for her. Kate, you haven't been scrubbing floors while I'm away, have you?''

Everyone openly laughed while Margaret turned away, defeated. Florence stared at the laughing guests, the color rising to her cheeks. Even in her inebriated state, she knew she had done something foolish. Eunice went to the doorway and gestured to a servant, indicating Florence. "I think Mrs. Eldridge might use a rest and a cup of tea. Would you mind taking care of her?"

More confused than ever, Florence accepted the servant's assistance. "Yes, I think a cup of tea would be nice. Especially with some brandy. Medicinal purposes, you know." She gazed one more time into the dining room, then back at Eunice. "Remarkable resemblance. Looks just like her! Please accept my apologies, Mrs. Scott."

"I'm sure." Eunice smiled as Florence left the room, still shaking her head. Returning to the table, she smiled discreetly at Katie, then accepted a glass of wine and laughed with the guests at the impossibility of Florence's claim.

"Too damned much drinking for a woman," Winston said sternly, then drank deeply of his own cup. "Now, what was I saying regarding the advisability of railroad bonds?"

The conversation resumed, and Katie gave a sigh of relief. Christopher alone noticed and squeezed her hand reassuringly under the table. No one noticed or cared that Margaret was silent, her plan to embarrass Katie backfiring.

Bertrice grinned reassuringly and Katie smiled back. Margaret had tried and failed, and for the time being, her secret was safe. But the incident cast a pall over the evening. The meal didn't taste quite so good, nor did the conversation seem so brilliant. Katie began wishing it would end long before it was time.

"Gentlemen!" Mr. Eldridge clapped his hands as the servant passed around coffee and dessert. "There is brandy in the sitting room and my cigar box. I know you ladies find both of them offensive, and rightfully so.'' He waved the air with a smile. ''So if you don't mind, we'll retire.''

''No, not at all,'' Nellie said cheerfully. ''I can't stand cigar smoke! It makes me . . . unwell,'' she added delicately.

Katie nodded at Christopher, but her tension mounted. This was the signal for the game to begin. Christopher had told her all about it on the way to the party. While the women and few remaining men sang songs and demonstrated their talent on the pianoforte, the gentlemen indulged in brandy, cigars, and poker. It was a closed game, and only the specified guests were invited to indulge. She watched as the men disappeared into the adjoining sitting room while Emily rose and indicated the parlor.

''We'll let them have their fun. Nellie, I hope you were going to play tonight. And Margaret, I believe you were going to recite? I'm sure we're looking forward to both treats. And Fan, you must promise us a song.''

''Kate,'' Eunice said with a grin. ''Christopher calls her Kate.''

''That's right.'' Emily took her arm and led Katie toward the parlor. ''We'll all have to call her Kate from now on. It's just too funny.''

Katie smiled and accompanied her to the parlor. She gave Christopher a concerned look, but he was already entering the sitting room. Everything Irish in her was filled with dread.

But there wasn't a thing she could do.

He guessed they were right about needing the money. As Christopher lost his third hand, he was forcibly reminded of what Jack had told him so long ago, about successful gamblers not needing their winnings. It seemed nothing was going his way. If he was conservative, he won and couldn't benefit. If he was impulsive, he lost grandly.

And he lost.

When his chips began to dwindle seriously, Charles offered a loan, but Winston slapped his son meaningfully on the shoulder. Christopher declined. The last thing he needed was to owe more debts to the Peppers. Drinking deeply of his whiskey, he realized that he should have gotten out of the game a long time ago, when he first started to lose. But dammit! He kept hoping that somehow the streak would end.

He didn't want to come home broke. He didn't want to admit another defeat to Katie and his aunt. Somehow he had to find a way to win, no matter what.

"Card?" Charles Eldridge asked.

He should stop now, he should decline, finish out the hand, and leave while he still could. In that moment he condemned himself. Nodding, he tossed in another chip, then accepted the card.

"Sure." He grinned and leaned back in his chair as if everything was fine.

Christopher Scott was never known as a quitter. And he wasn't about to start now.

"I am so sorry about what happened. I'm sure Florence will feel terrible tomorrow. She always does."

Katie smiled in response to Emily, then glanced around the parlor. Inside, it was bright and cheerful. The servants had arranged sherry and cakes, and the ladies indulged, some of them grateful for the respite from their mates.

But Katie could only worry. As she sipped her coffee and listened to the music, she wondered what was happening in the next room. Women were forbidden to enter; that was a rule that she didn't dare break under normal circumstances. But this wasn't normal, she reminded herself. Christopher was gambling with their lives and she had a feeling that something was wrong.

"I need some air." Katie rose, speaking softly to Emily, who instantly looked alarmed.

"Are you laced too tightly? Would you like to lie down? That dinner was a little heavy, perhaps that was the cause?"

"I'll be fine," Katie said softly. "I just need a turn in your lovely garden, if you don't mind."

"Not at all." Emily signaled for the servant to bring Katie's shawl. "Would you like me to accompany you?"

"No, please. Stay and hear the music. I apologize for not being able to sing, but I just need a walk. I'll be fine."

It took a little persuading, but when Emily realized that Katie was serious, she nodded and resumed her seat. Katie slipped out into the garden, then walked slowly around the house.

The parlor faced east, the sitting room west. Katie circled around the back of the huge mansion, hearing the bustle of servants inside. As she approached the sitting room, foggy with smoke, she could see the outline of a servants' door, just beyond the main wing of the house.

Katie entered the room and glanced about as if surprised to find herself in the middle of a card game. Charles looked up at her in confusion while Winston gave her a stern glare.

"Mrs. Scott! What a surprise!"

Katie looked abashed, then glanced apologetically at her husband. "Christopher, I'm so sorry. I must have come in the wrong entrance. I wasn't feeling well . . . I think I must sit down. Does anyone mind?"

"Not at all." Charles hastened to relinquish his seat while Christopher came to her side.

"Kate! Are you all right?"

"I'm not sure." She accepted a glass of water, then smiled weakly at the men. "It's just all the excitement, I suppose. Christopher, will you help me back?"

"Sure." He led her from the room, closing the door

behind him. As soon as they got a few feet away, Katie stood up and turned to him, her pallor gone.

"Is it going all right? I was so worried!"

"Katie!" Christopher said sternly, aware that he'd been taken in. "Do you mean to tell me that was all an act?"

"Charles has a full house, and Winston has three aces. Do you have anything?"

Christopher paled. "Are you sure?"

Katie nodded. "I saw them. My father gambled, I know what I'm talking about." She glanced at him questioningly. "It isn't going well, is it?"

Christopher shook his head. "No, but I just need to catch up."

"What if you don't?" Katie asked quietly. "Nothing is worth it, you know that."

He didn't respond. Turning angrily, he stopped and faced her abruptly. "I'm going back inside. I will see you when I'm ready to go. You can't come in here again—you understand that, don't you?"

Katie nodded, tears in her eyes. There was nothing she could do to stop him. He was a grown man and had to make his own decisions. And she knew he was furious with her for barging into the game and embarrassing him. She saw him reenter the room and close the door.

Technically, if he used the information she gave him, he was cheating. Katie knew that and wondered what he would decide. He needed this win—no one knew that better than she. Still . . .

She started to go back to the parlor, wiping her eyes with her hands, when the door reopened. Christopher came out and called the servants for his coat. Katie looked at him, but it wasn't until he said their good-byes and called for the carriage that he turned to her and gave her a wry smile.

"I quit the game. I couldn't stay in. It wouldn't have been . . . gentlemanly."

Katie grinned, then hugged him exuberantly. "I'm so proud of you—you did the right thing."

"Don't remind me. Ever," Christopher said, but Katie could tell that he was trying very hard not to be pleased. "When I think of all that money . . ."

"Don't think of it," Katie said cheerfully. "After all, I'm getting used to being poor again."

❋ TWENTY

"*I*'m sorry, Patrick. I never meant for this to happen." Samuel Riegan twisted his battered felt hat between his hands and stared at the old Irishman, his own face a study in compassion. Samuel's German accent grew heavier as he spoke, betraying his emotion. "I try to hold off as long as I could. But I got bills to pay." He indicated the house. "I can no longer wait."

"I understand." Patrick sighed, lifting his gnarled hand in resignation. "How long do we have?"

"There is a family who will rent the house and they want to move right in. They already give me money." Samuel displayed a few greenbacks. "I will take care of them. You take your time. You have family."

"I know." Patrick stared at the row house that had been home for so many years. It was odd, but he had thought he would escape this landlordism here, in the new country. But it appeared that for the O'Connors, the streets of America were not paved with gold.

Actually they had been making it until John Sweeney began his demands. True to Patrick's premonition, the fifty dollars was only the beginning of his blackmail. He'd shown up several times since then, asking for a few bills here and there, money that they just couldn't spare. John

Sweeney was convinced that Katie "rolled in it," and refused to listen to reason. Patrick couldn't convince him that the man Katie married was broke, and John Sweeney's threats grew worse.

And eventually it caught up to them. Patrick had managed to hide the worst of the situation from Moira and Sean, but in the last few days he knew it was hopeless. Katie had provided what she could, but even her resources were strained. There just didn't seem to be a way out, and today the inevitable struck.

"It'll just take me a day or two to get our things together. We don't have much, anyway."

"No, I know that," Samuel sighed, then dug deep into his pockets. "I don't have a lot, but take this. It may help you get a new start."

Patrick stared at the folded green bills. "Thank you, no. We'll find a way." He hadn't much left but his pride, and he'd be damned if he'd be reduced to charity. "We'll be gone by Sunday. Is that all right?"

"Fine." Samuel watched as Patrick turned and walked back into the house. The Irishman looked ten years older. Cursing, Samuel put on his hat and proceeded to the local tavern to drown his own pain.

Moira was waiting when Patrick reentered the house. Dressed as herself, the Miss Lillie garb discarded beside her like a glittering puddle, she saw the slump of his shoulders and the defeat on his face.

"Is it that bad, Paddy?"

He nodded, then sank down into the old sofa. "We only have two days to get out. I just don't have any more money, Moira. John Sweeney has drained us dry."

"Damn him to hell and back!" Moira said, her eyes flashing. "I knew from the first day I set eyes on that man . . . didn't I tell you I'd seen a raven that morning?

Ah, it boded ill, and now the devil has come home to roost.''

''Well, he's going to find the nest empty,'' Patrick said resolutely. ''I've given the matter a lot of thought. If we pack up and leave quietly, he won't be able to trace us. At least we can continue to protect the boy.''

Moira nodded. Paddy was so strong and safe; but then, he'd always been so. Somehow he'd take care of them. Gathering up her dress, she stood childlike and trusting before him.

''And where will we go?'' It was a question she dreaded asking.

Patrick sighed. ''We're going to live with Katie.'' At Moira's startled expression, he continued softly. ''We don't have any other choice.''

''My God, you make me happy.''

Katie snuggled in Christopher's arms, loving the way his naked body felt against hers. They were sequestered together like spoons in a drawer, her body curved into his, his leg over hers, holding her close.

They had just made love, and Katie felt that wonderful contentedness that follows sexual bliss. But something else was different, something she almost didn't dare hope. There had been a deepening in their relationship, an understanding that hadn't been there initially. It was something in the way he looked at her, the way he called her name when they made love, even the way he held her now. Yet he never said anything, never committed himself.

Just be happy, Katie. You've waited so long for this.

She could hear her father's ghost and she smiled, pulling Christopher's arm more closely about her. He stroked her hair, playing with the silky black length of it, then he traced the outline of her profile.

''Are you happy?'' he questioned softly.

''What do you think?'' Katie giggled, unable to resist the

urge to tease. "But I would be happier if you had won that card game."

"Don't remind me," Christopher groaned, and Katie laughed playfully.

"What will happen now that the notice will be published?" Katie dreaded the question, but she had to know.

Christopher grinned. "It just so happens that the publisher of the *Ledger* made a considerable amount of money last week from an investment that I advised he make. In return, he agreed not to print the notice. He just accidentally left out the Scott name."

"I am so proud of you." She turned to look at him, her eyes shining. "You are doing so well at your job. And I know what it took for you to walk away from that game."

She kissed him and he looked at her with that warm expression she was seeing a lot of lately. He grinned, smoothing the hair from her face, then spoke quietly.

"I'm glad we've reestablished you as Katie in the eyes of society. There have been too many lies between us. Maybe now we can really start to build something together. If only we could figure out the money part . . ."

He talked on for a few moments while Katie struggled within herself. She had to tell him the truth about her son, and now was the perfect opportunity. Even though he hadn't emotionally committed himself to her, she felt it was time. She had to trust that, and had to trust him. Taking a deep breath, she spoke softly, vowing to tell the truth and let the chips fall where they may.

"Christopher, there is something I have to tell you. It's about my past." Katie blushed, feeling the dreaded shame creep up inside of her.

Christopher saw her expression and smiled, gathering her up in his arms. "Your past doesn't matter. Mine neither. Katie, we have a fresh start, we can build our own life together however we want. I don't believe in dwelling on what has been.''

''You don't understand.'' Katie shook her head. Her stomach tightened as she tried to explain. ''There is something you need to know . . .''

''The only thing I need to know is this.'' Christopher leaned up and kissed her. Katie sighed, wrapping her arms around him as they tumbled into the sheets. He felt so good, so warm and comforting, that she forgot everything but holding him in her arms.

There was a quiet knock on the door, and it was a full minute before Katie, giggling, could disentangle herself. Brushing aside Christopher's teasing hands, she sat up in bed.

''Yes?''

''Kate, it's me. Eunice.'' The voice on the other side of the door sounded oddly strained. ''Do you mind . . . may I come in?''

''Just a minute.'' Katie reached for her robe, tossing Christopher an admonishing glance as he groaned and fell back into the covers. Tying the robe securely, she opened the door to his aunt.

''I'm so sorry.'' Eunice glanced from Katie to Christopher and looked mortified. ''I didn't mean to disturb you, but this is important.''

''Eunice, what's wrong?'' Instantly alarmed, Katie saw that Christopher's aunt looked pale and upset. Something had shaken her. ''Here, take a seat.''

''No. I have to go back downstairs. I think you should come In fact, you both should come with me.''

''Eunice, you're frightening me What is wrong?''

Eunice looked at Christopher, then at Katie, her expression guarded.

''We have visitors.'' She paused, then continued hurriedly, as if unable to think of a polite way to say this.

"Katie, your family is downstairs. The O'Connors. It appears that they have come to stay."

The silence that followed Eunice's statement was pregnant with emotion. Katie stared at her, her mouth open, then she shook her head.

"That can't be . . . it just can't!"

"Come and see for yourself." Eunice turned softly and glanced at her nephew. Her expression changed to concern, and she spoke quickly. "On second thought, maybe you should let Katie handle this—"

"No." Christopher rose and wrapped a sheet around himself. "Kate, I'll be right down. Whatever's the trouble, I'll help you."

He touched her comfortingly beneath her chin, then retreated to his own room for his clothes. Katie felt the pounding of dread as she descended the stairs. Surely it was some horrible joke, or Patrick needed something . . . there couldn't be something wrong with Sean. . . .

She raced down the steps, her mind leaping with a thousand possibilities. She heard Christopher behind her, and Eunice's whispered explanations. Coming into the parlor, she stood frozen as Patrick sat on a crate like a gnome, quietly smoking a pipe as if there were nothing odd about his appearance. Moira smiled, her lips quivering as she stared at Christopher, her Miss Lillie dress gathered softly around her. But it was Sean that everyone stared at. The little boy was busy examining every nook and cranny of the grand house, and when he heard voices, he turned and ran toward Katie exuberantly.

"Mama!" he cried.

Eunice slumped into a faint.

"Get her some water!" Patrick shouted to Moira, and immediately went to the older woman's side. Katie stood, in a torrent of confusion, her arms around her son, while Christopher and Patrick carried Eunice to the one remaining chair. Moira returned with a glass and helped the older woman sip the cool liquid.

"What . . . happened?"

It was Christopher who answered, and his expression changed from disbelief to anger.

"You fainted." Turning to Katie, he stood there looking at her, disillusionment in his eyes. She could see all the warmth disintegrate, replaced by a coldness that made her gasp with fear. Sean clung to her skirts, staring in wonder at the furious young man and his pale aunt.

"Christopher, please. I can explain—"

"There will be time for that later. Aunt Eunice, are you all right?"

"Yes, it was just the shock. Katie, I'm sorry, I just didn't know—"

"No, none of us did." Christopher glared at Katie, fury turning to rage. "It seems there is a lot we don't know, although that shouldn't be a surprise. May I ask one question. What the hell is going on here?"

Patrick came forth and extended a rough and callused hand. "I'm Patrick O'Connor, Katie's grandfather. This is her aunt Moira, and Sean you've met." Christopher returned the handshake, and Patrick continued, his voice calm: "I know this has come as a surprise to you, but we're in a bit of trouble and couldn't abide by the formalities."

"What kind of trouble?" Somehow Christopher managed to speak, but Katie could hear the hoarse emotion choking him.

"We were evicted." Patrick turned to Katie and nodded apologetically. "I couldn't pay the rent, so Mr. Riegan was forced to give notice. We need some help and a place to stay for a while."

Katie gasped, her hands pressed to her mouth in shock. "But I didn't—"

"I know," Patrick said reassuringly. "I didn't want to cause you any more worry. Lord knows, you've had enough of your own. But I can't continue as I've been. For a lot of reasons, I am forced to depend on your mercy. Mr. Scott, if you don't want us here, say so and we'll go."

Katie saw the fierce pride in her grandfather's eyes. Her own filled with tears and she turned her head, holding her son close, waiting for Christopher's verdict.

"You don't have to leave. I won't have Kate's family in the street," Christopher said quietly, and Moira fell to her knees.

"Bless you, sir! An angel, you are! I knew it from the moment I saw you!"

Patrick slumped, relief overtaking him, while Eunice stared about her, stricken with shock. Christopher turned to leave and Katie disengaged Sean from her robe, then ran after him.

"Christopher, you must listen to me—"

He turned, and she winced at the fury in his eyes.

"Katie, I don't want to hear anything you have to say. Not now or ever."

"But I tried to tell you."

"Liar!" He glared at her, then forcibly restrained his anger as the sound of voices reminded him that he could be overheard. "We will talk about this later. I can't right now. I have to go to work, and I need time to think."

"Please . . ." Katie tried to take his hand, but he withdrew it from her immediately.

"We will talk later. Now I just want you to leave me alone."

His eyes were distant, as if he was so hurt he couldn't bear the pain. He stared at her as if she was a stranger, then he turned as if he couldn't wait to get her out of his sight.

Katie crumbled against the steps, sobbing helplessly as he disappeared.

This time the lies had gone too far.

And both of them knew it.

"I'm so sorry, Kate. John Sweeney was blackmailing us, and I couldn't pay anymore. I was afraid he'd get to Sean." Patrick stood beside her in the garden, his hand heavy and comforting on her shoulder. "I had no idea that your husband didn't know about your son."

"It's all right." Katie leaned her cheek against his hand and wiped at her tears. "It's my fault—I really should have found a way to tell him. But it was so hard. And every time I thought of people's reactions, of the way they treated me when they found out, I got more scared."

"I know. It's a damnable world, lass. There are no two ways about that." Absently Patrick picked off a dead leaf from the boxwood shrubs, then glanced around the garden. "It needs work," he commented, indicating the overgrown flower beds and neglected lawn. "I could help him with this."

"I'm not sure how much of our assistance he'll take," Katie said slowly, the anguish in her voice. "Or if he'll forgive me at all."

"He will, Kate. Just give him time. I sense that he's a good man, for all that he is angry now."

"That's not it. You should have seen his face." Katie shuddered as her grandfather embraced her, and the tears flowed freely. "He looked at me as if he didn't know me! The worst part is, he was just starting to trust me. Now . . ."

"Now you must make him trust you again," Patrick said consolingly. "And there's only one way to do that. If you leave him now, he'll always believe you were nothing but a liar or worse. But if you stay, endure his anger, and see it through, he'll come to know you the way we do. And love you just as much.''

''Oh, Paddy.'' Katie hugged him back, overwhelmingly glad that he was with her once more.

''We have to make plans, however,'' Patrick continued, embarrassed by her reaction. ''He may not want us to stay. You need some money help—I can provide an income. And there's Sean to think about. John Sweeney will find us again, sooner or later. We have to find a way to deal with him.''

''The troubles never end, do they?'' Katie questioned softly. But her grandfather's words had made her dry her eyes. He was right—and she needed all of her resources to deal with the inevitable.

''No, they don't. At least, not for us.''

''May I come in?'' Charles Pepper knocked lightly on the office door, stunned to see Christopher seated behind his desk with a brandy bottle before him. It was late afternoon and most of the clients had gone, but it didn't take a genius to figure out that something was terribly wrong.

''Shut the door,'' Christopher said abruptly. Charles complied, and Christopher nodded. ''Good. The last thing I need is for your old man to see me like this. Charles, I really want to be alone.''

''I don't think that's a good idea.'' Charles took a seat, then indicated the bottle. ''May I?''

''Sure.'' Christopher pushed it over to him, then indicated the bookshelf. ''There are glasses in there.''

Charles retrieved a glass, then poured a drink, more alarmed by the moment. He sipped the brandy, waiting for his friend to speak, but the silence continued. Finally Charles began.

''Do you want to tell me what's wrong?''

"No." Christopher finished his glass and then refilled it. Charles saw the half-empty decanter and shuddered.

"Is everything here all right? Father says you are doing extremely well, so that couldn't be the cause."

"Your old man is correct." Christopher laughed sarcastically, then drank down the potent liquid. "In fact, I make more damned money for his clients than any of your other bankers. Doesn't that strike you as ironic, Charles? Tens of thousands of dollars cross my desk every day, and I can scarcely afford lunch."

Charles struggled, as if wanting to say something, then sighed in frustration. "But you are paying off your debts. At the rate you're going, Chris, you'll be solvent within a month. Then you can start clearing up the debt at home."

"And within another year, I can hold up my head again. But what do I do in the meantime? I have Aunt Eunice to take care of. And Katie." Christopher laughed bitterly. "My beautiful, deceitful wife."

"Chris!" Charles seemed shocked. "How can you say something like that? Why, Katie has stuck by you in a situation that would make most women run. And she is devoted to you—even Bertrice says that."

"Ha." Christopher poured another drink with the steady precision of the very drunk. He refilled Charles's glass, ignoring his protest, then lifted the glass eye level. Swirling the amber liquid, he spoke softly, almost to himself.

"Brandy is so deceiving, isn't it? The color of it is beautiful, like soft gold. And the smell of it . . ." He rolled the glass, then breathed deeply of the scent. "It's like the finest of perfumes. One would never think of the effect it can have on the unsuspecting."

Charles's brow knotted. "Chris, did something happen between you and Kate?"

"The man is a genius." Christopher bowed, ignoring the angry flush that came to Charles's face.

"Are you going to tell me what's wrong?"

"No," Christopher said softly. For a split second Charles glimpsed the pain in his face, but it was gone in a moment, replaced by the sarcastic scowl. His anger dissipating, he thought of Bertrice and how terrible he would feel if something happened between them. He rose and put a hand on his friend's shoulder.

"Come on, let me take you home before my old man sees you."

"I can't go back there." Christopher stared across the room at nothing. "You see, they've taken over my house. There's a leprechaun, an actress, and . . ." His face convulsed with pain.

Charles nodded, unable to understand a word. "All right, let's go to my club then. You can sleep there."

Christopher hesitated a moment, as if he hadn't heard him, then rose reluctantly to his feet. He turned to his friend, then spoke seriously.

"Charles, when this is all over, will you do one thing for me?"

"Certainly," Charles said earnestly.

"Good." Christopher took a deep breath, then indicated the brandy bottle. "Tell your father his liquor stinks."

Charles stared at him, then broke into laughter.

✳ TWENTY-ONE

*C*hristopher walked into his house and stared with aston-ishment. Patrick sat on a wooden box, a checkerboard between his knees, and a sodden old gentleman sat across from him, contemplating his next move. A gin jug sat beside them, and as each man took a turn at the game, a little of the liquor disappeared as well.

Aunt Eunice sat on the floor, playing with Sean and a tabby cat that appeared to be the newest addition to the household, while Katie energetically whisked dishes from the table and poured tea. Sean, basking in Eunice's attention, laughed merrily as the kitten chased light beams from the chandelier overhead, which was newly ablaze with gas. Everyone seemed to be having a good time, and Christopher leaned against the door, feeling like an outsider in his own home.

"Oh, there you are." Eunice handed Sean the cat and turned to her nephew. "Christopher, where have you been? It's been two days! We were worried."

"I can see that," Christopher said sarcastically. No one seemed concerned in the least. Patrick gave him a question-ing look, then returned to the game.

"Who the hell is that?" Christopher gestured to the other gentleman. "Not another O'Connor?"

"Why, no." Eunice laughed merrily, in a way he hadn't heard in weeks. "That's Tom Gallagher, Mr. Armstrong's groom from next door. He and Mr. O'Connor have become good friends. Do you want to hear the most hysterical thing? He actually shoots the game—Mr. Armstrong has been faking it for years."

"It's a known fact to his household." The groom belched, then took another swig of the gin. "The man couldn't shoot the side of a barn. I get the game for him and he takes the bows. It seems a fair exchange."

Christopher nodded, still bewildered. He glanced up at the lights, then recalled the newly trimmed hedges and flower beds outside. "And the gardens? Who—"

"Paddy," Katie volunteered quickly. "He is a gardener, you know. He cleaned up the yard and, with some of the money he made by doing Mr. Armstrong's hedges, got the gas turned on."

"I know one of the men who lays pipe," Patrick said modestly, as if reluctant to take full credit. "He said he'll let me make payments."

"Where is the milk?" Eunice glanced up from the icebox, then shared a wink with Sean. "I'll get the kitty a drink, but I can't find—"

"What about those?" Christopher pointed to the lace curtains that hung from the wall, and the pretty valances that covered them. "Where did they come from?"

"Moira," Katie said. "She is an excellent lacemaker. Eunice had some material, and Moira made the headings. She also did the dining room and the hall."

"Where is that milk?" Eunice continued.

Patrick jumped three of his companion's checkers, then guffawed as the groom slapped his knee in disgust. "Told you you weren't watching. Never play checkers with a man that drinks. That's what I always say."

"Well, give me another." Tom wiped his lips, then

turned to Eunice. "The actress has your milk. Says she's taking a bath in it."

"Moira?" Eunice looked to Kate.

"Oh, yes. When she's playing Miss Lillie, she likes to take milk baths. She'll be down directly."

Christopher leaned against the wall, staring at the chaos that was now home. It was as if everything had gone mad. Turning furiously to Katie, he indicated the garden.

"I want to talk to you. Now."

She nodded quickly, then removed her apron and followed him outside. He stopped beneath a huge oak that had already been denuded of leaves with the coming of winter. Fighting to catch his breath, he stared at her as if unable to decide what to do with her.

And she looked so damned beautiful. Just having not seen her for two days made him newly appreciate the glossy blackness of her hair, the clear blue of her eyes, which now stared at him, full of fear, and the slender curves of her body. Her lip quivered and he was newly angry. How could she stand there, looking so innocent, when . . .

He'd done nothing but think about it, about her with another man. He knew it was foolish, but he couldn't help comparing that image with the one of their lovemaking. Had she made the same sounds, assumed the same expressions as she did with him? What did any of this mean to her?

And to hide a child from him! It wasn't so much that she had a baby out of wedlock. Christopher was enough of a sophisticate to understand that these things happened. But that she'd never told him, that she'd hidden all of this from him . . . it was that which he couldn't forgive or forget.

He didn't want to think about it, or about her. In those two days he had made a decision. In some small part of his mind, he hoped that she would fight him on this, but the stubborn part of him, the hurt part, insisted that he say it anyway.

"Katie." She continued to stare at him like a little girl, trusting and yet afraid. *Damn her!* "Katie, I have come to a decision. I can't adjust to this. You have a son which you've told me nothing about, I have a house full of your family . . . my God, what are you doing to my life?"

"But—"

"No. No more explanations. No more assurances. This time I'm taking control. It won't work—it hasn't from the beginning. Kate, I think it's best if we separate for a while."

Her eyes filled with tears and she looked quickly away, hiding her expression in the shadows. "Is it just because of Sean?" she asked quietly.

"No." Christopher found himself choking. "No, it's everything. Katie, I can't believe in you anymore. This isn't a little thing you kept from me. How can I trust you ever again?"

"But I tried to tell you! I did—"

"Maybe you did. But Kate, if you really wanted to tell me the truth, you would have. I know you don't have money, nor does your family. I'm not proposing to throw any of you into the street. I'm going to stay at the club temporarily. In the meantime I think it wise if we both start to see other people."

"What?" Katie's head snapped up and she stared at him, incredulous. "Do you mean . . . courting?"

"Yes." Christopher regretted the words as soon as they left his mouth. The pain on her face was open and raw, but then it was gone in a moment. Determinedly he went on. "Look, Kate, what I'm saying makes sense. Every gambler knows when to throw in his hand. We married for money and we both lost. I think we have no choice but to go back to our original scheme."

Katie looked down at the ground. "I see. And what do you have in mind?"

"I suggest we give a party. You know, a housewarming.

Somehow I'll have to find a way to buy some secondhand furniture. We can meet prospective people there."

"And what of society?" Katie asked softly. "Won't people wonder?"

"By the time word gets out, we'll have this marriage annulled. But I don't have the luxury of time, and neither do you. We'll just have to make the best of it."

"I see."

"Dammit, Kate! Can't you say anything other than that?"

She stared up at him, looking absolutely stunning in the moonlight. Christopher waited for her to contradict him, to cry in outrage at his suggestion, but she didn't seem in the least disturbed. There was nothing in her manner or expression that gave him any reason to hope that they could work out their problems. Instead she simply nodded.

"If that's what you want. I know many society women now—I could help you find someone else."

"And I you," Christopher said, more furious than ever. "I'm glad we were able to come to such a reasonable decision. I'll get my things and meet with you later in the week to make the arrangements. Is there anything else?"

Katie shook her head. Christopher turned and strode into the house, slamming the door behind him. This wasn't turning out the way he'd expected.

And this time he had no one to blame but himself.

Nothing had ever hurt as much as this.

Crumbling in the garden, Katie sobbed endlessly, unable to stem the flood of tears that welled up as soon as Christopher stormed away.

How could he do this? How could he suggest such a thing? Pain enveloped her as she pictured Christopher with another woman, laughing as he did with her, sharing secret jokes and charming presents, then holding her in his arms and making her cry out in ecstasy. She had to close her eyes, the image was so agonizing.

Didn't their relationship mean anything to him? Katie could have sworn that it did, that he was beginning to care for her. But what did she know? My God, it wouldn't have been the first time she made such a mistake. Tears flowed more freely now and she hugged herself beneath the oak tree, wishing there was some way she could change things.

It wasn't meant to last. Happiness never was for her.

"Mama?" a small voice called out. Katie quickly wiped her eyes with the sleeve of her dress and tried to appear normal.

"What is it, Sean?"

"Mama, what's the matter?" Her little boy took one look at Katie's tear-streaked face and ran into her arms. "Did something hurt you?"

"No, it's nothing for you to worry about." Katie hugged him fiercely. It seemed as if it was just the two of them again. His small body pressed comfortingly against her and she was reminded of how desperately she loved him.

No matter what, she'd never regretted him. In spite of the hardship, the names, the difficulty in finding work, and the struggle to survive, he'd always been an addition to her life. She knew that was hard for people to understand, but truthfully she found them hard to comprehend. How could anyone look at this child and not love him?

His presence helped her with the pain, as it always did. She ruffled his hair and managed to smile back at his grin. Somehow she'd find a way to protect him, even if she had to do it alone. . . .

"Sean? Get yourself into that house! 'Tis chilly out here," Moira called from the doorway, then emerged when she saw Kate. "Go on, get inside."

Sean looked from his aunt to his mother. Katie nodded, then Sean ran into the house while Moira remained.

"What's the matter, girl?" Moira soothed Katie gently, her perfume clinging to her in the evening air. "Is he very angry?"

Katie nodded. "He's more than angry. Moira, he wants to give up on our marriage. He even wants to start seeing other people and wants me to do the same."

"What?" Moira stared at her as if she were addled.

"That's what he said. He wants to have a party so that we can both meet suitors . . . oh, Moira, how can he even think of such a thing?"

"Men," Moira said in disgust, wrapping her glittering shawl more closely about her. "At the first sign of trouble, all they can think about are greener pastures. Don't cry, lass. They just don't think the same way we do, nor love the same way." She peered at her niece with an oddly wise stare in spite of the ridiculous outfit she wore. "Did you tell him how you feel?"

"No." Katie faced her defiantly. "I won't. I should have told him about Sean—I was wrong for keeping that from him. But I won't apologize for him! I love my son, and he is a wonderful little boy. If Christopher can't see that, then he's not the man I thought he was."

"There, there," Moira said consolingly. "Ye have pride, lass. I'm glad to see that, for in the end that's all that matters. Yet you can't sleep with your pride. Now don't look at me like that," Moira scolded. "You know what I say is right. When is this affair?"

Katie shrugged. "Sometime within the next week or so, I imagine."

"Good." Moira nodded. "Don't you worry. I think he's angry now, and rightfully so. But sometimes the best thing to do with a man is to give him enough rope to hang himself. Let him have his way and let him find someone else. She won't compare with you, Katie. Perhaps he'll see that for himself."

*   *   *

She followed Moira back into the house. Sean played with Eunice on the floor while the kitten marched amid a tangle of yarn, Patrick and Tom were still arguing over the checkers, and Moira took a seat at the piano. Everything seemed so normal and yet . . .

She heard the door slam as Christopher left. He wouldn't be home tonight. Her bed would be empty, and as Moira said, she couldn't sleep with her pride.

She had to stop this, she had to do something positive. Instinctively she knew that if she confronted Christopher now, when he was still so angry, she would only push him away from her. She had to change his mind, had to make him see what he was doing. And she had to make him want her back, and accept her child.

It was a formidable task and Katie knew it. But the thought that had occurred to her when she talked to Moira kept coming back to her, nagging at her as if it contained an answer. . . .

Christopher wanted to meet someone else, someone without a past, without a flaw, who had nothing to hide from him. Someone of the same societal stature, no doubt, and who would have an income that could solve his financial problems.

A slow smile came to her face. No, she couldn't. It would be too . . . impolite. But the alternative, living without Christopher, was much worse. Katie bit her lower lip, wondering if she had the courage.

Christopher wanted to meet someone else, someone who had all of his qualifications.

And Katie thought she knew just the girl.

"La la la la la," Gertrude bellowed, her voice loud and without the slightest interest in tone or beat. Katie winced, then stopped the music.

"Let's try again," she said patiently, aware of Gertrude's sigh of disgust. "I'll play the notes, like this, and you try to sing them the same way."

Katie lightly struck the keys of the beautiful grand piano and the air was filled with the lilting song. "Now you try," she said encouragingly.

Gertrude frowned, her unattractive face looking even rounder and fuller. It wasn't that she was downright ugly; it was just that she went out of her way to neglect herself, making her plain features seem worse. Her hair, a coarse brown, was pulled into a simple braid that made her face look moon-shaped, while her thin lips and hearty complexion drew unwarranted attention. She was burned from too much sun, and her aunt had spent the last few weeks using milk compresses and cucumbers, trying to minimize the unfashionable effect.

"La la la la la . . . This song is boring," Gertrude said, flopping down on the sofa and reaching for a tin of bonbons. "Can't we go outside and feed the ducks?"

"When we're done," Katie said, trying to maintain her patience. "You know your aunt wants you to learn music. And you've made so much progress." Instantly Katie wondered if God had heard that lie, and wished that He hadn't. "Let's just give it another chance."

Gertrude groaned, then clapped gleefully as her aunt Isabelle entered the room, carrying a lunch tray.

"You two have been working so hard, I thought you could use a break. Thank you so much, Kate. Gertrude sounds lovelier every day."

Gertrude beamed, then without the benefit of a napkin or silver, devoured the lunch with her hands. Katie swallowed hard as the young girl picked up a chicken leg and gnawed on it like a dog with a bone, then tossed it casually onto the plate and reached for another.

Isabelle forced a smile and spoke softly. "You know,

Gertrude is from the country. She hasn't been exposed much to life in the city, nor to society people. I've been trying to teach her the social graces, but without much success.''

Katie nodded. Gertrude's eating habits were the talk of the town. She had to turn her head when the young girl gulped three helpings of potato salad, then drank a full glass of milk to wash it down.

''That's why I'm so grateful to you for the lessons, and so pleased that you will accept some remuneration. I couldn't possibly have a real tutor like the maestro; he just wouldn't understand.''

''No, I can see that.'' Katie suppressed a giggle as Gertrude wiped her hands on her dress and then reached for a slice of chocolate cake. Smearing it liberally over her face, she devoured the cake, smacking her lips as the last crumb disappeared. Katie was fascinated. Then, finishing it all up with more milk, the girl belched loudly and contentedly.

Isabelle forced a smile. ''Now, Gertrude, I've told you that isn't polite. Young ladies don't . . . belch in public.''

''Then what do they do?'' Gertrude asked, looking puzzled.

''They eat slowly, and sensibly. When one is wearing stays, one cannot gulp down food. One must take little bites. Men like women who eat like birds. It makes them seem . . . delicate.''

''Rubbish,'' Gertrude said, belching again. ''It's a good thing I don't wear stays then. Contraptions, that's what I call them. Keeps a body from enjoying good food.'' Getting to her feet, the young girl yawned. ''I'm ready for a nap now. Good-bye, Kate.''

Gertrude bounced from the room while Isabelle sighed. ''She really doesn't want to fit in here. Her mother was hoping that she would meet a nice young man, but I'm afraid none of them will look at her.''

"She's not unattractive," Katie said thoughtfully. "If you dressed her hair, and she wore a pretty gown—"

"That's just it," Isabelle said softly. "Gertrude has her heart set on a young farmer who lives out in the country. Dorothy, my sister, married quite well, a country gentleman. They have so much money, but that isn't enough. She wants better for Gertrude and is trying to impose a life that doesn't suit the girl. I know eventually Gertrude will return to the farm and everyone will be happy. But until then . . ." Isabelle looked helplessly at Kate. "It's like trying to make a silk purse . . ."

Katie smiled. "Isabelle, we are having a housewarming party this week. Why don't you let Gertrude attend? I can watch out for her and see that she meets people."

Isabelle smiled gratefully. "That would be wonderful. At least Dorothy would know that I tried. But if you are certain you don't mind . . ." She looked doubtful. "She can be embarrassing, you know."

"Don't worry." Katie grinned. "For what I have in mind, her manners are absolutely perfect."

❋ TWENTY-TWO

A sleek black carriage pulled up to the doorway of the Main Line mansion, and an elderly woman stepped out, her face shrouded against the chill with a veil. Pausing for a moment, Ella Pemberton surveyed the immaculate lawns, the manicured hedges, and the neat shrubs of the great house. She walked slowly to the door and rang for the servant.

Eunice Scott opened the door herself and stared in surprise at their guest. "Ella! I didn't know you were back! Come in!"

"I just returned," Ella said, then entered the house and stared with astonishment at the lack of furniture and the addition of the O'Connors. The four of them comfortably took up the living room, and Eunice glanced back, understanding her confusion. "What in the world . . ."

"A lot has happened recently," Eunice continued. "Our finances, unfortunately, haven't fully recovered. But we are confident that they will. And this is . . . well, I'll let Fan explain." Eunice looked helplessly at Katie, suddenly remembering that Ella still thought of her as her niece.

Katie rose from the floor where she sat with Sean and ran to envelop Ella in a fierce embrace. "I'm so glad you're back!'' she whispered, and she started to see tears on the old woman's face.

''I've missed you, too.'' Unaccustomed to displaying emotion, the older woman sniffled, then wiped quickly at her webbed cheeks. ''Look at us, two blubbering fools! Do you think we might have a cup of tea and spend some time talking? Alone?''

''Of course.'' Katie smiled, then returned to the kitchen to boil the water. Ella gingerly removed her shawl, then followed, watching her with a puzzled expression.

''You do not have servants yet?''

Katie shook her head. ''No. We used the money you sent for the most pressing bills, but the debts were in dreadful shape. Everything is really wonderful, though,'' Katie reassured her. ''I'm making a little money singing, and Christopher is doing so well at investment banking. We just need time.''

''I see.'' Ella's sharp eyes took in the quiver of Kate's lip when she mentioned Christopher's name. There was a wistfulness in her voice, and Ella could have sworn she seemed about to cry. Accepting the tea, Ella stirred the liquid thoughtfully and waited for Katie to join her.

''Fan, what's wrong?'' Ella placed a parchmentlike hand over Kate's. ''Now, don't try to tell me that everything is fine. I can see that it isn't. Where is Christopher?''

Katie stared at the tea, then suddenly raised her head, tears starting in her eyes. ''I don't know,'' she whispered, then broke into sobs.

''There, there.'' Ella patted her hand comfortingly. ''Tell me all about it. I knew something was amiss. As soon as I got here, I had to come see you. I sensed that you needed me.''

Katie choked back tears. ''Oh, Ella, everything is as bad as can be. No one will take me seriously as an instructor, and I've only managed to convince one woman to really pay me. Christopher is doing well, but Winston Pepper is taking most of his salary to pay off his loans. As it is, we've scarcely two pennies to rub together.''

"Winston Pepper—that old fool! Why didn't you tell me this?'' Ella demanded. "Fan, I would have helped you! You know that! I only forwarded part of your dowry because of the problems between you and Christopher! He has come to his senses, hasn't he?''

Katie remained silent for a moment, then spoke softly. "Aunt Ella, I have to tell you something. You are going to be shocked—you may even hate me forever and never want to speak to me again. If that is the truth, then I understand, but I've learned that lies only destroy all trust and I can't keep this from you.''

"I would never hate you, no matter what.'' Ella's hand tightened and the older woman made Katie look at her. "Fan, when you were a child, I never listened to the rantings of our family about you. You've made some powerful enemies; I'm sure you know that. But from the time you were a little girl, I've always felt you and I had a kinship that could never be broken. Tell me the truth, dear, and I promise to forgive you.''

Katie sighed, then looked at the sweet old woman, her blue eyes brimming with pain. "Ella, I have a child. A son. And . . . I'm not married to his father.''

"The little boy I saw you playing with?'' Ella asked softly, and Katie nodded.

"Yes, that's Sean. I'm sorry, Ella. I know how disappointed you must be.''

"Don't say another word.'' Ella turned toward the parlor. "Eunice, bring in that young man so I can meet him.''

Katie stared at the woman across from her, wondering if she could possibly have heard correctly. Eunice brought Sean to the makeshift table, allowing Katie to perform the introductions.

"Sean, this is Ella Pemberton. Ella, Sean."

"How do you do, young man?" Ella extended a hand, and Sean took it, confusion on his small freckled face. "You don't know me, but you are about to. You see, I love your mother very much. I always took care of her, and I will always take care of you."

Katie felt her throat tighten, particularly as her son gazed up at the elegant woman in wonder. "You will?" Sean asked, incredulous. "Why?"

Ella smiled, then ruffled his blond hair. "Because your mother is very special to me. She gave me back my life, Sean, and though I know you don't understand that, someday you will. She is a very special person, Sean. Don't ever let anyone tell you differently."

"I won't." Sean grinned, then fished into his pocket. "Do you want to see my frog? Paddy says I'll get warts, but I don't think so."

"I don't think so, either." Ella extended her hand and solemnly inspected the creature. "He's a very nice one." She handed the reptile back to the boy. "But I know where you can catch frogs that will make him look like a tadpole. There's a creek behind my house, and my gardener will be more than happy to show you. Would you like that?"

"Mama, can I?" Sean asked, his eyes round with excitement.

Katie nodded, trying to repress a smile. "Yes, you can. I'd like to finish talking with Ella now. Why don't you help Eunice with the dishes?"

Sean sped away, being careful to replace his frog first. Ella smiled fondly, then turned to Kate. "He is a fine boy."

Katie hugged her, feeling safe and secure in her embrace. "Oh, Ella, thank you. I'm so grateful that you accept him."

"What are you talking about? He's a wonderful child. Is that the reason you and your husband are quarreling?"

"Yes," Katie admitted. "Christopher cannot trust me

now. I know I should have told him about Sean—I just couldn't. And when he found out—''

"He self-righteously took himself off," Ella finished.

Kate nodded. "The worst of it is that he wants an annulment. He also wants to start looking for someone new. We're having a party this Friday just for that purpose. I still can't believe it.''

"What nonsense is this?" For the first time ever, Katie saw Ella get really angry. "He can't be serious! Wait until I get hold of that boy. Doesn't that man understand what a vow is?''

"He wants to start over. I've tried to reason with him, but he's too angry.''

"We'll see about this." Ella rose to her feet, looking formidable in spite of her small stature. "Do you know where I can reach him?''

"At his offices during the day. I believe he's staying at his club. But Ella, I don't know if he'll see you—''

"He'll receive me," Ella said purposefully. Then she turned to Katie and wrapped her arms around her. "Now that I'm back, I want to see more of you. And I'm having some furnishings delivered here—I won't have you living like this! You are, after all, my niece!''

Katie sighed. It seemed she had to tell everything, much as she hated to break this woman's heart. But she couldn't let Ella learn the truth the way Christopher had. The woman might truly hate her now, but she had to be honest. Taking a deep breath, she took Ella's hand once more, her own trembling.

"Ella, I have to tell you something else. I'm not Fan Pemberton. I am Katie O'Connor. Those people are my family. I never was your niece.''

Ella smiled, then tears filled her eyes. "My dear, don't you think I know that?''

*   *   *

Christopher didn't want to return to the club. He sat behind his desk, staring at the endless paperwork, wishing that everything could be different. But he couldn't go home, couldn't walk through that door as if nothing was wrong, as if he hadn't been lied to and deceived, as if there wasn't a hoard of O'Connors where peace had once reigned.

The few times he had stopped by to get some personal things, he'd been deeply insulted. No one seemed to miss him. Eunice was delighted with her newfound family. He'd never realized how lonely her life had been until he saw her with the O'Connors. Patrick had taught her to drink gin and play checkers, and now she was becoming formidable competition to him and Tom. Moira and she were writing a three-act play, with the two women taking turns at the various parts. Katie, Eunice had always loved.

And then there was Sean.

Frowning, Christopher recalled his aunt's obvious affection for the boy. It was as if Sean were truly her grandson, for all the attention lavished on him. The facts surrounding his conception didn't bother Eunice in the least; apparently she had longed for the sound of children in the old house, and now she had that.

The O'Connors themselves didn't seem to notice or care that they were infringing on his territory. Patrick had done a marvelous job with the gardens and provided some needed income. As a result, some of the bills were actually getting paid. Moira didn't seem to have a firm grip on reality and merely blushed and fluttered whenever she saw him.

And Katie. Christopher's frown grew even deeper. Katie treated him with all of the coldness that one would treat a stranger. She was unfailingly polite, but that was all. And she didn't seem at all troubled by the thought of leaving him. She acceded to his every wish, but made no move to reconcile their differences.

So now they were going to have to go through with their

plans, and find other mates. Christopher could only surmise that he'd been right all along. Katie had married him for a name and, of course, the money. Now that she would have neither, she was already mentally apart from him, a situation that didn't seem to concern her in the slightest.

Damn her! Christopher flung his papers to the floor just as the door opened and an elderly woman stared back at him.

"Ella!" Rising to his feet, Christopher saw her looking at the papers scattered around him. "This is a surprise."

"So I see." Ella softly closed the door behind her and stooped down to help him gather up the files.

"There was a draft," Christopher explained feebly. The last thing he wanted to explain was his own confused emotions. "They blew off my desk."

"Ah." Ella glanced at the closed window, but did not comment. Taking a seat across from him, she gave him a weak smile. "It is good to see you again."

Christopher slowly sat down, becoming alarmed. Ella didn't look well—there were odd circles beneath her eyes and a gray pallor to her complexion. "Are you all right?" he asked, his own anger forgotten. "Would you like some tea or something?"

"No, thank you," Ella said. "I'm just tired. You know, that's the problem with being old. There are so many things I would do differently. I'm beginning to think it's a fool's joke the Good Lord plays on us. Why is it we become wise when it's too late to be of use?"

There was a wistful quality to her voice and Christopher grew more alarmed by the moment. "Ella, have you seen a physician? I would like my doctor to speak with you."

"Bah!" Ella waved her hand at the suggestion. "Yes, I have seen a doctor. And he has seen me." The older woman coughed delicately, then shrugged as if in answer to an unspoken question. "It's done, dear. One knows that. But

I'm not afraid. I've lived a good life. And there are times when I've been very happy."

"I'm glad." Christopher found his throat tightening with emotion. Good God, if anything happened to Ella . . . he cursed himself for thinking about Katie. When would his thoughts stop filling with her?

"But lately I've been very concerned," Ella continued softly. "Christopher, I've been to see Fan. She told me everything."

The silence hung between them like a dead weight. Christopher glanced out the window, then back to the older woman, his face suffused with anger.

"Before you speak, Christopher, please, hear me out. I understand how you must feel. It came as quite a surprise to me to hear about the boy. But can't you find it in your heart to understand and forgive her? The girl was young—she made a mistake."

"I know that." Christopher's voice was tight. "But she hid it from me. I can't forgive that, nor forget it."

"What choice did she have?" Ella leaned forward, her handkerchief knotted between gloved hands. "Christopher, put yourself in her place. This society is very unforgiving of a woman in trouble. God knows it happens enough and it's nothing to be ashamed of. It's only Mother Nature reminding us that we are human. But other people don't see it that way. Fan has learned to protect herself."

"That's not the point." Christopher glared at the older woman. "Kate, I mean Fan, has had good reason to hide the child, it's true. But she didn't have to hide it from me."

"Didn't she?" Ella smiled wisely. "Christopher, if she had come to you at the outset and told you the truth, would you have married her?"

He turned to the window once more, unable to respond, but his teeth tightened with outrage.

Ella nodded. "You see? Fan had to protect her secret or

risk losing you. Don't you understand, you thickheaded man? She loves you—she always has.''

Christopher looked at her in astonishment. ''You actually expect me to believe that?''

''Why else would she be so frightened to tell you, then?'' Ella prodded gently. ''If she didn't care for you, she wouldn't have been afraid.''

''Fan married me for money,'' Christopher said wearily. ''And, to a lesser extent, for my name.'' He gave Ella a penetrating look. ''If you only knew the deceit she was capable of . . .''

''I won't hear your accusations.'' Ella choked, then was seized with a coughing spell. His anger forgotten, Christopher got to his feet and poured her a glass of water. Holding the vessel beneath her lips, he helped her take a few sips. Slowly the coughing ceased, and Ella looked at him apologetically.

''Thank you. Being old is so inconvenient and undignified.'' She waited a few minutes to catch her breath, then continued softly: ''Then what you're saying is that Fan married you for the same reason you married her. Wealth.''

''No, that's not true.'' Christopher flushed, feeling like a schoolboy whose knuckles have just been slapped. ''I always cared for Fan.''

''You have an odd way of showing it. An annulment is not a laughing matter, as you know. This is a scandal that neither one of you can easily overcome. Society mistrusts an ill-conceived marriage in a man as much as a woman. And when the talk gets out concerning the details of your arrangement . . .'' Ella fixed him with a steady stare. ''Especially this nonsense I hear about a gathering. Do you really think to begin courting other women while you're still married? And you expect my niece to do the same?''

''Ella, with all due respect, this really isn't any of your business at this point. I know you love . . . Fan, but I have to do what I feel is the right thing. I've talked to her—she's in total agreement that we should look for other prospects. So the next time you lecture me on how much my wife cares, I suggest you remember that.''

"Fan . . . agreed?" Ella asked in disbelief.

Christopher nodded. "She offered no resistance to the idea.''

"I see.'' Ella rose to her feet and clung to the table for support. "Then I suppose I'm wasting my time. If what you say is true, Christopher, then money means more to you both than I thought. To say I'm disappointed doesn't adequately express my feelings. Thank you for the water and your time. I have a cab waiting; please, don't bother.''

Ella walked slowly from the room, her head held high. Christopher suddenly felt a strange premonition. He strode to the hall and glanced down the corridor, but Ella had already gone.

"May I bring you another whiskey, sir?"

Christopher glanced up in annoyance at the waiter who was standing solicitously nearby. He wanted to get drunk—not just tipsy, but dead drunk, roaring drunk, the kind of drunk where he could forget everything and everyone.

"Yes. In fact, make it two.'' Christopher replaced his glass on the tray, waiting for the cold heat of the liquor to warm him.

He was still smarting from Ella's lecture and he didn't have the faintest idea why. Ella was blinded by her affection for Kate; Christopher was well aware of that. Yet her words kept coming back to him like a chant.

She loves you, Christopher. She always has.

God, if he could just believe that. Christopher stared at the roaring fire in the elegant library, ignoring the curious glances of the men around him. If he really and truly thought that he meant something to Kate, something other than a safe haven, then he would reconsider. But he had absolutely no reason to think that he did. If anything, her actions indicated the exact opposite.

Unless . . . Christopher stared thoughtfully into the flames, an idea forming. If Katie really felt something for him, could she actually stand by and watch him court someone else? He remembered the Mitchells' reception, when he'd escorted Margaret Chester. Katie had been livid. Much as she tried to hide it, her jealousy had been transparent and had assured him that he wasn't mistaken about her feelings.

But could he really live up to his end of the bargain and find someone for her? The very thought of Katie in another man's arms was repulsive. He stood to lose everything by his own damned cleverness. What was it Ella had said? That wisdom was wasted on the old?

"Here you are, sir." The waiter appeared with the drink, then lingered for a moment. "You didn't have any supper tonight. Is everything all right?"

"It's fine." Christopher stirred the drink, then sipped deeply of the whiskey, dismissing the waiter. The liquor burned, but it did make him feel better.

There had to be a solution. Pensively Christopher sipped his drink, staring into the flames. When he felt a familiar tap on his shoulder, he started with annoyance as he recognized the man behind him.

"Theodore." Christopher was forced to acknowledge him.

The older man grinned and pulled up a chair, ready to settle in for a long chat. Inwardly Christopher groaned. The last thing he wanted to do was spend time talking with this perennial bachelor who wouldn't have the slightest idea of what it was like to love a woman. Theodore Worthington recited a long list of his ailments, obviously happy to have an audience.

"You know I still have that trick knee. I can't ride or do much exercise until the swelling goes down. I've been putting ice packs on it. You know, cold for hot and hot for cold. Then there is my gout. Damnable thing, my boy! They all have their reasons for it, those physicians that charge by the minute, but I swear it's the cooking here. The service is poorer by the day. For what we pay for this club, one would think . . ."

Christopher closed his eyes while Theodore rambled on. He was tempted to excuse himself, but he felt sorry for the older man. Theodore had lived alone most of his life and was the most particular human being he'd ever met. He was so set in his ways that even the slightest disturbance was enough to set him on edge. He was known as a tightwad, which, in his youth, discouraged most of the women from looking favorably on him. Even if he paid the slightest attention to a woman, which he never did, he was woefully unsuited for marriage, a fact that caused no end of concern to his family.

A terrible idea came to Christopher. No, he couldn't. Instantly dismissing the thought as unkind, he glanced up and saw the man accept another drink, then pat his rotund belly gratefully.

Christopher grinned. All was fair in love and war, and in this case, it was war. Here was one man Katie would be perfectly safe with. He could have his answers, yet at the same time protect his own interest. "You know, Ted, you're right. The food here is terrible. I really think you need to get out more. How would you like to attend a party?"

❊ TWENTY-THREE

Katie still couldn't believe this was happening. Perched on the window ledge of the great house, she watched as workmen carried in the new furnishings, provided by Ella. Moira and Eunice oohed and aahed over the luxurious sofas, the wing chairs, the lovely cherry tables, and the crystal and china. Everything would be perfect for the party, except . . .

She fought the tears that stung her throat. She had to go through with this; she didn't have any other choice. Still, in the deepest part of her mind, she was hoping that Christopher would come to her and say that he really didn't mean it, it was all some horrible misunderstanding.

"My, Katie! Look how beautiful these pieces are! What a wonderful woman is Mrs. Pemberton!"

Katie forced a smile as Moira exclaimed over a silver bureau. The older woman pulled out the flat drawers, filling them with the serving implements, then reverently replacing them.

Her family didn't know. At least she thought they didn't. Neither she nor Christopher was anxious to publicize the real reason for this party. And Moira was like a little girl, always in a dream world. It was enough for her that she was living in this grand house, filled with pretty things, and that they were giving a real party tomorrow night.

Sean was equally excited and talked of little else. Only Patrick frowned and gave her a questioning stare. It was no secret that she and Christopher had quarreled, and she could read the question in his eyes. Why, then, were they celebrating?

Hugging her knees, she wished she could just do away with the pain. She had somehow to find the strength to get through this night. Maybe she could make Christopher see what he meant to her. If she could only think of a way—

"Mrs. Scott?" One of the workmen paused and wiped his face with a cloth. "There's a rough-looking bloke outside asking for you. You want me to tell him to get lost?"

"No, I'll take care of it." Slipping from the seat, Katie brushed the dust from her skirt with a frown. Surely it must be one of the workmen who wanted her, ostensibly to ask a question regarding the placement of the furnishings. Yet . . .

A cold dread filled her heart when she saw him. He was standing across the street, his hands thrust arrogantly into his pockets, but she wouldn't mistake him anywhere. Her breath quickened as she recognized his blond hair, his boyish profile that even from a distance looked charming. Glancing fearfully back at the house, she saw that everyone was inside, the door closed. Crossing the street, she approached him, her legs weak and trembling.

"What do you want?" Katie's voice broke, betraying her fear.

John Sweeney laughed, though his tone held little mirth. "That's a fine greeting after all this time, Katie love." His eyes ran over her appreciatively. "You look good, Kate. But then you always did."

Fear touched her spine like a cold wet hand. She couldn't let him know she was afraid; he would use it, as he used so much against her before. Patrick had insisted that he'd be back. Surely he didn't mean to . . . Katie couldn't finish the thought. "I'm just surprised to see you," she responded cautiously. "It has been a while."

"Six years." John pulled a rolled cigarette from his pocket and put it between his lips. He looked older, Katie noticed with surprise when he bent down to strike a flint and the light illuminated his face. There were lines that she didn't remember. He smiled, as if reading her mind. "Six long years. They haven't been as good to me as they have been to you."

"No?" Katie smiled bitterly. "You ran out on me after I discovered I was with child. I loved you—you knew that and it didn't matter. It must have been a grand joke to you. Do you have any idea what you've done to my life? What these last years have been like?" Fiercely she wiped at the moisture that sprang to her eyes. "No one would give me a job. No one would befriend me. I was, after all, an unwed mother, a sinner, while you walked away without shame."

"Katie, Katie." John tried to reach for her, but she stepped far away from him. "I'm sorry. I couldn't accept the responsibility of a child. For God's sake, I could barely take care of myself! Surely you can understand that!"

Katie stared at him and felt a measure of disgust and pity. He left her and his child, and now he wanted forgiveness! If it hadn't been for her family, she would have starved, and Sean along with her. This man, this child, she amended silently, cared for nothing and no one but himself.

"John, I think you should go. If it's my forgiveness you'll be wanting, you have it. But I cannot forget. I've gone on with my life and I suggest you do the same. I have nothing more to say to you."

She started to leave when, to her surprise, he detained her. "Now, lass." There was a subtle threat in his voice and Katie felt the fear once more. "I would think you'd show a little more affection for your son's father. Where is the boy?''

The blood drained from her face, and for a moment Katie thought she would faint. "You have no right to him," she whispered, her nails digging into her palms as her fists knotted. "Stay away from him. And me. There's nothing for you here."

"No?" John Sweeney's smirk disappeared and he leaned closer. "I think there is. He is my son, for all that you'd like to forget that. I don't give a damn who you've married or what you're doing with yourself. But that boy is mine and I have rights as his father." His grin reappeared and his voice became like silk. "Or should I discuss all this with Mr. Scott?"

Fury filled her and Katie stared at this man with horror. How could she have ever thought she loved him? A blackguard, a thief, and a liar . . . it was all written on his charming face. How could she have been so blind?

"You wouldn't . . . do that," she whispered, her voice filled with fear.

John Sweeney grinned. "Not now, I wouldn't. You see, Katie dear, I think we can come to some agreement. You seem to have done quite well for yourself. Christopher Scott, no less, as a husband. You're living in style in this house . . . even the gown you have on is worth more than I'm paid in a week. I don't want to disrupt your life. I just want what's coming to me."

"You cad!" Katie stared at him in outrage. "You don't care about your son—you never did! You just think to use this, to blackmail me!"

"That is such an ugly word." John leaned against a tree, obviously not at all concerned by her accusations. "I prefer to think of it as an agreement. I agree to stay away from Sean. You can go on with your life, as the elegant Mrs. Scott. And I get rewarded for my cooperation."

"How could I have ever thought there was good in you . . . ?" Katie stared at him in disbelief. "My God, I must have been ten times a fool."

"That's enough." John's face reddened and he glared at her. "I don't think it's too much to ask. I'm being deprived of my son. You have so much—a little money here and there won't kill you."

"You are the reason my family was thrown into the street. You bled them dry, and now you think to do the same to me. It won't work, John Sweeney. I'll—"

"You'll what?" John grinned, more confident now. "Tell your husband? Where is the dear boy? I've been watching this house for days. Bring him on out so I can meet him."

Katie felt the walls close in. If John met with Christopher now, it would all be over. There was a limit to anyone's patience, and John Sweeney's presence would push her husband right over the edge. And Sean . . . tears filled her eyes as she thought of her son, and how hard they'd worked to see him raised right. John Sweeney would have nothing but a corrupting influence on him. At all costs, she would protect him.

"How much?" Katie whispered, pain filling her voice.

John smiled. "Just a few dollars here and there. I think a hundred is a good start."

One hundred dollars. He might as well have said a thousand. Realizing that there was no way she could hide her financial condition, Katie opened her eyes and looked directly at him.

"I don't have it," she said softly. "As you know, Christopher and I aren't . . . getting along right now. I can't go to him with such a request. He would want to know the reasons, and might even want a divorce."

"I wouldn't expect you to get the money right off," John Sweeney said. "But you're a clever girl—you always have been. I'll settle for a token now to give you time. But then I want my money.''

Katie nodded. ''Wait here.'' Returning to the house, she reappeared a few minutes later with a box wrapped up in her hands. ''Take this.'' Tears moistened her eyes as she gave him the box. ''It was a gift. Christopher gave it to me.''

John Sweeney opened the wrapping and saw the music box inside. ''This will do. I can hock it. But I want to see the real cash, love. Figure out a way to get it. Or else.''

Katie watched him disappear into the shrubbery. Despair filled her and she clung to the tree to keep from falling.

John Sweeney wouldn't stop with a hundred dollars. Even if she could find the money, he'd be back again. And again.

''Dear God,'' she whispered. ''Haven't I been punished enough?''

''Katie!'' Moira called from the doorway. ''Come inside, it's chilly out there. And we need your help with the tables.''

Katie nodded, then returned to the house with a heavy heart. Why was it that everything went wrong at the same time? She didn't think she could bear it, especially when she reentered the house and Sean enveloped her in a bear hug. Somehow she had to find the strength.

And an answer.

''. . . and it was beautiful then. The fields were green, every green the mind could conjure! From the pale sweet lime of the new leaves, to the kelly of the grasses, to the dark green black of the lakes and bogs. Ah, and the rivers are silver, glistening like veins on the sides of the mountains. And in the morning, when the mist rises, one can see the ghosts of kings and queens, long since buried beneath the sod.''

Eunice sat entranced as Paddy talked of Ireland. Katie,

who had heard the tales a hundred times, felt a calm reassurance to hear them again for the hundredth and one. Moira scowled from the sofa where she stitched a new lace cloth for the table.

"Bah, you old fool! I remember it not that way. It's an island, and the rains pour down, drowning a soul. There was nothing to eat, no theater . . . why, it's a damned good thing we came here."

"Is that right, woman?" Paddy rose from the fire and came to stand over her. "Is it contradicting me you are?"

"No, not at all." Moira batted her eyes shamelessly, then turned to Eunice. "I just recall it differently."

Katie laughed, looking up from the sink where she washed the plates and cups, and handed them to Sean to dry. It was just like home. If she closed her eyes, she could pretend she was little again, and the only difference would be that her father would walk through the door about now and put an end to their arguing.

It was almost as if she could forget the past, forget John Sweeney, forget the threat that hung over her head. Dear God, would it never end? Would there never be a time when she could be at peace?

And now tomorrow was the party. Katie couldn't even picture herself, laughing and entertaining guests, all the while Christopher sought out another woman. She suppressed a smile, thinking of Gertrude and Christopher's reaction when he met her. Somehow she would have to find a way to reach him before it was too late.

"Katie, would you get the door?" Patrick called, reluctant to leave his argument. Drying her hands on her apron, she went to the hall and opened the oak panel, her greeting dying on her lips.

"Christopher?"

"Kate." His eyes held hers for a moment, as if wanting to say something. Instead he glanced awkwardly around her, then indicated the clothes he carried. "Haven't the servants arrived?"

"No, not until tomorrow." He looked so good that she wanted to cry. Could he feel the same way as she? Maybe he, too, had thought about it and wanted to call off the party . . . Katie wished fervently, but her hopes were dashed with his next words.

"I thought I'd stay tonight to help for the housewarming. Aunt Eunice said most of the people intend to come." His face looked intense and he glanced at her with an odd expression. "By the way, I've invited someone for you to meet."

Her heart dropped into her shoes. Katie stared at him, crushed, aware of what he meant. "That was very kind," she replied, trying to keep the bitterness from her voice.

He nodded. "I always keep my word."

Katie watched as he strode past the living room, where everyone talked and laughed. Her eyes followed his and she saw his aunt and the O'Connors, settled in like a real family. Then his gaze fell on Sean. Katie waited, expecting him to say something else, but he turned, hoisting his clothes over his shoulder.

"I think I'll retire to my room. Good night, Kate."

She watched him go, wanting to stop him, but her feet felt like lead. There was only one thing that she could say to him that might make a difference, but she didn't think she had the nerve.

If she confessed what she felt for him, it might make him return.

Or, just as easily, could drive him away.

"Come in." Christopher put down the book he wasn't reading and glanced up as Katie stepped into his room. His chest felt tight when she moved closer to him and he could see the black silk hair that fell down her back and the soft blue nightgown she wore. She looked so lovely that for a moment his breath stopped and he could hear a pounding in his ears.

"Kate. What are you doing here?"

He didn't dare hope that her presence meant what it implied. My God, did she have any idea of what she was doing to him? Was this some new kind of torture?

She smiled uneasily and stood before him like a little girl, afraid to ask for a favor. "Christopher, can we talk? I mean, really talk?"

"I don't think that's a good idea." He had to look away from her, so intense were his emotions. "I've had a long and frustrating week. The last thing I feel like doing is engaging in some heavy conversation."

"Christopher, don't do this." Her voice was a plea and she looked at him with glistening eyes. "Don't shut me out like this."

"Kate, what else is there to say?" He put the book aside and stood up to pace the room. It was easier than looking at her. "I can't change the past and neither can you. You lied to me—it's that simple. I can forgive the Fan Pemberton masquerade, because I understand that. I can't forgive . . ." He couldn't finish the sentence.

Kate stared at him, her chest rising and falling with suppressed emotion. "How dare you!" she whispered softly, the vehemence in her voice astounding him. Before he could react, she hit him squarely in the chest with a not particularly ladylike hand. Stunned, he grabbed for her before she could take another shot.

"Kate, have you lost your mind?"

"How dare you!" Her eyes flashed, an even deeper blue than before. He held her wrists, but she no longer struggled, instead she glared at him, all hell in her expression. "All this time I was feeling bad, thinking that I had hurt you. Now I see it's nothing more than your damnable pride! You can't let me close to you again—it might mean admitting that I mean something to you, and that I haven't been punished enough! Damn you!''

''Kate, you listen—''

''No, this time you listen.'' She stood still, magnificent in her outrage. ''That little boy downstairs is innocent of this. He hasn't done anything wrong, nor have I done anything that you haven't. My God, how can you be so condescending? You lied to me about your financial condition, and I don't believe for a moment I was the only woman in your life! How can you, of all people, sit in judgment of me?''

Fury gripped him. His hands tightened on her wrists, but she continued to glare at him.

''You are all such hypocrites! Do you think I don't know that Charles Pepper has an illegitimate child, one that he doesn't acknowledge? The boy stays with a woman in Baltimore, who cares for him and sends him to school? Is that what I should have done?''

''Damn you, Kate! I don't make up the rules, I just live with them!''

''And condemn me by them!'' Katie wrenched herself free from his grip and stepped back, looking furious. ''Well, I'm not playing by your silly rules anymore. What there is between us means something. But if you're too stubborn to acknowledge that, then there is nothing I can say or do. Be happy, Christopher. I certainly intend to.''

With a swirl of her gown she turned from him and strode from the room. Smarting, Christopher wanted to go after her, to put her in her place, but something stopped him. He couldn't face her tonight, after everything she had said.

Especially when a small part of him feared that she was right.

❈ TWENTY-FOUR

"*C*ome down, Mr. Tip. Please come down."

Christopher awoke to a plaintive cry outside his window. Struggling into his robe, he tied the belt and glanced outside.

Winter was fast approaching. There were very few leaves remaining on the huge oak tree, and those that did rattled like paper in the cold wind. It was therefore easy to see the tabby cat, perched miserably on a branch, and the blond hair of the small boy beneath.

Sliding open the window, Christopher called to the boy. "Don't scare him. Keep talking to him while I climb down."

The boy glanced up, tears streaking his face, and he nodded quickly as Christopher stepped through the window and onto the rooftop.

His feet were freezing, but if he remembered correctly, it was easier to climb the oak without shoes than with them. The only time he'd ever fallen when he'd done this as a boy was when he'd been dressed for a dinner party and his good shoes slipped. Tucking the robes more securely about his waist, Christopher grabbed the closest branch and eased himself down.

Somehow this had been easier when he was six. Looking

at the ground, he winced, wondering at his own childhood bravery. It was at least a fifteen-foot drop, maybe more. The wind whipped through the naked branches, chilling him thoroughly, but he managed to find a secure grip and swung down to the next branch.

"Mr. Tip, you stay there. Be a good kitty," Sean called up to the kitten, his eyes wide as Christopher struggled from one branch to the next. "Don't fall, kitty. You'll be fine."

The kitten mewed loudly and pathetically while Christopher hugged the tree trunk. His foot, numb from the cold, slipped once, but he managed to grab a branch and pull himself to safety. Within a few minutes he was eye level with the cat and secure on his branch.

"Here you are." With one free hand, he lifted the kitten, ignoring the claws that swung frantically, then tucked the cat inside his robe. The little animal mewed, frightened by the motion, but Christopher petted him reassuringly, then, inch by inch, climbed down to the ground.

"You did it!" Sean stared at him as if he were a hero. Grinning, Christopher pulled the kitten from his pocket and handed the trembling animal to the boy.

"Here. And tell him to stay out of this tree. It's too high for these rescues."

The boy smiled gratefully, patting the cat and pressing his small face into the animal's fur. Christopher watched him, remembering himself at that age, when a kitten was the most important thing in the world. Turning, he started to walk back to the house, well aware of the chill temperature, when Sean's voice stopped him.

"Are you my father?"

He should have known this was coming, but it still caught him by surprise. Hugging himself against the wind, he turned to the small boy, who stared back at him. He looked so little, the kitten held against his small body as if for protection. He remembered Katie's words. *He alone is innocent of all this—*

"Why don't you come to my room for breakfast? We can eat together."

Sean's face lit up with a grin. "Do you mean it?" he asked, with the exuberance of youth.

Christopher nodded. "I always get too much food as it is. And we've got cakes this morning, for the party tonight."

Sean raced ahead of him toward the huge house. Christopher entered the backdoor and, ignoring the shocked glances of the new servants, ordered breakfast.

"And please have someone bring it to my room," he said. "I have a guest."

The servants nodded, keeping their opinion to themselves as the man of the manor retreated to his room, still clad only in a robe, and shoeless.

Sean was there before he entered. The little boy walked slowly around the bedroom, still holding the kitten, exploring everything with his eyes. Much of the original furnishings had been sold, but there was still the ebony bureau, the huge mirror, the tray holding tobacco and brandy, the jars of scented limewater, and the shaving mug. It was a masculine room and, to the little boy, obviously fascinating.

"Don't touch that," Christopher warned as Sean picked up a straight blade. He immediately put it back as Christopher laughed. "You could get cut. The blade is sharp."

"Paddy has one." Sean nodded. "He does this with his face." The boy imitated shaving, then slapped his cheeks.

Christopher nodded. "Pretty soon you'll be old enough to use one of those." He let the boy examine his things, answering his questions, until the servant brought the tray. Instantly, upon the arrival of food, all else was forgotten and Sean put down the cat and climbed onto the horsehair seat, gazing expectantly at the covered dishes.

"There. Eggs, bacon, toast, cakes, fruit . . ." Christo-

pher opened each dish, grinning as Sean licked his lips and
piled the food onto a plate. He waited until the boy had
enough before taking his own.

They ate in companionable silence. Christopher grinned
as Sean helped himself freely to more of everything, then
washed it all down with a huge glass of milk. It was
amazing that so much food could fit into such a small body,
but it did. Yet his manners were perfect. Christopher was
forced to reevaluate his thoughts regarding this boy, an Irish
illegitimate child. When the boy finally seemed full, Christopher spoke slowly.

"Sean, why would you think I'm your father?"

"You're married to my mama," Sean said matter-of-
factly. "I heard them talking when we got here. I thought
that meant you're my da."

Christopher felt a tightening in his chest and he took the
small boy's hand and spoke seriously. "No, I'm not your
father. Whoever he is, he is a very lucky man, because I
think you're a great boy."

"Do you know who he is?" Sean asked thoughtfully.

"No." Christopher shook his head. "You'd have to ask
your mother about that."

"She doesn't like to talk about it," Sean stated flatly.
"She talks about other things when I ask her." He stared at
Christopher, then shrugged. "Will you be leaving us soon,
too?"

Christopher's mouth dropped, but to himself he had to
admit it was a logical question. Sean obviously felt that
since his father had walked out, he was liable to do the
same. What made the situation worse was his relationship
with Kate at the moment. He honestly didn't know what
would happen, and didn't want to lie to the boy. Taking a
deep breath, he tried to explain.

"Sean, your mother and I . . . have some problems.
We're trying to work them out, but we don't know if we

can. There is nothing for you to worry about, though. Whatever happens, we'll both see that you're always taken care of.''

Sean looked at him with eyes that were far too intelligent and street smart for a boy his age. Nodding, he picked up the cat and slipped from the chair.

''I'm going downstairs now. Moira's baking some pies for the party. She said I could help.''

Christopher watched the boy go. Sean had understood exactly what he'd meant. And what he hadn't said.

She just had to get through this night.

Katie stood before the mirror, surveying the midnight-blue gown she wore and the glittering sapphire that hung from her throat. The jewel was borrowed from Ella Pemberton, and it seemed to bring Katie courage as she turned, seeing the brilliant fire from the gem.

She had to admit, she didn't look anything like the poor Irish woman she was, or even the lady's companion or maid that she'd been the last few months. Something had changed. By assuming Fan Pemberton's identity, she had grown into the part.

Inside, however, she was still Kate O'Connor, and she was terrified. Once more she had to reach down to that secret place where she kept her strength and draw from it again. God, it was getting harder and harder. Katie was afraid that one of these times the well would be dry.

She was also still furious with Christopher. She hadn't seen him since their conversation last night, but she hadn't forgotten their bitter words. If this was what he wanted, she would give it to him. It was almost like the reminder Paddy used to whisper: Be careful what you pray for, Katie, you may get it.

''You look grand, dear,'' Moira whispered approvingly, pausing to smooth one curl into place and to brush imaginary lint from her shoulder. "Like a duchess. That man of yours won't be able to take his eyes from you."

Katie turned and hugged the older woman. She had been forced to explain everything to Moira, even though she hadn't wanted to. But with the party imminent, she didn't have much of a choice. To her surprise Moira had been wonderfully sympathetic and supportive. "Oh, Moira, thank you. Thank you for everything. You've always been there for me, better than any mother."

"Nonsense," Moira said, but Katie could tell she was pleased. "As for that husband of yours, well, this is a damned sorry state of affairs if you ask me. What kind of man looks to introduce his wife to other men and expects her to provide him with amusement? Although, I was in a play once . . ." Moira frowned musingly.

"What happened?" Katie almost shook the answer from her.

"There was a man and a woman in it. Lovers, I believe. Anyway," Moira said quickly, blushing at her own description, "they came to a parting of the ways. Both of them agreed to see other people, but when each of them saw the other with a new mate . . ."

"Yes?"

"They killed each other." Moira sighed heavily. "It was out of jealousy, you know."

Katie's arms dropped and she stared heavenward. The last thing she needed was that kind of a prophesy. "I think I'll go downstairs. Have most of the guests arrived?"

"Yes." Moira nodded, her brow furrowed. "Run along, dear." When Katie left the room, Moira muttered to herself, "Was it a murder? Or was that the one where they confess their love and live happily ever after?"

For the life of her, she couldn't remember.

Downstairs, the Scott house was ablaze with light and merriment. As Katie descended the steps, her heart in her throat, she paused in amazement at the transformation of the house. The new furnishings looked splendid in the parlor, setting off Moira's drapes admirably and looking elegant in the crisp gaslight. The chandeliers glittered, the fireplace crackled. Servants dressed in good wool suits circled the room, pausing with fluted glasses of sparkling wine, while maids brought tempting trays of mushrooms and oysters to the guests.

And the company! Even from the steps Katie could see that everyone had come. Bertrice and Charles waved from across the room, the Misses Chandler sat like crows on the new horsehair couch, the Mitchell girls giggled with several handsome young men, while Aunt Eunice and Florence Eldridge talked quietly. The Pembertons took up one wall, looking anything but happy to be present, while the Scotts dutifully ignored them. Isabelle and Gertrude stood near the serving table, and Katie saw the young woman's aunt cringe every time her niece snatched a morsel from the maid.

One of the young ladies softly played the pianoforte, and Katie saw Patrick, dressed elegantly in a suit, greeting some of the guests. He smiled at Katie reassuringly and gave her a gesture that meant an Irish blessing.

It was all absolutely perfect. Everything looked wonderful, the guests were elegant and having a good time, the food looked marvelous. The only blight on it all was the real reason for the party. As if in answer to her thoughts, she froze, seeing Christopher for the first time.

He looked so handsome she thought she would melt. Dressed in a dark blue suit that coincidentally complemented her gown, he stood beside the fireplace, talking with an older, fidgety man that Katie didn't know. As if feeling her gaze on him, Christopher glanced up and their eyes met. She could have sworn she saw an uneasiness in them, much the way she was feeling. His gaze swept over the gown she wore, and she could see the tension increase in his face. Her heart pounding, Katie managed to keep smiling and sweep into the room, aware only of him.

"Kate! You look lovely. That gown is beautiful with your eyes," Emily said sincerely, and Katie took the young woman's hands in gratitude.

"Thank you, but your gown is far lovelier. You look enchanting, as always."

Emily grinned, pleased. It was getting easier and easier to fit into this group, Katie realized, but after tonight, she might no longer need her skills. Should Christopher decide to court someone else, she and her family might find themselves in the street.

"Wine?" A servant paused at her arm and Katie nodded, accepting a glass as she greeted the guests. She felt Christopher's eyes on her as she made everyone comfortable, introducing Gertrude and Isabelle and pausing to laugh at the outrageous compliments she received. She wouldn't show him how much his presence upset her; no, not after last night. Even if it killed her, she would play this role out.

"May I have everyone's attention?"

Katie turned in surprise as Ella entered the room, holding Sean's hand. The little boy looked wonderful in a dark suit, his golden hair shining. He glanced inquisitively at the guests.

"I would like to formally introduce my grandnephew. Sean, this is Nellie Mitchell, Mary, and the Misses Chandler. Say how do you do."

The conversation ceased as the guests murmured to themselves with shocked expressions. Stunned, Katie watched as Sean, obviously tutored by Ella, extended a hand, then shook Nellie Mitchell's.

"How do you do, miss?" Sean asked politely.

Nellie stammered, glancing helplessly at her mother. Confronted with what might well be the illegitimate child of Fan Pemberton, she didn't know how to comport herself or whether to acknowledge the boy at all. The room seemed to wait in a collective silence while Mrs. Mitchell looked shocked and began to fan herself indignantly.

Katie's cheeks flushed crimson. My God, what was Ella thinking? How could she have chosen tonight, of all nights, to introduce Sean to society? Yet she trusted Ella, and knew the older woman would never hurt her. What then was she doing?

Before Mrs. Mitchell could comment, Eunice stepped forward and draped an arm around Nellie, speaking to the boy with a laugh. "She thinks you're so handsome, Sean, she doesn't know what to say."

The girls giggled nervously, then Ella turned graciously to the Misses Chandler, whose mouths looked like perfect *O*'s.

"Did I forget to mention Fan's son? The boy has been ill for quite some time. After his father died in that mine explosion, he did quite badly. I always thought the two events were connected. Even the physicians seemed to think so. But thank God, he has recovered, and has come home to stay."

Katie drank down her wine in a gulp as the ladies pressed forward. She saw more than one uncertain expression, and she didn't dare to look at Christopher. She held her breath as Alice Chandler smiled, pushed Nellie aside, then took Sean's hand.

"You are a handsome young man, and I am very pleased to meet you. Ella has told me so much about you. When we go to the seaside next year, do stop by for a visit. I make a wonderful lemon ice that a little boy like you will love."

The wind expelled from Katie's body and she stared in wonder as the women all spoke to Sean, apparently accepting him. One by one they obtained an introduction and promised the small boy everything from candy to a ride on a new carriage. Even Mrs. Mitchell, aware that everyone else seemed to know about Sean, was forced to smile politely and take his hand. Speechless, Katie felt a reassuring pressure on her elbow and she turned to see Aunt Eunice smiling gently.

"Ella's been speaking to most of the women about your son. It took a little doing, but she's managed to circulate the story about his father dying. Most people willingly believed that, since they all thought Fan left for a man anyway. Sean's appearance only solidifies what they already thought." Her smile broadening, Eunice sighed. "People. Give them something to talk about, Kate, and they'll always forgive you."

Katie stared at her in amazement, then her eyes went back to Ella. It wasn't so much the gossip, Katie realized, or the story. It was Ella's nature that made people listen to her, in spite of her reputation. Even the other Pembertons looked duly quelled as they spoke to Sean and outwardly accepted him.

It was hard to believe, but tonight, the impossible had happened. Ella Pemberton made Philadelphia society accept her son. Her throat tightened, and Katie looked up to see Christopher watching her, his expression full of approval. Paddy smiled proudly, his own eyes glistening. Even Moira had stopped chatting and was beaming at Sean from across the room, her Lillie Langtry pearls dangling dramatically in her hand.

If nothing else, Katie thought chokingly, she would always be grateful for this. Sean would know that he was accepted. He would have other resources now if he should ever need them; he would have society contacts. Best of all, he would know in his heart that he was as good as other people, in spite of his parentage.

It was a gift beyond measure.

When Ella approached, Katie took her hands in gratitude. "Ella, I don't know what to say—"

Ella flushed, but Katie could tell she was very happy with herself. "Nonsense! Did you actually think I'd let these old biddies treat Sean with anything less than respect? He's a fine young man, and you deserve much of the credit for that. You've done a wonderful job with him." Fixing Katie with a stern stare, she spoke firmly. "So, have you and Christopher come to your senses yet? Are you back together?"

"No," Katie admitted. "You know why he wanted to have the party tonight. He hasn't changed his mind."

"I see." Ella nodded. She lowered herself into a chair, and Katie noticed how pale she was, how fragile. Her complexion was like English china, translucent and pearl-like, while her eyes seemed wise and otherworldly. "Then I suppose there is nothing more to be said."

There was something queer in the older woman's voice. Katie started to comment, but Christopher called to her and she glanced up, startled. He indicated the young man who stood beside him.

"Come, Katie, there's someone I want you to meet."

Ella nodded to her, indicating that she should go. She pressed Katie's hand softly and smiled. "I want you to remember something for me, dear."

"Anything."

"What is the real reason you and Christopher married? Was it for money?"

Katie stared at her, surprised by the question. "Well, Christopher thinks—"

"Or for love?" Ella questioned, nodding to herself. When Katie looked at her in confusion, Ella smiled softly, her webbed cheeks wrinkling like an old summer rose. "I want you to remember that, dear. You married for love. No matter what else. Do you promise?''

"Yes." Katie nodded, more alarmed by the moment.

"Good." Ella sighed. "Run along now, dear. Your husband awaits. And don't forget. Ever."

❈ TWENTY-FIVE

"Katie, I want you to meet Theodore Worthington. Ted, this is Katie. I've been telling you about her."

"Charmed." Theodore bowed slightly, his eyes roving over her with little interest. He turned back to Christopher, indicating Winston Pepper. "Wonderful businessman, but I really can't admire his attire. One would think he'd realize that cravat pins went out two years ago, wouldn't you think?"

"True." Christopher looked annoyed, but managed to hide it from his guest. "I thought you and Kate might have some things in common. My wife has an excellent singing voice, and I know your love for good music."

"Ah, yes." Theodore turned to her out of necessity. "Is this so?"

Katie smiled, but her eyes did not meet her husband's. "I wouldn't call it excellent. I suppose when one is married, one exaggerates both the faults and the virtues of one's spouse."

Her arrow hit its mark. Christopher looked at her, his expression closed, then he nodded to Charles Pepper.

"If you two will excuse me, I have some business to discuss." Turning, he walked abruptly away, leaving Katie with his companion.

"So, Katie, would you care to dance?" Theodore asked, unable to refuse doing so without insulting his host.

Katie hesitated a moment, hating Christopher for putting her into this position. But she wouldn't cry, she wouldn't get upset. If he could treat her so coldly, she could reciprocate. "Yes, I would. Very much."

All eyes were on her as she walked to the center of the room and took his hand. She could hear the whispers and conjectures of the company as Mrs. Scott chose to waltz with this fussy old man instead of her husband. Her heart breaking, she forced a smile as the music began and she swirled on the floor, looking unbelievably lovely.

She couldn't resist searching through the whispering crowd for Christopher. He was standing against the wall, talking with Charles, but he didn't so much as glance in her direction. How could he be so uncaring? she wondered miserably. Katie held her head higher and laughed openly at something Theodore said, even though he was complaining about his chilblains. To all outward appearances, she seemed taken with this man, but to the person who mattered most, it was no cause for concern.

Patrick frowned disapprovingly, Moira glared, and Ella stared in dismay. Katie heard Margaret Chester's vicious laugh, and Bertrice's gasp of astonishment. The waltz seemed to last forever, and when the music finally slowed, she thanked her partner breathlessly.

"Thank you for the dance, but I must say this is a relief," Theodore said, fanning himself. "I can't wait to sit down."

"Then you'll excuse me. I have to see to my guests." Humiliated, Katie disengaged herself and walked to the table, where Gertrude indulged in every kind of food imaginable. Sending Isabelle a sympathetic smile, Katie took the young woman by the hand.

"Gertrude, there's someone I especially want you to

meet. We'll be having dinner shortly, don't worry," Katie added.

Gertrude nodded, obviously reluctant to leave the table. Shoving a few hors d'oeuvres into her pocket, she obediently followed Kate through the crowd to where Christopher stood.

"Christopher, this is the young woman I've been telling you about. Her name is Gertrude Meade. She is Isabelle's niece, and is very well connected. Her father is a country gentleman. Gertrude, Christopher Scott."

Charles looked from Christopher to his wife and shook his head, confused. Gertrude stood before them, obviously unimpressed, her mouth still munching. Dressed in a dove-gray gown that hung shapelessly from her round form, she looked like a plump pigeon. Christopher stepped forward and, with perfect manners, took the young woman's hand and kissed it.

"Charmed, I'm sure." If he was at all upset by Gertrude's appearance, her figure, or her unattractive hairstyle, he didn't indicate it in the least. "May I have this dance?"

Flustered, Gertrude giggled then slipped her arm through his. Immediately a small square of toast covered with chicken pâté fell from her pocket to the floor. Charles looked appalled, but the young girl shrugged as if it hardly mattered. Forcing a smile, Christopher kicked the offending morsel beneath the table, then led his fair lady out to the floor.

"Kate," Charles began slowly. "Have you and Christopher made up? What is going on here tonight?"

"I'm afraid I can't answer that," Katie said apologetically, aware of Charles's confusion. "It's just that some men are extraordinarily stubborn." She had barely finished speaking when Theodore approached, obviously nudged by Christopher. He sighed, then indicated his arm once more.

"Will you dance, my lady?"

"Of course." Katie accepted his arm reluctantly, leaving a puzzled Charles behind. Charles shook his head and glanced at Bertrice. If this was what happened within a few months of marriage, maybe he wouldn't wed at all.

He could hear her laughter.

Christopher tried hard not to look, but he couldn't resist. Instead of fuming with jealousy, as he'd hoped, Katie actually seemed to be enjoying herself in another man's arms.

Anger streaked through him, and he forcibly reminded himself that this was his idea, that he had nothing to worry about with Katie and Theodore. He was sure the man was an old maid and quite happy with his present arrangement. Hadn't he verified that with Theodore's mother, who had long since given up on her son? Yet as he covertly watched them he couldn't help the stab of insane jealousy that coursed through him. She was his wife, dammit!

He forced himself to smile at Gertrude, even though she still stuffed herself whenever he turned his head. He held her close as they danced, the way Katie liked, and he paid her full attention, smiling and laughing, trying to appear infatuated with the young woman. But his eyes kept wandering to his beautiful Kate, who apparently was having the time of her life.

This was supposed to be her punishment, not his. She was the one who was to be writhing in outrage. Desperately he tried to think of a way out of his plan, but now it seemed hopeless, especially after everything she'd said.

And the worst part of it was he now knew she was right. He'd thought of her words many times in the past few hours, and they came back to haunt him. He was guilty as charged. He'd judged her for doing exactly what he'd done, and what several of his friends had done. Truly it was a man's world, but he couldn't fix that, but in his heart he didn't have to live by it, either. He owed her more and, for the life of him, didn't know how to undo what he'd done.

He saw Katie leave the dance floor, pleading fatigue, while several other men begged for her hand. She declined all of them, but it made him burn to see their interest in her, particularly with her husband so obviously distant. They were like dogs in heat, he thought furiously, watching as his friends were enchanted by her looks and vivacious personality. Laughing, Katie held them at bay and accepted another glass of wine, drinking it down as if it were water. When her eyes lifted to his, Christopher had to look away.

"Are they serving dinner yet?" Gertrude whined. "I'm starving."

Christopher forced another smile and answered in his most gallant manner. "No, but we can go to the table again if you really want to."

She nodded quickly in assent, then slipped her arm through his as he escorted her to the food. Christopher tried to hide his repulsion as she belched, then helped herself to more. While Gertrude ate, Theodore joined them and eagerly fetched a glass of wine.

"I must say your wife is an excellent dancer, though I think you are very wrong." When Christopher looked at him murderously, Theodore continued quickly: "She doesn't seem at all lonely. In fact, I had to fight off the men for her. I don't think you'll be needing me to dance with her anymore."

Furious, Christopher could barely speak, but somehow he managed. "Nonsense. My wife is really very shy. Why, without your help . . ." His voice trailed off as Katie accepted a dance with one of his college friends and was immediately swept off to the floor.

"See?" Theodore grinned happily. "Now we can continue our discussion. I've looked forward to it all evening, and I don't really socialize with anyone else here. Now, as I was saying about my sinuses . . ."

This couldn't be happening. Outraged, Christopher watched his wife laugh and dance with a league of men while he stood by and fumed, Gertrude on one side of him, stuffing her face, Theodore complaining on the other. What the hell had he done?

Somehow this whole situation had gotten out of hand. Desperate, he looked around the room for help and spotted Kate directly across the floor from him.

Her eyes studied him, Theodore, and Gertrude, and her expression changed from confusion to . . . amusement. Theodore was wringing his handkerchief, reciting his woes, while Gertrude sat on the edge of the table, to be closer to the food. Fighting frantically to maintain her dignity, Kate, unable to help herself, broke into laughter.

Christopher was furious. The angrier he got, the more Katie laughed. He saw her fetch a handkerchief and try to control herself, but every time she glanced in his direction, fresh tears flowed down her face and she nearly collapsed with merriment.

"If you'll excuse me—" Christopher turned from Theodore and Gertrude, so outraged that he wanted to hit something. He strode across the room, intending to give her a real set-down, to tell her exactly what he thought, but even from a distance, he could hear her infectious laughter.

This time he'd really done it. He'd made a complete fool of himself, and Katie was enjoying it to the utmost. Deep down, he couldn't blame her. How could he be angry with her when, if he had to be truthful, it was funny?

A chuckle started somewhere within him, then a smile, then a full-fledged laugh. When Katie saw his expression, she appeared relieved, but it didn't stop her from giggling. She managed a semblance of a straight face as he approached, obviously expecting him to berate her. Instead, Christopher grabbed her hand, startling her.

"Madam," he said meaningfully, leading her onto the floor. "I believe this is our dance."

It was a gorgeous waltz. Ella smiled, watching the two young people she loved so much circling the dance floor. Other dancers moved, appreciating the handsomeness of the couple, Katie smiling beautifully at her husband, Christopher's eyes full of warmth.

"They are so much in love," Eunice remarked, taking Ella's hand. "It's so nice to see."

The older woman smiled, then coughed. She struggled to regain her breath and, when she could speak, nodded in agreement.

"Yes, but they are both stubborn. Christopher, for all his virtues, is extremely strong-willed, as is my niece. I just hope they learn to express that love before it's too late."

Eunice nodded, enveloping Sean in her arms as the young boy approached her. He watched his mother and Christopher for a moment, his blue eyes shining with admiration, then he turned to Eunice.

"Does this mean that he won't go away? Like my da?"

"I certainly hope so, Sean," Eunice said fervently. "I hope so."

"How could you laugh at me like that?" Christopher chided her as they glided beneath the chandeliers. The light brought out the rich blackness of Katie's hair and the brilliance of her eyes as she smiled mischievously.

"I'm sorry, I just couldn't resist. Christopher, when you plan a party, you don't forget anything. Even the drama."

"That's enough." He spoke firmly, but she could see the laughter in his eyes. "Kate, I'm sorry. Can you forgive me?"

Those words meant everything. Katie looked at him, her heart pounding, wishing he would tell her how he really felt, what this really meant. But he didn't seem inclined to continue the conversation, and with a group of people surrounding her, she wasn't comfortable with the discussion, either. Instead she gave him a breathtaking smile and whispered, "Of course."

He held her closer, and Katie felt an overwhelming love for him. "Please God," she whispered. "Please let him love me. I won't ask for anything else, ever."

As if in answer to her thoughts, Christopher bent down and kissed her hair. It wasn't the response she was looking for, but it was a start.

The last guest finally left and Katie closed the door and turned to Christopher, utterly exhausted. "What time is it?" she questioned, feeling as if she would collapse in a heap right at that moment.

"About four," Christopher replied. "It seems the party was a success."

He took her hand, helping her up the stairs. He made her feel so special, so cared for, just like before. Katie sighed, then giggled.

"What?"

"I was just thinking. Who would have thought that Theodore and Patrick would hit it off so well? Teddy didn't seem like the type to appreciate gardening, but he apparently raises roses. He found Paddy's methods fascinating."

Christopher grinned. "I know. And Gertrude seemed very relieved when I left her alone with her food. It seems that only Isabelle wanted her to be courted."

"Don't you dare mention that again," Katie said, though her voice was filled with mirth. "The last thing I want to think about is you courting another woman."

They entered her bedchamber and Katie sank down onto

her comforter, enjoying the soft luxury of rest. Christopher
came up behind her and indicated her stays.

"The maids are all abed. Can I help you?"

"Please." Half rising, Katie turned her back to him,
feeling the pressure of his hands as he expertly relieved her
of the gown and undergarments.

"Did I tell you how beautiful you looked tonight?"
Christopher whispered as he undid the laces of her stays,
pressing a kiss along her spine.

Katie shivered, loving the feel of him against her bare
skin. "No, not in so many words."

"Well, you did." Kissing her again and again, he pressed
his mouth at each place where the laces came undone, down
along her spine, until Katie was trembling. Holding her hair
out of the way, she shivered with delight as he slipped his
hands inside her dress, caressing her breasts until her
nipples hardened beneath his palms.

Nearly shaking with suppressed want, Katie faced him
and ran her fingers through his hair, wondering why, of all
men, she loved him so deeply. Pulling his head down to
hers, she whispered teasingly, "You looked lovely tonight,
too. Especially dancing with Gertrude."

There was just enough sincerity in her voice to make him
look up at her. Katie was still smiling, but it was an
uncertain smile. Christopher grinned, then pushed back her
hair from her throat, kissing the nape of her neck enticingly.

"I wouldn't talk. If I hadn't thought Theodore was a
confirmed bachelor, I would have been even more furious.
As it was, I could barely contain myself."

Katie caught her breath as he slipped her gown from her
shoulders. Was he admitting he was jealous? His words
penetrated her passion-cloaked mind, and she suddenly felt
wonderful. Christopher had planned this. He had deliberately selected the man, knowing that Katie was safe with

him. Hitting him playfully, she saw his look of surprise as he struggled out of his own clothes.

"That was terrible," Katie said, though her mouth twitched with humor. "Asking poor Teddy to be my companion, when all along he didn't want a wife."

"I know." Christopher came to her and enveloped her in his arms. His hot, muscular body felt wonderful against her own, and she gasped with pleasure as he pressed closer. "But I don't think you had my best interests in mind when you selected Gertrude."

"Whatever do you mean?" Katie asked, giggling as Christopher began to nuzzle her neck. Sweet sensations shot through her entire body, ending at the junction of her thighs. "Oh, my . . ." she whispered, trying to maintain the conversation. "I mean, Gertrude was what you wanted. Rich, well connected . . ."

"Katie." Christopher growled, looking up at her. The intensity in his eyes made her shiver. "Let's not talk about it again. Please."

Nodding, she let him push the rest of her shift away, then melted in his arms as he purposefully aroused her. She had him back again.

And nothing else mattered.

Ella sank down into her bed, the cool sheets, the warm comforter. Her attorney sat at her side, frantically taking down each word as she coughed and struggled through every sentence. When she finished, he handed her the document, which she read and signed, indicating her approval. Then she lay back on her pillow, a strange contentment coming over her features.

"Is that all, Miss Pemberton?" the attorney questioned, seeing her exhaustion and air of finality.

"Yes," Ella whispered, then opened her eyes once more. "I appreciate you coming all the way out here, Martin, especially at this time of night. But the changes to my will are crucial. You understand all my instructions?''

''I think so.'' The attorney nodded, his expression sorrowful as he watched the older woman struggle for breath. ''You know, Ella, many people feel worse than you and recover. I won't have you giving up hope.''

''I haven't.'' Ella smiled at him, and she looked sixteen once more. ''I am full of hope, Martin. I'm just not full of life anymore. But I need to make sure my wishes are carried out explicitly. You are clear on everything?''

''Yes.'' Martin nodded again. ''But you do know the Pembertons will not be happy.''

''I know.'' Ella smiled, and if she felt bad about the idea, she certainly didn't betray it. ''I wish I could be here to see their faces. But promise me you will hold firm. They are a powerful family, Martin, and will try to sway you. Promise me.''

''I promise.'' Martin packed up his papers and put on his coat. ''No matter what they do, I'll see your wishes are carried out.''

When he reached the door, Ella was seized with another coughing spell. Worried, Martin hesitated. ''Would you like me to send for a doctor?''

''No.'' Ella waved her hand. ''Please. I just need some rest. I'm so tired these days. Thank you, Martin. Please send your bill.''

Dismissed, the man left, and Ella was alone. Waiting until the door closed, she gave herself up to the pain once more, letting it envelop her until she could hardly stand it. When it finally receded, she closed her eyes and dreamed.

She was young once more. The fields were green, and she ran through them, laughing, snatching up a bachelor button and holding its slender stalk between her fingers. She could smell the grass, clean and fresh, and hear the steady buzz of bees as they searched each flower for nectar. The air was filled with the sweet scent of summer, and the sky overhead was a robin's-egg blue. It was beautiful, restless and clear, everything so intense. Then she saw him.

A young man waited for her, his body silhouetted against the sunlight. She wouldn't forget that profile anywhere; it was engraved on her heart. The flower dropped from her hand and Ella ran into his arms. "Michael, is it you?" Tears flowed down her face, and when he caught her, lifting her high, she thought she would burst with joy.

"Yes, it's me, Ella. I've come for you, as I once promised. You'll never be tired again. You'll never hurt again. You'll be with me forever. Come."

Ella looked back, wanting to say good-bye to Katie and Sean, but they weren't with her. Smiling, she turned back to Michael and followed him through the field.

He was right. The pain was gone.

❈ TWENTY-SIX

"*I* still can't believe she's dead," Katie whispered to Christopher, holding his hand tightly as they slipped into the church.

Christopher nodded, unable to speak as they both stared at the coffin in front of the altar. Ella. Tears stung Katie's eyes, but she wiped them away fiercely, knowing that Ella would not want her to grieve. As the minister began speaking Katie could only think of the day when Ella confessed that she had spent much of her life waiting for happiness.

Had she ever had a lover, a man who held her the way Christopher held Katie? A man who made her feel as if she were the most special woman in the world? Someone who had touched her hair, made her laugh, read her poems, and brought her flowers? Katie wished fervently that she had, for no one should pass through this life without love. And of all people, Ella deserved it the most.

May you rest in peace, Katie prayed, her throat tight with pain. My God, she loved her. And missed her.

It was as if her fairy godmother had disappeared. Strange, but she never seriously thought of anything happening to Ella, in spite of her age. The old woman was the family matriarch, a presence to be reckoned with, yet she was also kind and gentle, with a heart that Katie knew about firsthand.

Just yesterday she'd been playing with Sean. Katie had watched them in Ella's kitchen, laughing as Ella indulged her son in making cookies, the two of them devouring much of the dough before it ever reached the oven. Sean adored the woman and never seemed to mind her admonishments concerning hand washing or bedtimes. He shared secrets with her, let her hold his frog, and allowed Ella to tutor him in everything from etiquette to mathematics.

Katie wanted to think that she had been able to give something back to Ella, in return for receiving so much. She knew she would be forever grateful to the woman for opening up this world to her and, best of all, giving her Christopher.

"To all who knew Ella Pemberton, she was a good woman. She gave to the church and the charities, was an important influence in the ladies' clubs, and was a popular member of society."

Katie had to repress a smile. How Ella would have hooted if she'd heard this eulogy! Apparently the minister had asked the family for a few words to say. The Pembertons knew less about their relative than they did the fly on the wallpaper. As Ella had once said, they were waiting for her to die.

And now that day had come.

The people began filing out of the church and Katie stepped behind the Pembertons. Grace turned toward her, her handkerchief knotted pathetically, and gave Katie a pointed look.

"I believe only family are permitted to the home after services," Grace said sharply.

Katie gritted her teeth, but Christopher stepped before her and smiled charmingly.

"We understand that, Grace. But Martin Shuler asked

that we join you. Apparently Ella considered Kate family
and made some provision for her.''

Grace turned on her heel and stalked off while Stephen
Pemberton looked at Christopher and shrugged apologetically. Katie wasn't at all surprised. Grace had never been a
fan of hers, and she knew the Pembertons intended to cut
her off, now that Ella was gone.

Sean snuggled closer to her, his little hand moist as they
stepped inside Ella's house once more. Everything was so
familiar and yet so strange, Katie thought. How was it
possible that the curtains remained, the gaslights, the rich
furnishings and portraits, yet Ella was gone? It was as if the
very life force of this house had disappeared and could not
be persuaded to return.

''Oh, 'tis good to see your face, Kate. I still cannot
believe it. She's gone.'' Eileen sobbed, and Kate took her
hand comfortingly.

''I know. But you were good to her, Eileen. She'll
remember that.''

''Do you think so?'' The housekeeper brightened, then
wiped her eyes with her apron. ''Thank you, Kate. I'd like
to think that.'' She indicated the hallway with a tilt of her
head and her expression became sarcastic. ''Her loving
family are in there. Bastards! They're like a pack of
vultures. Go right in.''

The Pembertons were all waiting in the library. Kate and
Christopher took a seat in the back of the room, neither
acknowledged nor appreciated by the company. Truthfully
Katie didn't care. The Pembertons were a cold, cruel family,
and she was just as relieved to be rid of them.

Martin paged through his papers, then looked up at the
family. His eyes flickered for a moment when Grace wailed
plaintively, then he looked to Kate and Christopher, an odd
smile on his face.

''Before I begin reading the last will and testament of

Ella Pemberton, I would like to say a few words. Ella was a remarkably strong woman, both in mind and body. She has made some changes to the original documents, particularly in the last few weeks, but she was perfectly within her rights to do so. Ella had been examined repeatedly by Dr. Morris, so if anyone has any concerns about her state of mind, please feel free to contact him.''

The Pembertons murmured and Katie shifted in her chair uneasily. Something was wrong; even she could sense it. Martin shuffled through the papers again and began to read.

"I, Ella Pemberton, being of sound mind and body, do hereby bequeath all of my worldly possessions, with the following exceptions, to the church.''

There was a collective gasp from the family, and Grace appeared about to faint. Martin continued.

"To my good and faithful servant Eileen, I leave the sum of ten thousand dollars, to provide a retirement income to a woman who truly deserves it. May she live long and continue to demonstrate the honesty and values that I have always admired in her.''

Eileen sniffled in disbelief while the Pembertons shuffled nervously.

"To Sean O'Connor, I bequeath the sum of fifty thousand dollars, to be held in trust by his mother until he is twenty-one years of age. The money shall be used for the purposes of his education, with the balance allowing him a successful start toward becoming the man I know he will be.

"To Kate and Christopher Scott, I leave one hundred thousand dollars each, with the provision that they divorce and deny all future contact with each other. I feel personally responsible for the unhappiness of these two people, both of whom mean so much to me. They have been forced to stay together due to their financial difficulty, a situation that was encouraged by both myself and Eunice Scott. Hopefully this money will alleviate their need to remain in a loveless marriage, and both of them may go on to find true happiness.''

There were protests from the Pembertons. Martin gave them a stern look, and the noise died. Only when the room was quiet did he continue.

''To my immediate family, Grace, Stephen, my brother George, I leave what they gave to me in life: my prize roses and their thorns. May they receive the same comfort and beauty from them as they've given me and know, each time they prick their finger, that somewhere I am laughing.''

Martin closed the papers and looked up at the family. Grace slumped to the floor while Stephen shouted in outrage, ''She can't do this! We'll go to court, we'll contest—''

''Now, now.'' George put a hand on Stephen's shoulder and called to a servant for Grace. ''There's no need for emotionalism. Ella always was a prankster. Something tells me that wherever she is at this hour, she is enjoying this.'' Turning to Martin, George's face hardened. ''You will be hearing from the family attorney.''

Martin nodded. ''I was expecting to.'' He rose and shook hands with Kate and Christopher. ''Congratulations. You two seem to have the winning hand.''

All hell broke out as the Pembertons realized that he was finished, that Ella had really left them nothing more than her roses. Kate sank down into a chair, her mind whirling.

One hundred thousand dollars. A fortune. Katie numbly thought of what that much money meant. She could get nice clothes for Sean, buy a house, and pay for it with cash. She could provide peace and security to Paddy and Moira, something neither of them had ever known. Paddy wouldn't have to garden anymore, and Moira could play Lillie Langtry in the finest of costumes.

And for herself . . .

Katie felt a rush of pain. For herself, she would have a

home. An income. Money could be invested, and she'd never have to scrub another floor or teach another tone-deaf child to sing. She would have pretty gowns and friends, for people forgave anything if there was enough money involved. She would have the security she'd always longed for, and the respectability that had always eluded her. Sean was accepted by society as it was; now, with this inheritance, she would be, too. It was all perfect, except . . .

Christopher. Katie struggled with the ache inside of her. How could she possibly leave him? Looking up, she saw Christopher's gaze on her and knew he was thinking the exact same thing. Their eyes met and she had to look away, so intense was the exchange between them.

". . . and I knew she would do this! She wheedled her way into Ella's good graces, just so she could benefit—"

Grace's voice rose above the rest in a screech. Sean shifted uncomfortably beside her and Katie took his hand and turned to Christopher.

"I'm going to take him home. I don't want him to hear this."

Christopher nodded. His lips parted as if he would say something else, then he was drawn back by Martin, who indicated that he had the necessary papers to review. Katie's hand tightened on Sean's, but she merely nodded, then accepted her cloak from Eileen.

She had to get out of here, away from these Pembertons, to a place where she could find peace and quiet.

She needed to think.

"Cabbie, stop." St. Paul's Church loomed ahead, looking dark and gloomy in the cold. Sean had already been dropped at home, but Katie just couldn't go back there yet. She needed some time alone, to sort through her own feelings, and felt somehow drawn to the church.

Inside, it was dimly lit. Candles flickered at the altar,

creating a comforting light beneath the feet of the statue of the Blessed Mother. Dipping her fingers in the holy water, Kate felt the chill, then instantly touched her forehead, making the sign of the cross.

It was like home here. For all that this church had rejected her, so much of her childhood had been spent behind stone walls like these that Katie felt a comfort in being there again. Sitting in the first pew, she felt closer to Ella, as if this air of spirituality connected her with the older woman's soul. Strangely it was a good feeling, and Katie suddenly knew that wherever Ella was, she was happy.

God bless your soul, Katie prayed.

Tears stung her eyes, but she wiped them away. Ella had known her and loved her. She had known all along that Kate wasn't Fan Pemberton, but had wanted to help her, to make her life better. For that, Katie would always be grateful.

Why then had Ella given her this terrible choice?

She could have the money, and all that it meant, or she could have Christopher. She couldn't have both. She could take the money, and everything that it represented, and live out her life like a grand lady, never have to worry again, never have to wonder where her next meal would come from or what would happen.

But she would be alone.

Staring at the crucifix in the center of the church, Katie closed her eyes in pain. She knew, beyond a shadow of a doubt, that she loved Christopher, loved him with all her heart and mind and soul. How could she walk away from him, knowing she would never see him again?

Yet how could she not?

My God, Katie prayed. Please . . .

It had once been so easy. She had married him for money, and for a name and security. When had she started to love him? Was it their wedding night, when he had loved her so completely that she'd lost all touch with reality? Or had it happened long before that, from the first time she saw him at the Drexels' party and felt that odd confusion? Why had she really married him, of all the men she could have encouraged?

The candles flickered silently. A charwoman entered the church and began rubbing the pews with lemon oil. Katie looked down, blinking away the stinging moisture in her eyes.

She would always love him, even until the day she joined Ella. There would be no other man for her. She might live out the rest of her life in comfort and ease, but she knew with a certainty that when she closed her eyes each night, it would be his face she would see, his name she would say.

And remember.

Putting her face in her hands, she leaned back in the pew and sobbed.

"So if you'll just sign these forms, it will all be taken care of. The money will be deposited into the bank of your choice. You will have one hundred thousand dollars, as will your wife. But you must start the divorce proceedings immediately, and you must sever all relations with Kate. Do you understand?"

Christopher nodded, staring dumbly at the papers before him. Martin smiled and put down his pen, then placed a comforting hand on Christopher's shoulder.

"I know this seems odd, but many wills have strange stipulations placed there for reasons known only to the maker. In this case, Ella genuinely sought to right a wrong. She was firmly convinced that she'd caused both of you unhappiness in bringing you and Kate together. And she wants to correct that now, in the least painful way possible."

"I see." Christopher stared at the paper, unable to take

his eyes from the figure. One hundred thousand dollars . . .

"Do I have to sign these now? Can I take some time to think about it?"

"Of course." Martin nodded. "Though I admit, I am a little perplexed. This appears to be the ideal solution to a problem. But I understand, with your grief, that you may want to consider everything. And speak with Kate." He indicated a line on the page. "She has to sign this as well."

Christopher nodded, then turned to leave. Martin stopped him momentarily. "I'm sorry, son, about Ella. But she thought the world of both of you. I understand your financial difficulties. This is really your lucky day."

Turning, Christopher walked out the door. His lucky day. He should be on top of the world.

Why, then, did he feel like his life had just ended?

It was late when Katie got home. As she stepped into the grand house she saw Paddy and Moira, Sean and Eunice, all of them in their places as if nothing had happened, as if their entire world hadn't changed overnight.

Moira saw her first and smiled. "There you are! We were beginning to worry. Christopher stopped by—he has some papers for you to sign. He said he'll be back later."

Katie nodded, her throat tight. "So I guess that's that."

Moira stared at her, obviously puzzled. "What do you mean, girl? Of course, that's that. You're about to become a very rich woman, Kate O'Connor. Just think of what that means! We can have a fine home, gowns." Moira indicated the dress she wore. "Miss Lillie never wore the same gown twice, you know."

Eunice interrupted. "Now, Moira, Kate's been through a lot today. Ella was just buried. I don't think it a good idea—"

"You aren't thinking about this, are you?" Moira came to stand beside Kate and put her hand to her forehead. "My, lass, what is this sorrowing look? Don't tell me you aren't sure?"

"Moira, I don't want to talk about it—"

"That's it!" Moira stood back, aghast. "Kate, don't make another mistake now. For God's sake, lass, when it comes down to it, one man's as good as the next! You can buy a hundred husbands with that money!"

"Moira, that's enough," Paddy grumbled, then turned to Eunice. "Would you mind leaving us alone? I'd like a word with my granddaughter."

Eunice nodded, then led Sean and the protesting Moira by the hand out of the room. "What are you saying to her, Paddy? Make sure she does the right thing, for once!" Moira waved a scented handkerchief, Miss Lillie style.

Kate gave Patrick a grateful look, then sank down by the fire. Patrick came to stand beside her, then smoothed his hand through her hair as he'd done when she was a child.

"Katie, I want to make certain of something before Christopher gets here with those papers. I don't want you considering me or Moira or Sean when you make this decision."

Katie looked at him, her smile sad. "Paddy, you know I can't do that."

"Of course you can." Sitting beside her, Patrick took her hand. "Look at me, Kate. I know what you're thinking, and God love you, lass, it's one of the reasons you are such a special girl. But no matter what you decide, we will be fine." Patrick waved a hand toward the grand house and its furnishings. "I don't need any of this to live out my life. I wasn't born to it; I don't need it when I die. All I want now is a good jar of gin, someone to play checkers with, and to watch Sean grow into a healthy strong man. We don't need money to make that happen."

Katie stared at him, surprised. "But the house, the gardens—"

"Doesn't mean a damned thing to me. And Moira, she's always wanting something she'll never have. She wants to be Miss Lillie, and no amount of money will buy her that. Moira isn't your responsibility, Kate. I've taken care of her for all her life, and I'll always do that."

"But Sean." Kate smiled at Patrick, her eyes tired. "What of him? The additional money will provide him with a much better life. You know that."

"Do I?" Patrick sat for a moment, then turned to his granddaughter with an odd expression. "There was a time when I would have thought so. But now, living in this grand house, meeting some of these people . . . Kate, they are the same as us. Some of them are great men and women, hardworking and good, while others are rapscallions, same as if they'd been born in the street. Look at these Pemberton people."

"Yes, but I want a good life for him."

"And he'll get that, Kate. Ella's seen to it. Sean's a strapping lad, and well able to work. He'll always have a home. He's got enough money from Ella that he can pay for his schooling and start his own business. He'll be fine, Kate." When Katie looked up at him, her eyes full, Patrick took her other hand. "Have I ever lied to you?"

"No," she choked.

"He will be fine. I promise. So when your husband comes tonight, and you make your final decision, I want you to do it from here"—he lightly tapped his heart—"and not from here." He indicated his head. "Do you understand me?"

Katie nodded, her voice choking. "Paddy, I love you."

"I love you, too, girl. Now don't disappoint me. Whatever you decide, it must be what you want. I'll back you one

hundred percent if that is the case. Now be off with you.
He'll be here soon and you need to freshen your face.''

Reaching up, Katie pressed a kiss to his gnarled cheek.
''Thank you,'' she whispered.

''Don't be thanking me,'' Paddy said gruffly. ''It's the
simple truth. Now go.''

Katie smiled and did as she was told. If nothing else, she
still had her family. As always.

He now had everything he'd wanted. Christopher stared
at the back of the driver's head, thinking of the irony of that
statement.

One hundred thousand dollars. That was enough to pay
off all his debt, including the taxes and mortgage on his
home. It was enough to ensure him a comfortable future,
especially with his knowledge of banking and investments.
He could gamble, drink, have a hell of a good time, live out
his life the way he'd always envisioned it. He could buy
new suits, frequent the expensive restaurants he loved, play
the best games. He'd be rid of those O'Connors, with their
musical brogues and strange ways. He'd never have to see
Paddy again, with his damnable Irish wit and legends, hear
Moira's flutterings, or have Sean racing through his house.
It would be just like before—

Except that it never would be again. Cursing, Christopher
wished he had a drink, something to drown the despair he
felt.

Of course it was the ideal answer. Christopher had no
doubt that Ella had been appalled at their party and wanted
to make amends. Their marriage wasn't working; it never
had. He and Katie just had too many problems, too many
misunderstandings, and were too lacking in trust to make
their vows meaningful. For Christ's sake, he didn't even
know her real name until after they were wed.

Why then did it tear him apart to think of leaving her?

Even Eunice had been strangely silent since she'd heard about the will. Christopher had been hoping that she at least would be happy with the prospect of having her home to herself again, of reentering her social circle, this time with money, but she wasn't. Although his aunt didn't attempt to influence him, he knew she had grown to love the O'Connors and didn't want them to leave.

Dammit! It had all gotten so complicated so quickly. He'd intended to marry Fan Pemberton for purely practical reasons, and now . . .

Now he couldn't dream of his life without her.

For all her faults, for all her lies, he loved Katie O'Connor, and loved her desperately. Christopher stared out the carriage window, nearly laughing at the thought of that. Yes, dammit, he loved her, and he realized it now, when it was far too late.

The horse stopped and Christopher walked up the path to his home, a heavy feeling oppressing him. Somewhere the gods were laughing; he could feel it.

She was waiting for him. Christopher paused in the doorway, just watching her for a moment. Dressed in a simple mourning frock, her hair pulled back demurely, she appeared so beautiful that his heart stopped. Her expression was sad, but even that didn't take away from the classic lines of her face or the intensity of her eyes. Sensing him before he spoke, she glanced up, and he saw a strange mix of emotions on her face before she composed herself.

"Christopher." She forced a smile. "You've brought the papers."

His heart sank. He wasn't sure what he was hoping, what he thought she might say. Apparently she wanted to go through with this. Taking out the forms, he lay the parchment before her.

❊ TWENTY-SEVEN

Katie felt the pen in her hands, as heavy as a lead weight.
The parchment waited beneath her fingers, the dotted line
empty. She needed only to sign her name, and she would
gain everything.

And she would lose everything.

Raw emotion tightened her throat and she closed her
eyes. She couldn't do this. No matter how angry he got, she
couldn't sign this sheet unless she was absolutely certain
that that was what he wanted. Stretching forth her hand, she
gave the writing instrument back to him.

"You sign it."

He stared at her, then took the pen from her fingers. Katie
waited expectantly while he perused the document, even
though he must have read it thoroughly already. Finally,
after agonizing minutes, he put down the pen and looked at
her.

"I can't."

Her heart pounding with hope, Katie saw him turn away
from her to lean on the table in a gesture of torment, then he
whispered. "I just can't! Katie, I'm sorry." Turning back,
he faced her, his eyes full of emotion. "I know this is what
you want, but I just can't do it. I love you—I think I've

always loved you. And I can't trade you for money, no matter how much.''

''Oh, my God, Christopher!'' Joy suffused her face and she flung herself into his arms, holding him tightly, as if to make him irrevocably part of her once more. Tears streamed down her face, but it didn't matter—none of it did. She had him back now, and all would be well. ''I love you . . . I can't believe you love me! I didn't dream—''

''Katie, do you mean it?'' When she nodded quickly, he tightened his arms again, this time with happiness. ''I'm so sorry. I never meant to put you through so much. I love you, and I'll never leave you again.'' His voice was hoarse, and when Katie looked up, she saw the same tears in his eyes. ''God, I've been such a fool! Please forgive me, and don't ever leave me.''

''I won't,'' she whispered fiercely. ''God, I won't.''

They were like children, laughing and crying, overcome with joy. The parchment slipped to the floor, forgotten as Christopher leaned down to kiss her thoroughly, possessing her in a way that made her feel sheltered and protected and . . . loved.

When his mouth finally left hers, he spoke softly, caressing her hair and face. ''Katie, I know it will be hard, but bear with me. My debts are nearly paid off, and soon I will be receiving a salary at work, just like everyone else. In truth, I like this job and don't want to leave it. Disgraceful, isn't it?''

He was smiling, and Katie hugged him fiercely. ''No, it isn't at all disgraceful. It's one of the reasons I love you so much. We've wasted so much time, Christopher. Let's not waste any more.''

Her kiss was passionate, telling him in a timeless way just what he meant to her. Restrictions forgotten, inhibition gone, he returned the kiss with a burning desire, making Katie shudder with need. She clung to him, her knees weak

as his hands swept over her, making her want him so badly
that she whispered his name in a ragged plea.

"Christopher. Please."

She trembled in his arms and he swept her up, taking her
into his room, their room. Clothes became a barrier to be
gotten out of the way. When they were naked and alone,
Katie unashamedly ran her hands down his chest, loving the
feel of him, loving him.

"My God, you're gorgeous," she spoke admiringly, then
gasped as he took her in a violent kiss that made her lose all
control.

"No, you are. Katie, my sweet Katie."

There was no need for conversation, no reassurances.
Both of them knew what they'd long denied, and gloried
now in the physical expression of that feeling. When
Christopher filled her with his male heat, Katie cried out in
sheer ecstasy, clinging to him, wanting him to stay like this
forever, a part of her and she a part of him. Softness yielding
to hardness, woman surrendering to man, their minds and
bodies joined, they communicated everything they felt, but
most of all their love.

When it was over, Katie lay sated in his arms like a
contented kitten. Somehow she knew that nothing would
come between them again. The commitment they shared ran
deeper than a marriage license, deeper than a wedding vow.
They were together because they chose to be and because of
their love.

She would never doubt him again.

"I promise you, Kate, I'll make it up to you," Christopher said, kissing her hand as if reading her thoughts.
"Everything will work out, you'll see. I don't even mind
your family staying with us. As long as I have you."

Katie grinned. "Unfortunately Paddy has other ideas.
He's secured a position working as a gardener for the
Morris family. They have a small cottage on the property,

large enough for him and Moira. They plan to leave in the morning.''

"I see." Leaning up in bed beside her, Christopher frowned. "Will they be all right? I mean, have you seen this place? Is it adequate?"

She smiled as she held him close. "It's very nice. And Moira is so excited. Eunice gave her a few gowns, and she can't wait to try out the Miss Lillie act on a new audience. And it's within walking distance, so I'll still see them a lot."

"Good." Christopher's expression eased and he smiled back at her. "Eunice will miss them terribly. Please ask them to come by often."

"They will. They want to see Sean."

A silence followed her words, then Christopher spoke thoughtfully. "Kate, I've been meaning to talk to you about him. I think now is the time."

Her heart froze. Surely he didn't mean to send her son away? It was a real possibility—most men didn't want the responsibility of some other man's child. Her breath stopped, Katie waited as he spoke once more.

"I really care about Sean, and want him to have a good life. Ella's taken care of his schooling, and for that I will always be grateful. But do you think he would let me adopt him? And would you be agreeable to the idea? I would really like to be his father, and take care of him."

Hot tears stung her eyes and she tightened her embrace. "Do you mean it? Really? You want to—"

"Adopt him." Christopher laughed, lifting her face and smoothing away the tears. "Come on now, Katie, I'm not that bad. I know I'm not the ideal father figure, but I'm trying. And I can teach him things, like how to play cards and drink."

"Christopher Scott!" Katie threw her pillow at him and giggled as he pulled her into his arms once more. "I think you'll be a wonderful father,'' she said, grinning. ''But it's a lot of responsibility. Are you sure?''

''I'm sure.'' He spoke earnestly. ''I think you've done a wonderful job raising him, and so have Paddy and Moira. But I do think he needs contact with a man who can help him through the difficult years ahead, take him hunting and fishing. There are some sporting clubs for boys his age; I could help him to learn some of the games and to meet other boys so he'll have more friends. He seems a little lonely.''

Her heartstrings tugged within her as Katie realized what he meant. Christopher had thought about this for some time before making his decision. That was very reassuring, and he evidently spent some of it thinking about what would make Sean happy. Overwhelmed, she wrapped her arms around him and cuddled him close.

''I'm so glad you feel that way, especially now,'' Katie whispered, feeling his arms tighten around her.

''Now?''

''When we're going to have a baby of our own.''

Delight brightened his features and he stared at her in amazement. ''Kate, are you sure? I mean, do you really think? Don't you have to have tests and things? Are you all right?''

''Yes.'' Katie laughed. ''There is no mistake. I've already had one baby, you know. You're going to be a daddy.''

''My God, I love you.'' Christopher hugged her tightly. ''A baby! I just can't believe it.''

They lay together, anticipating a future that seemed very bright, in spite of the odds. Katie smiled, content. ''You know, at this moment I am perfectly happy.''

''Even without the money?'' Christopher asked cautiously.

Katie nodded. ''I've got you—the rest is just arithmetic.''

*　　*　　*

"And you really mean to walk away from two hundred thousand dollars?"

Martin Shuler sat on the other side of the desk, his expression incredulous. Christopher nodded.

"I'm sorry, Martin, but that's what we've decided. Ella made it clear in her will that the only way we'd get the money was to separate. Well, neither of us wants that. It wasn't really a decision at all."

"I see." The lawyer sat back in his chair, an odd look on his face. "Are you absolutely sure, then? I should just tear up these documents?"

He looked from Kate to Christopher. Both of them nodded, then Katie, snuggling closer to Christopher, spoke.

"Tear them up."

"All right." Martin did as he was told, assuming a resigned air. The only sound for several minutes was that of the parchment tearing, the money disappearing into nothingness. Christopher winced, but Katie held his hand tightly. They would regret the loss of the money, but never their decision.

"That's it then. Before you two leave, there is another issue," Martin said as Katie and Christopher rose, prepared to go. Sharing a puzzled look, they sat back down as Martin withdrew another envelope and gave them a secretive smile.

"When Ella made out this will, she spoke to me of her concerns about your situation. She felt responsible for bringing you both together, and didn't want you to stay in a loveless marriage."

"We know," Christopher said impatiently. "But we discovered we really did love each other."

"Enough to walk away from two hundred thousand dollars."

Christopher glanced at Kate, but when she squeezed his hand, he nodded. "Yes."

"Good." Martin fingered the envelope, then slid a silver

letter opener beneath the seal. "I need to be absolutely certain on that point. You see, Ella thought there was a possibility that you might come to that conclusion. In fact, she rather hoped you would. In which case, she added a codicil to the original document."

"What is this?" Katie turned to Christopher as Martin handed the document to him. Frowning, Christopher read the paper, his expression changing from puzzlement to incredulity, then finally to joy.

"Kate." He handed her the paper. "The codicil . . . it says we inherit the estate if we stay together."

"What?" Her hands shaking, Katie read the paper, then stared up at Martin numbly.

"That is correct." Taking the paper back from Christopher, Martin grinned. "Ella isn't playing games like you would think. She simply had to be sure that you both loved each other and that you were willing to make a real commitment. She knew that if you both turned down the money, you must be in love, for no one else would do anything quite so foolish. As you can see, she was right."

Katie turned to Christopher and shrieked, falling into his arms with laughter. Overwhelmed, they embraced like children, then Christopher disengaged himself and shook Martin's hand.

"How can we thank you?"

"It isn't me," Martin said, though he seemed pleased. "Ella cared for both of you very much. She did what she thought was right, and even in death it seemed she was. She was a grand old dame, and smart as a whip. We'll miss her." Martin folded the paper and chuckled at the two young people. "You can be sure there will be trouble with the Pembertons over this, but I'll handle that. Congratulations. You've inherited a fortune."

Dumbly Christopher and Katie stared at each other, then

once again Christopher shook Martin's hand. They started to leave when the lawyer stopped them at the door.

"One more thing. Christopher, I work with Winston Pepper at the bank. He's one of my clients. Anyway, he spoke to me the other day and informed me that you've done quite well at the job."

"Thank you," Christopher said dryly.

Ignoring his tone, Martin continued: "Evidently, in addition to paying off your debts, he invested some of your earnings into your own recommended stocks. It seems the strategy has paid off handsomely; even on your own, you are a rich man."

Katie hugged him exuberantly. "I knew you could do it! I just knew it!"

Chuckling, Christopher turned to Martin and smiled. "Thank you again. That was very nice of Winston Pepper. I'll tell him on Monday."

"Then you don't mean to leave your job?"

Christopher shook his head. "I find, much to my chagrin, that I like being respectable. If there's one thing I've learned from all this, it is that there is no such thing as security. Ella's fortune will provide that, but should there be an economic crash or some other catastrophe, we could wind up in the same position again. I'm not afraid of being poor, but I'd rather have a solid income, just in case."

"Well said." Martin nodded. "Your father would have been so proud of you."

"And so am I," Katie whispered.

Christopher grinned, then walked through the door with Katie. Martin watched them go with a smile.

Somewhere they had made an old woman very happy. He could feel it.

"Come here, boy. I want to talk to you."

Sean glanced up from his tree fort in the corner of the

garden. A man stood silhouetted against the field, his back
to the sun and his hands in his pockets. Curious, the little
boy stepped down the wooden planks to the ground, keeping
a respectable distance between himself and the man who'd
addressed him.

"Don't you know me?"

Sean stared at the golden-haired man with the charming
smile. There was something familiar about him, and
yet . . . Nodding his head, Sean answered wearily,
"You're a stranger. I'm not supposed to talk to strangers."

"That's very good." The man grinned, then hunched
down on his knees to face the boy on his own level. "Did
your mother teach you that?" When Sean nodded, the man
continued: "That's good. Your mother wants to keep you
safe. I'm a friend of hers. Did she ever mention me?"

Sean shook his head in the negative, and the man
continued: "Ah, well, she might not have. But we were very
close friends at one time. I knew her and Paddy and Moira."

Sean stared at the man, more confused than ever. "Why
don't you come for tea then? Most of their friends come for
tea."

"I suppose your mother wouldn't think that a good idea.
You see, her . . . husband may not like it. Sometimes men
don't like their wives to be friends with other men. Do you
know what I mean?"

Sean nodded, though he hadn't the slightest idea.

"I see you're a smart lad. I am very glad we met. I've
wanted to know you for a long time, and I'd like us to be
friends. Do you think you'd like that?"

"Sure." Sean shrugged.

"Good. I'll come to see you every now and then. But
Sean, I don't think you should mention it to Mr. Scott. He
might get angry at your mother."

"All right."

"It will be our secret. Next time I come, I'll bring you a present. What would you like?"

"A red ball." Sean smiled as he envisioned the gift. "I saw one in the store yesterday. Christopher said he would get it if I did my chores."

"I'll get it for you anyway." The man stood up and extended a hand, which Sean took. "Nice to meet you, boy. By the way, if your mother should ask, my name is John Sweeney."

There was something familiar about that name, some conversation he remembered between Paddy and his mother that only partially made sense. He couldn't recall what it had been about, but he remembered that Katie was crying and that it hadn't been good.

"Just remember, son, it's our secret."

Sean watched the man walk off, then returned to his play.

Katie tucked her son into the large bed, smiling as he snuggled down into the covers. He looked so small, his blond hair spilled against the white pillow, his eyes an intense blue that reminded her of a time she'd sooner forget.

"Mama?" Sean spoke softly, his eyes already heavy with sleep. "Are we going to stay here now?"

"Yes. This is your home and we don't ever have to leave it. Ella took care of all that."

Sean smiled, his freckles crinkling. "Is she like an angel, Mama?"

Katie grinned as she smoothed the little boy's hair. "I guess you could say that. She said she'd always take care of you and me, and she's still doing that. I suppose that makes her a guardian angel."

"Like the one in the picture."

Katie nodded, remembering the print that Sean saw in a picture book. He'd been entranced by the appearance of the beautiful angel, watching over two children who were crossing a broken wooden bridge. For some reason that image brought him comfort, and now Ella had taken the place of the spirit.

"I miss her."

"I miss her, too," Katie agreed. "Now go to sleep. You have a big day tomorrow. Christopher is taking you horseback riding, and Paddy wants to take you to church."

Sean nodded, then snuggled back into the covers. Katie pressed a kiss on his forehead, then started for the door. Her hand was on the doorknob, when Sean spoke softly again.

"I saw your friend today, Mama. He said his name was John Sweeney."

Her breath stopped. Frozen, Katie turned toward her son, unable to believe what she'd just heard.

"Sean." Forcing herself to remain calm, Katie questioned him quietly. "What did you say? Who did you see?"

"John Sweeney." Sean yawned, his eyelids fluttering. "He was in the garden. He said he knew you and Paddy and Moira. He's nice, Mama."

Panic seized her, but she struggled not to show it. "What else did he say?"

"He said he wanted to be my friend. He's buying me the red ball—you know, the one Christopher promised me. But he said I didn't have to do the chores to get it. He'll bring it next time." Sean yawned once more. "I'm going to sleep now."

"Sean." Katie came to stand beside his bed. "This is important, and I want you to think hard. Did he say anything else?"

She dreaded the answer, and when it came, she didn't know whether to be relieved or more puzzled. Sean opened his eyes and thought, then shook his head.

"No. He didn't say anything else. Just that he wanted to be friends. He is your friend, isn't he?"

"I know him." Katie forced herself to breathe slowly and

not to reveal her emotions. "Sean, I don't want you speaking to that man. If he ever comes to see you again, I want you to tell me. Do you understand?"

"But why?" Awake now, Sean stared at his mother in confusion.

"Because he isn't a good person. I don't want you meeting with him or accepting anything from him. Will you promise me?"

Sean nodded. "I will."

"Good. I know you don't understand, and when you are big enough, I promise I will tell you everything there is to know about John Sweeney. But until then, stay away from him. And Sean." Katie leaned closer, her tone intense. "Don't tell Christopher he was here."

"All right." The little boy buried his face in the pillow. "Good night, Mama."

Katie kissed him, then softly retreated and closed the door. Outside, she leaned against the wooden planks, her mind awhirl.

John Sweeney. She'd almost hoped that he'd forgotten his threats once he realized their financial situation. He couldn't possibly have learned of their inheritance; it had all happened too quickly and too recently.

Yet his visit could only mean one thing—that he intended to make good his threats. Katie choked, bile rising in her throat as she pictured him confessing his parenthood to Sean.

My God, Katie thought, forcing down a sob. John Sweeney would corrupt her son; she had no doubt about that. And even if he didn't do it intentionally, just Sean finding out what kind of man fathered him would leave an impression that Katie couldn't easily erase.

This couldn't be happening, but it was. Somehow she had to get him out of her life. She would get the money to pay his bribe, but Katie knew that wouldn't suffice. John

Sweeney's visit to Sean had proven that. He knew she'd do anything to protect Sean, anything at all, and he intended to use that knowledge.

"Katie? Are you all right? You look like you've seen a ghost."

Christopher stepped into the hallway, seeing his wife standing against the door, looking pale and wretched.

Katie forced a smile and nodded. "I'm fine. I just . . . felt ill for a few moments, but it's passed."

"Good." Christopher took her hand. "Come on to bed. It's late. Are you sure you're all right?"

"I'm fine," Katie said. "Just fine."

✦ TWENTY-EIGHT

"Could you spare a dime, friend?"

Christopher looked down and saw a beggar sprawled beneath the window of a pawnshop, calling to the passersby. Clad in a ragged coat, his pockets frayed and hanging from the weight of a liquor bottle, the beggar stared pathetically into the crowd, ignored by most.

Digging into his pocket, Christopher pulled out a few bills and handed them to the astounded man. "Bless you, sir!" the beggar cried, then folded the money reverently and scuttled off in search of food.

God, it felt good to be rich again. Christopher sighed with satisfaction, pleased that he'd been able to help someone else.

His newfound wealth didn't change much else. He had his home, his family, and best of all Kate. But knowing that there was money again, food on the table, and enough to help other people, made him feel like a different person.

In truth, he was doing quite well on his own without Ella's money. The investments that Winston had put aside for him were paying off handsomely, and he continued to reinvest the dividends in new enterprises. By doing this, he had the satisfaction of assisting newly formed businesses and still continued to reap a handsome profit for himself and his clients. It was, he had to admit, gratifying.

Everything, in fact, was perfect, with one exception. Staring absently into the pawnshop window, Christopher thought of Kate.

Something was wrong; he could sense it. She was carrying their first child and wasn't due for several months, but she acted distant and depressed, and sometimes, he could tell she had been crying. When he questioned her, she would always reassure him that everything was fine, but deep within himself, he knew it wasn't.

Eunice thought it was the child. She told him that many women experienced ambivalent feelings when in a delicate way, and that he shouldn't worry. But for all their problems, Christopher knew Katie like the back of his hand and sensed it was more than that. Yet if she refused to tell him, there was little he could do.

He started to walk on when a glimmer from the window caught his eye. Curious, he glanced back, then froze as he spotted a small lacquered box positioned in the center of a piece of blue velvet, displayed to draw attention.

It was the music box he had given Kate. Christopher wouldn't forget the tiny box, with its ivory roses and trailing leaves. He'd bought it with the last pennies he'd possessed, wanting to make her happy and surprise her. She had seemed genuinely to like the present, so it was doubly odd to see it returned to the pawnshop.

He stepped into the shop and waited until the rotund Italian owner put down the glass he was polishing and came to the counter.

"I would like to purchase that music box in the window," Christopher explained, then reached into his pocket and withdrew a wad of bills. The merchant's eyes grew wide and he hurried off to get the box.

"Yes, sir. Anything else, sir? I have a lovely new set of

china, imported from England. And a nice rosewood table that a lady would love.''

"No, just the box.'' Christopher studied the piece, then glanced up at the eager shopkeeper. ''You wouldn't remember who brought this in, would you?''

"Oh, yes. A handsome man, with blond hair. John Sweeney was his name. He said it belonged to his wife, but she no longer liked the tune.'' His smile fading, the shopkeeper leaned closer with a worried expression. ''He said it was his to sell. There is no problem, is there?''

"No.'' Pocketing the box, Christopher paid the man and walked from the store.

A handsome young man. Instantly he dismissed the thought. No, Katie was a lot of things, could impersonate Fan Pemberton and manage to keep her secrets to herself, but she wasn't a cheat. He couldn't imagine her carrying on a secret affair. And yet . . .

Doubt tormented him. Why then had she sold the box? Who was this man, and how did he come to possess this intimate gift he'd given his wife? There seemed no easy explanation.

He had to stop this. No one knew better than Christopher what mistrust would do to a marriage, and the last thing he wanted was to return to their previous relationship, full of doubt and insecurities. He loved Kate; there wasn't anything he wouldn't do for her. And he sensed that she returned that love. Yet he still felt uneasy.

He would ask her tonight. He wouldn't let this fester, nor would he continue to wait patiently while something else ate away at her. He would demand an explanation and would clear the air. Surely Kate would have some logical reasons, and he would laugh and it would all be over. Easier now in his mind, he hurried back to work.

". . . I really don't know why you're so upset. All I did was see the boy."

Katie stared at John Sweeney, her blue eyes full of grief. "You know I don't want you to see him. For the love of God, John, don't do this. Sean is innocent of everything. He deserves a chance in life—don't take that away from him."

"Well, now, I didn't say I couldn't be persuaded." John Sweeney grinned, but the smile vanished as quickly as it came. "But I warned you what would happen if you didn't pay up. I haven't a cent from you for weeks, Katie darling. We'll have to remedy that, or else."

"Here." She thrust a handful of bills at him, hiding her disgust. What had she done to deserve this?

She didn't dare tell Christopher, and didn't have the first idea of how to get rid of Sean's father. That the man didn't care at all for his son was obvious. Sean was merely a tool to blackmail her, but how could she stop him?

As if reading her mind, John pocketed the bills and smirked. "That will do for now, but it's been a cold winter. I need coal for me fire, some whiskey at night—you know, all the comforts you're used to."

"What would it take to make you go away once and for all?" Desperate, Katie nearly pleaded with him. "Think of your child, the future . . . what would make you leave us alone?"

John Sweeney shrugged, but there was a gleam in his eye as he calculated his price. Finally, after what seemed forever, he grinned.

"I think fifty thousand would do it."

Stunned, Katie stared at him as if he were mad. "Fifty thousand dollars? Surely you're joking. There's no way I could get that kind of money—"

"I'm afraid that's your problem, Kate," John said, unconcerned. "I don't mind taking my share in payments. In fact, I kind of enjoy it. I made my acquaintance with Sean the other day, and I could continue to, ah, visit him. But if you really want to get rid of me, that's my price."

"You would do this." Katie felt the emotion well up inside of her. "You would risk ruining your son, just for a little money."

"It's not a little money, Kate." He cupped her chin in his hand, seeing her expression of scorn. "You and I both know that. And we both know the value of it. You have my price, Katie love. Pay it or my son and I will become even closer." He grinned. "And we both know how much you'd love that."

Katie watched him go, her fists clenched in despair. My God, how long would she pay? And how could she be sure, even if she got the money, that he would stay away from them?

There was only one way she could be sure that John Sweeney would never come near her again. She dismissed the thought as it came to her mind, but it stayed within her soul.

Only in his death would she ever be free.

"Kate, we need to talk."

Katie glanced up from her sewing, surprised at the tone in Christopher's voice. The parlor was empty, Sean and Eunice having retired moments before, and Kate realized that Christopher must have been waiting for this time. Apprehensively she put down her sewing as he retrieved something from his pocket.

"I know I told you that we were going to start over, and that there would be no more secrets between us. I really believe that mistrust destroys a relationship, and that we need to believe in each other. Do you agree?"

The walls were closing in. He knew something; Katie could sense it. She nodded and waited, trying to stop the panic that was building inside of her.

"Then I want to ask you about this." He placed a package wrapped in burlap into her lap.

As she stared at him dumbly Katie's gaze dropped to the parcel and she pulled at the twine. The package fell open, and she saw the black lacquered music box nestled inside.

How did Christopher find this? She had given the box to John Sweeney when she had no money . . . had Christopher seen the man? Did he already know?

"Where . . ." Her voice was almost a squeak. Surely he hadn't confronted Sean's father, her ex-lover . . .

"I bought it from a pawnshop near the bank. It's the same box that I had given you, do you remember?"

"It can't be," Katie protested. "I don't know how—"

"Why don't you tell me what happened," Christopher pleaded. "And what's troubling you. Kate, I know something's wrong. I can help you, or at least I'll try. Please, you've got to trust me."

He made it sound so easy. All she had to do was explain, then he would share her burden in all this. But she couldn't. Katie couldn't bring herself to risk their newfound happiness by confessing John Sweeney's blackmail. Christopher had barely recovered from the shock of learning about the scandal without seeing her lover face-to-face. No matter how much Christopher cared for her, there were limits to any man's patience, and she didn't want to test his.

Worse, even if he knew, there wasn't much he could do about it. John Sweeney would torment her and Sean for as long as he thought he could prosper from doing so. They wouldn't have a moment's peace. Christopher might be tempted into a confrontation, and the thought of that gave her chills. No, it was better this way. John Sweeney was her mistake, and a problem she'd have to solve on her own.

"There's nothing wrong," Katie insisted, fingering the box and refusing to look up. "I just . . . haven't been feeling well, that's all. It's common when expecting. I remember such with Sean."

"I see." Christopher's voice betrayed his hurt. "And the box?"

Katie shrugged. "I didn't know it was gone. Perhaps one of the workmen picked it up when we had the new furniture delivered. Or a servant. I really don't know how it wound up in the pawnshop."

"Katie, look at me."

Forced to do so, Kate raised her face, her lips trembling. Christopher sighed with frustration. "I can't help you if you don't let me! Why can't you tell me what's wrong? Haven't we learned from our mistakes in the past?"

Katie got to her feet, clutching the box. "I'm sorry, Christopher, but you have to believe me. If you don't mind, I feel a little ill. I want to go to bed."

He nodded, watching as she rushed from the room, holding the box tightly. When she reached her bedroom, she closed the door in relief.

She had to solve this problem soon. John Sweeney would destroy her marriage if she didn't. But she'd only been able to come up with one solution. Carefully Katie placed the music box inside her bureau drawer, then pushed aside her lacy underthings.

There, beneath her corset, gleamed an 1846 Colt revolver.

"Are you sure this is it?"

Christopher stared at the police report, frowning at the number of entries listed.

The clerk nodded. "We've got quite a dossier on Mr. Sweeney. Mostly petty stuff, but there is that one charge that could see him hanged." The clerk indicated the last line. "Some states don't take too kindly to armed robbery, and Colorado is one of them."

"I see." Folding the paper and thrusting it into his pocket, Christopher thanked the man and left.

So John Sweeney was a criminal. From the dossier, it

seemed he specialized in petty crimes, like robberies and blackmail. He'd never been arrested for violence, but that didn't always mean everything.

How could his Kate be involved with this man? None of it made sense. He had come to the police station on a whim, desperate for information, and hadn't really expected to find anything on the man. He certainly didn't expect such a complete listing of crimes that the man had committed or to discover that the police were actively looking for him.

Frowning, Christopher walked swiftly toward home. If Kate's story was right, that she hadn't known the box was missing, perhaps someone did steal it, and in that way John Sweeney came into possession of the item. He'd heard of the thieving rings in Philadelphia, some of which made Dickens's stories look tame. Was John Sweeney a Fagan? Or was there more to it?

That theory had one huge hole—it didn't explain Kate's unhappiness. She had been having dreams lately, nightmares that left her trembling and crying in his arms. He begged her to talk to him, but she withdrew more and more each day. He was getting frightened for her. As angry as it made him to know she didn't trust him completely, he didn't want to press her. Their love was too new and too fragile.

She was sleeping when he arrived home. Christopher smiled as he saw her, sprawled across the bed, her hair spilled out over the white pillows like black lace. Clad in a demure white eyelet gown, her pregnancy barely visible, she looked lovely, like a sleeping goddess he'd wandered upon.

A rush of love came through him as he smoothed her hair and pressed a kiss on her forehead. *Whatever it is, Kate,* he vowed, *I will find out what's troubling you and we'll face it together. I promise.*

*   *   *

There was silence when Katie woke. Outside, the full moon poured into her window, bathing the covers and the sheets in silver.

Crossing herself, Katie shivered. Madness. Sleeping in the moonlight made one addled—everyone knew that. She was about to draw the blinds when she heard the barely perceptible chink of pebbles against her window.

He was back. Her heart sinking, Katie fought the nausea that threatened. She'd given John Sweeney a huge sum of money the last time she'd seen him, hoping against hope that he would finally stay away. But that had been barely a month ago and he was back, like a vampire, ready to draw blood.

She couldn't go on like this. Christopher was suspicious already, and would eventually discover her secret. What would happen then was anyone's guess, but none of the alternatives were good.

More importantly she had to protect Sean. Katie's mouth filled with bile as she envisioned John Sweeney, tempting her son like the devil himself. Sean was happy, was doing well, and was full of confidence. What would happen to her sunny little boy when he learned about his father? What would happen when society found out?

He had to be stopped, Katie vowed. Reason left her; she only knew one fact, and that was that she had to get rid of John Sweeney, once and for all. Tears choked her, and she slipped her hand inside her drawer and pulled out the gun, feeling the cold, metallic weight in her hand. She put on her cloak and put the gun inside her pocket.

Outside, it was cold. Wind ruffled the trees, and the leaves sounded like bats in the night sky. Moonlight poured over everything, making the paths luminous and deadly.

He stood near the gazebo, smoking impatiently and glancing toward the house. When he saw Kate, his face became relieved and he threw his cigarette onto the ground.

"So, you've come." He forced a smile, which vanished instantly when Katie didn't return it. "I need some money, love. I'm almost out of whiskey."

"Johnny, don't do this." There was a crazed look in her eyes that made John Sweeney take a step back. "Please. For the love of God, have some decency and leave us alone. Please."

There was something odd in her voice. John Sweeney frowned, then shrugged as he envisioned the money she surely carried beneath her cloak. "I can't do that, me darling," John said, reaching out to touch her cheek. For once, Katie didn't move and he took that as a good sign. "You know I can't do that. You've found your fortune, love. I still need mine."

"I'm begging you," Katie whispered, her voice breaking. "Go away from here. Don't ever come back. Please. Don't make me—"

"Make you what?" John laughed. "Tell your husband? Go on, tell him. I have a feeling that when you do, you'll lose everything. You think so, too, love, or you would have told him by now." His brow furrowed as another thought occurred to him. "Of course, if he divorced you, he would have to pay you a nice settlement. We could live on that, Kate. You, me, and Sean."

Horror filled her as she stared at the man before her. He meant it. John Sweeney would stop at nothing to get rich, even if it meant destroying everyone else. He would ruin her son, ruin his chances, make him just like himself, a liar, a blackmailer, and a thief. Helplessness seized her, and she withdrew the weapon from her pocket, unable to think clearly.

"Please." Katie's brogue deepened as emotion filled her. "Don't make me do this. Don't make me kill you."

John Sweeney stared down the barrel of the Colt.

❄ TWENTY-NINE

Christopher awoke, an unsettled feeling within him. Outside, it was dark, but the full moon gleamed eerily over the landscape, lending it a ghostly hue. Turning in his bed, he saw the dented pillow and the empty place beside him.

Katie. She was gone. Puzzled, Christopher got to his feet. Sometimes in the night she felt ill or had to use the convenience. She was still shy about displaying such personal needs before him, so he wasn't too alarmed to find her gone until he searched the house.

She was nowhere to be found. Standing at the backdoor, Christopher fought the uncertainty that filled him. Surely she didn't plan some clandestine meeting with a lover while he slept beside her? That was beyond the realm of belief, but still, it was the middle of the night and she was gone.

Voices came from the garden, and he glanced outside. Maybe that was it. Maybe she saw something and went to investigate. Putting on his coat, he moved stealthily outside, hushing the door closed behind him.

Katie was there. He could see her clearly in the moonlight, standing beneath the gazebo. Her voice sounded tearful, full of pain and pleading, but it was to the other person that his gaze quickly went and his breath stopped.

A man stood beside the garden gate, young and handsome

even from a distance. Christopher froze, all of his doubts rushing back to the surface.

Katie had taken a lover before him. She never talked about the man, but it had always made Christopher uneasy. Did she feel the need for another lover, someone else to satisfy her? Was the child she was carrying even his?

Blood rushed madly through his brain and he approached the couple, barely able to think. The idea of Kate with another man nearly drove him insane. Could she have fallen in love with someone else? Was that the reason for her unhappiness and weeping? Was she just using him?

". . . Please leave me alone. Don't make me do this. Please, John, if you feel anything for Sean, leave us."

She had a gun. Stunned, Christopher saw his wife pointing the weapon at the strange man, saw his shock and disbelief as she pulled back the trigger, her hands shaking.

"Kate!" Christopher called to her. She turned instantly, and in that moment the other man attacked her, knocking the gun from her hands. Gasping, Katie turned, her face full of fright, but Christopher grappled for the weapon and retrieved it before the other man could. Harmlessly the revolver discharged, and Christopher thrust the smoking weapon into his coat.

"What the hell is going on here?"

"She tried to kill me, that's what," the other man replied, still looking at Kate in disbelief. "You saw it."

"Kate, who is this man?" Christopher questioned his sobbing wife, knowing the answer before he heard it.

"John Sweeney. He's Sean's father. I'm sorry, Christopher, I couldn't tell you. He's been taking money from me for months to stay away from Sean. I couldn't let that happen, and I couldn't tell you."

Nodding, Christopher turned toward the man who stood arrogantly before him.

"That's right, I'm the boy's real father. I have rights, and

I just wanted to get my fair share. I didn't think she was crazy enough to pull a stunt like that.''

"Get out," Christopher said between gritted teeth. "And don't come near my wife or son again. Ever.''

"Well, now, there's something to say about that.'' Recovering from his fear, John Sweeney grinned insolently. "I'm the brat's father. How do you think that would make him feel? And what about your fancy friends? I'm a bit of a nuisance to get rid of, but two businessmen like ourselves can surely come to an agreement. I'm not unreasonable.''

Blindly Christopher struck him, his fist connecting neatly with John Sweeney's jaw and bringing the other man to the ground. Shocked, John Sweeney stared up in a red haze of pain as the gentlemanly-looking lad before him wrenched him to his feet and hit him again.

Struggling, John swiped back, but Christopher's rage was so intense that he didn't stand a chance. Again and again John Sweeney got to his feet; again and again Christopher sent him back to the ground. Katie sobbed as John became more bloody, and finally he collapsed to the hard earth.

"You come here again and you'll think that was a tap dance," Christopher said, breathing hard from exertion. "I have your police records; they have enough on you to see you hanged. If you ever cause my wife or son trouble, even speak to them in the streets, I'll have you put away for good.''

John Sweeney got to his feet like a doddering fawn, wiping at the blood that streamed into his eyes. "You'll pay for this!'' he swore, then stumbled off toward the road.

"Anytime," Christopher promised. "Come back and see.''

"Christopher, I'm so sorry. Are you hurt?'' Katie touched his hands, soothing away the pain while Christopher shook his head.

"No. Not from him." Lifting her face toward his,

Christopher looked at her seriously. "Katie, don't ever keep anything from me again. Do you understand?"

His voice was so firm, so threatening, that Katie nodded quickly. "I won't. I just thought—"

"Do you realize what could have happened to you? My God, he could have killed you and our child! Kate, I'm strong enough to help you, no matter what the trouble. But if I ever find out that you've kept something from me again, so help me—"

"You won't." Katie hugged him fiercely. "Christopher, I love you. I wanted to protect you and Sean. You don't know what he's like."

"I know exactly what he's like," Christopher said, returning her embrace when his anger eased. "Kate, you and Sean and our new baby mean everything to me. Do you think I'd ever let John Sweeney hurt you?"

Katie shook her head in the negative. "No, you're right."

"Then no more secrets?"

"No more secrets," Katie promised. "But Christopher." She gave him a wan smile. "Don't say I didn't warn you."

"It doesn't matter, Kate. I love you and will always be there for you. Do you believe me?"

She nodded. She did believe him. And always would.

They walked back into the house, barely aware of the lights or the commotion as people, aroused by the sound of shots, appeared at the house. Eunice was waiting, her handkerchief knotted between her hands, and Sean looked worried until he saw Kate. He ran into her arms, trembling, while Eunice spoke in a demanding tone.

"Are you both all right? What happened?"

"We ran into a bit of trouble," Christopher said, acknowledging their neighbor, Mr. Armstrong, and his groom. "Everything is fine, though. Thank you for your concern."

"I heard the shot through my hedge." Mr. Armstrong looked genuinely concerned, his normal bravado gone. "I rushed over immediately. Are you certain you don't need help?''

"No," Christopher reassured him. "Katie thought she saw something and fired the gun prematurely. She gave herself a bit of a scare."

Mr. Armstrong glanced at Kate, who nodded apologetically as she soothed her son.

"I'm sorry to have disturbed you."

"It's nothing." Mr. Armstrong tucked his robe about him and accepted the coffee Eunice offered. A smile came to his stern features and he winked at Eunice. "It reminds me of that hunting trip in India. Did I ever tell you . . ."

Katie smiled as Eunice listened attentively. The older man joined Christopher's aunt in the parlor, obviously delighted to be there to comfort her. Katie wondered if there was more than a casual interest between them as Eunice laughed, enjoying his stories. She honestly hoped that there was, and that Eunice could find some happiness, even late in life.

"Is that what really happened?" Sean asked quietly. His arms were still tucked around his mother and he looked up at her, his freckled face full of trust.

Katie wanted to reassure him, to tell him not to worry, but Christopher's glance caught hers. She had almost cost them everything tonight because of deception, even in a good cause. Taking a deep breath, she faced her son and spoke directly.

"No, Sean. I didn't want Mr. Armstrong to worry. But I think you need to know the truth, even though it may be hard. Your father was outside tonight. The man called John Sweeney."

Sean's eyes widened and he looked to Christopher for verification. Christopher nodded, then Sean turned a confused face to Kate. "And you were shooting him? Why?"

"Sean, how can I explain?" Katie choked, but bravely

continued: "There was a time when I loved your father. He was a good man then, but he's changed. He wants to cause us trouble, Sean. He is wanted by the law for committing crimes. He doesn't belong here. I was afraid of what he'd do, especially to you. Do you understand?"

Sean nodded, hugging his mother tighter. "Will he come back?"

"I don't think so," Katie reassured him. "He has no reason to now."

"Sean." Christopher rose and took the little boy's hand in his own. Sean stared at the man who'd been more of a father to him in the past few months than any blood relative, and he accepted Christopher's hand. "Sean, I want to be your father, in more than just name. You may never see John Sweeney again, but I want you to know you'll always be my son and always have a place with me. The child that your mother and I are having will be your sister or brother. I know I cannot take the place of your father completely, but if you will let me, I will do everything I can to make up for the loss. Do you understand?"

Sean nodded, then reached out and hugged Christopher as well. Katie's eyes stung with moisture and then they lifted and met her husband's.

She had never expected this, to find a love that would make her feel so tremendously complete. She was sure now that God had forgiven her, and fate had done its part, too. Trembling with emotion, she silently whispered, "I love you."

Christopher smiled in response, his eyes full of emotion. They were a family, and nothing would come between them, ever again.

✿ EPILOGUE

"Kate, are you sure she's all right? She's not moving." Christopher poked at the sleeping infant with his finger while Katie glared at him in exasperation.

"Christopher Scott! Will you please leave that baby alone! It took me an hour to get her to sleep, and you're going to have her awake again!"

Her tone was scolding, but Kate smiled as she spoke. Christopher's fascination with his daughter was wonderful to see. He just couldn't believe that he'd helped to create this tiny, perfect human being with her jet-black hair and ivory complexion. He had insisted on calling her Ella, a name that Katie heartily agreed was appropriate.

Momentarily chagrined, Christopher finally relented and left his daughter's side to stand next to his wife. "She just looks so helpless like that. I'm afraid she isn't breathing."

"She is," Katie assured him. "All new parents go through this. You worry about everything."

"Is that right?" Leaning down, he kissed her forehead, then his expression grew serious. "At least we don't have to worry about John Sweeney anymore."

Katie nodded in agreement. John Sweeney had been arrested on several charges and was in jail for a good many years. "But what happens when he gets out?" she wondered out loud.

"I doubt if he'll be any trouble." Christopher grinned. "I don't think he wants to spend the rest of his life in prison. The man isn't that stupid."

Katie smiled, nuzzling against him. "Thank God we have him out of our life. Sean is doing so well and is so happy. He's number one in his riding classes and all of the boys really like him."

"There hasn't been any trouble with the gossips?"

Katie shook her head. "The Scott name is an impeccable one, it seems. Ever since you adopted him, no one asks a thing. And you are so good to him."

"Hmm." Christopher pulled her closer into his embrace and began to kiss her neck softly. "How about if we practice something else I'm good at? Or have you forgotten?"

In answer, Katie placed her arms around his neck and gave him a seductive smile. Slowly, enticingly, he slipped her gown from her shoulders, massaging her back so that she stretched like a cat in pure pleasure. Nearly purring, she raised liquid blue eyes to him and sighed.

"Have I told you today how much I love you?"

"Yes." He grinned, slipping his hands around her waist. "But tell me again. I like hearing it."

"I love you, Christopher Scott," Katie whispered. "Now and forever."